"Thank you, Keary, for a wonderful evening. I hope you will allow me to see you again before I sail."

"Sail!" She was stunned. "Where? When?"

"I'll be sailing to England as soon as the repairs on my ship are complete," Morgan replied.

Searching his face she asked softly, "Will you be gone long?"

"Yes, permanently."

She lowered her eyes to hide the quick despair, feeling a lead weight had dropped to her stomach. "I see. I'm sorry to hear that, Morgan." The pain in Keary's eyes was more eloquent than words in expressing her true feelings.

Morgan started to say something but a sharp twinge of regret engulfed him and he quickly placed a hand on each side of Keary's face, kissing her forehead tenderly. Withdrawing his hands he saw, by the flickering candle, tears trembling on her eyelids. Keary felt him shudder as he drew in a sharp breath and, with a sweeping motion, pulled her roughly, almost violently to him. She locked herself into his embrace, burying her hands in his thick hair while his mouth covered hers hungrily. She became conscious of a low, tortured moan as he quickly released her. To physically untangle from her arms was a simple matter, but emotionally he felt the pull of his heart to hers forever. . . .

CAPTIVATING ROMANCE
by Penelope Neri

CRIMSON ANGEL (1783, $3.95)
No man had any right to fluster lovely Heather simply because he was so impossibly handsome! But before she could slap the arrogant captain for his impudence, she was a captive of his powerful embrace, his one and only *Crimson Angel*.

PASSION'S BETRAYAL (1568, $3.95)
Sensuous Promise O'Rourke had two choices: to spend her life behind bars—or endure one night in the prison of her captor's embrace. She soon found herself fettered by the chains of love, forever a victim of *Passion's Betrayal*.

HEARTS ENCHANTED (1432, $3.75)
Lord Brian Fitzwarren vowed that somehow he would claim the irresistible beauty as his own. Maegan instinctively knew that from that moment their paths would forever be entwined, their lives entangled, their *Hearts Enchanted*.

BELOVED SCOUNDREL (1799, $3.95)
Instead of a street urchin, the enraged captain found curvaceous Christianne in his arms. The golden-haired beauty fought off her captor with all her strength—until her blows become caresses, her struggles an embrace, and her muttered oaths moans of pleasure.

JASMINE PARADISE (1170, $3.75)
In the tropical Hawaiian isles, Sarah first sees handsome Dr. Heath Ryan—and suddenly, she no longer wants to be a lady. When Heath's gaze rakes Sarah's lush, soft body, he no longer wants to play the gentleman. Together they delight in their fragrant *Jasmine Paradise*.

Available wherever paperbacks are sold, or order direct from the Publisher. Send cover price plus 50¢ per copy for mailing and handling to Zebra Books, Dept. 1828, 475 Park Avenue South, New York, N.Y. 10016. DO NOT SEND CASH.

Noreen O'Neill
Ecstasy's Dream

ZEBRA BOOKS
KENSINGTON PUBLISHING CORP.

ZEBRA BOOKS

are published by

Kensington Publishing Corp.
475 Park Avenue South
New York, NY 10016

Copyright © 1986 by Noreen O'Neill

All rights reserved. No part of this book may be reproduced in any form or by any means without the prior written consent of the Publisher, excepting brief quotes used in reviews.

First printing: May 1986

Printed in the United States of America.

Chapter I

An early morning sun appeared sporadically between fast-moving clouds, casting long shadows on the dew-laden fields of Lord Fenleigh's estate. In the center of more than two thousand acres of well-cultivated rolling hills, on the south coast of Ireland, stood the old stone mansion.

Keary didn't know when she skipped lightly to the barn for a secret rendezvous with Bruce, this second day of June, 1776, that it would trigger a chain of events which would change her life completely.

His hot breath came in short gasps, flooding the side of her neck as his hand, traveling in ever-widening circles over her rib cage, came closer and closer to its intended destination. As his lips closed on hers, she reached down and held his wrist, stopping the motion just as the knuckle of his thumb lightly brushed the outline of her breast.

"That's enough of that, my love."

"But, Keary darlin', 'tis an awful achin' I'm havin' for you."

"'Tis a worse achin' you'll be havin' if you don't learn to behave, Bruce darlin'." She pushed against his chest with one hand while pulling a few strands of hay, which had fluttered down from the loft, off her hair. Unable to entice her to the stack of hay as he had planned, he instead maneuvered her against the side of a stall in yet another attempt to seduce her.

She was not the first maid he had lured into this position, she was sure, for Bruce was a handsome lad with a poetic tongue and an innocent, engaging smile. She had always been able to hold off his advances, not because of a lack of desire on her own part, but rather because she was a lass with uncommon common sense. That she would surrender to him in time was a foregone conclusion but, as she had told him several times, "Only after the reading of the banns and your placing that plain gold band on my finger, Bruce darlin'."

"But, Keary love," he would counter, "how can I wait that long? The torture of it is a hard cross to bear."

Today she answered his spurious pleas with, "The longer you procrastinate about talking to Father O'Connell, the longer the torture. If you were to talk to the good man today, the first banns would be read Sunday and I'd be sharing your bed within three weeks. Now wouldn't that be better than a romp in the hay?"

"But, Her Ladyship has not yet given permission."

Keary drew back from his encircling arms and, looking into his forlorn eyes, she said in biting tones, "Have you asked her?"

Bruce shuffled his feet, afraid to see the angry fire in Keary's dark blue eyes that appeared every time he wavered in his determination to face Lady Fenleigh. His fear made him stammer.

"No—ah—I'm afraid what her answer might be. Ah— if she refuses and we marry without her consent, it's the old heave-ho she'll likely be givin' me." Pleading for her understanding, he lifted beseeching eyes and asked, "What kind of a husband would I be without a position?" Keary stood her ground, determined his excuses would not undermine her resolve.

"And if I grew big with child, wouldn't she be givin' us both the old heave-ho? Wouldn't that be a fine kettle of fish now?"

"Bru-uce." Lady Fenleigh's feigned soprano echoed through the stable and Bruce froze in terror. Trying to push Keary into the background, he caused her to fall into the hay mound. His frightened eyes pleaded with her to remain hidden as she jumped up and stood resolutely beside him. With only one entrance to the stable, there was no way for her to leave unnoticed and she felt no reason to hide.

"Bru-uce." The call came again, Her Ladyship pronouncing Bruce as if it had two syllables.

Keary, seeing how shaken Bruce was, said reassuringly, "We've done nothing to be ashamed of and, though she's our employer, she certainly doesn't own us. Come now, take my hand and hold your chin up; this is a good time to tell her we're betrothed."

"Oh, there you are, Bruce. Why didn't you answer?"

"I was just on my way, Milady." He started for the door then stopped as Lady Fenleigh was already in the wide doorway adjusting her eyes from the bright sunlight to the dim interior of the stable. Recognizing Keary, her eyes narrowed and a malevolent frown chased away the inviting smile she had carefully prepared for Bruce.

Her Ladyship was well-proportioned and the slim-waisted riding dress showed this off to its maximum. Her oval face had been stunning once and still retained features of classic beauty, with large brown eyes, straight nose, and full, sensuous lips. But it was a frail beauty unable to withstand the ravages of time and a mean temperament. Years of scowling had creased the fair complexion and the coquettish smile, once able to charm a saint into adultery, now appeared as a tight smirk, as though held in place by a coat of varnish. The long ash-blond hair, which had crowned her beauty in youth, had long since faded and now framed a habitual frown and slightly drooping eyes that flashed with hatred as she approached Keary.

"Keary, my dear, whatever are you doing here?" She purred as her eyes roved up and down the younger one's form, looking accusingly for telltale signs of a recent tumble in the hay. Keary brushed her skirt and instantly regretted it, knowing the gesture would be interpreted as guilt. She moved to stand beside Bruce, hoping he would take her hand and tell Her Ladyship of their betrothal. Instead he ran to the stall and, mumbling excuses, led out the big hunter and placed the well-polished sidesaddle over the animal's back.

"Be careful with him today, Milady. He's a bit skittish." Looking guilty, his eyes riveted to the floor, he touched his cap obsequiously—a gesture which never failed to stir Keary's ire.

"Perhaps you had better accompany me then, Bruce, in the event he proves too much to handle." The sardonic smile from one of the best horsewomen in all Ireland was meant to impart to Keary that Her Ladyship owned Bruce lock, stock, and barrel. Raising her foot for Bruce to help her mount, she managed to show considerably more silk-clad leg than was absolutely necessary and, once aboard the prancing hunter, her adjustment of tangled skirts displayed even more.

Bristling with anger at Lady Fenleigh for her supercilious insinuations and Bruce for failing again to stand up to the old shrew, Keary picked up her skirts, also showing a little more leg than necessary, and sailed haughtily out the door. All the way up the path to the manor house, she seethed at the veiled sneer Her Ladyship had flashed in parting. As she gained the main entrance, Keary turned to see the two of them cantering across the meadow to the bridle path, which wound up the hills to cliffs overlooking miles of jagged shoreline. The romantic spot was one she and Bruce had ridden to many times, and she was angry at him for going there with another woman—despite the fact he had no choice in the matter. Her heart labored earnestly, causing her cheeks and neck to flush as she watched the two distant forms being swallowed by the forest.

Striding angrily into the manor, the only sound in the cavernous entry hall was her clogs clicking across the flagstone tile. As she approached the twelve-foot wide stairway, she found her path blocked by a large man leaning against the bannister, glass in hand. Lord Fenleigh's bloodshot eyes brazenly appraised that which her clothing was intended to hide and he flashed a lascivious smile.

"Keary, m'dear, you look beautiful today—but then, of course, you always do."

"Thank you, Milord." Sidestepping, she tried to continue up the stairs but, anticipating her action, he moved just enough to halt her advance.

"Yes, m'dear, you are no longer a child. You have

blossomed into a young woman—and a ravishingly beautiful one at that." His crooked index finger nestled under her chin and slowly tilted her face back, his hand traveling deliberately, caressing her cheek until two fingers snaked under long black tresses to fondle her ear. The gesture, as usual, was supposed to appear almost paternal and, as usual, Keary was not one whit beguiled.

"Thank you, Milord. I hope I please both you and Her Ladyship." With a quick backstep, she managed to unhitch the hand, which had crept further to the back of her neck and was attempting to pull her closer to his aroused body.

"What's wrong, my child? You appear uneasy. Don't tell me you have developed fear of your loving patron after all these years?" He tottered on unsure legs, his leering, bleary-eyed countenance belying the concern he tried to impart. Whiffs of stale rum assailed Keary's nostrils and she stepped back further.

"Oh no, Milord. But in your own words, I've grown up and, as a woman, it's improper for you to fondle me as you would a child."

In the four years since her arrival in the Fenleigh household, Keary's dread of being alone with His Lordship had increased steadily. Actually, they were never completely alone in this house that employed a dozen servants. However, servants could not be counted on to come to her rescue in the event he tried to carry out the intentions so plainly written on his face.

"Please, Milord, let me pass." Her cool stare disarmed him for an instant and she quickly ducked out of reach. Facing straight ahead, she ascended the steps, ignoring his pleading eyes.

"Keary dear, you don't understand, I only wanted

to—" The rest of his words faded away as her determined gait added distance between them. She closed the door to her bedchamber wishing there were a way to lock it, but only Lord and Lady Fenleigh's chambers and the guest rooms were equipped with locks.

"Oh Bruce," she thought, "you must do something soon; I can't tolerate this situation much longer." The thought stunned her, as this was the first time she had actually put it in words. Now that she had, she saw her problem more clearly.

Keary Cavanaugh had arrived at Fenleigh Manor four years past, at the tender age of fourteen, to act as tutor and governess to the Fenleigh's only child, Cynthia. Keary was conceived in late childbearing years and her mother died shortly after the long, painful delivery. Her father, the village schoolmaster and a firm believer in education of both sexes, had introduced her early in life to the wonderful world of books. When a scourge of cholera swept through the small village more than half of the inhabitants succumbed, Keary's father among them. Father Quinn, the village priest, befriended Keary and through his intercession she obtained the coveted position at Fenleigh Manor.

When she first arrived at the estate, Lord Fenleigh often pulled her onto his lap professing paternal interest while making vague references to a future in which her status would be much higher than that of the other servants, almost familial. But along with these promises his fondlings became more intimate, and as her body blossomed so too did her awareness of his real intentions. As knowledge supplanted innocence, Keary also developed the skills to parry his advances and a sixth sense to evade his company.

Lord Fenleigh was in his early forties, the last fifteen years of which he was unable to relate an accurate history due to the alcoholic shroud covering his memory. Beneath the sweat-stained periwig was a glistening forehead that extended all the way to a thin fringe covering the back of his skull. The meat of his once powerful chest and shoulders now resided around his waist and hips, creating a bulge the most talented tailors could no longer disguise. Though he was the fourth generation of Fenleighs born in Ireland, he proclaimed his English heritage proudly while looking derisively down his aristocratic nose at all Irishmen and farm animals on an equal basis.

In strict Fenleigh tradition, he received a classical education at Harrow, acquiring speech and mannerisms that were English to the core. Despite the subtle trace of a brogue, which occasionally invaded his sterling diction, self-discipline had immuned him against ever uttering an Irish expression.

Since Cynthia's death of smallpox, six months ago, Keary's duties were not defined. His Lordship had often mentioned making her an assistant clerk. However, when Mr. Radcliffe, the chief clerk and bookkeeper of the estate, was approached, the rotund little man looked through his pince-nez glasses and snorted.

"By jove, M'Lord, ye'll be telling me these Irish are civilized."

"But, m'dear man—"

The Lord of the manor was rudely interrupted by the little bantam rooster as he declared, "I'll not hear of it. No, M'Lord, I won't!" He considered the position above the station of an Irish man—let alone an Irish maid. And, for reasons Keary had never been able to fathom, the irascible old bookkeeper was the one person on the whole estate who seemed to routinely defy the master with impunity.

Though her employment status was somewhat vague, Keary was still Irish and, as such, she could never surmount the barriers to a social status resembling equality. Lady Fenleigh had assigned her menial tasks such as tending her elaborate wardrobe, but these chores were designed more to keep the younger girl out of His Lordship's sight than because of an actual need for an additional maid.

Lady Fenleigh didn't consider Keary a rival, as she cared little about His Lordship's romantic escapades. Rather, her jealousy was rooted in a timeworn feminine anxiety: Her bloom was wilting and Keary's was just unfolding. Both women understood this intuitively and knew such a tense situation could not long endure.

That Lord Fenleigh rarely visited Her Ladyship's chambers was a fact well-known to the servants and thus to the entire south coast of Ireland. His few attempts to force entry into his wife's personal sanctuary, which were met with vitriolic rebuffs, were common knowledge.

Lady Fenleigh reined in her horse at a crest overlooking the pounding surf.

"Will you help me down please, Bruce?" Disengaging her foot from the stirrup, she held her skirts out, preparing to dismount. Bruce's eyes were quickly drawn to the slim ankles and legs she purposely displayed.

"Yes, M'Lady." He quickly dismounted and ran to her, the flush of his countenance revealing the response she had hoped for. His large hands closed around her waist, and she slid seductively down his body managing to brush one breast against his face in her slow descent.

"Bruce, you've grown so tall and strong. I remember when you could barely lift me into the carriage." Her hands remained on his shoulders and her body pressed against his.

"Sure there's nothin' to liftin' you, M'Lady. 'Tis like a feather you are."

"Why, Bruce, what a sweet thing to say. For that you deserve a kiss." Her lips brushed his cheek and swept across his mouth. His hands on her waist froze, wanting to travel but lacking the courage.

"Are you afraid of me, Bruce?"

"No, M'Lady, that is—"

"Then show me." She lifted his hands from her waist, wrapping them closer around her body as she tilted her face back, her eyes boldly challenging.

"But, M'Lady!"

"Show me—kiss me the way you want to, the way you were kissing Keary before I came into the stable." As their lips met and their bodies came together, his hands began to explore and his breathing labored. She allowed his passion to mount to a point and then, pushing against his chest gently, said, "That will be enough for now, love."

They walked along the cliffs silently for a while and Bruce tried to interpret Her Ladyship's strange behavior. On the one hand she appeared to want him to be more aggressive, but just as he was becoming so, she had gently but insistently stopped his advances. As much as he wanted her body, he valued his position more.

"M'Lady, I—ah—" He reached for her tentatively, his eyes questioning.

"Not now, Bruce. I'm not one of your farm lasses. There is a time and place for everything and I'll decide when and where." She caressed his cheek, pecked his nose softly, and added, "Soon—very soon, love."

Keary evaluated herself in the mirror and frowned as she pondered Bruce's reluctance to inform Her Ladyship of their intentions. The figure staring back from the long, oval cheval glass confirmed the remarks others had been making of her flowering womanhood. The body had a fullness that erased any hint of adolescence and suggested every womanly attribute that men find so alluring—firm full breasts and rounded hips. Her raven-black hair, which lay in soft curls around her face, enhanced her violet-blue eyes and creamy, soft skin. A small straight nose and full red lips above a square chin gave her the determined and independent look inherited from her Irish forefathers.

But was such beauty a blessing or a curse? she wondered. It had not been enough to make Bruce agree to a wedding date, and it had only earned her Lady Fenleigh's enmity and her husband's unwelcome advances. She slowly untied the tightly laced crocus bodice and the strings of the paragon petticoat and hung them carefully on the rack. Relishing the freedom of the soft chemise, she decided to remain in the privacy of her own room to read.

She lifted a romantic novel from the bookshelf but, after leafing through the pages, decided instead on a John Locke selection. She had begun studying his theories on the "Natural Rights of Man" and found them fascinating. The book was one of the cherished library she had inherited from her father, and when His Lordship first saw it, he had snorted.

"M'dear girl. Certainly you can find a better way to spend your time than reading that claptrap work from revolutionaries!"

"But Milord," she had replied defensively, "John Locke is brilliant; I find his works enlightening."

"Humph! By Jove, if it were up to me, I'd burn that trash. Natural Rights of Man bedamned, girl! God ordained those who rule by birth and, I swear it's high time men such as Locke realized it." Keary didn't argue further, neither did she refrain from reading the book.

She opened a window to allow both the breeze and early summer sun to enter then, tucking her feet up by her side, settled down for a few hours of relaxation. The air was refreshing and she inhaled deeply of the fresh ocean scent. Her eyes scanned the print of the open book but her mind refused to assimilate Locke's wisdom, obstinately focusing on her present problems instead. With no immediate solution to her troubles, she forced herself to read on and eventually became so engrossed in Mr. Locke's theories that she was unaware of either the lowering sun or the handle turning on her door. When a shadow fell across the page, she looked up, startled to see His Lordship clad only in a dressing gown and reeking of stale brandy. Her first impulse was to make a dash for the door, which she should have heeded rather than try to reason with him.

"Please, Your Lordship, it's not proper for you to be in my bedchamber."

"Damn the proprieties, Keary. Do you have any idea how long I've wanted you—how long you've had the power to drive me insane just by walking across the room? I have indulged you above every other servant in this house and I have waited patiently for you to come around—more than I have for any other woman—but my patience has worn thin." His pent-up desire, reinforced with a large dose of bottled courage, placed him out of reason's reach.

Her quick action of bounding out of the chair to avoid his lunge only trapped her in the corner to face his oncoming attack. Keary ducked under his outstretched arms, but her frantic dash for the door was abruptly stayed by a savage yank on her trailing black tresses. The stone walls of the great mansion were still reverberating with her scream when his other hand clamped over her mouth and he began half dragging, half carrying her kicking, twisting body to the bed. He flung her to the mattress and floundered on top of her writhing body, snarling.

"Now, my little ingrate, I'm going to take what I've dreamed of these last years."

"No, don't! Please, Milord. I'll tell Lady Fenleigh, I swear it!" The words were muffled by his hand, which now pressed harder into her mouth in an attempt to stifle her. Feeling his fingers close to her teeth, Keary savagely bit until, with a pained curse, he pulled them from her grasp. She screamed again and clawed at his face. Attempting to wedge her legs apart, he committed the critical error of leaving one of them between his. With his attention centered on her nails now digging savagely at his eyes, the Lord and Master of Fenleigh Manor was not prepared for the knee Keary drove forcefully into his noble manhood. He froze as if turned to stone. Encouraged by her surprising advantage, she repeated the knee thrust. His face was the color of his slightly askew powdered wig as she added one more for good measure. Collapsed on top of her like a wet rag, it took considerable time and effort to roll his inert form over and crawl from under him. As she struggled to free her leg, a feminine voice stopped her cold.

"Well, what a pretty scene, and right after your little romp in the hay! Tell me, Keary, how many men do you usually bed in one day?"

Pulling tangled hair from her face, Keary looked up to see Lady Fenleigh standing in the doorway, hands on hips, her expression a mixture of anger and surprise. Lord Fenleigh, hearing his wife's voice rolled over on his back groaning, his robe falling away from his body to reveal a little soldier, bruised and battered, who would be unable to stand at attention for quite some time.

Lady Fenleigh approached the bed and, for an instant, Keary was too shocked to move. Then, springing up, she tugged at the chemise and pushed back her hair as she gasped.

"He attacked me, Milady. I was reading and he crept up on me."

"Of course, dear, and right in the middle of this attack you removed most of your clothes and hung them neatly on the rack. My, you are a cool one!" Lord Fenleigh rose still groaning and, wrapping the robe around himself, stumbled toward the door.

"Milord, please wait! Tell her the truth—please, Milord!" Keary's words trailed helplessly as he trudged out the door in a stooped-over posture. "But, Milady, couldn't you see the scratches on his face? You can see he is hurt in—ah—other places as well. I fought as hard as I could!"

"I'm sure you did, my dear. Once a man has been enticed into a wench's bedchamber and properly aroused, a small token resistance is usually part of the game. In fact, it probably adds a touch of spice." Keary tried further to explain but realized it was useless. For Lady Fenleigh to accept her story, she would be admitting her husband's infidelity and that was more than her frail ego could bear.

"What a pity, Keary. We've always treated you like a daughter. But then, you Irish are never appreciative of our efforts to civilize you. Until further notice you will keep to your room. Your meals will be sent to you and, in the meantime, I'll try to arrange another position for you. You do realize, of course, that it is now quite impossible for you to remain here. In years to come, I'm sure you'll live to regret your promiscuous conduct of this day. And one more thing, Keary dear, much as I dislike the thought, I will have to inform Bruce of this little episode. It wouldn't be fair not to, in the event his intentions toward you were serious."

Angry tears flooded Keary's eyes and she thrust back her shoulders, announcing defiantly, "Bruce is going to marry me. He'll see the truth in this matter. Tell him what you will, but before I leave he'll hear the facts from me. And I'm also going to talk to His Lordship when he is sober. I'm sure he will confess it was his doing."

"Do as you wish, Miss. I have been trying to handle this in a civilized manner, even to the point of getting you another position, so it's best you heed my warning and not press your luck." With this, she sailed through the door, closing it with a loud crash.

Keary crossed to the window and stared out at the dusk settling on the countryside. Her mind was unwilling to believe the events of this day. Little by little frustration was supplanted by anger and closely followed by resolution. She would wait until dark, slip down to the stables, and confront Bruce with an ultimatum.

She knew the Fenleighs were expecting a dinner guest tonight and Lady Fenleigh, allowing for her usual three-hour toilet, would probably not have time to approach Bruce beforehand. Keary would have ample opportunity to confront Bruce with her version of the story first and he would realize that the decision had been made for him. If he truly loved her and wanted to be with her, they could leave together immediately. It was on this hope that she began to formulate a plan.

The stationery with the Fenleigh coat of arms was kept in the upper right-hand drawer of the large walnut desk in His Lordship's study. Keary planned to appropriate a few sheets late tonight. Tomorrow she would write a glowing recommendation for each of them and, with their combined savings, they could go far away, maybe even as far as Dublin. With Bruce's experience caring for horses and hers as both governess and tutor, they shouldn't have too much trouble securing new positions, especially with references. But if Bruce refused to leave, she would go without him—and soon.

Keary leaned against the window jamb, aimlessly watching the approaching carriage wind up the long, curving drive. As it came to a halt in front of the main entrance, the tall passenger waited patiently as the footman opened the side gate and lowered the swivel step. He made a commanding figure in his maritime uniform—not royal navy but rather the merchant service. Stepping down, unmindful of the bowing footman, he strode confidently toward the main entrance. Although she couldn't see his features, Keary guessed him to be handsome, or at least manly attractive. She remembered hearing his name that morning when Lady Fenleigh announced to her husband, "My dear, Captain Shelby will be dining with us tonight so try to be partially sober—or is that too much to ask?"

Now that Keary saw the captain, she was sure her mistress would gladly pour brandy down her husband's throat herself, hoping he would remain facedown on his big four-poster the remainder of the evening.

Keary had heard the captain's name before and the stories connected with him filtered through her mind. His reputation was that of a rogue and an invader of ladies' boudoirs, and she felt sure Her Ladyship was cognizant of these stories before she issued the invitation. She sighed, wondering if the day's events would in any way dampen Lady Fenleigh's usual flirtatious ways. With Milord undoubtedly incapacitated for the evening, Milady would certainly be at her charming best.

Thank you, Captain, Keary thought, smiling. *I believe your visit tonight will make my plans much easier to execute.*

Greeting the captain in the hall with an exuberant smile and outstretched hands, Lady Fenleigh gushed, "Good evening, Captain, I'm so happy you could come. I have bad news, however. My husband is indisposed for the evening—a wretched fever." The captain smiled appreciatively, knowing she was just as happy with her husband's absence as he was.

"I'm sorry to hear that, Milady, although I must confess with your dazzling beauty to keep me occupied, I would probably never have noticed his absence." He bent over her hand and prolonged the kiss somewhat more than custom dictated—or convention allowed. Enclosing his other hand over hers, he squeezed intimately, imparting a message that required no explanation. Lady Fenleigh smiled and inwardly blessed her husband for his earlier indiscretion and subsequent indisposition. Actually, his timing couldn't have been more perfect.

"Shall we retire to my sitting parlor until the dinner announcement, Captain?" She took his arm, managing to brush him with her body in the process. Handing him a goblet of Madeira, she sat as close as possible on the curved settee so that in replacing her glass on the low table he would have a teasing view of her scandalous décolletage, as the low-cut bodice struggled heroically to contain her ample bosom.

Captain Shelby smiled contentedly. He usually preferred more of a challenge in his seduction of women, but with an eight to twelve-week voyage ahead, he was now more interested in a sure thing. He knew her type so well—the once great beauty who was valiantly struggling to keep the flower in water. A few choice compliments and she would drag him to bed. Lifting her hand and studying it, he laced strong fingers through hers.

"How very beautiful! You know, my dear, there is one sure way to identify a true lady even though she be dressed in peasant's clothing. Nothing can disguise true noble hands." Bending over, he kissed each finger before turning the hand over and pressing his warm lips to her palm, his tongue tracing every line of the quivering flesh.

"Captain, really you shouldn't; you arouse very strange feelings." She made no effort to withdraw, however.

"Forgive me, Milady, but your beauty overwhelms me." He reluctantly released the hand, laying it on her lap. In the process, he delivered the faintest pressure on her thigh and to this bold advance, only her eyes commented.

She sighed contentedly, assured the captain was everything she had heard from her close, gossipy friends. Yes, her husband's misadventure was certainly well-timed and the captain could not have come at a better . . . Sitting bolt upright, she stiffened as a fresh thought surfaced. He shot a puzzled look in her direction, trying to understand her sudden change of mood.

"Oh, I'm sorry, Captain." She slowly traced his ear with one finger and purred, "It's just that suddenly I thought of something that may be of mutual interest"—her fingers fluttered to his neck and began a sensual massage—"something we can discuss later." His arms encircled her waist, pulling her closer, their lips meeting hungrily. Even as she savored each delectable sensation, one side of her brain was plotting revenge on Keary. . . . *And now, my dear,* she gloated, *I know the perfect way to settle your hash.*

Dinner was accompanied by a stream of silent messages transported back and forth across the huge table by four passionate eyes as liveried servants traipsed to and from the kitchen wearing studiously innocent expressions. Lady Fenleigh's little romantic escapades were a secret about as well kept as a coronation. Once the last drop of wine had been sipped from the dainty Waterford crystal goblets, the return to the small parlor was only a way station on the journey to Milady's chambers.

Her Ladyship turned to the small oak table beside the bed and, leaning on one elbow, poured wine that she held to the Captain's lips, giggling.

"Here, Amos. I think you need nourishment."

Taking the proffered goblet from her hand, he finished it in one gulp and chuckled, "Aye, Lady. My pipes were fair dry from your burning passion."

She returned the glass to the table and stretched lazily as she gazed at the ruffled covering of the curved canopy. A contented satisfaction masked her face as she thought, *Yes, Captain. Your reputation is well-deserved.* Before he departed, they would have time to make love at least once more, and with more control it would be even better. Perhaps now was the time to talk business. Once serious conversation was out of the way, she could devote herself solely to recapturing the rapturous mood that would carry her to dizzying heights of passion.

"Amos, darling. I have a proposition for you."

"I have a proposition for you too, my lovely." His hand cupped her breast. "But tell me yours first." She felt the pressure of his expanding maleness against her leg.

"It can wait, darling, but we must talk business before you leave."

Keary tiptoed down the hall past Lady Fenleigh's chambers and, seeing a light shining under the door, she stopped and listened. First a giggle then muffled voices of a man and woman wafted through the closed door. Pressing her ear closer, she could detect heavy breathing and groans of enjoyment. The captain hadn't left and His Lordship, in his own chambers, would be snoring, oblivious to his wife's adulterous conduct.

Keary snorted derisively and continued down the hall. She knew this was not the first time her mistress had entertained a gentleman in her bed, yet the she-devil had played the self-righteous part to perfection while unjustly accusing Keary that very day.

The servants had retired and she left the house unnoticed. Fortunately, there was a night lantern burning in the stables, lighting her way to the narrow stairs that climbed up to Bruce's loft room.

"Bruce?" she called softly, then waited in the deadly silence. "Bruce?" a little louder this time with desired results; there was a stirring in the loft. "Bruce, I must talk to you. It's urgent!"

A drowsy voice answered, "Keary, what are you doing here this time of night? Come up here, darlin'."

Having a fair idea why he wanted her in the loft, she quickly vetoed the request. "No, you come down here, and hurry!"

A candle flickered tentatively and then spread into a steady glow as he appeared at the top of the stairs clad in a knee-length nightshirt. She waited anxiously as he descended the narrow steps, the light bouncing eerily off the huge overhead beams. Before he reached the bottom step she blurted, "Bruce, something terrible has happened! Lord Fenleigh tried to rape me in my chambers today! Lady Fenleigh came to my room when she returned from riding and saw me fighting him off but, Bruce, she blames me! I have no choice but to leave now. Will you come with me?"

Rubbing his eyes, trying to shake sleep from his muddled brain, he muttered, "Leave here—leave my position? Where would we go? What would we do? I don't know, Keary. This will take some amount of thinkin', and without references 'twill be mighty hard to latch on to somethin' else."

"If I can obtain the references, then will you go?"

"She's not about to give us references." He was

digging his toes into the dirt floor, his legs bare below the thin nightshirt.

Keary clutched his arm, shaking it crossly. "No, but his Lordship will—once he's sober and remembers what he did." She saw no reason to tell him how she intended getting the letters of reference.

He turned his back, not wanting to meet her eyes, and began slowly picking long splinters of wood from the rough stall. "Did he actually—that is, ah—did he have his way?"

Grabbing his nightshirt she spun him around, crying furiously, "Of course not! I'd have killed him first. I gave him a good knee, and he was so sodden with drink he had little fight in him. If that old witch hadn't come in when she did, I think I would have killed him."

Bruce's downcast eyes reflected his mood. "I don't know, Keary. This is the only place I've ever worked. How can I be sure I'll get on somewhere else—even with a letter?"

She released the grip on his shirt and turned her back, defiantly issuing her ultimatum. "Bruce, if you don't want to marry me or if you're afraid to leave here, just say so, but I'm leaving in the next few days."

He approached her rigid back and played with the shining curls. Noting the angry toss of her head, he dropped his hands on her shoulders, burying his head close to her ear as he wheedled softly, "Maybe you could talk to her—try to explain."

She shrugged his hands off in exasperation. "Don't you care that I was almost raped today? Do you expect me to go on living under the same roof with a man such as that? The next time he may not be as drunk and I may not get away."

She bolted for the door, stopping abruptly when he pleaded, "Keary love, wait! I'll talk to Her Ladyship tomorrow."

"Talk! About what!" She couldn't believe his passivity! How could he be in love with her and not be furious over His Lordship's conduct or Her Ladyship's terrible accusations? She had been so confident he would gladly leave rather than subject her to this treatment.

"We could try to straighten this thing out. Maybe—"

She cut into his rationalizations, suddenly very tired of his limp excuses. "Bruce, I'm leaving. All you have to decide here and now is whether you are coming with me or staying."

"Keary, there's so much to consider, how can I decide right this minute?" His whining voice grated on her ear. Unable to control her patience, she strode furiously to the door, banging it loudly in her wake.

The following day Keary waited anxiously, hoping to see Bruce's strident form charging the manor, his resignation in hand. The hours crept slowly by and the hot sun began its descent, turning finally into a large red ball resting on the ocean. Still no sight of Bruce. Turning from the window, she crossed to the bed and sank disconsolately on to the bright-colored quilt, knowing there was only one course of action left. After dark she would slip to the study and take the stationery.

The next few hours Keary spent wrapping her few belongings in her shawl and pacing back and forth across the room waiting for time to pass. Lacking means of transport, she would have to sacrifice all of her wardrobe she could not carry to Cork. When the big clock downstairs finally struck ten and she assumed everyone was in bed, Keary crept quietly from her room.

One wall sconce lit the main entrance hall and its meager light did no more than enhance shadows as she stole down the long stairs. Opening the study door, she slipped through and proceeded slowly, feeling her way between furniture to the large desk. She slid the drawer open and quickly withdrew two sheets of stationery, slowly easing the drawer closed again. She was making her way back across the large book-lined room, preparing to step into the hall, when she heard the creak of the outside door. Startled, she stood frozen and stared through the slightly opened door at the figure crossing the main hall. Her hand flew to her mouth to stifle a gasp as she recognized Bruce's tall, masculine form. Her heart leaped; he had not given up!

She pulled the heavy door closed behind her and ran the length of the hall, hoping to catch him without creating a noise, but Bruce's own haste as he bounded soundlessly up the stairs put him out of sibilant range. When she caught sight of him at the top of the steps, it was evident her room was not his destination. One quick tap and Lady Fenleigh's door opened, swallowing him before Keary was totally aware of what was happening.

Dumbstruck, she walked slowly to her room, her thoughts whirling. It was obvious Bruce had made previous arrangements to have been admitted so readily after one short tap. At a loss to understand his intentions, she sat on her bed too preoccupied with her thoughts to compose the letters of reference. If Bruce was informing Lady Fenleigh of their plans to leave the estate, he would surely not be doing so at this time of night and in her Ladyship's bedchamber.

Hours passed. Tormented hours in which Keary walked the floor of her small room, occasionally opening her door to peer down the hall or walking to the window to stare listlessly at the moonlit yard. Bruce did not appear and, finally exhausted, she threw herself across the bed and fell into fitful sleep.

The following morning she moved about the small room wishing there were more to do. Everything she could carry was already packed and hidden under the bed. She had written her letter of recommendation, signing it with a flourish "Lady Elizabeth Fenleigh," and it, too, was tucked safely in the shawl. She would steal away after dark.

Delicious smells from the kitchen wafted upstairs and, feeling hungry for the first time since her unfortunate encounter with His Lordship, she hurried down the back stairs to the kitchen. The serving maid and cook looked up in surprise as she greeted them. "Good morning, Sarah. 'Morning Mindy. May I have some breakfast?"

"Yes, Miss, but I'm supposed to bring your tray to your room." Sarah giggled and shot Mindy, the cook, a sly glance. "Her Ladyship gave strict orders before she left this morning that you weren't to leave your chamber."

Keary knew Lady Fenleigh would have told her version of the story to one of the servants, knowing it would make the rounds of the entire house in a matter of minutes. It was evident she was an outcast and the servants were afraid to associate with her. "Where did Lady Fenleigh go?"

"To Cork, Miss. Bruce had the carriage waiting at first light and she told Cook she wouldn't be taking lunch or supper."

Since neither woman seemed inclined to go against their mistress's orders and serve Keary breakfast, she rose. "Very well. Bring a tray to my room when it's ready. In fact, since I'm known to entertain gentlemen in my chambers, maybe you had better bring two trays." Their horrified expressions followed her as she whirled and stomped from the room.

Lady Fenleigh didn't return until dusk and, going straight to her room, sent her personal maid to summon Keary.

"Sit down, Keary." Lady Fenleigh gestured toward a straight-backed chair facing the soft cushioned settee, where Her Ladyship lounged in satisfied ease, sipping a glass of wine. Sitting nervously on the edge of the chair with her hands clasped tightly in her lap, Keary waited for her mistress to proceed.

"Now, my dear, I have had time to think and I realize that sordid affair the other day was not entirely your fault. My husband had been drinking and was probably not in complete control. At a time like that, any man could easily misinterpret an innocent flirtation."

Keary stared at her, stifling the urge to shout, "It was not one bit my fault and you know it. His Lordship is a lecherous old man with or without drink." But she waited, biting her lips and trying to control her anger.

Lady Fenleigh rose and began pacing the room, unable to meet Keary's stare. "Of course, under the circumstances you can no longer stay here, so I have arranged another position for you. There is a ship leaving for Dublin on the morning tide the day after tomorrow. Here is your reference and you will note I have been charitable in not mentioning your promiscuous conduct. The envelope also contains your back wages. If you will pack your things, there will be a carter come by tomorrow afternoon to transport them to the ship. You may take the two old reed chests from the attic. Those, along with your trunk, should be ample for everything you own. The carriage will be ready at sunrise the day after tomorrow to drive you to Cork. That will be all, girl."

"Milady—" Keary's voice was hesitant.

Without looking up, Lady Fenleigh waved her out of the room. "No need to thank me, girl. You are dismissed."

Thanks was the furthest thing from Keary's mind and she felt like saying so. However, since so many of her problems were solved, she decided to leave well enough alone. It was a relief to know she had a position waiting, her back wages, passage paid to Dublin and, most of all, she could take everything she owned and loved with her.

The following morning after packing her belongings, she wandered through the garden. Unwilling to return to the mansion with its distasteful inhabitants, she sank down on a small bench amid the spring flowers she loved. The sun was setting when she finally returned to her room to stare out of the window at the darkening sky.

Rising long before dawn, Keary was dressed and ready to leave when a soft knock broke the silence. Thinking it was Bruce, she flung the door open, ready to vent her wrath. Instead, she saw the frightened eyes of Sarah standing timidly holding a tray.

"Oh, thank you, Sarah. This will be the last time you will have to bring me a tray. I'm leaving this morning; I'm afraid this is good-bye."

"Yes, I know, Miss." She handed the tray in the door

and left without another word. Keary shook her head sadly, aware she was an outcast and that no amount of effort on her part could change one mind in the entire household. Even those who were discerning enough to see the truth of the situation would pretend to accept Her Ladyship's version rather than endanger their own positions.

"I should have a red gown so I could dress the part," she thought ruefully.

The carriage pulled up in front of the manor and Keary spied Bruce sitting high atop the driver's seat.

"Well—would you look at the great philanderer perched high and mighty on Lady Trollop's carriage, now! I thought curs ran along beside the coach. I can bet your mistress has taught you some new tricks." She walked to the front of the carriage, patting the nearest horse and continued, "Are you afraid even to look at me?"

"Get into the carriage, girl. We don't want to miss the ship." Keary whirled to see Lady Fenleigh treading daintily among the pebbles of the long, curved driveway. "Bruce has been embarrassed enough by your conduct, girl, don't make things harder for him. Now, get in the carriage before I change my mind and leave you to fend for yourself."

"Oh Bruce has a right to be embarrassed, Milady, but not from anything I've done. You can easily find the reason for his shame by looking in a mirror." Bruce remained as if carved from stone and said not a word. Lady Fenleigh's mouth dropped open and her eyes glittered venomously as Keary flounced into the carriage. The two ladies, sitting opposite one another, rode the eight miles to Cork in silence.

Chapter II

As the large carriage twisted and turned down the narrow waterfront streets, Keary was amazed at the amount of activity. She had heard Cork was a major supply depot and staging area for His Majesty's armies now putting down the rebellion in the American colonies, but she wasn't prepared for anything of this magnitude. There was not an open berth at any of the docks they had passed already nor on any as far ahead as she could see. The entire harbor was a forest of masts and redcoats were everywhere. This was her first trip into Cork in several months, and although others had spoken of the increased military buildup here, she never envisioned anything on this scale.

Ireland had always been in a state of perpetual rebellion but seldom had much success. Whether the colonies would ever be able to throw off the yoke of mighty England, she seriously doubted, but from the looks of things here, they had certainly gotten King George's attention. As the carriage stopped in front of a sleek three-masted vessel, Keary broke the silence.

"Milady, you haven't given me instructions. Whom do I see in Dublin? What is my new employer's name?"

Grudgingly, Lady Fenleigh slowed her hurried steps. "I'll tell you once we're aboard, girl. Now hurry on. I must see the captain and pay for your passage. From the looks of those sailors with the mooring lines, there isn't much time."

As they ascended the short gangplank, sailors were already going aloft to set some of the smaller sails. These would propel the ship slowly out into the channel where it would catch the ebbtide. Without asking directions, Her Ladyship made two turns and entered a hatchway that descended to the darkness of the lower deck. It was evident Milady had been aboard this ship before.

"Ah, Lady Fenleigh, I see you've brought the wench as promised, and not a minute too soon. Have you got her papers?"

Perturbed because the captain's eyes were raking Keary, she stepped between them. "Yes, Amos—er—Captain." She thrust an envelope in his hand and, trying to be her coquettish best, continued, "It's a shame we don't have more time; the traffic along the waterfront held us up."

"The fortunes of war, M'dear." He nodded in Lady Fenleigh's direction but his smile was all for Keary. "Next trip, Milady." His lips brushed the offered hand almost in dismissal and she turned angrily back to the gangway. It was evident she had planned a more fond farewell in the captain's cabin and was much more disappointed at the lack of time than he.

"But, Milady, you haven't given me instructions for Dublin!" Keary felt sudden panic; she recognized the captain as the man who had shared her Ladyship's bed the other night.

Lady Fenleigh stopped. Her rage at being so easily dismissed while the captain so openly admired Keary showed in her beet-red face. Turning to Keary, she said sarcastically, "Captain Shelby will give you your instructions; I'm sure he has had ample experience dealing with whores." She wheeled and fairly flew up the steps.

Keary turned to the captain, "Please, Sir, do you know who I'm to contact in Dublin?"

"Why—I assume, Miss, it's all written in this envelope. I must see to the ship now but if you care to join me for supper, I'm sure we can straighten everything out then."

"Thank you, Sir." Feeling something was amiss but not knowing quite what to do about it, she followed his directions to a small cabin as he disappeared down the gangway. Even as she opened the door, the deck beneath her feet felt unsteady and she realized the ship was under way. She glanced around uneasily, searching for her belongings but seeing nothing other than sea chests and other gear belonging to sailors. Was she in the wrong cabin? Running back on deck, she headed for the captain, who was now standing on the quarterdeck, feet firmly planted, staring out over the channel.

"And where might ye be goin', Miss?" A sailor stood with arms akimbo, blocking her path.

"I must talk to the captain; he assigned me to a cabin but I can't find my chests." She attempted to brush past him but he stepped sideways, continuing to obstruct her passage.

"The captain can't be disturbed 'til we clear the channel, Miss, and that'll take all day."

Turning, she saw the dock and Lady Fenleigh's carriage falling away rapidly. Bruce was standing on the driver's seat staring out at the departing ship and, as Keary watched with tears in her eyes and a lump in her throat, he sat down hurriedly and snapped the reins. Keary could almost hear the sharp command that had been issued from within the coach.

As the ship rode the ebbtide down the channel under the royals and topgallants, the captain nodded to the first mate who, in turn, lifted a speaking trumpet to his mouth. "Set mains'lls."

Immediately huge sheets of canvas fell loosely from the spars and sailors began securing the lines according to instructions from the quarterdeck. The ship shuddered then heeled under on a starboard tack, growing ever smaller to the man and woman watching from a cliff on the east side of the channel.

"You'll not miss her, Bruce; you still have your horses—and me." Her hand squeezed his thigh then moved slowly upward.

Turning to her and cupping her breast, he asked, "Do you think my wages could be adjusted, Milady? They're not all that good, you know."

She laughed at his sudden brazen attitude. "Let's see . . . it depends on whether you continue to treat me as well as you do my horses."

All of Keary's attempts to see the captain that day were unsuccessful, but she did manage to find out he dined at seven bells. Without her chests, she was unable to dress for supper or even repair her appearance to any degree. At the appointed hour, she arrived at the captain's cabin still clad in her traveling clothes, her long black curls tangled from the fresh breeze cutting across the ship. Still, the captain's expression as she appeared before him, showed she made a favorable impression.

"Come in, Miss Cavanaugh." He stepped aside, gesturing her toward a table set for two in the center of the cabin, his smile friendly and disarming. She was perplexed to see her own trunks standing near his bunk.

"Oh, here are my chests. Someone must have put them here by mistake since there is nothing but sailor's gear in my cabin."

As she started toward her belongings, the captain said, "Yes, well—ah—we can straighten that all out after we sup." He stepped to the back of a chair and drawing it out, bade her to sit.

Since this was the first night out of port and the ship was well-provisioned with fresh meat, fruits, and vegetables, the meal was a banquet. Keary, who had never made an ocean voyage before, would soon learn a ship's diet changed radically after a few days at sea, and even the captain's table would not escape the monotony of salt pork, dried vegetables, and hard biscuits.

Captain Shelby repeatedly filled her wine glass but Keary sipped sparingly, feeling uneasy about his motives. After the seaman had cleared the table and they lingered over their wine, she asked, "Do you have my instructions for Dublin, Captain? I would like to retire to my cabin as soon as someone can transfer my chests. It's been a very tiring day."

"Dublin, Miss? Wherever did you get the idea the ship is headed for Dublin?"

"My passage to Dublin was paid by Lady Fenleigh. She obtained a position there for me. We discussed it clearly when we boarded."

"Hmmm, I was paying little attention. Preparing to sail is always an absorbing experience."

Keary was frantic. Something was very wrong; she had felt it all day. It was strange how Lady Fenleigh had arranged a new position in such a short time but, after scheming to leave on her own with forged references, her relief at this happy turn of events had discouraged analyzing the situation in depth. Eyeing him warily, she demanded, "If not Dublin, Captain, what is our destination?"

He leaned back in his chair and stretched long legs out to the side of the table. "Philadelphia."

"Philadelphia! Why, that's thousands of miles from here—in the colonies! There's war there and wild savages!" Her hands flew to her throat in horror as she anxiously cried, "This is all a terrible mistake. I can't possibly go to Philadelphia. How would I make a living there?"

Captain Shelby threw back his head and laughed. "Will you Irish ever learn anything outside of your own little island? Philadelphia is a city second only to London in the empire. It's larger than Dublin. I'm sure you'll not be bothered by savages."

"But the war? How can you land there?" Her mind was spinning and she desperately tried to comprehend the frightening situation.

"If you line the right pockets, Miss, you can land anywhere. The naval blockade only increases the price of my cargo so, in the long run, it's to my benefit." He was oblivious to the roll of the ship and was sprawled out completely relaxed, whereas Keary kept both feet planted firmly on the floor and her arms tight on the table. His roguish grin explained how easily he had attained Her Ladyship's bed.

Still alarmed, Keary asked again, "But how will I be able to find employment there?"

Straightening in his chair, he leaned across the table. "Your employment is guaranteed for the next seven years."

"I'm afraid I don't understand."

He looked up from under thick black brows, feeling just a small prick of conscience. "That's the period of your indenture."

"Indenture! Why I'm free! I tell you this is all a terrible mistake. I demand you turn this ship around at once and return to port. I would never agree to indenture—in Philadelphia or anywhere!" Her blood began to boil in indignation and, oblivious to the roll of the ship, she jumped up and began to pace the cabin.

"That matters little, Miss. The magistrate signed the papers and, in return for your immediate deportation, Lady Fenleigh agreed to waive the charge of adultery, which seems to me a very magnanimous gesture after finding you in bed with her husband."

"Magistrate! When could she have been to court? And why wasn't I summoned to tell my side of the story?"

"I don't know the particulars, Miss, but it probably all transpired the day before yesterday. Her Ladyship spent most of the day in Cork."

She wanted to ask other questions: How much did the captain pay for her indenture? When did Lady Fenleigh approach the captain to take her to Philadelphia? But suddenly she knew this line of questioning was useless. The captain probably knew the whole story already but, since he stood to profit and was involved up to his ears, would tell her nothing.

In truth, Her Ladyship spent only a couple of hours bribing the magistrate and the remainder of the day she spent in this very cabin; however, the captain felt that part of the story was better left untold.

Keary whirled around, feeling a sickness in the pit of her stomach unrelated to the roll of the ship. "I don't suppose it would do any good to tell you he forced himself on me and that nothing really happened between us?"

"Not a bit since I'm not the judge. I only know I hold indenture papers on you for seven-years service and intend selling them in Philadelphia. Now, it will be an eight to twelve-week voyage, depending on the weather, and it's entirely up to you whether or not you make it in comfort." Strolling over to the curved, multi-paned porthole, he stood with his hands clasped behind his back. His body remained erect, seemingly without effort despite the roll of the ship. Years of sailing had taught his legs to adjust naturally.

Glancing toward her chests, Keary said, "Captain, then I gather my bags were not brought here by mistake?"

"That's a fair assumption, Miss."

"Then you are in league with my former employer? The very trollop with whom you so recently shared a bed?"

He grinned wickedly as he turned from the window. "Why, what a terrible accusation, Miss. Especially from one who has fornicated in the very same house."

"And, if I refuse the comfort of your cabin—then what?"

He approached her with cold, piercing eyes. "I suggest before you do that, you inspect the accommodations of bound slaves and appraise your duties in the galley."

"There will be no need for that, Captain. Regardless of what you've been told, I am a virgin and intend remaining one. Will you please have someone help me with my belongings?"

An angry flush spread across his features and, raising his hands in disgust he said, "As you wish, Miss. It will be a long voyage and I'm sure you'll change your mind in time."

"Not if the voyage were to China and back," she flung over her shoulder as she attempted to stomp out of the cabin but lurched drunkenly instead on the rolling ship. She made her way to the rail, breathing deeply of the clean breeze until a young sailor came with her chests and directed her to the indentured quarters.

The sailor in his flat hat, striped body shirt, and petticoat trousers shook his head in disbelief when the captain had commanded, "Move the lady's gear forward to the bound passenger's quarters; she seems to prefer their company to mine."

Now all the way down the long, dark passageway, the sailor chuckled, and shaking his head, finally said, "Miss, ye brain must surely be addled."

When she saw where she would be spending the next couple of months, Keary could understand his reasoning. Three lads and another girl were cramped into this storage area in the bow of the ship. There was no door or curtain for privacy and no portholes or ventilation of any kind. One dim lantern swung from a beam, casting shadows through the deep darkness.

The sailor dropped her trunk and was returning for the rest when Keary called after him, "But where is my berth?"

41

"Wherever you make it, Miss." His laughter echoed through the grim passageway as he left.

A young voice came out of the darkness, "Well now, this jaunt bayn't mebbe so cursed as whut I thot." Peering through the dimness, Keary saw a sandy-haired lad of about her own age patting a blanket he had rolled out between two large crates. Grinning up at her, he continued, "Ye kin be sharin' me bunk, lass."

Tossing her head, her eyes flashing, she shot back, "Put your tongue back in your face before you trip on it, lad." At this she turned to search in the darkness for room to store her belongings, leaving space to lay her head.

"It's here ye kin be comin', luv. 'Tis room right here I'll be makin' for ye." The girl sounded friendly and Keary, holding onto a large crate, made her way toward the voice. The sea was running heavier and the ship's bow was riding high and plowing hard. Hearing groaning to her left, Keary guessed one of the lad's stomach was not taking to it kindly and she hoped he would not add to the already overpowering stench.

In the shadows, Keary could barely make out the plain round face and long straight hair of a buxom lass smiling at her as she heaved and pushed her trunks. "'Tis Molly Gallagher I be, Miss. 'Tis a lady I took ye fer when first ever I see'd ye b'ard this marnin'. Saints above, lass, whatever are ye doin' here?"

"It's a long story, Molly. I'm not sure I understand myself. But, at any rate, it seems I'm bound."

"Oh, an' a genulman was involved, I be thinkin'—ye bein' such a fair lass and all. Oh, 'scuse me wanderin' tongue, Miss. I run on so."

"My name is Keary and you aren't saying anything

42

others haven't already said. Do you know where the galley is? I'm supposed to be there at five bells."

"Aye, 'tis there I be workin' too. Ye just come wi' me in the marnin'." She was shoving bales and boxes around as easily as a robust tar, making room for her newfound friend and happy that now she wasn't the only female in this crowded little hole. She kept up her chatter as Keary lay down beside her. But much of what she said fell on deaf ears, as the rolling of the ship and the fact she hadn't slept well the last few nights had lulled Keary to sleep.

Each day became the same as the next, the monotony broken only by the changes in weather. When a storm raged for two days, they found themselves confined to their dark, damp quarters. With the galley closed and the crew living on hard bread and cheese, Keary and Molly should have viewed it as a reprieve, but after being cooped up in their "quarters," both were happy to return to their duties at storms end. Keary's only pleasure during the voyage was spending time on deck between meals. Being the only two females aboard, Keary and Molly at first created quite a stir every time they appeared but, for the most part, the crew accepted them now. Although their deference was probably due to the captain's hostile scowl at anyone who approached her, Keary was nonetheless grateful.

Once their galley chores were finished, the women were free to roam the open deck, feeling the salt water spray on their faces and relishing the cool, clean-smelling sea breeze—and they cherished these times.

The quarterdeck was for the sole use of the officers and helmsman. She often looked up there to see the captain, standing with hands clasped behind his back, watching her but pretending no interest. When caught, he would smile knowingly, taking in her worn dress and rough appearance. His look intimated he expected it would only be a matter of time before she gave up her foolish pride and returned to his cabin.

"Miss Cavanaugh, are you enjoying the voyage?" Whirling, she saw the captain's tall form looming even taller as he spoke down to her from the quarterdeck, some four feet higher than the main deck on which she was standing.

"Oh yes, Captain." She recovered sufficiently to offset his advantage, and sarcastically replied, "The quarters are so spacious and the food so palatable. It's really unforgivable of me not to have taken the time to thank you properly, however, the tremendous social demands on my time have made it impossible."

"Then you plan to continue in your present quarters, I presume?"

"But of course, Captain. After all, I couldn't bear to leave my pet rodents. We've become so close."

"Well, when you change your mind, please let me know."

Ceremoniously lifting the corners of her ragged skirt, she executed a deep curtsy and, flashing her sweetest smile, called back loud enough for all on deck to hear, "That will be a cold day in hell, Sir." The smile became genuine as she watched him stomp across the deck and disappear from view amidst stifled laughter from nearby sailors.

Keary had become acclimated to the roll of the ship, the mouldy biscuits, the dried vegetables, and even the rats racing back and forth through their quarters at night. She had spent little time thinking of the future or what the new land might hold for her. Her only dream was a large tub of simmering water and a glob of scented soap. Washing with salt water left her feeling as dirty afterward as before. With no privacy or facilities for a bath, hurried rinsings behind a blanket held up by Molly were all she could manage. The same old gamblet gown and coarse apron, which she had worn since coming aboard, were now faded and ragged from repeated dowsings on a rope over the side of the ship. She refused to sacrifice more of her wardrobe to the salt water thrashings, only liberating her apparel from the old reed chests to air or to satisfy Molly's curiosity.

"Keary, if ye had a mind to pick yer own master, whut cut of a man would he be?" Molly and she were leaning over the rail looking at the star-studded sky, too tired to walk the deck and unwilling to retire to the hold.

"Well Molly, I've already decided General Washington is going to buy my indenture and set me on a white charger so I can lead the American army just like Joan of Arc."

"Can I be yer aide then and take care of all yer uniforms?" To Molly, who had enjoyed little of life's luxuries in her twenty years, just feeling rich materials was a thrill.

"Yes, so long as you bow every time I enter and say, 'yes, milady' and 'no, milady.'"

"Seriously now, Keary, ain't ye secretly hoped yer master would be rich and handsome?"

"To tell you the truth, Molly, I haven't given it much thought. I just hope I'm not sold to some lecherous old man who wants me for the same reason Lord Fenleigh did."

Molly's eyes widened; from the first day she had suspected there was a man involved for someone as beautiful and well-bred as Keary to be bound, but had no idea of the details. Hesitantly, she asked, "Did he—that is, did the bugger try to—?"

"He tried to rape me but I gave him a knee where it hurts most. And it's true, men are very tender there just like I heard. Ah, you should have seen his expression, Molly." Keary rolled her head back on her tired neck and closing her eyes chuckled softly, recalling the scene. "His eyes crossed and he turned whiter than cow's milk; the hot air went out of him and he fell like a punctured pig's bladder."

"Saints preserve us, Keary! Ye kneed an English lord in his private parts and got nuthin' more out of it than indenture? Why, if I'd done somethin' like that, I'd expect at least the noose, if not torture first."

"Well, really Lord Fenleigh didn't do anything about it, it was his wife who had me kidnapped. And why are you bound, Molly? What terrible crime did you commit?"

"None. I chose servitude meself as a way t'free meself of Ireland. America's a land of opportunity, ye know. O'course I ain't hopin' to make a fortune meself, but I hear simple artisans own their own cottages and shops, and farmers—even the wee ones—own their own land."

"You chose servitude voluntarily? I find that hard to understand even if America is all you say. How could you share in its prosperity as a bound girl?"

"Well, me aunt came o'er years ago an' was bound to a wee farmer. She be only fourteen at the time an' it was like one of the family the good man treated her. When her time was up her master even found her a husband an' now she's livin' on her own land wi' a good steady man."

"If what you wanted was a good steady man, why didn't you just stay in Ireland and try to find one?"

"Sure, an' grub on some Englishman's land 'til he decides he can make more money turnin' it to sheep grazin', at which time he gives ye the boot. I'm knowin' just to look at ye an' talk to ye, ye have never lived on a tenant farm. 'Twas tenant farmers me parents were, an' me mother died of nothin' more than plain hard work when I was only eight. We never had enough to fill our bellies and me father's spirit was broken as far back as I can remember. The only time he ever drew a sober breath was when he couldn't raise the few coppers fer a jug of poteen."

"Where is your father now?"

"In purgatory. I made up me mind years ago to come to America as soon as ever he died. I planted him one marnin' and walked to Cork that same day. I walked down the wharf askin' fer a ship goin' to America and offerin' to sign indentures fer me passage. Captain Shelby was the first one to take me up on it so here I be."

"Well, I certainly hope America is all you hope for. Suppose some mean old man buys you and treats you like a slave?"

"That's the chance I have to take. The other bad possibility is that I'll be bought by some rich man."

"What's wrong with that?"

"Fer ye nothin'. Ye would be a governess, a lady's maid, or even somethin' better. But I don't have yer looks or manners. Sure as the stone on me sainted mother's grave, it's emptyin' chamber pots I'd be doin' or, at best, a scullery maid. That way I'd never be treated like part of the family. But I'm not goin' to be thinkin' about such as that. Me dream is that I'll be bought by some wee farmer or artisan, and it's a very fine wife he'll be havin'. I will eat at the table with them and mebbe even go to church with them on Sunday. Then when me time is up it's a good man me master will be findin' me. It'll be a man whut doesn't drink and we'll live on our own land just like me Aunt Nora."

Keary looked out at the rolling waves of the unruffled sea and wished her own dreams could be as simple and well-defined as Molly's. Even the three lads who shared the hold looked forward eagerly to life in America. And, despite the stories told by the sailors of savage Indians and a fierce civil war engulfing the country, the future still held promise for them. But what did the new country hold for her? According to the captain, Philadelphia was the second largest city in the empire, and the continent of North America was a hundred times the size of Ireland and England combined. Would she become part of a rich banker's household or that of a simple artisan? *Whatever my fate,* Keary thought, *I have no control over it for the next seven years so I'll not be carking my brain about it now.*

The sailors generally ignored the women, except for one who made lewd advances early in the voyage before he had the opportunity to feel the lash of Keary's sharp tongue. Molly, mouth agape, had been utterly horrified at the scathing rebuff Keary had laid on him the time he had taken advantage of her thin skirts to squeeze her buttocks. When the veteran of a hundred waterfront brawls and countless encounters with doxies was not easily dissuaded, she waved a belaying pin menacingly above his head and barely missed trying to part his hair.

Details of the incident quickly made the rounds of the ship and did wonders in defense of her chastity.

Also her refusal to accept the captain's hospitality was well known and few sailors were arrogant enough to expect success where the captain had failed, or be willing to face his jealousy even if they were. When she talked to the crew at all, it was usually to ask questions about the operation of the ship or to inquire if they thought this interminable voyage would ever end.

After two weeks at sea the weather turned favorable, with just enough wind to keep the bow of the ship ploughing the waves at a steady pace. According to the sailors they were making excellent time, and both Keary and Molly worked hard and efficiently, thus having the opportunity to enjoy the open deck. The further into the voyage they traveled, the more the diet became a tasteless routine of salt pork, dried vegetables, and hard biscuits. The daily gill of rum and the ever-present limes were the only other additions to the diet, and only the rum was taken willingly. The limes, now standard practice on British ships as a prevention against scurvy, were distasteful to the crew, not only because of their tartness but also because the practice had given birth to the nickname "limey," which the Americans had bestowed upon all British sailors.

Though the monotonous diet was as hard on the women as the rest of the crew, it had a beneficial side effect. Galley duties became simpler and they were able to spend more time on deck. Keary was standing at the rail enjoying the late afternoon sun when a young sailor approached.

"Are you looking forward to America, Miss?" Barney, a dark-haired lad, had become more talkative of late. He was well-mannered and she enjoyed speaking with him about the operation of the ship, a subject she found fascinating. She marveled at the sailors' skill, amazed the ship could sail either east or west regardless of the wind's direction.

"Yes, Barney, although I'm not sure why. Maybe I just want to leave this ship and enjoy a hot bath. Really, I don't know how you can stand the life, confined to a ship all the time."

"That's why this is my last voyage. Though I like the work and the sea, I don't like being at sea so long at a stretch."

"You're leaving the ship? You mean after the return voyage?"

"No, Miss. I mean as soon as we reach Philadelphia."

Keary looked around to see if anyone else could overhear before asking, "You mean you're going to jump ship?"

"No. I just signed on for this half of the voyage and when we reach Philadelphia, I'll be free to go. Of course, I had to do it without pay to get the captain to take me along."

"I didn't think you could do that; I always thought you had to sign on for the whole voyage."

"With most captains that's true, but Captain Shelby is a decent man. He allowed me to come so long as I worked for my passage."

A brisk wind blew the dark curls over her face and she lifted the handkerchief tucked into the neckline of her bodice, quickly wrapping it around the recalcitrant curls and tying it under her chin. "Humph. I think he's a horrible man."

"Guess you would considering the circumstances, but

remember this—with most captains you wouldn't have a choice. You would have shared his cabin and no bones about it."

"Well, you don't know the whole story. But if he's your idea of a good man, I hope you never meet a bad one."

"All I know, Miss, is that if you do your duty on this ship, no one bothers you. I've known of ships where hardly a week went by without some sailor feeling the lash. I've only seen Captain Shelby order the lash twice and both times the men deserved it. He insists on discipline and won't tolerate shirkers but he never issues punishment just because he's in a bad mood."

"If you're leaving the sea why are you going to America? Why not go back to England where your home and family are?"

"What could I do in England? Wages are twice as high in America and anyone willing to work can find it. I don't know how long it will take, but some day I'll own my own land."

"Why does everyone think they can own land so easily in America?"

"Because there is a hundred times as much of it and there ain't a bunch of earls and lords controlling it."

Keary wondered if land was as available as everyone seemed to think. In Ireland she never even dreamed of owning land. But, if it were possible in America, some day she would like to have a beautiful farm. As she stared over the rail the swells became a landscape of gentle rolling meadows and timber and it was all hers, as far as the eye could see. Suddenly there was a burning desire within her for land—a desire, the likes of which she had never felt before. A tap on her shoulder disturbed her reverie and she turned to see one of the crew.

"'Scuse me, Miss. The captain would like to see you in his cabin."

Keary ran her fingers through her dirty hair as she hastily tucked the handkerchief into the neck of the bodice. She ran her hands down the soiled skirt, smoothing it as well as she could although she told herself she had no interest in impressing the captain. Still, she didn't like to appear before anyone looking so bedraggled.

Answering her hesitant knock, Captain Shelby said, "Come in and sit down, Miss. I assume you are still enjoying the voyage." She felt ill at ease in her soiled clothing and, covering work-worn hands in the folds of her skirt, tossed her head back with a venomous stare.

"Oh yes, Sir. I'm ever so grateful for your kindness. You know it isn't every man who would provide the luxurious accommodations you do, nor would he work ladies like slaves ten hours a day and callously sell them at the end of the voyage. It's really difficult for me to express my thanks for your generosity."

"Spare me the sarcasm; I offered to share my quarters and, by the way, that offer is still open."

A sarcastic hoot followed his words and she bent over the desk, sparks splintering the blue eyes so close to his as she ground through tight-set jaws, "I don't give a tinker's damn. Your offer can stay open 'til an Irishman's made king of England for all I care." She pushed away from the desk and he was smitten with the flushed cheeks and fiery eyes now turned almost violet from her anger. "If you'll tell me the purpose of this summons, I'll get back to my duties."

A momentary frown creased his rugged features and he

attempted to keep his composure. "You are a stubborn wench but that's your problem. Tell me then, have you made friends with the other indentures?"

She stared at him haughtily. "If you are insinuating that I have been sharing my blanket with one of the lads, you're flapping your gums in the wrong direction. One of them tried, but a borrowed knife from the galley flashed in his face, showing him the error of his ways. Now that we understand each other, we all get along fine. And, if it's in your mind to punish me for filching the knife, I've already returned it."

"You are a cold, cold lass." He wagged his head slowly in disbelief and added, "I hope you have a long and happy spinsterhood."

"If I have to choose from men such as I've known so far, spinsterhood would be paradise. Now will you please tell me the reason for this summons?"

Her haste to end the meeting irritated Captain Shelby in a way he could not hide with his manufactured smile. "At any time now we will be stopped and boarded by a royal naval officer from the blockading squadron. In the event you have any idea of telling them your little tale of woe—your alleged kidnapping—I strongly advise you to hold your tongue."

"And if I don't?"

"The royal navy is desperate for sailors right now and even the press-gangs can't supply enough men. Normally they can fill their quotas from waterfront grogshops but, at the rate things are going, press-gangs will soon be raiding the churches. And, if the preacher objects, he'll find himself climbing a rigging too. They will take anyone from this, or any other ship, on the slightest pretense and no questions asked."

"I fail to see how that concerns me."

"How about your friends, the three bound lads from Ireland and the seaman, Barney, you seem so friendly with lately?"

"Do you mean the royal navy would press them without provocation?"

"Oh, they can invent the cause very easily. Say—charge them with desertion from a British man-of-war, anything to put the right coat of paint on things. So, if you try to tell your little story, I could put a bug in the officer's ear and the lads would be pressed into naval service immediately. In return for my cooperation, your story would be ignored and this ship would be allowed clear sailing to Philadelphia while the navy looked the other way."

"Oh, but that would cost you money, my dear Captain, and I've learned that is very near and dear to your heart."

"Yes, I would hate to lose the price of the bound servants but it's a price I would rather pay than face a charge of kidnapping for such as you. As for Barney, a stint in the royal navy would be just deserts."

Her square chin jutted out and she wrapped her arms tightly under her breast, her head jerking up and down in a few quick nods. "Humph, I knew I was right."

His eyebrow quirked up and, leaning over the desk, his voice fairly dripped disdain. "Right about what, my dear lady?"

"Barney was just saying you were a decent man and I wholeheartedly disagreed with him."

"Don't try to play on my sympathies; this is strictly a business decision. Now there will be a naval officer come aboard and tell us we cannot proceed to Philadelphia because it's under blockade. After—shall we say—ah, certain arrangements have been made, the navy vessel will continue on her way and we'll sort of get lost and end up in Philadelphia. Now, in light of what I've told you, do you anticipate exposing the circumstances of your unusual exile to the boarding officer?"

"No, Captain. It seems Lady Fenleigh isn't the only one who schemes well in advance."

"I'm glad to hear that. Had your answer been different, I would have been forced to put you in irons until after the boarding party left."

"Your benevolence never ceases to amaze me, Captain."

"See here, Miss. I started as a common seaman and now I not only command this vessel, but own most of it as well. I didn't accomplish all that by being charitable."

"Bully for you, Sir. I have not labored under any misconceptions regarding the possibility of noble blood in your veins. In fact, I would be willing to wager canine blood could be found on the maternal side of your immediate ancestry. Now may I go?"

Ignoring the barb, he warned, "Yes, but just in case you should change your mind, if this ship is deterred to the Sugar Islands for any reason, I'll sell you to one of the planters for the very same services you denied me. A wench so well educated in obscenities should have no trouble being accepted into a society where women serve only one purpose. Do we understand each other?"

"Perfectly."

He raised his hand and waved her off. "Then you may go."

Keary left shaking her head. She had not thought of asking anyone for redress of her grievances, especially the British. Still, she wondered how he knew she would be willing to suffer her own fate rather than betray another human being. There was no doubt in her mind that, in the same position, he would sell his own brother if there was a profit to be made.

The day after Keary's meeting with Captain Shelby, a British frigate pulled alongside and two officers came aboard. After a short conversation with the captain, the officers departed and they were again under way—but on a changed course. Rumors quickly spread through the ship that they would not be able to proceed to Philadelphia. One of the officers had been overheard saying as he was leaving the ship, "You may try the Sugar Islands, Captain. I'm sure you could dispose of your cargo there."

Keary was despondent. She had assuaged her fears lately thinking of all the wonderful opportunities the others spoke of in the new country. All she had heard of the Sugar Islands were heat, fever, and black slaves. Had the captain been unsuccessful in his attempts to buy off the officers or were the rumors wrong? She shuddered. If the rumors were true, would her fate be white slavery in the chambers of a remote planter?

Glancing up at the quarterdeck, she took note of Captain Shelby's smug expression and suspected the rumors were untrue. At the first sign of darkness, the ship heaved hard to starboard and sailors began scampering aloft to crowd on every inch of canvas. The next morning, Keary saw land on both sides of the ship and the sailors confirmed they were on the Delaware River. Her mounting excitement over the prospect of seeing Philadelphia was dampened, however, when she learned it would still be three or four days depending on the winds.

For two days the ship tacked back and forth across the river, making very little headway. Keary and Molly hung on the rails at every opportunity, enjoying the sights and noting the tiny settlements and the ever-growing assortment of river boats. They were standing exclaiming over some of the beautiful homes along the shore when a sailor approached.

"Cap'n wishes to see you on the quarterdeck, Miss." He nodded to Keary.

Perturbed at having to leave the loveliness of the shoreline to confer with the arrogant captain again, she faced him with a pronounced scowl. "You sent for me, Captain?"

He ignored her evident displeasure. "Yes, I did." Handing her a key, he continued. "A man is filling a hot tub in my cabin. You can lock the door from the inside and, if you think I am planning to seduce you, there is a slide bolt on the door. You will bathe and join me for supper and, for God's sake, select your best dress! I'm sick of seeing you in that rag."

She flashed a sardonic grin as she mimicked Lady Fenleigh and, with a deep curtsy said, "Why, Captain, I didn't think you noticed." She winced and scampered away under his withering look, afraid she had jeopardized this rare privilege. Unsure of what had developed to cause this wonderful opportunity or exactly what he had in mind, she ran to the cabin dreaming of hot water perfumed with scented soap, not allowing herself to speculate further. All other problems would be addressed later.

The relative stability of the ship in the calm river

enabled the sailor to fill the tub more than halfway without sloshing over the side. Keary danced from one foot to the other in her haste to be rid of the sailor so she could lower herself into the steaming tub. Once the door was locked, the slide lock secure, she fairly tore at her clothes, scattering them in all directions. She languished in the tub until the water was lukewarm. Reluctantly emerging from the spicy smelling water and wrapping a huge towel about her body, she proceeded to dress while her mind happily created a new coiffure. She had decided on the mauve taffeta as it was the least wrinkled and was not too daring. Its primly rounded neckline edged in lace and the fitted bodice with small flounces decorating the sleeves at the elbow gave a nice contour to her firm breasts. The full overskirt was separated at the waistline, falling away to display a purple and white striped petticoat. Lady Fenleigh's dressmaker had made the gown for her to attend a musicale with Milord and Her Ladyship.

Unlocking a small metal box, Keary carefully withdrew the amethyst earbobs, a gift from her grandmother many years ago. She gathered the clean, shining curls atop her head and, using the horn poll combs and a few bodkins, secured the raven mass except for one long strand. This she wrapped around her finger to form a perfect curl trailing softly over her shoulder.

Pirouetting in front of the mirror in the black satin slippers, the long ribbons laced around sturdy ankles, she felt like flying on weightless feet after weeks of wearing heavy clogs. Keary was pleased with the results and even the unladylike burnished complexion, acquired from the hot sun and sea breezes during the long voyage, couldn't detract from the pleasure of seeing herself properly dressed once again.

Captain Shelby opened the cabin door to her soft knock and she was surprised to see two other officers, standing wide-eyed and open-mouthed, unable to conceal their delight. Captain Shelby, his dark eyes admiring the loveliness before him, took her hand.

"Good evening, Miss Cavanaugh. This is First Officer Hampton and Second Officer Davis. They are going to dine with us tonight."

Keary dropped a demure curtsy as both officers acknowledged the introduction. She was not acquainted with either of these officers despite having seen them every day for weeks. After a few cursory remarks, the gentlemen pretended total involvement in the conversation concerning the cargo they would pick up and details of the return journey, all the while stealing covetous glances at the refined, beautiful young lady sitting at the captain's side.

Keary was pleased, no longer fretting over the prospect of an intimate supper with the captain. She enjoyed the delicious meal of fresh beef, tiny new potatoes, suet pudding with thick brown gravy, and green vegetables, which small river boats, swarming along the side of the ship, had delivered that day.

It was only after the two officers left that apprehension began to take hold. Captain Shelby stretched until he tilted the chair back, balancing it on two legs. His mocking smile at her obvious discomfort unnerved her.

"The first mate will double up with one of the other officers tonight. You will use his cabin and wear either that gown or something else suitable tomorrow."

Cautiously, she asked, "And to what do I owe this kindness, Sir?"

"It's simple. You will be going on the block tomorrow and this way you will bring a better price."

"Thank you for the first bit of honesty you have shown me. However, I have had other advice."

"Oh? From whom?"

"My friend, Molly. She told me to dress plainly and tie up my hair or I may be purchased by a lecherous old man who has similar ideas to those of a ship's captain."

Her barb found its mark and jumping up furiously, he leaned over the table. "Go to hell, wench. Dress any way you want because I don't give a damn about you or what price you may bring. If you prefer those surroundings, sleep in your hole again tonight. My intention was to help you get a decent start now that I'm sure you were telling the truth about the affair with His Lordship." He strode furiously to the porthole.

Still uncertain of his motives but not wanting to capitulate at his first sign of kindness, she asked, "Why, Captain, do I denote a trace of remorse? Could it be you do have a conscience under that malevolent exterior?"

Without turning he said quietly, "If you dress as a peasant, you may find yourself scraping hides in a tannery or milking cows. If you dress as I tell you, you could conceivably be bought by wealthy folk to serve as a governess or lady's companion. I planned to inform the auctioneer of your ability to read and write and also that you had served in the house of a nobleman." He turned abruptly and threw up his hands. "But suit yourself; after tomorrow I'll not see you again."

Her look was one of pure amazement. In the back of her mind dwelt the suspicion that the bath, dinner, and cordial treatment were nothing more than bait to lure her into accepting his final invitation to share his berth.

Along with relief at seeing this hurdle passed came pure euphoria at the prospect of spending her last night in a regular bunk rather than the hold. Still, his last remark, "I'll not see you again," produced an unexpected emotion. She passed it off as an injury to her pride but for reasons she could not explain, her happy spirits of a moment before were somewhat dampened. "Which cabin is the first mate's?"

"The first one on your left."

He strolled to the desk and examined the log as she rose and meekly replied, "Thank you, Sir," and hurried to the door.

Chapter III

Morgan Baines did not stand to inherit any of his family's holdings. The Baines family was governed more by custom rather than law—and he was a second son. They were loyal to the king and mother country and were bound firmly by tradition to the Anglican church and the Tory party. Most importantly, the family name and position were perpetuated through the practice of willing the bulk of the estate to the eldest son to insure it would survive intact, rather than be decimated in a few generations by division among all the heirs.

A reasonable trust was set up for the widow, including a provision she could not be removed from the plantation for the remainder of her natural life. The provision was no longer valid since Mrs. Baines had preceded her husband to eternal rest by more than two years. This proviso remained in the will, however, as a guideline for future generations whose wills, hopefully, would be identical to this document.

Marilynn, Morgan's sister and the apple of her father's eye, was bequeathed a dowry large enough to tempt a

Byrd or a Randolph. Simon, the eldest son, received the manor house with its accompanying fifteen thousand acres, all livestock, one hundred and twenty-seven slaves, four hundred shares in The East India Company, a one-third partnership in a flourishing London brokerage house, three ships, several mortgages and other commercial papers—and seventeen thousand pounds sterling.

Morgan received one thousand pounds cash, two hundred acres in the western frontier, his black boy, Benji, two blooded Arabian stallions, and a trust of two hundred pounds a year. He didn't resent his father's will notwithstanding the fact that Simon was a drunk and a gambler and, in his entire lifetime, had never shown the slightest interest in the plantation. It was the custom and in no way reflected the squire's feelings for his sons since he had always held a special place in his heart for Morgan. From the time he had been a strawberry-blond tad with mischievous eyes that glinted like sparks from a fire when aroused and softened like melted honey when the devilish grin broke across his features, Morgan had captivated not only his father, but everyone with whom he came into contact.

The arrangements for the frontier acreage had been completed, providing him with extra income, and the young couple who had leased it had an opportunity to eventually own a farm. He had magnanimously refused their meager savings as down payment, urging them to use it for operating capital. The lease was unique in that after ten years, title to the land would revert to the tenants.

Morgan would have liked to carry out his late father's wishes regarding the land; however, the frontier held no attraction for the man whose aspirations gravitated naturally to English drawing rooms and the female companionship to be found there in abundance. He recalled the last conversation on the matter as he and his father traversed Banetree's acres one spring morning.

"Morgan, I've received two hundred acres of land in the Shenandoah as payment for a debt. I've thought of leaving it to you in my will." Morgan's mount shied at the sudden pull on the reins.

"Why, thank you, Father, but—ah—what would I do with land on the frontier? I just can't picture myself in buckskins."

"I know it wouldn't be much considering the manner in which you have been raised, but you will also get a nominal trust and by investing it wisely, in time you could build a great plantation on that land."

"It's a noble thought, Father, and most men would jump at the opportunity. Somehow though, I—I don't feel the urge to build empires."

"Don't decide too quickly. You have qualities neither I nor Simon have. If anyone can do it, I believe you're the one. I'll leave it to you in my will and you'll always have the option."

"Thank you, but with my style of living, you'll probably outlive me." Morgan couldn't know that less than a month later, an unknown fever would put his father in his grave.

With most of his preparations complete, only two matters needed attention before Morgan could leave for England. First, he had to free Benji. It was not practical to take a slave along. The cost and inconvenience of caring for a servant would tax his pecuniary position and his carefully planned investments.

The signed manumission papers were in his desk; still, he was reluctant to tell Benji, fearing a painful farewell. Though everyone would view freeing a valuable slave as an act of great charity, guilt pangs assailed Morgan as he stood at the window gathering courage. Benji was busily laying out his master's attire for the evening.

"Benji, there's something I must tell you."

"No need to tu'n ya back on me, Mistah Mohgan. Ah knows ya ain' gonna tek me wif ya."

Morgan turned and met his lifelong servant's eyes squarely. "Dammit, Benji. Can't I ever keep a secret from you? Who told you?"

"No one tol' me. Ah knowed soon as ya start t'look away ever time ya talks 'bout Lon'on. Whut I gonna do now, drive de cah'age?"

"You can do whatever you like now; you are free." Morgan crossed to the desk and handed the sheaf of papers to the tall black. "Here are your manumission papers and fifty pounds hard money."

"Ah sho am beholden', Mistah Mohgan, but why ya doin' dis?"

"Because I can't afford a servant now and I don't know how well you would fare in London. There wouldn't be many Negroes there for you to associate with, while here you would be with your own people. Simon said you can stay here as long as you want or leave whenever you want."

The slave studied the ticket to freedom as if he could read. "Ah won' be stayin' heah on'y long 'nuff to tek keer of a few things den ah be gone."

"Gone? Where?"

"If'n ah gon' be free den it's 'bout time ah starts fightin' fo it. Ah be leavin' to jine Gen'rul Wash'nden's ahmy. Ah knows ya doan holds wit' da rebels, Mistah Mohgan, so if'n ya wants to stop me, ya bettah tek dese papahs back right now."

Morgan laid his hand on his friend's shoulder; pictures of a young shadow running at his side to the fishing hole flooded his memory. The sigh that escaped Morgan's lips wasn't from his friend's decision and he suddenly grasped Benji in his arms.

"You're right, Benji. I don't hold with the rebels but you are a free man now. What matters most is what you hold with."

It had been exactly one month since his father's death and the house had entertained a constant flow of visitors. Several of the mourners had stayed on for some time after the funeral and, once Morgan had announced his intentions of sailing for England, a new stream came.

Morgan would have enjoyed spending this last night with Pearl, the other matter he had to attend to, but since the great house was full of guests who had come to bid him farewell, he would have to be content with one hour in Pearl's cabin. She knew of his plans to leave and would be expecting an all-night farewell.

He had been an innocent lad of fourteen, recently expelled from school for clumsily trying to seduce the headmaster's daughter, when Pearl, the coffee-colored Negress, took him under her wing and initiated him into the mysteries of sex. She was two years older and loved him dearly, but knew well the limits of their relationship. She had served him well as a lover and teacher, instructing him in all the tender techniques and subtleties that turned even free women into slaves. By the time Morgan was eighteen, he had seduced a vast array of both single and married women in an area reaching far beyond the borders of Virginia. Pearl always insisted he tell her the intimate details of his conquests, receiving perverse enjoyment out of hearing of those prissy little ladies having their legs spread. She would usually try to wheedle him into divulging his latest seduction.

"Mistah Mohgan, honey, yo sho' nuff done planted yo pitchfoke in dat lily-white hay mound? Whut di' she say—'Oh, my! Ah nevah gwine be de same—Ah cain' lib a'nudder day wiffout ya?' Den ah bet she sweah dat be de fust time an' iffen ya doan mah'hy her she gwine die."

"That's about the size of it. I don't know why I let you drag these tales from me. A gentleman should never divulge such things. If you ever breathe a word of this, I'll come after you with a real pitchfork."

"Huh! Who ah gonna tell out heah—de field hands? Whut dey cah 'bout white folk's goin's-on?"

Morgan's education had been the classic type with emphasis on Latin, Greek, and the social graces. Nothing in it prepared him in any way to earn a living in the commercial world. In fact, most of his schoolmates were from the noble class and considered trade beneath their station. He had acquired a firm belief in the virtue of class distinction as a prerequisite of an ordered society, and a God-given right to a place near the top. According to this tenet, gentlemen were born to rule and the lower classes to serve.

His social opinions were more democratic than most of his peers, in that he would encourage those of the lower stations who, by their own industry, were able to better themselves. Yet he abhorred the concept of eliminating class distinction, not on moral grounds but rather because it was impractical. His vision of the social structure was a ladder with every rung filled, and his own rung being near the top.

For the past several years the colonies had revolted against these beliefs and Morgan had reacted with disgust—not at the rebels, but rather at the Crown for not resolutely putting the rabble in their proper place. The demonstrations, boycotts, and tea parties were one thing but, for a year New Englanders had been in armed rebellion. Finally the king, tired of his subjects misbehaving, had sent a large expeditionary force to New York to settle the issue.

"Are you all packed, Morgan, or did you forget such an unimportant detail? I wouldn't put it past you."

"Come in, Marilynn. I've packed all I can cram into my saddlebags and the remainder will be shipped. Hopefully, my clothes will not be too far outdated by English fashions. Out of my princely inheritance I will have to budget enough money to supplement my wardrobe once I reach London."

"Oh, those poor London maids! The most beautiful one will capture you and the others will be destined to a life of sorrow or a convent." Marilynn, now twenty years old, had the same sandy hair as Morgan and it wouldn't take a stranger a full minute to decide they were brother and sister.

"I hope you're right—on one condition that is."

"Condition!" Her soft brown eyes widened that anyone would attach conditions to marrying the most beautiful woman in London.

"Yes. She will have to also be the richest—or at least one of the richest."

"Oh, how mercenary! And I always considered you a romantic."

"I always was and still would be if I could afford it. But unfortunately I'm afraid from here on the purse will be taking precedent over the heart."

"Strictly business, huh? Tell me more, brother dear. The day you can't find time for the ladies is the day Sam Adams will be made prime minister of England. If you are serious about marrying for money, why not stay here? Do you realize how many maids there are around here who would browbeat their fathers unmercifully for large dowries if they thought it would ensnare you?"

"Yes, I'm sure I could make a profitable match here in Virginia, but after studying the situation, I've come to the conclusion there are too many drawbacks."

"I see no drawbacks in making a profitable marriage and still staying close to your family."

Bothered by her hurt expression, he took her hands in his. "Come here and sit down for a minute. We've always understood each other pretty well, so maybe I can explain. If Banetree were mine, I could work hard, find the right woman, and be content. But Simon is the eldest and the one who should rightfully inherit."

"Not if it were up to me—why I'd—"

"Shh." He put his finger to her lips and continued, "It's a good custom; though Simon has his weaknesses, I'm sure responsibility is exactly what he needs right now, and that leaves me in a position to fare for myself. If I married a local girl, I'm sure I could pick up a dowry large enough to start with a few hundred acres and, in time, build it into something substantial. But with this infernal war on, I'm not sure this is the time to try, eve[n] if my heart and soul were in it. However, in London I ca[n] circulate in society and watch for widows with larg[e] fortunes. Then if I'm something less than a dutifu[l] husband, at least I'll have a lot of company."

"And here that life would not be so easy?"

"Exactly. Here a man has a wife, a mulatto concubine and occasionally a tryst with a love-starved neighbor. Bu[t] on the whole, he better lead a pretty straight-laced life t[o] be accepted in society and not disgrace his family."

"So you want to carouse with the macaronies, is tha[t] it?"

"No. I have no desire to wear lace or decorated hose, o[r] even to bathe in perfume. In fact, if I could find a woma[n] of wealth who I could also love, I might become a devote[d] husband. But here I just haven't found a wealth[y] woman I feel could keep me close to the hearth on a col[d] winter night."

"Well, at least you have made the rest of my visi[t] much easier. I have been charged by two different maid[s] to make last minute pitches on their behalf and, now tha[t] I know your specifications, there's no need to go throug[h] with it."

"Thank God for that! I have a fair idea who the maid[s] are and have no desire to spend the rest of my life wit[h] either, regardless of the size of their dowries. But tell me what are your plans? Will you marry soon or keep thos[e] suitors of yours dangling a while longer?"

"I don't know; most of the eligible men are off to war.' She laughed, "At least with you gone, those left will no[t] be so afraid to press their suits."

"What has my leaving to do with it?"

"Morgan, how can you be so sophisticated and at the same time so stupid? Ever since you cut Byron Wells'[s] arm in that duel, every gallant in Virginia has been hesitant about making advances toward me."

"Sorry, but I fail to see the connection. I challenged Byron because I felt he was cheating at cards."

"Oh, brother—do you think I'm still an innocent little girl playing with dolls? I am well aware a lady's name is never publicly mentioned in a gentlemen's quarrel. However, it's awfully strange that within minutes after he made a slurring remark about my virtue, you just happened to walk over to the table and accuse him of cheating in a game in which you were not even playing."

"But, Marilynn, it was not like that at all. It was—"

"Don't worry, Morgan. I never resented your action, although it did put a crimp in my social life for a while. I was proud of you for upholding family honor. And now that it is out in the open and you are leaving, there is one thing I would like to add: I never gave Byron any reason to say the things he did. In fact, he was angry because I refused his advances, and after several drinks could no longer contain it."

"I know that. And the fact he was drunk at the time he said those things is the only reason I stuck him in the arm instead of the chest. Now, Simon is going to need help and I hope you will be a pillar of strength for him."

Tears formed in Marilynn's eyes as she clung to him. "I'll try, Morgan, but don't be surprised if you see me in London before long. I don't see any more future here than you do."

"Can't say that I blame you. Still, you had better find a husband first. It's much easier for a man to go out into the world to seek his fortune than a woman."

"I know. Oh God, how well I know."

* * *

The guests that evening included a few in the uniform of the new American army, and Morgan was amused at these gentlemen playing soldier. They secured commissions, dressed the part, but never seemed to leave home. Some, he figured, were simply making a gesture to hide their true allegiance so they could protect their property from the hated Committees of Safety. These were unique organizations set up without the slightest legal justification, holding almost unlimited power over the citizenry. In the political vacuum caused by the flight of Crown authority these committees simply appointed themselves to fill the void. They had been known to seize property and punish citizens on any charge, proven or not, and this reign of terror, Morgan mused, was executed in the name of liberty.

The dinner was similar to many held at the Baineses' plantation over the years. The long table and huge sideboard gleamed under a chandelier of numerous flickering candles displaying linens, crystal, and silver that had graced this table for almost a hundred years. Servants moved back and forth bringing one course after another of succulent meats, puddings, vegetables, and freshly baked bread and rolls. Various wines enriched each course, and later rich black coffee would be served in demitasse cups to be enjoyed over mouth-watering desserts.

The only way this dinner differed from hundreds of its predecessors was the sprinkling of uniforms and the political discussions being held in the presence of ladies.

George Jamison, his neighbor of many years, was seated directly across the table from Morgan, dressed in the new blue and buff of the Virginia Line. He was a serious-minded, honest owner of a small plantation on the Rappahannock River and wouldn't don the emblem in a cause without true dedication. This interested Morgan, who had offhandedly termed all American soldiers "rabble."

"Are you raising a company to serve in Squire Washington's legions too, George?" The sarcasm was directed at the many gentlemen who were supposedly raising companies but, in truth, were using the failure of recruits to respond as an excuse to sit home and wait.

"No, Morgan. We have enough gentlemen already filling that role." With this he acknowledged the causticity and applauded its intent. "I've secured a commission and along with a few neighbors will be leaving for New York to join an existing regiment. Perhaps you would like to join us?" A satisfied smile was his vehicle for returning the barb, since Morgan's loyalties to the Crown were well-known.

"I'm afraid you'd regret the invitation, George, for on our arrival I would be offering my services to General Howe."

George laughed easily. "In that case, I withdraw the invitation because, seriously, I feel we should all examine our conscience carefully these days before choosing sides. And to be perfectly honest, my decision did not come suddenly."

This intrigued Morgan, for although he had resolved not to discuss politics this night, he knew George was a man of unusual intelligence and not one to be coerced easily. "That fascinates me, George, for if anyone could justify this rebellion, it would definitely not be a politician, but a man such as yourself. Is it tyranny, taxation without representation, or perhaps the usurpation of the rights of free Englishmen?"

A hush fell over the table as all eyes moved to Lieutenant Jamison. The whole area had been a bulwark of loyalists until the Committees of Safety had made that persuasion untenable. If the king's troops were to march in tomorrow they would be greeted with open arms, but the absence of Crown authority had created a vacuum in which only rebels could survive. Discussions that used to be free and open were fast becoming guarded, and opinions expressed were not necessarily dictated by one's conscience. Thus, everyone was interested in George's opinion without having to express his own. George looked around the table at the questioning faces and then, addressing Morgan again but speaking loud enough for all to hear, he replied.

"You seem to have put me on the spot, Sir. First, let me say that I would be ready at any time to work for reconciliation even though I know it would not last long. This continent is too large and diversified to be ruled by a tiny island three thousand miles away. The population is a third of England's and growing a hundred times as fast. In the last few years, there have been more than seventy-five thousand new immigrants to Pennsylvania alone. In a few more years the population of this continent will exceed England, and shall we then receive all manufactures through English ports?" He sipped his wine and the room remained quiet for him to continue.

"I tell you all the ports of England would not be capable of handling the tonnage. Instead of arguing on how best to tax us—and this after forty years experience in which the actual revenue didn't equal the cost of collecting it—Parliament and the king's ministers should be planning ahead for such a golden age of trade."

No one challenged him and he toyed with his

silverware, seeming to weigh his next words carefully. "I, for one, would not object to taxation with or without representation, for who in England has representation? No Sir, it's not representation I want but the damn rights as English merchants and—that is to sell my produce anywhere in the world I can find a market. For years I, and my father before me, have lived on credit from English merchants."

Hunching himself over the table, he spread out his hands to Morgan and asked, "Why should we not be allowed to establish manufactures of our own and be free to market our wares? I tell you, if it were not for our proficiency in the art of smuggling, these colonies would live in a state of perpetual poverty. In the last war, which by the way added the entire Dominion of Canada, a country which could put all England in one of its lakes, our reward for helping was a law prohibiting us from settling beyond the mountains. Are those vast, rich regions to remain in perpetuity as a refuge for a handful of Indians?"

At the murmurs along the table, he shook his head and said, "I'm not a rebel by nature; that title was forced on me by circumstances. But I do know separation from England at some time is as sure as the changing of the seasons, so it may as well be now."

The room remained silent as a tomb and, by way of breaking the spell, Morgan asked, "So you do believe Parliament has the right to tax us? That's quite an admission from a rebel."

Looking up, George agreed. "Yes, I do; I always have. But along with that right is an obligation to grant free trade to all."

A conversation buzzed along the length of the table a

small furor erupted at the front door. An excited messenger pushed past the servant and burst into the room. "I've just come from Philadelphia and Congress has passed the Declaration of Independence."

Morgan sat quietly through the pandemonium caused by the announcement, thinking to himself, *I couldn't have decided on a better time to leave these shores.*

Excusing himself and tapping Morgan on the shoulder, Simon bade his brother to accompany him to the study. Sitting behind the large walnut desk, he poured each a glass of brandy.

Simon was only thirty, five years older than Morgan, but could easily pass for his father because of dissipation and a bad liver, the result of incessant, heavy drinking. He had acquired the drinking habit while attending Harrow, a prestigious English school, and his constant need for spirits grew each year.

The brothers were very fond of each other and as he looked across the desk at his sibling, so much in command of himself, Simon said, "Morgan, I want to give you a parting gift." Reaching into the drawer he withdrew a sheaf of papers tied neatly with a worn black ribbon. Handing them across the desk, he continued, "Here are the necessary papers which convey title of the *Banetree Princess* to you. Since you are leaving for Philadelphia, the timing is perfect as she is berthed in Wilmington, and I've already sent a rider instructing the skipper to proceed to Philadelphia and place himself and the ship under your orders. Though I doubt you will be able to turn much profit on this small vessel in transatlantic trade, I'm sure she could provide a good income around the British Isles."

Pleased with Simon's generous offer, Morgan replied,

"Thank you, Simon. I'm sure I can pick up a cargo in Philadelphia to at least cover expenses in crossing."

Morgan loved the *Banetree Princess,* a sleek two-masted vessel that the family had used primarily for coastal trade. Over the years, he had sailed her to New York, Philadelphia, and Charleston as well as taking several shorter voyages in the Chesapeake Bay. She was only a forty-ton burden but a fast sailing ship with low maintenance, which required only a small crew.

Simon pointed to the unopened packet in Morgan's hand. "You'll also find power-of-attorney in there to conduct family business in England. I will probably have to swear allegiance to the damned Congress before long in order to keep Banetree. With you in England swearing allegiance to the Crown, the family should be protected both ways."

Morgan was pleased. With control of his brother's money in England, it would enhance his social position with wealthy females even though he would never use it for personal needs. When the family of a prospective lady checked with his banker, Morgan would appear to be a man of wealth.

Chapter IV

Even with the luxury of her own cabin at last, Keary spent little time below. She stood at the rail most of the time with Molly, staring transfixed at Philadelphia. Despite the captain telling her this was the second largest city in the British empire, she still expected to see small groups of log cabins and colorfully painted savages creeping stealthily through the underbrush.

As she watched the busy waterfront with square streets leading in all directions from it, she couldn't contain her excitement nor the underlying fear of being alone in this strange city. When the sailors told her it would be much busier were it not for the blockade, she couldn't believe them. The wharves were full of ships and several stood at anchor in the river. The place bustled with industry and for a reason she couldn't comprehend, the sky seemed so much larger.

After the first few days, when she had finally accepted the treachery of Lady Fenleigh and the captain, she tried to think of Philadelphia in a positive way. She was hurt by Bruce's deception but in her heart she knew he would never have been the husband she hoped for. Now was the time to set her sights ahead and leave that other life behind.

Molly and the lads had talked of America as a land of opportunity where no one had to kowtow to English lords; she fervently hoped they were right.

"Just think," Molly had said, "in America a man can own his land even if he is not born in England." Keary law awake long into the night, intrigued by the thought since it was difficult visualizing an Irishman owning land. The word "freedom" came to mind and she puzzled over how this would apply to her. Though rebellion was inborn in her Irish heritage, indentured servitude would restrain her untamed nature even in this new land where people fought for what they believed. Still, as she pondered the concept of freedom, a burning desire to see this promising new country raged within her.

The last morning aboard ship great black clouds scurried across the gloomy sky. Keary was concerned and hoped if she had to make a long journey with her new master, he would have a suitable conveyance. Looking over her shoulder, she saw a patch of blue here and there breaking through the grayness and took heart as she remembered old Mrs. Sullivan, the laundress at Fenleigh Manor, saying, "I be tellin' ye, Lass, if there be enough blue in the sky to patch a Dutchman's britches, 'tis safe to be hangin' the clothes out fer dryin'."

Keary's pale blue cotton petticoat and white chemise were snugly tucked into a tightly laced navy bodice. She had tied her flying mane back in an attempt to look older, but tiny tendrils escaping around her face gave her the appearance of a sweet, vulnerable maid. She had weighed the advice of both Molly and the captain and dressed halfway between the two. An urge to return to the cabin and change to one of her better gowns surfaced, but a sudden vision of Lord Fenleigh's lecherous eyes changed her mind. She would stand on the block dressed plainly and take her chances. Her clogs were worn but clean and donning a pair of white cotton stockings, she slipped them on and made her way to the deck.

"Oooh, that's cold!" Molly's hearty laugh could be heard all over the ship. "If a bucket I had, ye'd be after gettin' a dose of yer own medicine."

Molly and the three lads were receiving dousings of river water from a sailor. As they lathered themselves with lye soap, he would douse them again with a rinse. The lads in their wet drooping breeches and Molly, her whole body outlined by the soaked, clinging chemise, hooted and laughed as the cold water stung their skin, leaving them shivering and breathless. Their other apparel was drying on a line strung from the rail to the lowest spar.

Keary wondered if they would ever bathe unless forced. Maybe they occasionally threw water on themselves to alleviate the heat in summer but, like most people, they considered bathing a health hazard. As Molly walked over to Keary, bunching her long hair in her hands and squeezing the water onto the deck, the first mate approached.

"The sale will be at eleven bells, ladies. Please be ready a little before that."

"Are you taking us to the sale, Mr. Hampton, or has Captain Shelby reserved that pleasure for himself?"

"No, Miss. He went into the city early this morning."

Keary breathed a sigh of relief knowing the captain wouldn't be there to gloat over her embarrassment. Now that the sale was imminent, she was anxious to have it over with and know who her master for the next seven years would be.

Waiting for time to pass, she watched the stevedores running back and forth on the wharf. How different they were from laborers in Ireland! When a gentleman passed, the workers didn't bow and doff their hats—they ignored him. She pictured Bruce with his obsequious manners and thought how out of place he would be in this country.

The others joined Keary on deck and she was shocked to see Barney trailing behind them, his hands bound. "Barney, what happened?"

With a bemused half grin he made his way to her side. "It seems I'm to be sold in bondage too." The wind whipped his dark hair as he looked wistfully to shore. Then the seasoned sailor, not wanting to appear weak to the pretty girl he had come to know so well these past weeks, grinned as he looked into her concerned eyes. "I could hope to be sold to the same master as you and the seven years wouldn't be so bad."

"Have you talked to the captain? Maybe there has been a mistake."

"There's no mistake. He gave orders and had all the papers drawn before he left early this morning for Philadelphia. They say he won't be back today so there's no way I can talk to him. I'm sure that's the way he had it planned."

Keary wanted to say "I told you so," but what purpose would it serve? His remark about wanting to be sold to the same master so he could spend the seven years with her she hoped wasn't as serious as it sounded; she liked Barney but not in a romantic way.

"Come along, Miss." The mate led them single file

down the gangplank and up Market Street to a large pavilion.

Morgan checked in at the Queen's Inn on Market Street in Philadelphia on his way to Samuel Snyder's house. As he sauntered along the sunny street he was glad to once again be in a civilized city after a week of country inns and ordinaries. The inn at Elk Mills had been the one pleasant respite in an otherwise dreary trip. Not because the food or atmosphere was better—really it was quite primitive. However, bad weather had caused a delay and the innkeeper's bound girl more than made up for any inconvenience. The blond girl with the healthy tan of a country maid had needed only a few subtle suggestions to appear at the door of his small room after everyone else had retired. The violent thunderstorm raged unheeded as he enjoyed the serving girl's company in the feather bed.

Frolics like this helped alleviate the repulsion Morgan felt every time he had to pay for food and lodging in this mercenary north, where hospitality was rarely understood and little appreciated. At Banetree and many other southern plantations, travelers were treated entirely different. Each afternoon a slave was stationed at the main gate of the plantation and instructed to invite any genteel travelers to enjoy Banetree's hospitality for as long as they wished. But in his condemnation of Yankees, Morgan failed to realize few could afford such lavish conviviality. He had to chuckle as he recalled his father saying, "If the good Lord hadn't wanted to distinguish between southern gentlemen and Yankee mercenaries, he wouldn't have placed the Potomac River where he did."

Some of Morgan's wealthier friends in Philadelphia provided generous hospitality, but Morgan preferred to stay at an inn for reasons they would not understand. These reasons revolved around his conquest of the fairer sex, an occupation which occasionally made all-night demands on his time. This lifestyle would be impossible as a houseguest.

Many men of wealth and position had joined either the American or British armies and others, hating everything the rebels stood for but lacking the inclination to become soldiers, had flocked to the protection of the British army in New York. They were confident the rebels would not war with their families. The net result was a city to Morgan's liking—a city of lonely women.

Scores of wealthy loyalist women were tired of the war and ready to find refuge in England. If he could cultivate one in this group and entice her to accompany him on the *Banetree Princess*, the long voyage would be far less boring. In any event, his prospects would be much brighter if he stayed at an inn and didn't have to explain himself to a narrow-minded hostess.

Samuel and his plump wife, Beth, were happy to see Morgan, apologizing that war was not conducive to entertaining. As Samuel was an old schoolmate and lifelong friend, Morgan felt a short visit was his duty. He knew Samuel would expect him to stay longer and he had carefully rehearsed a speech explaining that due to business reasons this would be impossible. He hoped to sound convincing.

No sooner were the greetings concluded then Samuel began a long-winded tirade against Congress, Washington, and rebels in general. It was becoming dangerous to speak out within hearing of Whigs, and Morgan noticed his host continually checking the whereabouts of the servants and lowering his voice when one was near.

"Good God, Samuel! Are things reaching such a state one has to be afraid of his own servants?"

"You wouldn't believe the changes that have taken place this last year, Morgan, especially since that illegal body, which calls itself Congress, is in session here. Even six months ago a gentleman was free to speak his mind regardless of his political persuasion, but since they passed that ridiculous Declaration, it's treason to speak against them. Isn't that ironic—loyalty to one's government is treason? Do you realize if the Committee of Safety were to judge me a 'Tory,' as they term loyalists, that I could be turned out of my own house and all of my property confiscated?"

Morgan nodded and proceeded to tell how his own brother Simon, a stout loyalist, had outwardly reversed his sentiments and was now openly supporting the rebel cause. "He has not only accoutered several lads in the area but has also freed five good slaves to serve in Washington's army."

Samuel shook his head in disbelief. "I never thought I would live to see the day a Virginian would allow a Negro to carry arms."

"Neither did I. But this is one thing we can't blame on the rebels. It was due to the stupidity of our English Governor Dunmore. He and his slave army were the worst blunder any of His Majesty's ministers have made yet. I doubt his army ever numbered more than six hundred. They had no officers to lead them and the only result of the whole fiasco was to turn thousands of loyal southerners against the Crown."

Morgan's reference was to Lord Dunmore, the Royal Governor of Virginia. A typical Crown-appointed nincompoop, he had freed all slaves willing to join the British in putting down the rebellion. Washington, himself, could not have devised a better plan to aid the rebel cause, since the south feared armed slaves more than any other enemy. Many people of substance in the south still tried to write this off as a blunder of a Crown appointee rather than English policy.

Beth excused herself and left to oversee the preparations for supper as Samuel asked, "Whatever happened to his slave army?"

"Well, they had no officers or provisions and never really were organized. Actually it was only a mob and without discipline. Sanitary precautions weren't followed so most of them died of one disease or another. A few are still serving in His Majesty's navy. That pompous ass, Dunmore, is now living comfortably on his country estate in England while others are paying dearly for his stupidity."

Rising to pour another glass of wine, Samuel changed the subject. "You haven't told me your plans, Morgan. Are you going to offer your services to General Howe? He needs all of the good loyal subjects he can find. I would go myself but I fear the Committee of Safety. If they discovered I was in the king's service I'm afraid Beth and the children would be homeless."

Settling his six-foot frame in the corner of the settee, Morgan relaxed, stretching his long legs and crossing them at the ankle. Tenting his fingers, he replied, "I may be tempted if there was a determined general who would take the offensive and put the rebel scum to rout. But what have they done so far? Howe couldn't even hold Boston with almost ten thousand troops. Perhaps he will show some spirit at New York, although I doubt it. Some say Bunker Hill made him overly cautious and a cautious man will not win this war. At any rate, I'm returning to England to live in a civilized society. Simon was kind enough to give me the *Banetree Princess* and I'll be sailing as soon as she's ready. She weathered a hard storm on her last voyage and is berthed in Wilmington under repairs."

Samuel shook his head negatively. "Since this Declaration business, no ships are being cleared directly for England. You may have to go by way of the Sugar Islands." He grinned and punched Morgan on the shoulder. "That may be very much to your liking—a lot of dark-skinned beauties to help you wile away your time. If you're destined for England, why did you come here rather than Baltimore or a port closer to home?"

"I had business here. I hope to pick up a cargo to help pay for the crossing. My funds are insufficient to cross in ballast."

"And would I be accurate in assuming that most of your important business here concerns the fairer sex?" All of Morgan's friends knew of his weakness for the ladies.

"Now Samuel, you know me to be a serious, industrious, and virtuous man." Morgan's brown eyes crinkled with laughter and Samuel slapped his friend's knee as he rose. Jamming his hands in the pockets of the long, outdated waistcoat, he crossed the room to stare out the window.

"If you are any of those, I'm a general in Washington's army. Seriously though, a word of caution. If you plan to cross the Atlantic, you had better carry a couple of guns. Those seas are crawling with American privateers. I'd mount two long nine-pounders; they aren't much good in a close fight but they will discourage a privateer from closing in on you." He turned from the window and walked slowly back to the settee. "What is the *Princess*'s burden—about forty ton?"

"Yes, roughly."

"Well, no privateer will risk a few hits for a prize that small. Two nine-pounders should serve the purpose."

On his way back to his room, Morgan was deep in thought. So far his stay in Philadelphia hadn't measured up to his expectations. The gay parties, dinners, and balls were no more. There were just as many ladies willing—even eager—to share his bed but the opportunities for conquest were few, due to the lack of social events. He was not one to make formal calls or leave his card. This might cause the ladies to interpret his lighthearted intentions seriously. It was always better to meet accidentally and let the lady take the initiative. This also saved time in the weeding-out procedure.

Morgan preferred Philadelphia over all other places on the Continent. Despite the strong Quaker influence, the city on the Delaware was not only America's largest but easily the gayest. Next to Philadelphia the social life of all other American cities paled in comparison. Morgan usually spent at least one month a year here attending to family "business" and inevitably had to invent excuses to explain to his father the reason for his late return.

Chapter V

Keary, along with the others, was herded into the open pavilion where a crowd was already gathering, their murmurs intensifying as she passed. On the sidewalk she had noticed a sour-looking gentleman dressed in dark velvet—strange attire for the middle of summer. He had peered, mouth agape, when she drew near, and his stare placed her once again at the foot of the stairs at Fenleigh Manor, facing His Lordship. She looked away immediately, a cold shiver running down her back, and quickly followed the others into the pavilion. Glancing nervously over her shoulder, she saw him hurrying behind her, his eyes devouring, and she slipped behind a heavyset man, hoping to escape the narrow eyes smiling in anticipation.

Along one side of the open room there were close to a dozen black men—four chained together at the ankles—and the forlorn expressions on their heavily sweating faces made Keary turn away in revulsion at their pathetic appearance. She cowered in the back as men elbowed through to squeeze her shoulder, feel her waist, and check her hands and teeth. She was so busy defending herself against the seeking hands, the auction began without her noticing.

The auctioneer, a small man with greasy hair and pockmarked face, spoke in an inarticulate monotone as he gestured toward the black man now occupying the stump. Keary moved slowly backward as the crowd began bidding with a nod, a wave of the hand, or by voicing a number. She had unconsciously reached the brick sidewalk when someone bumped her.

"Excuse me, Miss."

Turning quickly, she was taken aback by a sandy-haired gentleman bowing and sweeping an elegant beaver tricorn in a well-practiced arc. His brown eyes danced to an elfish tune and his impish grin threatened to enslave her before she even ascended the auction block.

"It was my fault, Sir," she managed after a quick indrawn breath. "I should have watched where I was going."

"Wherever you were going, you shouldn't be called upon to watch. There should be an army of gentlemen to lead your way. In Virginia, Miss, one of such beauty couldn't take a single step without escorts vying for her attention."

Completely taken with the handsome stranger, she was surprised when someone grabbed her arm roughly. "See here, Miss, don't try to run away or I'll have to put chains on you." The fat, swarthy man started to hustle her back into the bedraggled group of indentures. His motion stopped suddenly and Keary turned to see his feet leave the ground as the sandy-haired gentleman clutched his shirtfront.

"Take your filthy hands off the lady or you'll never see

another sunrise—mark my words." Morgan's eyes flashed fire and the threat was uttered through clenched teeth.

Frightened at the hostility in the gentleman's face, Keary pulled on his arm. "Please, Sir, you don't understand. I am to be sold and he is only doing his duty."

"Sold!" His eyebrows shot up in disbelief then, collecting himself, he said gently, "Angels aren't sold, they are worshipped. If beauty had a measure of value, all the kings of Europe could not afford one such as you."

She was embarrassed at meeting this fine gentleman under such circumstances and a bright flush crept up her cheeks. "Thank you, Sir, but I'm indentured and someone will buy my services for the next seven years."

Careful not to touch her, the fat man, shaking visibly, led Keary back into the center of the pavilion. Morgan watched with rising anger as an old man in a black velvet suit felt her arms and lifted the shining black hair. Morgan walked farther into the pavilion, keeping his eyes on Keary, oblivious to the brisk bidding on the black slaves. His family had owned slaves for four generations but Morgan disliked auctions and the frequent sale of humans. Most of their slaves had been born on the plantation or purchased at a tender age. Once they became members of Banetree, all but the very troublesome stayed their lifetime. He could understand a planter selling his slaves for badly needed capital impossible to raise any other way, but speculating in human flesh was a degrading occupation. Indentures were not actually slaves and would be free after a specified number of years. In addition, they could get redress from a court if a master was proven cruel or did not feed and clothe them properly. However, the interpretation of the law decidedly favored the master often making the bound servant's life worse than some of the slaves.

As the last of the slaves were led away, the indentures were moved to the block. The professional auctioneer hesitated momentarily to add impact to his words before announcing, "Gentlemen, we have three healthy men, two lasses from Ireland, and an able-bodied seaman. They are from the ship *Scorpion*, which has bravely run the blockade. All are for the term of seven years and all are in good health. The first, a lad of seventeen, a skilled farmer, no criminal record, has come willingly to seek a chance to live in our free country. The papers are held by the ship's captain, Amos Shelby, and all bids will be in pounds sterling."

The auctioneer's voice drifted off into a garbled singsong as hands were raised. After a few moments the gavel slammed down and he droned, "Sold to the gentleman for eleven pounds eight."

The lad turned and nodded good-bye to his friends as a tall man in a plain brown coat and white homespun led him away. The buyer appeared to be a tradesman, which meant the lad might have the same training and advantages of an apprentice, albeit his start in business would take longer than usual.

Morgan knew the black-haired beauty would be held until last in order to keep the crowd interested. Even those who had no intention of bidding would remain to see who purchased her and what amount she would bring. He watched her standing defiantly, arms clasped around her waist, as one man after another inspected her. Her scorn belied her terror as the old man in velvet came back again, checking her minutely. Morgan's anger mounted at the old man's obvious intentions. He would buy her himself for service at Banetree, but it was impractical. Custom forbidding fraternization between white and black as well as master and servant would leave no place for her in the social order.

Of the two remaining lads who had made the voyage with Keary, one sold for fourteen pounds and the other for twelve pounds six. There were few bids for Molly, indicating female labor was not in great demand, but she finally went for eight pounds ten to Mr. Penrose, a baker. He led the smiling buxom girl through the crowd and Keary hoped Molly's dream of becoming a member of a regular household would be fulfilled.

A few moments later Keary's anxiety changed to pity as Barney was led away by a man wearing the same style uniform as Captain Shelby. It appeared that Barney would not be seeing his own land, or any other land, for a long time. He would be back at sea. Totally ignoring the other lads, the seafaring man had paid eighteen pounds for Barney, the only sailor in the group.

As Keary hoisted her skirts to mount the stump, the old man pushed and elbowed his way to the front, anxious to bid. Even the auctioneer was caught up in the excitement as the crowd moved in closer and he began extolling her virtues: "Reads, writes, accomplished in the social graces, served nobility as governess and tutor."

Keary cringed as the libidinous old man, impatient for the bidding to start, rapped his cane on the brick floor. Heartsick, her eyes fluttered over the crowd and met those of the sandy-haired gentleman who had so recently championed her. Would he bid on her? For a moment she fantasized, seeing him mounting a large white horse and, reaching down, easily swinging her up behind him. Her arms wound around the slim waist and, resting her cheek against his broad back, they galloped off, fading into a beautiful, enveloping mist. Her dream was shattered by the old man rapping his cane angrily and demanding in a loud voice that the bidding commence. Perspiration formed on Morgan's forehead. He understood clearly the old goat was determined to have the young girl and would bid highly for her. Not wanting to witness her being led away by the lecherous one, he was tempted to leave but was held there by some unknown force. At his elbow a familiar voice was saying, "Good day, Morgan. Are you planning to buy a servant?"

Turning around, Morgan reached for the other's hand. "Benjamin, how are you? No, I have no use for a servant, do you?"

Benjamin wiped the sweat from his forehead and chuckled, "Morgan, I couldn't afford to feed one if the auctioneer was giving them away. I just came in to get out of the sun for a few minutes since there wasn't a tavern close by, but it seems old Wentworth there is anxious to make the black-haired lass part of his household. I feel sorry for the girl, knowing that old reprobate as well as I do."

"Wentworth—I've heard that name somewhere before."

"Whatever it was you heard about him, I'm sure it wasn't good. That old skinflint is the biggest hypocrite I've ever known. Spouts religion from the rooftops but his only God is money. I sure pity that poor lass if that sanctimonious old bastard buys her indenture."

Benjamin Fowler was a short man, his shoulders rounded by leaning over a workbench for many years. As a tinsmith, he had once been very prosperous but in later years, with failing health and a lack of enthusiasm, his business had deteriorated badly.

"Now gentlemen, what am I bid for this fair lass?"

Before the last words were out of the auctioneer's mouth, the velvet-clad man had waved his hand yelling, "Fifteen."

A smile crossed the auctioneer's face, anticipating a good commission as a man across the room countered, "Sixteen."

Before the auctioneer finished, "Sixteen, who'll give seven—" Wentworth snapped, "Twenty."

"Twenty-one." Another bidder joined in and Wentworth pounded his cane defiantly and upped the bid to twenty-five.

After a short lull, the auctioneer resumed his chant, starting with, "Twenty-five once, twenty-five—"

"Twenty-six," the second bidder shot back.

"Thirty," Wentworth challenged, and at this no one else seemed ready to pick up the gauntlet.

"Come now, gentlemen"—the auctioneer tried to rekindle the spirit of competition—"only thirty pounds for this rare beauty?"

No one responded and Morgan edged closer to his friend. "Benjamin, I don't want to let that old bastard buy this girl. You bid and I'll cover it."

"But why don't you bid yourself?" Benjamin looked at Morgan, a puzzled expression on his round, cherubic face.

"I'll explain later. Hurry!"

The chant was, "Going once, going twice—" As the auctioneer scanned the crowd with raised gavel, Wentworth approached the stump, his hand outstretched for Keary's arm, his thick lips fairly drooling and his narrow eyes lusting.

"Thirty-one," came loud and clear and the crowd turned to see Benjamin's upraised hand.

Whirling, his face flushing in anger, Wentworth stammered, "Thirty-five." He wiped perspiration from his forehead and fixed Benjamin with a venomous stare, waving his cane menacingly.

"I owe him money," Benjamin whispered to Morgan, "and that gesture was a threat to call the notes if I continue to oppose him."

"Do you want to stop?"

"Hell no!" Benjamin was about to say thirty-six when Morgan nudged him and mouthed "forty." Benjamin, enjoying the rivalry, called out, "Forty."

Wentworth removed his hat and wiped the sweat from the brim as he glared hatefully at Benjamin. He reached in his pocket and removed his purse and, after niggardly fingering the contents, choked out, "Forty-one!"

Benjamin glanced at Morgan who, without batting an eye, mumbled "fifty." Grinning like a pixie and with a nonchalant wave of his hand reminiscent of his prosperous days, Benjamin scanned the crowd, waiting for absolute silence. In a conversational tone he said simply, "Fifty," and everyone in the room heard.

Wentworth reluctantly returned the faded purse to his pocket and cast one last look at Keary, who was visibly relieved. Benjamin chuckled, "The old skinflint could have paid five hundred and never missed it but his horror of spending money just won out over his lust."

"I hope this won't cause you any trouble." Morgan's face showed serious concern.

"No. The annual payment on the note isn't due for three months, and you can bet your best horse he'll be at my door that very day. But then, he would have done that whether I had bid or not."

The auctioneer wasted little time bringing the gavel down when Wentworth turned away, ending the bidding. Morgan deftly slipped a stack of gold coins to Benjamin. "There is an extra five for her keep until we can find a home for her." He gathered in the smile now crossing Keary's face and left immediately.

"Keary Cavanaugh at your service, Sir." She dropped a curtsy to the slump-shouldered man who had just paid the auctioneer, then taking both of his hands, she continued, "Thank you, Sir. I was so afraid the other man would buy me."

Benjamin fidgeted nervously, finally blurting out, "I hope you don't think I bought you for the same reason that old—"

"No, Sir." She smiled sweetly, "Of course not. There is a difference in your eyes. What will my duties be, Sir?"

"I don't really know, Miss. I am a tinsmith but business has been poor and I can't really afford the one journeyman and apprentice I have now. As soon as possible, I'll place you in a good home in a genteel position. In the meantime, I hope you don't mind my humble quarters—you being used to a nobleman's estate."

She patted his arm and, thankful for her good fortune she said quietly, "After that ship, anything will be a palace." As they turned down Market Street a small thoughtful frown puckered her forehead. "If you have no work for me, why did you pay that outlandish price, Mr. Ah—?"

"Fowler, Miss. To tell you the truth, I'm not sure why except that I didn't want that other gent to buy you. You see, Miss, all he wanted was to—"

Keary interrupted. "I know what he wanted, Mr. Fowler, and I am very grateful to you. Until you find a place for me I will be your housekeeper—that is, unless you already have a wife or housekeeper."

The little man shook his head sadly. "No, my wife has been dead for several years. I live alone above my shop."

Benjamin had hired a cart to haul her chests to his quarters and Keary strolled leisurely beside him, taking in the sights of the city. "Well then, at least I can earn my keep." Trying to hide her inquisitiveness, she nonchalantly asked, "Who was the young gentleman I saw you talking to, Mr. Fowler?"

"That was Morgan Baines from Virginia, Miss."

Keary's heart skipped a beat. She had assumed Mr. Baines lived in Philadelphia. "Virginia! Is that far away? Does he come here often?"

"Usually about once a year and stays about a month."

She hesitated, not knowing exactly how to ask the next question. "Did his wife come with him?"

Benjamin halted and peered into her anxious eyes; a slight grin crossed his features. "He has no wife, Lass, but there are a lot of ladies who would like to change that."

I'll just bet there are, she thought as they resumed walking. She was amazed at the wide roads and the sameness of the row upon row of brick buildings that lined the streets. The filth and offal in the gutters was ample to feed the scores of pigs who wandered the city oblivious to the pedestrians and bustling carts everywhere. Philadelphia on the whole though was much cleaner than Cork, the only other city she was familiar with.

Every few hundred feet they passed a pump, some of which had horse troughs. Passersby often stopped and drew water and Keary thought it strange the pump owners didn't object. A rough-looking man wearing a fringed hunting shirt, a garment she had never seen before, stopped by a pump and began working the handle. When no water was forthcoming he pumped harder for a few seconds then, kicking the pump in disgust, stomped off.

"Mr. Fowler, are all Americans so inconsiderate of other people's property?"

"The pumps are owned by the city, Miss, and most people give them a kick when they aren't working. Maintenance of pumps is a job often given more out of political consideration than whether or not the fellow knows anything about fixing them. Therefore, the people show little tolerance when they can't draw water. That man was probably not as angry at the pump as he was the politicians. He'll no doubt walk right on past the next one and head for the nearest tavern. If he gets drunk tonight he'll blame his big head tomorrow on the city fathers." He noticed her quizzical expression and asked, "Are things so much different in Ireland?"

"If we had pumps like this in Ireland, Sir, Englishmen would own them and an Irishman would have to pay for a drink." Walking along Second Street she was astounded by the length of the blocks. "There must be a lot of wasted space in this town, Mr. Fowler. The blocks are so long."

"Well, Miss, when old Penn laid out this town, he had visions of large lots and the populace living well spread out. A 'green country town' he called it. But the population grew much faster than anticipated and people began to subdivide their lots because street frontage was so valuable. This made a lot of narrow frontages with very deep backyards. Each block had one or two alleys leading back to coach houses, stables, work sheds, and whatever." Approaching a small opening between two buildings, he pointed. "As the population grew, there was so much demand for houses in town near employment, smaller houses were built on the alleys. Now there are really two cities—the one you see from the streets and the one you see in the back alleys. Some of the blocks have only one entrance to the alleys, which is a major problem during a fire. There is constant agitation to tear down a house or building here or there to make an access, but nothing ever comes of it."

"Is your shop on the Main Street?"

"Yes, with an alley in the back. But if you wanted to enter from the back, you must go by way of another street." They turned left off Second Street to Spruce, and halfway down the block he stopped in front of an old brick-front building with a large multi-paned window and opened the door. "Here we are, Miss."

Off the hall was a door leading to the shop and a staircase leading to the living quarters above. As they mounted the steps, she noticed the old man's breathing was very labored and his progress slow. The upstairs apartment had a huge common room, its chief use seeming to be for storage of junk of every description in the most haphazard methods possible.

Benjamin proceeded down the long hall to the first door. "This is my room, Miss. You choose whichever one you like. Now, if you'll excuse me, I tire easily these days and wish to lie down for a spell."

Chapter VI

Keary walked aimlessly through three other bedrooms, a kitchen, and a dining room. A narrow stairway at the end of the hall led to an upstairs attic. The very thought of putting order into this chaos was staggering but she was undaunted, as it did show promise. There was good quality in the old furnishings and Keary was sure she could brighten everything with a little soap and water.

One room was furnished with a grand old four-poster, a small writing desk, and a huge armoire divided into closet space and drawers; all of the pieces were of a rich cherry wood. This would be her room.

She tugged and pushed at the large windows until the sashes were halfway and, throwing the patchwork quilt and soft feather bed over the sides to air, removed the canopy and curtains and returned to the kitchen to find a laundry tub. A door led to a back porch enclosed with a wrought-iron rail and she hung her laundry carefully over the railing, allowing the breeze from the river to quickly dry them.

Her efforts were rewarded when the late afternoon sun, shining through sparkling windows, cast a burnished red glow on the gleaming cherry wood. A brisk breeze blowing in the open windows stirred the ruffles of the pillow on a dainty rocker in front of the corner fireplace and eliminated the musty smell Keary had encountered when she first entered the closed room. Taking one last satisfied look, she hurried to the kitchen to begin work on that rubble when she realized there was nothing to prepare for supper. She tiptoed down the hall and pressed her ear against Mr. Fowler's door. Hearing his heavy, rhythmic breathing, Keary decided against waking him.

She tied a kerchief around her hair and reached into her precious hoard, extracting a few coins. Grabbing a market basket from the clutter on the cupboard, she hurried down the steps. Looking both ways along the street, she finally decided to head back along the same route they had taken this morning. As she walked along Spruce Street, she spied an older woman lumbering along with a full basket.

"Please, Ma'am, can you tell me the way to the nearest market?"

The woman shifted her basket to the other arm as she appraised the young maid. "Hmmm, shopping this late, girl, you don't have much choice. The best bargains are at Market Street but it's too late to go that far. Are you new in town?"

"Yes, Ma'am."

The woman set her basket down, pleased to find someone to chat with. "A body should always shop early unless she wants to waste money. Now, I usually shop in the mornings but my husband has the ague and he was

right bad this morning. Thought for a while I was going
have to call a doctor. Why, he was as solid as a rock tw
days ago, then all of a sudden he started to complain
dizziness right after supper and by bedtime he had th
runs. Now if you ask me—"

Keary, trying to hide her impatience interrupte
"Please, Ma'am, I'd love to talk but my master is waitin
for his supper."

"Master! Are you a bound girl?"

"Yes, Ma'am."

The woman stooped and picked up her basket. "Shoul
have known with that Irish accent. Go up to Secon
Street and turn left. You'll run right into it and you'
better not dillydally or the place will be closed."

"Yes, Ma'am." Keary hurried past the woman
relieved to get away. She thought to herself, *Heave
forbid, is this the attitude everyone here has towar
indentured servants?*

The market, still called the "New Market" although
had been there for some thirty years, was much large
than any Keary had ever seen. The selections wer
unlimited but she shopped cautiously, not knowing th
value of the strange money.

"Do you take English money?" she asked a ma
behind the produce stand. His wide eyes told her th
money she carried was extremely valuable, whic
prompted her to bargain shrewdly. Dickering was secon
nature to Keary, and even without knowing the customs
she entered the fray with enthusiasm. With each iter
she asked for the translation in shillings and pence
frowning slightly as she said, "In Ireland I didn't have t
pay that much."

To the inevitable question "How much did you pay?"

she would quote a lower figure while holding a gold coin in plain view. She learned on this one errand that having hard money in this town was quite an advantage and she would have to learn how to exploit it.

Mr. Fowler beamed at the rack of lamb, the bright orange carrots, and the small onions placed before him but was only able to eat a small portion. Keary, worried at his lack of appetite, brought him a bowl of broth made from the drippings of the lamb and he sipped this to the last spoonful.

As Benjamin excused himself and made his way to the big, comfortable chair, Keary placed his pipe and tobacco and a small bottle of port and a glass beside him. She turned the wick high on the lamp and handed him his book.

"Now if you need anything, call me. I'll be close by." The old man nodded as he reached contentedly for his pipe and Keary returned to the kitchen.

Within a week every room sparkled, showing the hand of a woman had been hard at work. With the flat clean and orderly, and Mr. Fowler spending most of his time in the shop or resting in bed, Keary started to grow restless. She decided to familiarize herself with the city, and on her excursions would occasionally stop at a coffee shop to partake of delicious pastries and a cup of coffee. The first time she had ordered tea and received a hard look from the proprietor.

"Ye'll not be findin' tea in these parts, Miss." Suddenly she remembered hearing something to the effect that a tax on tea had played a major role in the revolution.

She puzzled over the revolution. People talked much of the recent Declaration of Independence, which had been signed by Congress here in Philadelphia, but there was no sign of military activity and all she had learned was that a large British force had landed around New York. She surmised that New York must be very far away because Philadelphians spoke of the Yorkers as if they belonged to a foreign race.

Keary was not sure why a people who seemed to have more freedom than she ever thought possible would rebel, or how it would affect her personally. It was evident some people thought of themselves as living in a new country while others expected the Crown forces to put down the rebellion and return the old government. For the time being, she had a kind master and freedom to come and go as she pleased, and politics didn't linger in her mind.

With time on her hands, Keary stopped in the shop daily to converse with Benjamin. As she walked by his side while he explained the various tools and machinery, she longed to bring some semblance of order to the disarray of the benches, racks, and shelves. She knew the shop could be a profitable business if properly organized. But Jamie, the journeyman, was loath to have her around. To her subtle hints of reorganization, he turned a deaf ear.

Deciding to make one last attempt, she vowed to find the key to Jamie's objections. All men could be drawn out by one method or another. As she came through the door of the shop this morning carrying a tray she called, "Good morning, Jamie. I brought you some cool lemonade and some fresh pastries."

He looked up from the bench, ignoring the tray. "Good

morning, Miss. Is Mr. Fowler up yet?"

"No, he isn't feeling well this morning."

"Well, let me know when he awakes. I haven't had my wages for three weeks and I'm going to have to get another position if he doesn't pay me soon."

Dismayed, she hurried to his side. "Oh, Jamie, I'd hate to see you leave. You do such beautiful work." Lifting a metal kettle and turning it around, she studied the smooth surface. "All that is necessary to make this shop pay is someone who can sell your tremendous talent."

He reddened and a broad smile broke across his plain lean face showing gaps in an uneven row of yellowed teeth. Pushing back the bush of yellow curls, he bent lower over the press.

Keary noticed his appreciation of her compliment and she quickly followed it. "In fact, Mr. Fowler told me you made the candle sconce on his mantel. A silversmith couldn't have done better."

"Why—thank you, Miss. I did put a lot of effort in that sconce. It was a present for Mrs. Fowler." He was standing a little straighter now, his chest thrown out and his pale eyes alight with pride.

Walking farther down the long bench, Keary reached for a small teapot setting among discarded metal and tools. "And what a lovely teapot. Who did you make this for?"

"No one in particular. There aren't many orders so I was sort of keeping busy. Would you like it, Miss?"

"Like it! Why I'd love it but I shan't take it right now."

He was bewildered and somewhat deflated. "Why not?"

"Because it should be displayed for other ladies to see. Right in that big window. Jamie, I'll clean out that window and you can make one of each of your specialties. I'll arrange a display and as the ladies pass by they can see your lovely work."

He shook his head unconvinced. "That's all fine and good, Miss, but what about my wages? My rent is already past due."

"Would two pounds hard money do until we sell a few things?"

"Sure, but where are you going to get that much money?"

"I have a little money saved and a lot of faith in your work. I know what ladies like and I can think of a lot of things to make." Her excitement was mounting as she pictured a neat, clean shop with many customers coming through the door. "You do beautiful work, Jamie, and I know I can sell it."

Before he could offer an argument she began cleaning out the window. Later, as she stood on a small stool washing the huge pane from the inside, Tom, the apprentice, smiled through from the outside as he stood on a ladder sloshing water. When they finished, Keary dashed upstairs for something she had seen tucked away in a drawer. Now blue curtains hung from the upper half of the window and the teapot set proudly on a folded length of white linen. After standing back admiring her handiwork she returned to the parlor and came back with the sconce. Jamie eyed her warily.

"Don't worry, Jamie. We won't sell it; the window needs more display to catch the ladies' eyes."

"If that's what you want, Miss Keary, there's a lot of other things around here. Sometimes people order things and they either can't pay or they never come back."

Whirling around, she asked excitedly, "What kind

of things?"

"Most everything we ever made. For instance, here is a lantern that has been here as long as I can remember. One of the glass panes is missing but I could cut a piece from stock. I'm sure there's some glass around here somewhere."

Looking at the lantern, her eyes widened. "Why, Jamie, this is brass. You replace the piece of glass and I'll clean it up. I'm going to start looking for other pieces."

He took the lantern, saying, "Check the attic, Miss. Mr. Fowler has been piling stuff up there for twenty years."

After Jamie left for the day she began searching under shelves, into old crates, and along benches. One treasure after another was uncovered, everything from solder and brass to tinplate. Unfinished items were thrown in with finished ones and unused tools and equipment lay everywhere. An excited glow lit Keary's face as plans began to formulate. She turned to the counter, resolved to put her ideas to work immediately, when the little bell above the door tinkled, announcing a customer. Turning around, she came face to face with the sandy-haired gentleman she had seen at the auction. Her heart raced, pumping a flood of warmth to her face.

"Good evening, Mr. Baines. I'm afraid the workmen have gone home."

"It was not the workmen I came to see," he grinned, "and not Benjamin either."

He withdrew a handkerchief from his wrist and wiped at a smudge of dirt on her nose. She was shamed by the disarray of her clothing and the mobcap that shielded her hair from the dust. She lowered her eyes and his hands reached for hers. Her effort to withdraw them was feeble as he raised them to his lips, kissing each in turn.

"I've had visions of you, Miss Cavanaugh, ever since the day at the auction. That black hair and those eyes have haunted my dreams."

"Mr. Baines, please! How did you learn my name? You should not talk this way—it's not proper. I mean—after all—" She was embarrassed at rattling on but was unable to stop.

"I learned your name from the same source that you learned mine. I paid a visit the other day but you were roaming the city. And why shouldn't I talk this way, my fair shopkeeper?"

"It's just not right. I haven't been formally introduced to you. Why, I hardly know you."

"And how long would it be before I could properly talk thus?" His grin and teasing eyes completely disarmed her.

She mumbled, "A year at least."

He set his tricorn on the counter and, laughing heartily, slipped his arms around her waist, gently pulling her forward. The feeling of his body against hers sent a thrill like nothing she had ever known.

She pulled back, trying to free herself. "Please, don't." His lips silenced her and one large hand pressed the middle of her back as her thoughts whirled in confusion. *This is madness. He's a gentleman and I'm a bound girl.* When he released the pressure, she pulled back again, saying, "Please don't, Mr. Baines."

He grinned and rubbed his nose against hers as the hand on her back traveled slowly, sending pulsating thrills through her entire body. He murmured, "I have never seen one so beautiful. Tell me, are all the maids in Ireland as fair as you?"

Her heart and mind were at war and her heart won as two small hands, rough and red from scrubbing with lye soap, crept around his neck and her lips found his. Her body sagged, forcing his hardening manhood against her trembling form.

She held tight as his tongue forced through the breach of her parted lips and her breasts were crushed against him. Her chest wanted to explode with the wild thumping of her heart against her ribs as his hand roved up and down her hip, burning through the single petticoat. With his tight breeches, it was as though nothing were between them. She felt his throbbing desire and unwillingly twisted against it as his mouth traveled down the side of her neck. Her fingers threaded his hair and pulled his head closer.

The bell at the front door shrilled through their senses and Morgan turned his back to hide a prominent bulge in the tight breeches.

Jamie, taken aback, stammered, "I brought you this, Miss; it's really too nice for my room. I can do with a candle in a cup." He held out a beautiful hammered brass lamp with tilted glass sides and a three-tiered conical chimney. "Sometimes when I have nothing to do at night, I come to the shop and make things."

"Oh, Jamie, it's—ah—" Her befuddled speech and high color betrayed her insouciant features.

"Is something wrong, Miss?" He stared at Morgan's back. "Maybe I came at the wrong time."

"No, Jamie, it's all right." Her voice was strong and the tone of relief was not lost on Morgan. Her whirling brain was beginning to clear. "It's just that your lamp is so beautiful, I'd hate to sell it."

Jamie waved his hand casually. "I can make more; go

ahead and sell it."

She turned to the window with the lamp creating distance between herself and this handsome rogue who, with one embrace, could make her want to drop her skirts. "Well, we'll see, Jamie. At least we can display it. I'm sure it will attract attention."

Morgan turned to her as she started for the window and Jamie looked from one to the other. "I was going to work some in the shop tonight but maybe I better come back later."

Keary turned quickly with a determined look at Morgan. "No, Jamie. Mr. Baines just came by to see Mr. Fowler; we were about to go upstairs to see if he was awake. This way, Mr. Baines."

With a devilish glint in his eyes, Morgan followed Keary's quick steps, humming a rollicking tune as she hurried ahead keeping several steps between them on the narrow stairway.

Benjamin, huddled under a shawl despite the warmth of the room, attempted to rise and held out his hand. "Morgan, it's good to see you; sit down and have a glass of port." As he eased back in his chair, Morgan leaned over and squeezed the hand, noticing a marked deterioration in his old friend's health in just the last few weeks.

"Have you seen a doctor, Benjamin?"

"No, and I'm not going to. All those quacks know is purging and draining your blood out. Seems to me the good Lord put that blood in us for a purpose and I can't see the sense in draining it all out."

Morgan nodded in sympathy. His opinion of doctors was no higher than Benjamin's.

Keary entered with a bottle of port and two glasses and, as she poured the deep purple wine into goblets, raised her eyes to Morgan. "Will you stay for supper, Mr. Baines?"

"No, thank you. In fact, I came by to invite you to sup with me after which, I hoped, we might attend the Southwark Theatre. There is an exceptionally good company there presenting *The Musical Lady*. It's an English satire on Italian opera and the music is quite good. I've seen the company perform in Williamsburg and thought you might enjoy it."

The casual invitation astounded Keary, whose background emphasized class distinction. She was aware that nobility, as such, didn't exist in America but knew well the wide social gulf separating a gentleman and a bound girl. Had she known Morgan's views, the invitation would have been even more of a surprise for he was a firm believer in the dominance of a select aristocracy. But when it came to the beautiful raven-haired Irish lass, whose kiss still remained fresh on his lips, his usual maxims were easily cast aside. He well knew the scandal that would be attached to one of his station escorting a bound girl to the theatre, but he worried little about social conventions. He even enjoyed scandalizing the Philadelphia gentry. At this moment he would be willing to present her at court.

Keary's heart raced. She wanted so badly to accept the splendid invitation but was afraid of what lay behind his impetuous offer. There were also her duties to Mr. Fowler. "That's very kind of you but I was about to prepare Mr. Fowler's supper."

Morgan was caught short. He was accustomed to women accepting him immediately—even forcing the issue—and usually it wasn't that important since he never lacked feminine companionship. Unsure of whether or not he had been rejected, her answer both unsettled and excited him.

Benjamin reached out and patted her hand. His tired, ailing eyes smiled gently, grateful for her concern. "Don't worry about that, Lass. Just leave me some cheese and bread and a full bottle. You run along and enjoy yourself."

"Are you sure, Sir? Will you be all right alone?"

Benjamin chuckled, rolling his head against the back of the chair. "Well, I managed a number of years before you came, although now I can't imagine how." Stooping down to brush the top of his head with a light kiss, she decided against further objections and fairly flew out of the room.

Morgan sipped the wine without tasting it and strained to keep his attention on Benjamin's conversation. All the while his mind tried to understand why her acceptance was so important to him when he had so recently made her acquaintance and his impending trip to England would become a reality soon.

To Keary, the exciting prospect of dining out and attending the theatre was overwhelming. She had seen a few traveling actors perform at Fenleigh Manor on special occasions but never a full company on stage before. She routed through the armoire, deciding on the mauve taffeta Lady Fenleigh's seamstress had made for her to attend the musicale. If it was appropriate for gentry, it should do for this evening.

As she hurriedly sponged off, her thoughts centered on Morgan Baines. Had he really meant the things he said downstairs or was he just trying to maneuver her into a compromising situation? She was sure he was experienced and had seduced more than his share of women, but the passion in his eyes had been more than a simple conquest. Fear seized her with the realization of how easily she would have surrendered her virginity if Jamie hadn't interrupted. She pictured the scene below again and knew, had there been no intervention, her body would have yielded. It was frightening—but also exciting.

The face in the mirror returning her gaze was a deep scarlet and over the pounding in her chest came a melancholy reminder. "He's a gentleman from a large plantation in far off Virginia and I will be bound for seven more years! Some day he will marry a fine lady." Sudden desolation gripped her but she immediately cast the mood aside, resolving to enjoy the evening.

She tied the violet striped petticoat at her waist and slipped the soft mauve taffeta gown over her head, making sure the divided overskirt revealed enough of the shimmering, striped petticoat. The simple lines of the bodice enhanced the high, firm breasts and she quickly dabbed a violet scent above the modest neckline. Fluffing the ruffles at the elbow-length sleeves, she viewed herself from all angles before dressing her hair. Showing no mercy to her tender scalp, she whealed the brush time and again over the unruly locks until finally they succumbed in a shining mass of soft curls on top of her head. The style displayed to perfection the slender neck and amethyst earbobs dangling from dainty lobes.

When she reappeared in the parlor, Morgan rose slowly, his eyes lazily roving over the tight bodice and small waist. He had seen richer attire but never on one so beautiful. The soft glow from the lamp reflecting on the mauve taffeta turned her eyes, usually the color of a dark, stormy sea, into pools of violet. She carried a soft lace shawl and as he draped it over her shoulders, a redolence of violets reached his nostrils.

Walking over to Benjamin, Keary worried over him for a few minutes, making sure he was comfortable. Patting his hand, she said, "I won't be terribly late. Jamie is working downstairs and I'll tell him to check with you before leaving for the night." She fairly floated down the narrow stairs and Morgan, following in a euphoric daze, couldn't imagine a more lovely companion than his indentured servant.

A thought, unbidden, clamored in his brain. *She's mine for seven years—this heavenly creature belongs to me. Maybe not as thoroughly as slaves belong to their master but very nearly.*

When they reached the street Keary turned to lock the door, the street lamp making her dark hair gleam with shadows of deep velvet, and Morgan was stunned at the new and unexpected warmth surging through him.

Chapter VII

The hired carriage took them first to the City Tavern, where the banquet aromas chased the smell of the chimneys smoking their pipes and the stench from the offal in the gutters. They dined on succulent oysters, braised beef, and a wide assortment of fresh green vegetables. Keary's eyes mirrored in the candle's bobbing glow radiated excitement, while Morgan was talkative, happy, and gay.

"Tell me what unfortunate circumstances forced one so beautiful and well-educated into indenture—family debts?" The question caught Keary by surprise as she was filling a short silence with wonderings of what life on a Virginia plantation would be like—especially with Morgan Baines.

Recovering quickly, she answered, "It's a long story and I'm sure you wouldn't enjoy sitting through such a boring tale."

"Keary, I can't imagine anything about you being boring." It was the compliment he had used many times to prime women's emotions but this time he was sincere.

In fact, he could have elaborated to the point of absurdity and still been sincere.

The use of her given name on such short acquaintance was contrary to convention; still, his casual use of it with the soft Virginia inflection made her feel deliciously alive until a cautious anxiety gripped her. Was this his way of informing her of their difference in station, a basic lack of manners, or—she desperately hoped—a term of endearment? Her thoughts traveled back a few hours to their encounter in the shop and the most thrilling experience of her life. She could still feel his arms about her and his probing tongue burning her mouth, his lean, hard body pulling her closer and closer. Snapping back to reality, she spoke with as reasonable a voice as she could manage. "Mr. Baines, in Ireland a gentleman would never use a lady's Christian name on such short acquaintance, and I can't help feeling customs are not that much different here."

"They're no different really. But then I was never governed by proprieties. I'll refrain from such familiarities if you insist—unless—"

Her eyes met his with a hint of challenge. "Unless what?"

"Unless you also cast convention aside and agree to call me Morgan."

Intense astonishment touched her face and she stared, tongue-tied. He was not demonstrating a difference in station; he was not informing her of the contrast between a gentleman and a bound servant. He wasn't raising a barrier between them at all. In fact, he was doing just the opposite. He was putting her on an equal basis by asking her to address him by his given name—Morgan. The sound of it echoed like a resplendent chord in her brain as she mouthed it secretly over and over. Many times since Mr. Fowler had told her his name she dreamed of calling him "Morgan Love" or "Morgan Dear" while she busied herself about the flat, pretending her station in life were different and they were madly in love. Now, joy bubbled in her laugh and shone in her eyes as she shook her head affirmatively and made a kidding gesture of spitting on her hand before offering it across the table for a handshake. "Done. Hello Morgan."

He laughed and pumped the small hand twice, continuing to hold it firmly and ignoring the halfhearted tug. A deep pink suffused her face and, lowering her eyes to her plate, she drew a deep breath, forbidding herself to tremble. "I hope you won't curse me for bringing you bad luck."

"Bad luck? I don't understand."

"Oh, an old Irish superstition 'tis." She grinned, using the brogue that her English master had taken such pains to weed from her speech. "Faith, the worst of luck will come to them who are after shakin' hands across a table, now. Why, it's turnin' in his grave me old grandfa'r would be doin' if he could see the likes of me temptin' fate in such an outlandish way." Keary mimicked the gestures of an old Irish peasant, causing Morgan to beam with delight.

"It's strange, but until now I hadn't noticed your lack of an Irish brogue. Your speech is more English than Irish."

"That's because my father taught me. He was a scholar and felt my opportunities would be better if my speech was 'thinned out a little.' And he was right. I'd never have gotten the position at Fenleigh Manor with a brogue so thick you could stir it with a spoon."

"What were your duties there?"

Emotions long extinct, buried, and forgotten surfaced and she said quietly, "I was governess and tutor to their daughter for four years until she died of smallpox."

"So then you chose indenture to pay for your passage? Tell me, Keary, wasn't there a gentleman or gentlemen trying to prevent your leaving?" There was more than ordinary interest in his question.

"No. I wish it had been that simple but unfortunately it wasn't. Lord Fenleigh tried to molest me and his wife refused to believe the truth. With the help from a detestable sea captain, she sold me into indenture and had me kidnapped."

"Sea captain? Who is he? Is he in Philadelphia now?"

"I'm sure he's not. Why?"

"I'd like to bring the rogue to terms. The very idea of accusing one so fine makes my blood boil."

"I'm sure he sailed shortly after receiving his soiled money for his human cargo. I don't know where and I hope to never see him again."

An inexplicable feeling of remorse befell Morgan and he squeezed her hand, seeing the dark look of shame in her eyes. "I'm sorry, Keary. I hope your troubles are all behind you now and that you have a much happier life here."

Her confidence spiraled upward. Unlike Bruce, who questioned whether or not Lord Fenleigh had succeeded, or Captain Shelby, who believed the worst without asking, Morgan had accepted her innocence as a foregone conclusion and was ready to take Captain Shelby to task.

Determined to keep her sadness at bay, Morgan changed the subject. "I've never heard the name Keary before. Where does it come from?" A glint of endearment lit his eyes. "I'll wager from a lovely flower or a precious stone."

"No, it comes from an old Gaelic name 'Ciara' meaning the dark one. My parents were going to call me Brigid until my grandfather—so the tale goes—saw a head of thick black hair and, rising to his full six feet, squared his shoulders and with chest out and tankard raised to the heavens proclaimed in a loud voice, ''Tis Keary she'll be named or the fairies' smile will niver be upon her.' Now my father didn't pay much attention to the old proverbs but couldn't quite master the courage to disregard this one. According to ancient custom, if a baby has a distinguishing feature, his or her name should reflect the Creator's handiwork. When we say 'the fairies smiled' on someone it means the same as God blessed them; they are destined for a life of good fortune."

With amused understanding, Morgan sat transfixed by her beautiful smile and light, bubbling chatter. The clock chimed the hour and he rose, handing her the shawl. "I'm not that familiar with Irish proverbs but I'm sure the fairies would smile on one so fair regardless of her name."

Dropping an abbreviated curtsy, she said coyly, "If it's a farthing's worth of influence you have with the wee people, Sir, I'd be ever so grateful if you'd bring it to bear, for up 'til now the fairies' smiles seem to have been reserved for someone else."

Leaving the theatre, they traveled along the river. Street lamps blended with the ship's lanterns to give a soft glow to the summer night. Keary thoroughly enjoyed the play and laughed as she recalled the part where Mask pretended to Sophie he understood opera. She had sat spellbound at Sophie's rendition of "Fonte Amiche" in her lilting soprano. She exclaimed over various scenes, gesturing like the comical Mask and imitating the bewildered looks of Sophie at the little man's ignorant observations. Though Morgan was amused by her effervescence, she noted a genuine affection in his eyes and to this picture she clung tenaciously.

When they arrived home Morgan lit a candle at the bottom of the steps and they made their way up the narrow stairs, their bodies casting long shadows so close on the dim walls Keary had to fight the urge to turn around and make the shadows one. To her surprise, Morgan halted at the door and gave her the candle.

"Thank you, Keary, for a wonderful evening. I hope you will allow me to see you again before I sail."

"Sail!" She was stunned. "Where? When?"

"I'll be sailing to England as soon as the repairs on my ship are complete."

Searching his face she asked softly, "Will you be gone long?"

"Yes, permanently."

She lowered her eyes to hide the quick despair, feeling a lead weight had dropped to her stomach. "I see. I'm sorry to hear that, Morgan." The pain in her eyes was more eloquent than words in expressing the true depths of her feeling.

He started to say something but a sharp twinge of regret engulfed him and he quickly placed a hand on each side of her face, kissing her forehead tenderly. Withdrawing his hands he saw, by the flickering candle, tears trembling on her eyelids. Keary felt him shudder as he drew in a sharp breath and, with a sweeping motion, pulled her roughly, almost violently to him. She locked herself into his embrace, burying her hands in his thick hair while his mouth covered hers hungrily. She became conscious of a low, tortured moan as he released her quickly. To physically untangle from her arms was a simple matter, but emotionally he felt like the fly entrapped in a spider web. His plans had been made and no one must stand in the way of their fulfillment. Her arm reached out to stay him but he turned abruptly and retreated down the stairs.

In the bedroom the tears Keary had so rigidly held back slowly found their way down her cheeks as she sat forlornly in the little rocker, gazing at the empty fireplace. Only a short time ago she didn't know Morgan Baines existed and now she felt a wretchedness of mind she'd never known before. In an attempt to convince herself it was for the best, she reasoned it wasn't wise for a serious relationship to develop. Soon he would sail and she wanted no part of a quick tumble in the hay, as the Irish called these hurried affairs. In trying to convince herself that this was logical reasoning an old expression of Andrew's, the gardener at Fenleigh Manor, came to mind.

"Faith, 'tis a lot of bull, Lass."

She returned to the parlor and, after lighting a carrying candle, blew out the lamp. A light shining under Benjamin's door caught her eye, and wondering if he needed attention, she knocked hesitantly and opened the door a crack. He was propped up in bed with an old nightcap dangling to one side. Hurt and longing lay naked in her eyes and Benjamin quickly put his book aside and patted a place beside him on the bed.

"Come in, Lass, and have a nip with me. Tell me all about your evening."

She toyed with the bedcover, averting his eyes as she replied in a low tormented voice. "It was a wonderful night but Morgan is going back to England."

"Yes, I know. Does that bother you?"

She managed a tremulous smile and, tossing her head back said quickly, "Oh, I hardly know him; it just surprised me. He didn't say why he was going." Her eyes begged Benjamin to enlighten her.

"I see. Well as far as I know, he has two reasons: First, he will be handling the family fortunes, which I understand are quite extensive; and secondly, he's not much in sympathy with American independence." Looking at her downcast face he asked, "Do you want to go with him?"

"He hasn't asked me, Mr. Fowler, and besides I still have seven years to serve."

He lifted her hand from the bed and held it between his emaciated palms. "I could arrange your freedom any time. If you want to go, just say the word."

She shook her head vehemently. "No, Sir. You paid good hard money for my services and I intend to make your investment pay. Besides, no gentleman would want to wed a bound girl."

His sad eyes appraised her sorrow and he debated whether or not this was the time to divulge the identity of her true master, but quickly decided it was not. He told himself this was because of his vow to Morgan; he told himself it would be improper for her to leave with Morgan as an indentured servant; what he refused to tell himself was how much he would miss her. He hesitantly compromised. "Well the offer is still good if you ever want your freedom."

She rose, straightening the quilt and tucking it under the feather mattress. "Thank you, but not now. There is a favor I would ask though." He looked at her, his eyes quizzical. "You mentioned finding a genteel home for me and I wish you wouldn't. I would like to stay here with you, if I may."

The warmth of his smile echoed in his voice as he said, "I can't think of a single favor I'd rather grant, Lass. You have brought sunshine into my old life again. I want you to stay as long as you have a mind to."

Chapter VIII

The following morning Keary arose at the crack of dawn and, gulping a bowl of gruel, carried a precarious cup of coffee as she hurried to the shop, hoping the sweat of her brow would untie the knot in her chest. Her head, protected by an old mobcap, was thrust into every nook and cranny of the shop, rummaging for treasure in a mountain of disorganized rubble. Her persistent efforts were rewarded with one finished product after another. The damaged pieces she set aside, confident Jamie could repair them.

Against the far wall stood an old oaken bench, the top of which had not been seen by the human eye in twenty years. Keary wagged her head in dismay at the mountain of rubbish it supported, realizing the dust it held was older than she. If Jamie could cut the legs down it would make a nice display table. The picture was clear in her mind. However, when she approached Jamie, his shock could not have been greater had she suggested moving his mother's tombstone.

"I don't know, Miss. Did you ask Mr. Fowler? That

bench has been there a long time and what would we do with all the stuff on it?"

It was on the tip of her tongue to say "Throw it out," but she knew it would be impossible to make her schemes work without his wholehearted cooperation. And, above all, he must never think a woman was giving him orders. Meekly, she agreed.

"You're right, Jamie. I had better ask Mr. Fowler. He really liked the idea of the window display, especially when I told him of your beautiful contributions. And by the way, would it be possible to inscribe your work?"

"What do you mean, Miss?" His look was curious, underlined by suspicion.

"You could scratch a little mark on each item in order to identify it. After all, something made by such a superior craftsman should sell for more money."

"You mean like the silversmiths do?"

"Exactly." She shook her head affirmatively, watching him out of the corner of her eye. The curve left Jamie's back as he grew about six inches taller.

"I guess so, Miss."

Keary's smile hid under a serious mask as she turned away. "Now, I'm going up to talk to Mr. Fowler. Can I bring you a cup of coffee and a piece of home-baked bread?"

His mouth watering, he answered gratefully, "Yes, Miss, if it ain't too much trouble." She paused heading for the stairs and saw him tying an old apron around his hips.

"Jamie, do you eat breakfast?"

"Oh, sometimes I have a chunk of bread or cheese, but my room ain't got a proper stove so mostly I don't bother much."

"Well, if you can get in here a half hour early each morning, I'll have a pot of gruel with hot bread and we can eat together. You should have a proper breakfast and since Mr. Fowler never arises that early, I would enjoy the company."

By mid-morning, after Keary had "gotten permission" from a sleeping Mr. Fowler, the bench had been cut down and draped with a curtain, and she was now busily arranging her merchandise.

Within an hour two women stopped and peered in the window but, after a few glances and comments Keary couldn't hear, continued on. Hardly a woman passed without giving the display at least a cursory inspection. Later that day as Keary swept and cleaned the front area of the shop, the bell over the door rang, admitting a short woman with a partially filled shopping basket. She nodded good afternoon and made her way to the display. After fifteen minutes of haggling over a flour sifter, Keary made her first sale. She still puzzled over the strange American money, her mind trying to convert it to shillings and pence even as her heart thrilled with her very first sale.

"What are you going to do with all of this, Miss?" She turned to see Jamie standing over the box of damaged goods she had been assembling.

"That's what I was going to ask you, Jamie. Most of it is broken or damaged. Can any of it be salvaged?"

"Won't know 'til I look at it." He pulled out a metal scoop and turned it over several times, examining it critically on his way to the workbench. Placing it over a conical piece of iron called a stake, he began tapping lightly with a convex-head hammer. Moving to a round stake and with another hammer, he began tapping again, his head tilted at an angle while his mouth formed various distortions willing the new shape of the metal. Within a couple of minutes he held the scoop up, turning it every which way as his expert eye questioned its shape. Satisfied, he handed it to a shocked Keary. It looked like new.

"Oh, that's wonderful, Jamie! Is there anything you can't do? I'll clean it up and put it on display."

"Just a minute, Miss Keary." He reached for the scoop. "I made that originally so maybe I'd better mark it." Going back to the bench he scratched a small *J* on the handle. Keary, looking over his shoulder, protested as he offered it back.

"Shouldn't you mark an *S* too? There could be many tinsmiths with a name beginning with *J*, but if you run the two letters together, it would be a more distinguishing signature and people would be sure it was a James Stuart original." She emphasized "James" instead of "Jamie."

Soon Keary had more merchandise than she could display and Jamie had Tom, the apprentice, scouring every inch of the shop for more. The next day she made four sales but after proudly showing Jamie the results, quickly sobered.

He scoffed, "Miss, that continental paper you got there ain't worth much; I wouldn't trade a teakettle for a bushel basket full of it." His disgusted expression took the wind from her sails.

"Well, what can I do if people insist on paying with it?" She studied the large bills, unable to believe the amateur printing and poor paper quality.

"Just refuse to accept it; everyone else does."

"But I thought it was illegal to refuse continental currency."

"Maybe so, Miss, but accepting it is the easiest way to go bankrupt I know." Her earlier enthusiasm evaporated as she pondered future policy of accepting paper money.

Her days were busy with the shop, running errands, and caring for Mr. Fowler, who now kept to his bed most of the time. There was never an idle moment, and for this she was grateful. Somehow empty hours were always filled with romantic thoughts of Morgan. Every day sales improved and more ladies were stopping to study the window display. She learned the names of the products and their uses, the selling points of different designs and, with Jamie's help, developed a system of pricing.

Without direct supervision Jamie was reluctant to allow Tom to perform even the simplest tasks on metal, so Keary used him to help her clean up the remainder of the shop. By inquiring, she learned of a foundry that would buy the mountain of scrap metal she and Tom had accumulated. If Jamie's estimate of the weight was accurate it would bring a tidy sum. She tried to discuss everything with Mr. Fowler but he merely chuckled and waved her off.

"Do what you think best, Lass." These days he showed little interest in anything except the ever-present bottle of port, which seemed to be his nourishment and medicine combined.

It was a crisp October day Keary chose to walk to the foundry to arrange the sale of the scrap metal. She decided her woolen walking dress, spun from the wool of the sheep at Fenleigh Manor, and several petticoats should stave off the chill from the brisk wind. The shade of indigo in the material made her blue eyes shine like cobalt, and the tight-fitting jacket with its gathered peplum emphasized her tiny waist. The full skirt flounced at the bottom swayed provocatively as she crossed the room, albeit hiding thick woolen stockings and stout walking shoes.

Stepping out the door of the shop wrapped in her paragon shawl, she took only a few steps before an impetuous spurt of cold wind sent her back for the gray wool mantle.

As she left the main streets of the city the countryside was awash in a multicolored blanket of new-fallen leaves. Children going "a-leafin'" played games with the elusive leaves dancing crazily on the sporadic wind, which had chased the hot summer odors across the river. Mothers would scold the children for dillydallying but knew no power on earth could deny youth their sport on this first crisp day of autumn. Each child was charged with bringing home enough leaves to line the oven all winter, adding flavor to the bread.

"But, Mamma, the wind was blowing them all over. That's why it took so long to fill my bag."

"The same wind blows piles against the buildings where you could fill your bag in two minutes. Would you try to make a snowball by catching one flake at a time?" This same conversation would be repeated all over town as it was last year and the year before—and would next year and the year after.

Keary sauntered along, enjoying the bright sunlight as crisp winds billowed her skirts around her ankles. After dealing successfully with the foundry owner, who was shocked to find a woman so young bargaining so shrewdly, she was in a lighthearted mood. She loved the fall weather; it brought back sweet memories of Ireland, the chill winds whipping across the moor, rustling the heather while lads blew on their hands as they dug turf from the damp marshes.

She was still immersed in thoughts of her homeland when Morgan approached. The staccato beat of her heart dulled as her eyes appraised the beautiful, richly attired lady holding his arm possessively. Keary slowed her steps, hoping to delay a meeting she wanted—yet dreaded.

"Miss Cavanaugh, what a pleasure to see you again!" He raised his tricorn and halted in front of her, bowing slightly. "Miss Cavanaugh, this is Miss Thornton."

Both ladies murmured, "How do you do," as their eyes swept over each other, searching vainly for deficiencies and conveying mutual envy. Morgan was unaware of the antipathy between the two as his eyes devoured Keary, wondering all the while how he had maintained the willpower to keep from calling on her these last few weeks. He had told himself she wasn't the type for a quick sexual experience and wouldn't fit in his social circle. What he didn't want to admit, however, was the deeper feelings rapidly developing, feelings he had never before experienced.

"Miss Cavanaugh has recently arrived from Ireland to live with her uncle, Mr. Fowler." Keary was stunned but appreciated his kindness in hiding her indentured status. She had ceased thinking of herself as such but at this moment would give her sainted place in heaven to keep Miss Thornton from learning it.

"Will you be living here permanently, Miss Cavanaugh?" Though the question was phrased hopefully, the voice inflection pleaded for a "no" answer.

"Yes, my—ah—uncle is quite ill and I no longer have family in Ireland." Keary's verdancy with bold-faced lies showed in the slow flush enveloping her cheeks. Morgan's usual devilish grin faded in wonder at Keary's natural beauty framed by the soft gray hood and wisps of curls playing gently around her blushing cheeks. These attributes were not lost on Deborah Thornton either as she dissembled her envy behind a sweet smile.

"One so beautiful must have left a lot of broken hearts in Ireland."

Keary shook her head slowly, feeling embarrassed and awkward as she replied without thinking, "No, Miss Thornton, only one—and I don't think it remained broken very long." Why this answer popped out she was unsure, unless it was a feeble attempt to advise Morgan she was available.

"Then you must join forces with me, dear, and see if we can't deter Morgan from this idiotic trip to England. I've thrown myself at him shamefully, even threatening to stow away on his ship in an attempt to break his armor, but with an ally such as you I'd be certain of success."

Glints of gold danced in Morgan's eyes as he touched Deborah's elbow and, in a conspiratorial tone just loud enough for both women to hear, whispered, "If you want Miss Cavanaugh's assistance, I suggest you invite her to your dinner this evening."

Miss Thornton's furtive glance indicated she was not prepared for his suggestion but, being well schooled in social etiquette, she recovered quickly. "Of course, dear. Having just arrived in Philadelphia, you must be introduced socially. I regret my lack of manners."

Astonished at the unexpected invitation, Keary stammered, "Well—ah—I'm not sure my uncle's health will permit it. I doubt I have a suitable gown and I'm—ah—unfamiliar with Philadelphia. I don't know where you live."

Deborah breathed a sigh of relief and made ready to depart, anxious to bring an end to this distasteful meeting. As her lips formed, "Another time," Morgan interrupted.

"From the little I've seen of your wardrobe, Miss Cavanaugh, it's quite appropriate and I'll be glad to come for you, shall we say, eight of the clock?"

Keary's heart raced as she struggled to contain her excitement. "Oh, that will be fine!" Nodding her head to both of them she said, "Good day," then, after remembering to thank Miss Thornton for the invitation, fought to restrain her feet from dancing down the street.

As Keary's lively form disappeared around the corner onto Walnut Street, Deborah Thornton appraised her tall escort. Since returning to Philadelphia this time he was almost like a stranger: quiet, pensive, easily angered at times, but most of all preoccupied. When this black-haired young woman turned up, Morgan magically transformed to his old self. It was not hard to see how Miss Cavanaugh could turn a man's head. She was beautiful. Deborah knew she had no choice other than to invite her to her home this evening but vowed she would not share Morgan's company with the Irish maid. Despite all efforts to dissuade him, Morgan still planned to leave for England soon; but however short his stay in Philadelphia, she had no intentions of sharing him with any other woman.

As Keary continued down the street she thought of

what a paradox Morgan was. He hadn't called on her or Mr. Fowler in some time, yet he promoted an immediate invitation at a chance meeting. Was it a ploy to pit one woman against another? Was he using her to make Miss Thornton jealous? She believed him capable of such schemes, treating a woman as an angel or a whore, depending on the situation. She pictured the venomous stare of Miss Thornton as they were introduced and was sure Deborah would fight like a demon for one she really wanted. The golden-blond lady with the pale blue eyes and dimpled chin would be a formidable foe. Forgetting her indentured state, Keary shrugged this danger away as she joyfully said to herself, *At least I have a fighting chance.* And her roistering Irish ancestry came to the fore.

She roused herself from daydreams and suddenly realized she must hurry home and ready something to wear. Picturing her wardrobe, she knew there were only a few gowns suitable for this time of year. The mauve gown she had already worn for Morgan and it was not stylish enough for a dinner party. The pearl gray florentine would be perfect if it were not so plain. Lady Fenleigh had grudgingly donated this dress to Keary, feeling it was too restrained and the color did nothing to enhance her pale beauty. Keary could dispense with the kerchief at the neckline, and with a few snips here and there and a little trim—a little trim! She turned abruptly and headed toward Chestnut Street and the draper's shoppe. Entering the dimly lit shoppe her eyes adjusted to the row upon row of materials. As she wandered farther into the depths of the large room, a clerk came to her assistance and directed her to the display of ribbons, trims, furbelows, and buttons. Her eyes settled on a dusky pink velvet trim embroidered in silver vines and tiny silver bells and, as she reached for a small bolt, Keary noticed a large piece of alamode, a thin glossy silk almost identical to the shade of the velvet trim. She quickly calculated the amount of each required and, after waiting impatiently for the slow-witted girl to make change, flew out the door, setting such a fast pace her cape billowed out behind her like a large gray cloud.

Bounding up the steps two at a time, she burst into the common room, jolting Benjamin out of his peaceful repose. Trying to assemble her plans, she spread the purchases out on the old settee, babbling incoherently. After several moments of careful listening, Benjamin deduced she had received an invitation and by being patient he would eventually learn the particulars. Suddenly she noticed Benjamin's ailing color and thought perhaps she should cancel her plans and stay home with him. As she voiced her concern, he shook his head firmly from side to side while his eyes brightened.

"I'm just fine; seeing you so happy and excited makes me feel young again. I wouldn't dream of denying such a pretty lass a wonderful evening such as this promises to be. Now stop fretting and get on with your preparations for whatever it is you're planning—and I'm sure you'll tell me what it is in time."

Running to her room, she threw open the door of the mammoth armoire and withdrew the gray florentine. Then hurrying back to the common room, she described to Benjamin her plans to redesign the gown.

"May I use Mrs. Fowler's sewing box?"

"Of course, my dear. It hasn't been touched since she used it last. I'm not much good when it comes to mending or sewing on buttons. Use whatever you need."

At the small closet in the kitchen she reached on tiptoe for the sewing box on the top shelf. Turning to close the closet door, she spied the wooden bucket and decided to wash her hair and create a becoming coiffure. Keary used so much water rinsing her hair that she had to pound the floor three times, her usual signal for Tom to come up and refill the water buckets. She separated two long shanks of hair behind each ear and quickly wound them around strips of cloth before tying them securely in knots close to her scalp. Gathering the remainder of her hair, she haphazardly pinned it atop her head until later.

Benjamin called from his room and thinking he was indisposed, she cast aside the bodice she was dismantling and ran to answer his summons. He turned from the open drawer in the high walnut chest as she entered the room.

"These belonged to my wife and I'm sure she would want you to have them." Resting in his shaky palm was a dainty string of pearls with matching earbobs. At Keary's incredulous stare, tears forming in her eyes, he tried to mask his discomfort. "They do me little good and when you explained the design of the gown, I thought these would give the added touch needed to make you the prettiest maid at this grand dinner tonight."

"Oh Mr. Fowler, dear friend, I couldn't." She ran her fingers lightly over the necklace as she frantically batted her eyelids, trying to dry the moisture gathered there. "These are so beautiful and such lovely keepsakes for you to treasure. You are very kind, but I just couldn't."

"Come, girl. What good are keepsakes for a sick old man with no other living kin? They were made to be worn by another lovely woman and it will give me great pleasure seeing you wear them." He raised her hand and gently pressed the expensive ornaments into her palm.

Throwing her arms around his neck Keary broke completely as she squeezed him, unable to utter a word between the sobs. He unwound her arms and giving her a little push, said, "Hurry now with that gown so I can see the finished work after you're dressed. I am going to rest awhile."

She worked steadily on the gown, cutting the bodice in a low, wide décolletage. A false front of the sheer alamode was attached beneath the laced bodice, the laces being replaced by tiny bows of the velvet trim. The trim was continued around the neckline and the edges of the elbow-length sleeves, to which were added small double flounces of the rose alamode. The remaining alamode, under Keary's skillful fingers, became an overskirt drawn up at the sides with ribbons, forming large, soft poufs over each hip.

Breathing a sigh of relief at the last stitch, Keary hurried to her bedroom with no time to spare. As she sponged herself and proceeded to dress, she trembled with mixed emotions at the prospect of meeting Philadelphia society. She told herself this would be no different than many of the Fenleigh dinners she had attended. Lady Fenleigh often invited extra gentlemen and Keary was called upon to balance the table. She grinned recalling Milady's subtle dismissals after dinner, which sent her to her room leaving Lady Fenleigh the center of the gentlemen's attention. She would not have to retire before the party was over tonight, however, as Morgan would be escorting her, and tonight she would use all her skills to be his center of attention.

She began to arrange her hair, the long curls springing back as she carefully unwound the rags. Bending over the old trunk, her rump in the air, she withdrew several small hair rolls that she pinned to the top of her head. The loose hair was piled high over the pads, allowing natural, deep waves to fall in place. Keary thought the natural waves much more attractive than the tight little ripples the crimping irons produced. The long curls released from the rags were brushed around her finger and lay in soft, shiny rolls extending well past each shoulder.

Benjamin, nodding in his chair before the fire, raised his eyes as she entered in all her finery. "You're a vision of loveliness and the pearl trinkets against your pretty throat belong there." She smiled her appreciation and was about to thank him again when she heard Morgan's tread on the steps.

Keary stood frozen in the center of the parlor as he entered and bowing slightly to Benjamin, said, "Good evening, Benjamin. Who is this lovely maid you're entertaining tonight?" The golden flecks were deep in his eyes as they roved over her form from head to toe and lingered boldly on the expanse of creamy bosom. He was completely enthralled with the vision before him as Keary stood with an uncertain smile curving her lips and a slight blush coloring her cheeks. "I swear, this lass is the prettiest I've yet to see in Philadelphia!"

Keary's heart beat wildly and her mind groped for an appropriate repartee as she thought to herself, *You are the handsomest gentleman I have ever seen—in or out of Philadelphia*. His white and gold brocade waistcoat and buff satin breeches blended beautifully with the rich brown frock coat. The snowy lace cravat and cuffs completed his elegant attire.

Trembling with hidden desire, Keary stooped and brushed her lips across the top of Benjamin's head as Morgan continued to appraise her. Then, stepping quickly to her side, he lifted her gray cape from her hands and slipping it around her shoulders, said huskily, "We'd better go." They bade Benjamin good night and she left the parlor on Morgan's arm, her heart singing.

He helped her into the coach and gave directions to the driver, then settled as close to her as the bouffant skirts would allow. With a glint of wonder in his eyes, he hesitantly touched the thick long curl hanging in a graceful curve over her shoulder and slowly moved his arm around until she reclined against him. As he gently kissed her temple and the escaped tendrils curling around her face, he spoke of her beauty in gentle tones. Keary lost all desire to attend the dinner party, wishing the coachman would lose his way and they could ride on forever. But all too soon the rattle of the coach's wheels against loose cobblestones reached her ears, and they eventually came to a halt in the long, curving driveway before a grand mansion.

If Keary had expected to spend a good part of the evening with Morgan, it was because she had underestimated Deborah Thornton. She didn't lack for male attention, surrounded by gallant gentlemen all evening, but Miss Thornton monopolized Morgan from the minute they entered the huge entrance hall. Deborah had skillfully maneuvered them to a small group and, after introducing Keary to a Mr. Jason Wentworth, pulled on Morgan's arm, pretending she needed his approval on something or other. The name Wentworth immediately recalled to Morgan the scene at the auction. He had met Jason before but had not connected the name to the old man who had bid so determinedly for Keary. Could the old skinflint have been Jason's father?

Miss Thornton's seating arrangement placed Keary too far away from Morgan to carry on a conversation. He was seated on Deborah's right at the head of the table and Keary was hidden between Mr. Wentworth and Mr. Langston, a short old man so hard of hearing it would have strained her vocal chords to get his attention. As Deborah smiled sardonically down the long table at Keary, the flashing blue eyes didn't betray her malicious musing.

That wench! She implied she hadn't a gown to wear and she appears in the latest fashion with the courage to flaunt custom by discarding the wig in favor of a becoming natural coiffure. Who, exactly, is she and what is Morgan's interest in her?

Socially the evening was a great success for Keary as she received numerous compliments and one invitation after another, but as the hours wore on and she was unable to be alone with Morgan, she longed for an end to the festivities, anxious to flee from all but him—to spend the rest of the night in his embrace. She attempted to show an interest in Mr. Wentworth's boring diatribe against The Declaration of Independence, nodding appropriately and murmuring noncommittal replies as her eyes constantly followed Morgan around the room. At this moment the butler, showing disdain for the man's station, reluctantly ushered a seaman to Morgan's side. After a brief conversation the sailor left. Keary saw the deep frown on Morgan's face and was about to excuse herself to Mr. Wentworth and make her way across the room when Deborah, ever close to his side, began an animated conversation with Morgan that ended when she flounced from the room in a fit of pique.

Morgan walked deliberately toward Keary, the seriousness of his expression making Jason Wentworth's tirade fade into oblivion. Nodding to Wentworth, he took both of Keary's hands in his and the sadness of his eyes alarmed her even before he spoke. "Miss Cavanaugh, I've come to say good-bye. I only wish I could have had the opportunity to know you better."

His eyes implored her to understand as she cried out, "Good-bye! Are you leaving now? Why—I don't understand!"

"I didn't expect to leave tonight but the captain wants to make the next tide and his timing, I'm sure, has to do with the blockade. I just received his summons and we will sail within the hour." Glancing at Jason Wentworth he said, "I'm sure Mr. Wentworth will be happy to see you home." As Jason nodded his approval, Morgan raised her hand to his lips and before she could grasp what was happening, he squeezed her hand saying, "I'm sorry, I must be on my way." He turned and hurriedly made his way out through the chattering crowd.

Chapter IX

Morgan felt as if his soul had been imprisoned as he leaned against the taffrail watching the sailors make final preparations to cast off. A quarter moon spread gray shadows over the city as two seamen scampered topside to set the main royal. This one small sail would propel the ship downstream on the ebbtide.

The plans that once seemed so perfect and the country Morgan would have so willingly left a short time ago were now overshadowed by an Irish lass with deep blue eyes and a quick tongue. As the anchor was lowered a few notches to drag in the swift current, the picture of Keary as she stood in the antiquated parlor this evening, a fresh rosebud in a bramble bush, appeared before him. Gripped by a morose feeling, Morgan briefly considered jumping overboard and swimming back to shore. Sighing deeply, he retired to his cabin and opened a bottle of brandy, intent on obliterating all feeling in a merciful drunken stupor. After a few quick gulps, however, he replaced the cork, knowing no amount of brandy would erase Keary's face and realizing the more he drank, the more melancholy he would become.

He paced back and forth across the small cabin cursing an unknown enemy. The whole idea of any kind of a relationship was insane. Though a second son, he was a member of one of the first families of Virginia and she a bound servant. Of course she could pass for a lady in any society and he wouldn't be above such a masquerade if it were only temporary, but something warned him there could be nothing temporary in a relationship with Keary Cavanaugh. And how could they live? His meager allowance wouldn't support the two of them in the style he demanded. No, he must get her out of his mind and focus on his own well-laid plans. With this resolve, he strode out on deck for a breath of fresh air. Leaning on the rail, he stared at the dark water below where the face of a black-haired lass was reflected on a shimmering moon path.

After sailing cautiously downstream, the ship lay at anchor for two days in a sheltered cove, waiting to put out to sea. Captain Towne had told Morgan he had no fear of the British blockade, as they were not carrying contraband and everyone aboard was a loyalist. "Still," he continued, "it would be much simpler if we slipped by the blockade unnoticed. The British have to see us to question us."

"But, how can you pass a blockade unnoticed, Nathan?"

"It will take three things in our favor: darkness, an ebbtide, and a fresh breeze. If we can slip past the blockade, the British will not bother to chase a ship this small and fast. Smugglers often use this ploy of sending out a fast vessel to draw pursuit so larger ones with important cargo can escape."

"Well this is your business, Nathan, so I'll leave everything up to you." Morgan was anxious to be on his way to England, hoping distance and time would erase memories of Keary. The small cabin, the lack of female companionship, and no diversion more exciting than reading or stargazing was not his idea of time well spent.

By evening of the second day the tide crested, and as the wind came up Nathan gave orders to ease the *Banetree Princess* into the main current. The whole ship came alive as one sail after another was unfurled, cracking loudly and ballooning in the wind as the halyards were secured. Morgan enjoyed watching the machinelike teamwork of the captain and the crew as commands were given and eager hands did his bidding. As each sail was set in turn, the ship heeled a little more to port and added speed.

"Set your maintop, set your fore-gallant, bring her closer to the wind, sou' by sou'west." Soon the beam was slicing waves in a smooth rhythm and the race was on. Though the crew labored with an air of purposeful nonchalance, underlying tension could still be felt and Morgan knew they would all spend an anxious night. Captain Towne remained on deck all night and Morgan, after several attempts at sleep, returned to keep him company.

As the first rays of a gray dawn washed the choppy bay, a sail was sighted off the starboard bow. Captain Towne held course, every few minutes extending his glass and studying the sail relentlessly bearing down on them.

"She's a British frigate, Sir." The voice crying out from the crow's nest was barely audible before being carried away on the wind. The captain studied the fading shore and light-brightened water as if watching for a change or a point to be cleared. After a few minutes he turned to the helmsman and calmly ordered, "Due east."

"Aye, aye, Sir, due east," the helmsman repeated as he cranked on the extended spokes of the wheel.

"Bring her closer to the wind," the captain barked and sailors began pulling and slackening lines as the huge sails turned slightly and responded with quivering tension. Turning to Morgan, he said, "If this breeze holds, we'll be beyond the frigate by noon. Now, how about a little breakfast?"

Since the water was too rough to cook or set table, the breakfast consisted of bread, cheese, and wine, but even this they were not permitted to enjoy for very long. Loud excitement broke out on deck and leaving his unfinished breakfast the captain, with Morgan a few steps behind, made his way topside.

"Another sail due north and closing, Sir," the helmsman greeted them. For a while they waited anxiously, the captain from time to time peering through his glass until finally he confirmed their worst fears.

"It's another British warship. No way to run now." He turned and resignedly issued orders to slacken sail. By mid-morning they were drifting under only the maintop and fore-royal as a longboat from the British frigate rowed toward them.

"Lt. Lawrence Layton of His Majesty's ship *Corvair*, at your service, Sir." The young officer who came aboard made the announcement as he bowed.

"Capt. Nathan Towne, skipper of the *Banetree Princess*, Sir. This is Mr. Morgan Baines, owner of the vessel." As Morgan bowed and mumbled a greeting, the young British officer continued.

"I see you carry a British flag. Now, where did you hide the American one?" His knowing smirk was a challenge and Captain Towne's back stiffened, his cheeks flushing red at the rude insinuation.

"We carry no such flag, Sir. We are all good subjects of His Majesty, George the Third."

"Tut, tut, Captain. Spare me such chicanery. If you are loyal subjects, why were you trying to run from one of His Majesty's ships after you were signalled to stand by?"

"I saw no signal. We are a peaceful merchant vessel and were merely holding our course in a fresh wind."

Ignoring Captain Towne's reply, the officer turned and motioning to one of the seamen who had accompanied him aboard the *Banetree Princess,* said, "Come forward, Willy." The seaman came to his side and turning to Captain Towne, the officer commanded, "Have your crew line up, Captain, and prepare your manifest for inspection."

After glancing through the ship's papers, the lieutenant rewrapped the pouch and, tucking it under his arm, muttered, "The usual forgeries." He walked up and down the deck, his hands behind his back as he studied the *Princess*'s crew. Then turning to the seaman following at his heels, he feigned inquisitiveness. "Recognize any of them, Willy?"

The weasel-faced one nodded his head and without hesitation, answered, "Yes, Sir, the lot of them."

Pretending surprise, the officer raised his eyebrows, "Really Willy? Everyone? No exceptions?"

The seaman's beady eyes slid back and forth as he grinned wickedly and stoutly declared, "None, Sir. They must have all deserted together. Everyone o' the scum served with me on the *Rhonda.*"

The lieutenant turned swiftly to Captain Towne and

with a sneer on his thin lips said, "It seems, Captain, you are not only operating a privateer, but are doing it with deserters from His Majesty's Navy."

Captain Towne took a step forward, his fists clenched at his sides as angry voices rose from the crew. Glaring at the wily sailor as if he would throw him overboard, he shouted, "This scurvy bugger is a bloody liar."

The lieutenant ignored the outburst and, holding his hand up for silence, said, "Deserters should be keelhauled or strung from a yardarm, but the Admiralty has decided to be lenient. You may return to your duties in His Majesty's service or you can spend the duration of this unfortunate rebellion in the hulks."

Morgan, furious and unable to remain silent, stormed at the lieutenant. "Now see here, Lieutenant, how can I get my ship to England if you take the crew off?"

The officer turned, sneering at the gall of the colonial rascal and retorted, "Your ship, Mr. Baines? This vessel is a privateer and, as such, now belongs to the Crown. It will be taken to New York and sold at vendue."

"Sell my ship! Why I'll have you know, Sir, the Baines family is well connected in high places and it will take very little effort to prove this is a peaceful merchant vessel."

"'Pon my word, Mr. Baines, do you expect me to believe you would be stupid enough to appeal my action?" He expressed pompous annoyance.

"Yes, Sir. To the Crown, if necessary." Morgan's temples pounded thickly, the cords of his throat contorting.

"Then tell me, Sir, exactly what is the purpose of this voyage?"

"Why trade, of course."

"Hmm, you are riding light, at least ten tons under capacity, carrying enough canvas for a vessel twice this size. You carry two nine-pounders and are well supplied with powder and shot. Perhaps you can enlighten me on why the rebels allowed you to take that much powder out of Philadelphia when they are so desperate for it themselves?"

"We paid off the right people; it's the same here as it is in England."

"And why did you try to outrun one of His Majesty's men-of-war?"

"As the captain explained, we had a fresh wind and were simply making the most of it."

"My dear fellow, please don't try to insult my intelligence. You are carrying enough canvas to risk snapping a mast and until such time as you found yourself trapped, ignored our signals and made every attempt to outrun us. Had my captain interpreted your action as anything other than a privateer, I'm afraid his superiors would consider him unfit for command." As the lieutenant laughed and turned to leave the ship, Morgan grabbed him by the shoulder, spinning the slight man around.

"By God, I'll not stand for this; no popinjay lieutenant is going to take my ship."

The officer recoiled in fear but quickly regained his arrogance as some of his men advanced. Straightening his jacket, the contempt he held for colonials surfaced and he turned to the seaman at his side. "Willy, are you sure this yokel is not a deserter too?"

Willy peered around the lieutenant's shoulder, his features registering pleasure at the predicament in which Morgan had placed himself. "Now that ye mention it, Sir,

I be saying he was for certain. For a little he had me fooled in them gentlemen's togs. But not even fancy togs kin hide an ol' shipmate from ol' Willy. No, Sir."

"Very well, Willy, I'll take your word for it; you've never lied to me yet." Motioning to the rest of the toughs he had brought on the longboat, the lieutenant smiled triumphantly at Morgan. "Throw him in with the rest of the scum."

The first time Jason called, Keary sensed tension in Mr. Fowler and knew something was wrong. She had heard the name Wentworth before but had never made a connection until she returned home that evening after dinner and found her master scowling.

"Mr. Fowler, you seemed to dislike Jason; if you would rather I didn't see him again, I won't."

"Oh, Keary lass, I'm not going to tell you who you can see and who you can't. Besides, I have nothing against Jason; Lord knows he has probably had a hard enough time of things already with that father of his."

"You know his father?"

"Yes, and so do you; he was that lecherous old skinflint who tried to buy your indenture."

"Oh!" A chill traveled down her back. "But Jason seems like a gentleman and I doubt he is anything at all like his father, unless—"

"Unless what?"

"Well, he is a bit narrow-minded. It's hard to explain but sort of like his was the only way and God himself had told him what was right and what was wrong. Is his father like that?"

"Exactly, only a hell of a lot more so. Righteous self-esteem is about the only way I can describe it. He has an outward code of conduct and feels the rest of the world is out of step." Keary wore a contented smile as she sat in the chair opposite him. "What is that smile all about, Lass?"

"Oh, it's just that after all those weeks of uncertainty on the ship and the fear of old Mr. Wentworth buying my indenture, it's a relief to be here where I feel safe and appreciated. Whenever I think of what my nights might have been with that old man, I shudder. What is he really like? Is he as bad as I thought that day?"

"Worse, Lass—a lot worse. He lives by two different sets of rules. One set governs outward conduct, and any breach of these rules is a mortal sin. The other set governs the making and hoarding of money. These rules say that every possible penny should come to Silas Wentworth whether by fair or foul means, or regardless of who gets hurt in the process. To him a man falling asleep in church is headed straight for hell, but there is nothing wrong with swindling a poor widow out of her last penny."

"Oh, no one could be that bad. Are you sure you are not exaggerating just a little?" Her eyes twinkled with merriment as she rose and turned up the wick of the lamp, illuminating the dark-paneled, comfortable old room.

"No, if anything I'm being very generous to him. He owns half the tenements in Philadelphia, and just let one poor widow be a day late with her rent and see how soon he takes the bailiff in tow and pays her a visit."

"Hmm, and you say he is a churchgoer?"

"Oh, he wouldn't miss church for the world. The pew his father bequeathed him has not been empty once in twenty years, nor has his tithe varied one penny in all that time. He pays the exact minimum amount to maintain his pew rental and not one day before it's due."

"Strange, he doesn't seem like the type who would buy a young woman; seems he would worry too much about what others would say."

"That's hard to figure because women, drinking, or gambling were never his vices—they were probably too expensive. Also, they are vices others could see and condemn. In your case, I'd say the old devil's lust almost got the best of him. He was about to break one of his own rules but changed his mind when the price reached forty pounds."

"Well, in this case I'm glad he's an old tightwad."

Benjamin was quiet for a few moments as if remembering something. "His actions really surprised me. I've never known him to show the slightest interest in any woman before, not even his wife. Up until the time of Jason's birth his wife received affection in the form of weekly visits of about ten minutes duration, and after that an occasional cheek peck. Once an heir had been created, Silas had no desire for more mouths to feed or more noise to pollute his staid world."

Keary giggled, "Now, Uncle Benjamin, how would you know such things about his personal life?"

His face lit up at the term "Uncle," which she used occasionally since Morgan had introduced her to Deborah as Benjamin's niece. "Well, I'm not entirely sure where that information came from, but it fits so well, I guess everyone just sort of accepted it without question. There's another story told on him that is almost folklore in this town, and it illustrates exactly what I told you about his deep concern for outward conduct."

Keary settled back happily. For a bound servant, her life was better than she had any right to hope for. The only dark spots were Benjamin's failing health and the agony that seized her every time she thought of Morgan—thoughts which seemed more frequent than less with every passing day. In the short time she had known her master, she had found him to be a great storyteller and their evening conversations were the highlight of his life. And by the amount of wine he poured into the glass, before picking up his pipe and relighting it with a taper from the lamp, she knew this one would be long and interesting.

"It seems old Silas had taken his pew in church one Sunday morning exactly one minute before the service was scheduled to begin. It was a day so hot you could cook a leg of lamb just by hanging it out in the sun, and so humid some of the fish in the river swam right down Market Street. The church was only about one-tenth full, indicating sensible people felt God had already punished them enough for one day and would excuse them from having to endure another one of the preacher's long, boring sermons. Now, whether Wentworth was there in order to prove to God he deserved a priority over less dedicated souls when it came time to select the chosen few to enter the pearly gates, whether it was to keep his long-standing record intact, or whether it was because he felt the pew rental was already paid and by missing services he would in effect be losing money, I'm not sure. It was probably a combination of all three. But regardless, there he sat, heavy coat, stiff cravat, and all."

Benjamin leaned over to rekindle the neglected pipe. "Now, Keary, you were not here ten years ago when the invasion of Brazilian ticks hit this town. Some say the sailors brought them, but regardless, of all the ornery crawling vermin the good Lord ever cursed mankind with, these had to be the worst. They multiplied so fast some folks said that within two weeks of the time the first male and female crawled off the ship in Philadelphia, fifty million of them had taken up residence in Pittsburgh. They never stopped crawling or biting. Fact of the matter is, one very observant gentleman figured out they bit exactly seven times to the inch.

Now as I said, old Silas had taken his seat and Reverend Brown had mounted the pulpit for his usual three-hour attack on Satan, when a full-grown Brazilian tick began to ascend Silas's left leg. Well, don't you know by the time God's chosen son got well wound up to his task of driving sin out of Philadelphia, that tick had reached Silas's upper leg in close proximity to his ample derriere." Benjamin took a long pull on his wineglass and paused expecting Keary to recoil in horror, in which case he would water down the account. But her interest showed in her wide blue eyes and he took courage.

"As the story goes, and Lord knows I have no way to verify its authenticity, that tick didn't stop there. No, ma'am, he explored old Silas's body in minute detail, biting several times to the inch as the ultra-religious gentleman sat perfectly still, apparently engrossed in the preacher's verbal onslaught against the frailties of human nature. Silas held that cane of his firmly on the floor with both hands closed over the silver handle and never so much as lifted an eyebrow. Though one close observer swore he noticed repeated contractions in the old skinflint's Adam's apple."

Benjamin glanced up mischievously, sure that by now Keary would be properly horrified, but found her convulsed with laughter instead. "To make a long story short, Miss, that preacher expounded virtue for two more hours while that tick reversed his route countless times and old Silas never so much as gritted his teeth. Now, I don't know where the verification would come from on a story such as this, since old Silas wouldn't tell such a tale on himself, but more than a few upright citizens have sworn to the gospelness of it. And unlike fables that fail to stand the test of time, this one seems to gain credence with age. And its most substantiating factor is those who have known old Silas the longest are the most likely to swear to the truth of it."

"What you are saying, I gather, is old Silas is not one to show his feelings." She shook her head, still chuckling at the tale.

"What I'm saying, Lass, is that before a man can scratch in public, he first has to learn to belch and spit. And, I swear, though Silas is not above a little thing like larceny in all its myriad aspects, to him clearing one's throat in mixed company is a mortal sin."

"If he's that prudish maybe I would have been safe in his house after all."

"He could get a cook and housekeeper for a whole lot less than he bid on you, so you draw your own conclusions."

"Well, don't worry about Jason. He's a suitable escort but that's all he could be to me." She patted his vein-covered hand and began to walk to her bedroom when his question stopped her midway across the room.

"Are you in love with Morgan Baines?"

153

"How did you know?" A strange, bleak expression replaced the smile and her eyes were glazed with hopelessness.

"You were not that difficult to read when he was around."

"I didn't realize that. But since I probably will never see him again, it doesn't matter much, does it?"

"I guess not, if you say so." Benjamin felt that it did matter though—it mattered a great deal.

Each day Keary threw herself more intently into her work, trying to erase the memory of Morgan. Nevertheless, she found herself wondering where he would be at a certain time, or what he might be doing. Remembering her own voyage, she knew every few ticks of the clock would see the bow of his ship slice a wave closer to England and farther from her.

Since the dinner party she had a new social life of sorts with Jason Wentworth, her constant escort. He was handsome in an un-rugged sort of way, fashionably dressed with impeccably correct manners and a foot in the door of all the best homes in town. Like his father he considered himself one of God's chosen, with an inalienable right to help the Creator select all others.

Keary tolerated Jason, even humored him, but the chances of his building a fire in her heart were about equal to his chances of igniting a tinderbox underwater with a worn flint. Jason was not alone, however, in his dearth of romantic appeal to Keary at this time. His company included every other male on earth, save one. Every man she met was unconsciously compared to Morgan and came up wanting.

She remembered that day in the shop when he took her in his arms and she wanted him to hold her forever. She had been so vulnerable and he was experienced enough to know it, yet he had not taken advantage. He found her physically attractive; his eyes had said as much. Each time she closed her eyes and pictured the scene it always produced the same longing.

One bright spot in Keary's life lately was the apparent improvement in Mr. Fowler's health. He stayed up for longer periods of time and occasionally ventured downstairs to look in on the shop. She and Tom had cleaned and discarded mountains of trash and everything was stacked neatly on shelves or in bins, and Tom was whitewashing the walls, giving the shop a bright interior.

She had helped Benjamin down the narrow stairs and stood aside as his amazed eyes took in his surroundings. His glance moved from the window arrangement to the display counters and freshly painted shelves stacked with neat rows of merchandise, before coming to rest on the neat, uncluttered aisles and Jamie working happily in the well-organized shop. Two workmen were hanging a new sign, a beautiful ornate piece of tin depicting an apron-clad figure holding a hammer, with the words "Benjamin Fowler, Tinsmith" printed across the bottom.

"Do you like it?" Keary asked softly, bending her head to see his reaction.

"Yes, very much. But how were you able to do all this? Where did you get all the money?"

"By selling and trading," she laughed, "probably more trading than selling." At Benjamin's questioning look she continued, "I sold all the scrap to the foundry and planned to use the money for the counter and shelves, but in the meantime I made a trade. Do you remember the cornice work you made for a customer who went bankrupt? I found another builder who wanted it and when I refused to sell it on credit, he agreed to make the shelves and counter in exchange for the cornice work."

"You say you sold the scrap to the foundry? Did they pay well for it?" Keary pulled an old chair closer to the window and helped Benjamin settle into it. Her spirits soared at the appreciative smile on his face because to Keary, who had endured four years of parental famine at Fenleigh Manor, his approval and appreciation were very dear. Her affection for this old man, who had spent his last farthing to save her fate, was unbounded.

"The foundry tried to pay me in continental paper but, thanks to Jamie, I knew the value of that. However, we were able to make a three-way trade. They were selling castings to an army contractor who had a good supply of tin sheet, sheet metal, copper, and brass, and the three of us were able to come to terms." As Benjamin watched the sign being raised outside the window, Keary nodded her head and continued, "That sign was also a trade to a certain extent. Jamie made the design and cut it from metal, and when we took it to Mr. Connors to paint, he liked it so well we agreed to create the design for another sign order he had in exchange for painting ours. He told Jamie he would be able to give us a lot more business."

Benjamin's eyes danced as he shook his head in disbelief. "You haven't gone into debt? I can't believe it."

"Rather than being in debt, we have more than forty pounds in the cash drawer and Jamie and Tom are both paid up to date." The old man laid his trembling hand on her head as the bell above the door tinkled and a woman entered the shop interrupting the tender moment. Keary touched the corner of her apron to her eye and swallowed the lump in her throat as she hurried to the woman's side, asking, "May I help you?"

"Yes. Mrs. Weinstock, my neighbor, bought a coffin tray here last week, an original James Stuart."

"Oh, yes. I remember her as being quite discriminating."

"I would like to look at a James Stuart teakettle if I may—about a three-quart size?"

"I may have one under the counter. I don't dare display them or other dealers would grab them up before anyone else could see them. You realize the price is much higher for an original than an ordinary teakettle?"

"That is no problem as long as it is a James Stuart original." Lifting a plain metal teakettle from beneath the counter, Keary held it up so the woman could see the *JS* scratched on the handle. "But I wanted it painted, Miss. You see I don't have the talent for such things."

Keary looked around the shop as if ready to divulge an important secret then, leaning over the counter, whispered, "There is a young maid employed by Mr. Penrose, the baker, who paints these beautifully and bakes the finish by putting them in the oven at night. She is the only one Mr. Stuart recommends to paint his work. Her name is Molly."

The woman paid the price Keary asked without haggling. As she left the shop, Benjamin, who had been trying to eavesdrop, asked, "What was that all about?"

"I don't know if you remember Molly, the girl who went on the auction block just before me? I ran into her last week and she stopped by the shop for a few minutes. She is very good with any kind of artwork and Mr. Penrose, her master, is kind enough to allow her to paint our tinware and bake the finish in his ovens at night in her spare time. That's the fourth lady I've sent her this week."

"What was that I overheard about an original?"

Keary pretended shock, her eyes widening and her mouth falling open. "Why a James Stuart original, of course. Jamie does such beautiful work, I came up with the idea of him initialling everything and we would say they were originals just as the silversmiths and coppersmiths do. Every day more and more people ask for them and the prices keep going higher and higher."

"It seems I'm making more money staying away from the shop than when I'm working." A wave of warm gratitude washed over Benjamin. "I don't know how to thank you, Lass."

"No need to thank me. 'Tis I who am indebted to you, and I shall be for the rest of my days. The day you bought my indenture and prevented old Wentworth from taking me as his personal chattel was the fairest day of my life." Benjamin turned again to the window, honor-bound not to tell her who actually bought her indenture, and wishing sadly it really had been him.

Chapter X

For the first time since Keary's arrival in America, Philadelphia buzzed with war news. General Howe, the British commander, was leading a huge expeditionary force of crack British troops and hired German mercenaries. They had already taken New York and were now marching across New Jersey.

Washington's ragged bunch of farmers and shopkeepers ran in terror before the neat rows of scarlet uniforms and flashing bayonets. Every day more American deserters poured into Philadelphia, not bothering to disguise their uniforms, or what rags remained of them. Horror stories circulated of plunder and rape, especially about the Germans. These were German troops, hired primarily from the province of Hesse-Hanau, which the Americans immediately nicknamed "Hessians."

The stories were reminiscent of those told by old-timers throughout Ireland and Keary, who had witnessed the problems her own countrymen had throwing off the yoke of England, had little hope the Americans could succeed. She was concerned more with the rapid rise of prices, which made business decisions difficult; with business prospering, her chief problem was figuring out how to produce enough to meet the demand. Despite all the steps she had taken to improve production, Jamie, believing in his old tried and true methods, inherently resisted new innovations. But since stubbornness can seldom stand up to a careful schemer, he faced a formidable foe. As demand outraced production, Keary began posting the orders on a nail at the side of Jamie's workbench.

Today, as she stood leafing through the backlog, a small, thoughtful frown creased her forehead and she approached Jamie. "I guess we'll have to hire more help; our backlog is really starting to mount up."

Jamie eased the weight to his sound leg and raised the lame one to the lower shelf of the workbench. Then, leaning on his elbows, he looked up at Keary. "That's easier said than done, Miss. I don't think there is a good tinsmith to be had in this whole town. With this war there is all kinds of work and everyone worth a grain of salt is already working."

She walked back and forth staring pensively into space, slapping the orders against her palm. Whirling and placing one elbow on the bench, her eyes on the same level and very close to Jamie's, she said, "There still may be a way, Jamie. If you drew the exact pattern on the metal couldn't Tom cut it out? Of course you'd have to watch him."

"Huh, if I had to spend all day watching him"—he shook his head disgustedly—"how would I get anything done myself?" His attitude warned her a little subterfuge might be necessary to convince him her scheme was worth a try.

"Well, maybe you wouldn't at first, but you could at least give him a chance. Once he gains experience he shouldn't need close supervision every minute of the day. Oh, Jamie, I know if anyone in the world could teach him, you could." Her eyes were only inches from his, expectant and trusting, and refusal was impossible.

"Well, I guess it won't hurt to try; the lad has to learn sometime." He raised up from the bench, the sweat forming on his forehead having nothing to do with physical exertion. His voice had an unfamiliar ring as it labored past the catch in his throat when he called Tom. Keary hid a satisfied smile and hurried to the front to assist a customer who had just entered. When the customer left, she peeked around the corner holding her breath as Tom, with Jamie's head almost resting on his shoulder, began feeding a piece of metal into the jaws of the bench shear.

"Jaysus, Mary, and Patrick help the lad do well or Jamie will not soon be giving him another chance." After offering up the hurried prayer she attempted to give the Lord a little help by maneuvering her head and arms, mimicking the motions she had often seen Jamie use as he cut the metal. Jamie's nose practically touched the metal as Tom cautiously lowered the handle and Keary could almost hear the instructions.

"A little to the left—a little to the right—slow down a little—easy now, keep your eye on the line."

After a few anxious days in which she mentally assisted Tom and prayed every time Jamie inspected the work, she was ready for the next phase of her production plans.

"Jamie, you never cease to amaze me. When you first

got the idea of teaching Tom how to cut the metal, I was thinking in terms of several weeks before he could actually turn out finished work. And here you have him working with only minimal supervision in a matter of days."

"Well, he does pretty well so long as I draw the lines for him." Jamie drew a file across the edge of a freshly cut part as they talked. Keary watched intently and suddenly "got an idea."

"It seems a shame for an artist like yourself to be filing when you could be using the time to create your masterpieces."

"Oh, it's not as wasteful as it looks, 'cause when I'm filing I'm also planning the next operation."

"But if you had someone to file for you, you could plan even further ahead. Ordinarily I wouldn't think of such a thing but after I saw how quickly you taught Tom the bench shear, I'll bet you could teach another lad to file in no time at all."

"Dunno 'bout that, Miss. A lad should spend at least a year running errands and cleaning the shop before he ever touches the metal." He quoted the familiar doctrine as if it were his own. "That's the way I had to learn the trade."

"I guess you're right; you always are. I shouldn't be sticking my nose into men's business." She turned to leave as if everything were settled, then called back over her shoulder, "Now that Tom has other duties, I'll hire another lad to clean and run errands." Keary hired another apprentice and smiled contentedly when, within two days, Jamie got the brilliant idea to teach the lad how to file edges.

Production began to climb as, with her gentle nudges, Jamie started assigning the lads more duties. But there were other problems to overcome: principally, the difficulty of obtaining materials in a wartime economy of shortages and a determination to accept only hard money for finished products. She welcomed any problems, however, that would keep her mind off Morgan. Even though she knew he was gone and out of her life forever, his handsome features continued to haunt her.

Sitting on the high stool behind the counter, she pushed the ledger away and stretched, tired to the bone. She wished she hadn't accepted Jason's invitation to the Allens' dinner party this evening. Jason was a doting gentleman, and despite a nose which reached a trifle too far into the atmosphere and a softness not to Keary's liking, many considered him handsome. Even if she could muster romantic feelings for him, the thought of being part of the same family as old Mr. Wentworth turned her stomach. Jason never mentioned his father and Keary sometimes wondered if he was aware of his father's attempts to buy her indenture.

She felt Jason would propose soon, but although money and position were important to her, she had no intentions of marrying for any reason other than love. She sighed and jumped down from the stool, thinking at least tonight's dinner would give her the opportunity to wear the new gown Benjamin had insisted she buy. She smiled, remembering the first time she had purposely called him "Uncle Benjamin" after telling him of Morgan's plausible introduction to Deborah Thornton. Handing Benjamin the profits from the shop that day, she had said, "I have paid Jamie and the lads and left a good amount in the cash drawer. This is your profit, Uncle Benjamin." He was so pleased with the endearing title, she called him "Uncle" regularly now.

Counting the profits, he smiled ruefully and said, "Ah, Keary, I wish you had come to me years ago. I never was a good businessman." Then he placed a stack of coins in her hand. "This is for a new gown."

"No, I won't take it. You should put some aside for a rainy day."

He forced her fingers back, enclosing the coins, insisting, "Keary lass, I'm a sick old man and have no use for money other than to get some enjoyment from it. And nothing would make me happier than seeing you in a new gown. Besides, if my niece is going to mingle in Philadelphia society, she must always look like a stylish young lady."

"But, Uncle Benjamin, I have plenty of clothes; I brought my entire wardrobe from Ireland."

He chuckled, wagging his head knowingly. "Lass, you can pull the wool over those young gents' eyes all you want, but don't try to fool an old man. Though my courting days are ancient history, I'm not too senile to remember a lass never has enough clothes. My only regret is there's not a dressmaker in this town with the skill to do you justice."

Planting a kiss on his bald pate, she hurried to the draper's and chose an apple-green brocade sack that hooked at the waist. The wide V of the open bodice displayed a corset of the same material, and a white satin petticoat was revealed by the divided skirt billowing out over oblong hoops. White lace chemise ruffles showed above the corset and fell in deep tiers from the elbow-length sleeves. With the remainder of the money she was able to purchase the green satin slippers with low French heels and tiny rosettes.

As they pulled up to the three-story red brick mansion, Jason helped her from the carriage and threw the reins to a small black boy. Keary looked up at the imposing house with its large symmetrically spaced multi-paned windows and long portico, its roof supported by snowy-white Roman columns. There were no spacious grounds surrounding the mansion, as this home, like most others in Philadelphia, set close to the red brick sidewalk amid a mixture of shops and other homes in a haphazard yet charming arrangement.

A liveried doorman ushered them in and recognizing Jason, consulted a card to find the name of his companion before making his announcement. Once his announcement of "Mr. Jason Wentworth and Miss Cavanaugh" was delivered in his usual practiced iteration, the servant would never again have to consult a card to know the name of this beauty.

"Why, Miss Cavanaugh, how nice to see you again." Deborah Thornton's dissembled voice caught Keary's attention. Its trained softness belied the venom behind her pasted-on smile as she glided across the room with both hands outstretched. After gathering as much attention as possible with the profuse greeting, she slid her arm into Jason's and led him off as easily as a drover would oxen. After only a few steps she turned and her face lit up as if a lost thought had just been found. "By the way, Miss Cavanaugh, I must inform you of some bad news. It seems a mutual friend has come upon misfortune." Keary waited patiently for the trite bit of gossip Deborah was taking her time telling now that a few gentlemen had turned toward her in anticipation. After a quick survey of her captive audience, she addressed Keary again. "Morgan Baines's ship has been captured by the British."

Keary's smile was replaced by wide-eyed shock as she cried, "Morgan!" Her body shook as she hurried to Deborah's side and seized her hands. "Is he all right?"

Disengaging her hands, Deborah curtly replied. "I'm sorry; there is no more information one way or the other. They say the ship has been sent to New York as a prize, but what has happened to the crew no one seems to know." She elbowed her way through the group with Jason in tow. Keary was unaware of Deborah's exit as she anxiously searched the group and directed her question to whomever had an answer.

"What usually happens in these cases?"

One of the gentlemen replied. "Miss Cavanaugh, it's as Miss Thornton said. The ship will be taken to New York and sold as a prize. The crew will, in all probability, be given a choice between joining the British Navy or spending time in the hulks."

"The hulks!" Keary's eyes mirrored fear at the ominous sound.

"Prison ships, Miss. Demasted old ships anchored in New York Harbor that have been converted into floating prisons. Life aboard them is said to be extremely harsh, and the mortality rate very high."

"Do you think they would send Morgan—ah—Mr. Baines there?" She glanced nervously from one face to another, seeking assurance.

A rotund little man with a large powdered wig and a scholarly expression said, "If they found a letter of marque, which is a letter from Congress or the state of Pennsylvania empowering his ship to act as a privateer, he will go to the hulks for sure."

Desperately she asked, "But if they don't find such a letter, they'll release him, won't they?"

The little man slowly shook his head from side to side. "They would probably suspect him of destroying the letter before they boarded." Seeing her bereft expression, he quickly added, "But they may give him the benefit of the doubt."

"That's a relief." She smiled weakly, clutching at straws. "I'm sure there was no letter because his intentions were to move to England permanently."

The tall gentleman she had talked to first now leaned toward her. "There are a couple of other possibilities, Miss. If someone had a grievance against him, they could have reported him as a privateer or a blockade runner. Or if one of the crew had become disgruntled for any reason, he may give false evidence to gain a reward or to secure his own freedom. The fact the ship was seized seems to indicate something suspicious."

Keary was no longer in a party mood and would have preferred to go home but, after having refused Jason so many times, she felt it would be the height of bad manners to ask him to leave early.

The lavish dinner consisted of several courses of rich food washed down with the finest wines, but Keary was unable to eat or concentrate on her surroundings. In response to the glib conversation surrounding her, she could manage only an occasional nod or an absentminded smile as her mind focused on Morgan languishing in a drifting, damp cell. After dinner, Keary was surrounded by several gentlemen vying for her attention, as the conversation centered on the war and how Washington's ragged army was being destroyed by the redcoats. With the fortunes of war now decidedly favoring the British, loyalist sentiments were being voiced more and the word "patriot" was often supplanted by the more derisive term "rebel," with a generous helping of sarcasm dripping from it.

Deborah slipped up to the group unnoticed and waited patiently for a lull in the conversation, then spoke in a voice elevated enough for the whole room to hear. "Miss Cavanaugh, I've just heard the most ridiculous story and I'm sure you would want to correct the obvious falsehood." Her fan fluttered happily, waiting for Keary to take the bait. Keary refused and after an agonizing silence, with the whole room waiting, she was forced to continue. "Someone, whom I'll not name because I hate malicious gossip, has intimated you are not Mr. Fowler's niece at all. In fact, they insist you are indentured. I declare I've never heard anything so absurd." Her truculent eyes gloated, never wavering from Keary's.

Only for a moment was Keary abashed and then her Celtic blood began to boil; through a white rage she scathingly replied, her Irish brogue rolling unchecked. "Faith, and I'm sure you do detest malicious gossip, my spiteful friend, and there now is why you didn't see fit to borrow Captain Smallwood's speaking trumpet." Walking insolently up to Deborah, hands on hips and the bouffant skirt swinging, she spat, "Yes indeed, I'm indentured to Mr. Fowler, and a more loveable man I'll never meet. He's a sick man with neither kith nor kin and treats me like a daughter. Does that answer your question or"—lifting her skirt enough to expose a dainty satin slipper, she challenged—"would you like to inspect my ankles for burns from the chains?"

The room buzzed, and through the cacophony surrounding her, the words "Irish wench" found Keary's ears. Throwing her head back, she looked down her nose at the assembled "ladies" and rasped, "Yes, an Irish wench, born and bred to dig potatoes and serve English whores."

Just as the crowd drew back to escape her scorn, an excited messenger was admitted to the hall announcing, "Washington is retreating across the Delaware and all of New Jersey is in British hands."

Despite the cold December weather, Keary refused Jason's offer to share the fur blanket as they rode home. She was still reeling from her recent outburst and this, along with the shame of being exposed as a bound servant daring to break into society, kept her so warm that her gray mantle was ample protection from the cold. Jason's silence on the way home was a blessing as her anger gave way to worry over Morgan. His spirit was akin to her own and putting him in prison would be tantamount to caging a wild animal. Arriving at her door, Keary felt Jason's arm on her shoulder as she stirred to alight from the carriage. With a patronizing sigh he leaned forward, taking her hand.

"Miss Cavanaugh, things may not be as bad as they seem; I believe I have a solution to your dilemma." Settling back, she waited for him to continue, more out of politeness than interest. "If this episode of tonight is allowed to die, you will receive invitations again. Maybe not right away or from the best families but, if you follow my counsel, eventually they will come. Naturally as a bound servant you could never be received, but I can take care of that. I would like to send you to a good school in Baltimore where young ladies are taught the social graces. With proper elocution lessons you will be able to cover every trace of that Irish accent, which seems to surface when you are angry. When you return in a year or so, I'll compensate Mr. Fowler for your services and arrange a proper home for you until the time is right for us to marry." His benign smile, blended with a contented sigh and a reassuring pat on her hand, made her anger rise in blinding waves.

She snapped, "Married!"

"Yes, my dear. Although it may be impossible for you to believe, I am quite serious. Some may say I've taken leave of my senses even thinking of marrying a bound girl but, ah—er—I'm really a very liberal person."

The hot Irish blood, which had begun to settle after the earlier ordeal, boiled anew as she listened to his sanctimonious speech, then spat, "You are a pompous ass."

The verbal slap widened his eyes and dropped his mouth. Finally he sputtered, "But Miss Cavanaugh, I am offering marriage in a situation where most gentlemen would simply take advantage."

"Advantage?" she asked scornfully. "Advantage of what?"

"Why your situation, of course. Surely you understand that in the present circumstances the best families will no longer receive you."

"I could care less what your so-called best families do; but tell me, exactly what constitutes the best families in your opinion—the ones with the most money?"

"No—ah—it's more than just money, there's—ah—

breeding as well."

Keary threw back her head and her laugh probably woke a few of the neighbors; then wiping her eyes, she retaliated, "Yes, I have seen what seven hundred years of careful breeding can produce in England—a pervert and a whore." She raised forward on the carriage seat, preparing to step down, then turning, added, "No, Jason, when I marry it will be for love. And I don't care whether or not the man has breeding, offers a country estate, or a log cabin in the wilderness. He will love me for what I am and care little what the rest of the world thinks."

Jason shook his head in disbelief. "Does this mean you're actually refusing my generous offer? Why I thought—"

"You thought"—she cut him short—"I'd be so anxious to find acceptance in your precious circle I'd willingly become your slave. Mr. Wentworth, as far as I'm concerned you can take your generous offer and go straight to hell." Jumping down from the carriage, she called back over her shoulder to her astounded escort, "Don't bother to walk me to the door; Irish wenches don't expect such courtesy." Her lilting laugh floated back to him in the quietness of the night.

Chapter XI

Prisoners were brought on deck, four or five at a time, to breathe fresh air and get a little exercise. After long hours in the hold, packed so close they had to take turns breathing, this was as close to heaven as Morgan could imagine. It had been two weeks since their capture and he, along with several of the crew, had been taken aboard the frigate and hauled to the dark, filthy hold where several other seamen from another captured American vessel were already languishing.

Captain Towne and the remainder of the crew had accepted service in the British Navy to avoid prison life on the hulks. Although Morgan had no political beliefs preventing him from doing the same, he chose prison, refusing to knuckle under the British who so unjustly confiscated his ship. Each day when his exercise turn came he looked over at the *Banetree Princess* sailing beside them as a prize and his anger at the British mounted.

Today the frigate was tacking through a channel between two large land masses that some of the more knowledgeable seamen called "the narrows," or the entrance into New York Harbor. The *Princess* was no longer in sight and Morgan was sure she had gone on ahead to be auctioned in Manhattan. Hundreds of vessels ranging in size from ships of the line to small shallops plied these waters, indicating a large military presence as well as a thriving commercial trade. Though Morgan was eager to be off this ship, he was troubled by the silent, withdrawn look of some of the other prisoners after seeing New York Harbor.

"Aren't you happy to be getting off this scow?" He asked this of a sailor who had been scanning the shoreline, nervous as a treed cat.

"No, Sir, not if it means the hulks." The man's gaze never left the shore.

"How could the hulks be any worse than this?"

"They are the oldest and rottenest ships in the British Navy, that's why they were converted into floating prisons. If you think the chow has been bad on this ship, just wait until you see conditions there. On a ship at sea no one profits by cutting our rations and we have probably been eating the same as the crew. But on the hulks it will be a different story. Everyone from the commissary down to the guards will be stealing from our rations and what little we get will be rotten to boot. At sea the sailors had regular duties to keep them busy and they left us alone. On the hulks the Royal Marines will be guarding us and they will have a lot of time to think of ways to make life miserable. The hulks are always crowded and the only relief will be if men die faster than new ones are brought in."

That night the ship rode at anchor and the following morning Morgan followed the others down the ladder, not as anxious to get off this ship as he had been before. They were placed in longboats and rowed to a demasted old tub, which was to be home for the next several months. Everything the sailor had said about the hulks proved to be true, but did nothing to prepare Morgan for the realities of this life. In addition to the hardships he had foretold there were rats, an overpowering stench, and they were anchored only a couple of hundred yards off the coast of Long Island, close enough to dream of freedom but far enough to realize the impossibility of obtaining it.

"All right, ye buggers, line up here and when the corporal reads your name, answer up." As the roll was read every man except Morgan answered to a rank as well as a name.

"What's your rank, Baines?" The corporal stared at Morgan's attire, unsure of who he was addressing.

"I'm not a sailor and don't have a rank. You can call me Mr. Baines." A guffaw spread down the line but was quickly silenced by the corporal's cold stare.

"Then what the hell ye be doin' on a privateer?"

"I owned the vessel you speak of and it wasn't a privateer." His gaze met the corporal's squarely.

"Well, ain't he the high and mighty one, now. All right, Baines, I'll assign ye to the officers' quarters on the forecastle."

Morgan didn't know it at the time but the corporal had just given him the best possible break. The forecastle was a hellhole by most standards, but compared to the hold, it was paradise. This was heavily outweighed, however, by the fact he was not listed on any military or naval roster and, therefore, was not in a position to be exchanged. Occasionally a British cutter would come alongside and an officer would come aboard to read off a list of prisoners to be exchanged for British prisoners held by the Americans. Though the odds were slim, the other prisoners had this one hope to cling to, but Morgan didn't even have that. For all intents and purposes he might as well have fallen off the end of the earth.

From the moment Morgan stepped aboard, he was obsessed with plans to escape. At first he thought only of getting to England, then little by little a new destination surfaced in his thoughts. It came to him so subtly he could not remember the first time he had pictured Philadelphia as his destination. But somewhere along the line a black-haired Irish maid supplanted those rich London widows. She was different from any woman he had ever met. That she was beautiful, there was no doubt. But it was more than beauty; Morgan had seen that clearly the first day he saw her on the auction block. With that straight nose, full mouth, and square chin she could look more determined than a beaver. Yet a simple smile could change that resoluteness to tenderness so easily, such as when she tended Benjamin. He smiled remembering how Benjamin had fretted at first over the responsibility of taking her into his house, but how quickly he invented excuses when Morgan had later suggested finding a more genteel home for her.

He could read Benjamin like a book. Within two days of Keary's arrival his old friend's eyes sparkled anew, and all the doctors and all the medicine in the world couldn't have improved his health as much as she. Yes, it was easy to see how Benjamin felt about her. He suddenly had the daughter he had always wanted.

But Morgan was having more trouble analyzing his own feelings. She was beautiful; anyone would agree on that after a single glance. Yet his mental pictures of her were not those of one posing for a portrait. He usually pictured her laughing, staring in wide-eyed expectancy as she listened to an interesting story, or setting her determined chin when she had a purpose in mind. She had all the feminine charm he could ever hope for in a woman; still, she reminded him of a cornered fox when her temper was ignited. But above all she was easy to talk to. There was never any of the artificial romantic jargon he habitually encountered in other women.

Yes, she had many wonderful qualities to make her likable and an unlimited number to make her desirable, but what was it about her that made his loins ache, ruined his appetite, and made other women seem so alike and lifeless? Sometimes when he was totally immersed in escape plans a dizzying, overpowering feeling would engulf him. It was a need to see her, to be near her. It was a need beyond logic or reason—a hunger of the soul, an overwhelming desire to possess her. These were not the welcome yearnings of which daydreams are made, for he fought valiantly against the intrusions but to no avail. He could no more purge his thoughts of Keary than he could deprive his lungs of air. He chided himself for such immature behavior and tried to remind himself of his usual ability to control any relationship.

Rationally he would tell himself it was fruitless to moon over someone he would probably never see again. He would tell himself these feelings were caused more by his being in a lonely prison than an actual desire to see her again. Any man used to sharing women's beds on a regular basis would feel this emptiness when those beds were no longer available. Why then didn't his thoughts drift back to one of those exquisite creatures he had bedded instead of always picturing a bound girl with midnight hair who had so abruptly changed his life? Was he in love with her? No, that was nonsense. He was Morgan Baines and women were in love with him. They connived to be with him. They flirted outrageously and when this failed they became more direct. How then could he be in love with a woman he had never even bedded?

He had escape plans to consider and determined to put Keary out of his mind. This he resolutely did but within a few minutes she returned.

After two months of thinking escape day and night—of which maybe an hour or so was uninterrupted—he still hadn't come up with a feasible plan until today. With the late autumn weather already upon them, he visualized a winter without heat, since there was not even enough wood for cooking. He vowed not to spend a winter here regardless of how desperate an attempt was necessary. For wasn't it better to die attempting escape than face certain death by disease? All morbid thoughts vanished, however, once he conceived a realistic escape plan.

Much of Morgan's education had been in the social graces: how to hold one's liquor, how to perform the latest dances, and even how to lose money gracefully. He mastered these subjects easily, plus one not included in the ordinary curriculum: how to win gracefully. Social obligations often dictated spending many hours at games of chance, and he realized early in life those hours could be utilized winning money just as easily as losing it. His father had always given him an ample allowance by most standards, but Morgan didn't live by most standards. His accelerated lifestyle always demanded large amounts of money and games of chance were usually a dependable subsidy.

This talent was of immense value to Morgan now, since gambling was one of the few recreations available. The only source of wealth was the constant flow of new prisoners and he wanted to direct as much of that wealth into his own pockets as possible, to be available when his escape opportunity finally came. Now with a plan, life took on new meaning and winning became more important than ever. The following morning was the time to start the first phase of his plan. He stood at the forecastle entrance as the guard bellowed out the morning calls.

"Bring up the slop buckets, fill the water barrels, turn out the dead." With dysentery, smallpox, and putrid fever cutting a swath through the prisoner population, hardly a day went by without at least a few bodies to bury in the sands of nearby Long Island beaches, and some days eight to ten. Morgan could see a long stay on the hulks was an almost certain death sentence.

Sergeant Cranby of the Royal Marines ruled this ship like a dictator and every privilege he granted was in direct proportion to how much he personally stood to gain. Morgan understood this and hoped to turn the sergeant's avarice to advantage.

"I'd like to volunteer for the burial detail, Sergeant."

"Oh ye would, would ye? And what does a big shipowner like yerself know about diggin' holes?" It was easy to see the sergeant hated all people born above his station and Morgan decided it was best not to antagonize him.

"I was raised on a farm and digging holes is nothing

new to me." He was careful not to mention the "farm" was fifteen thousand acres and the holes he was familiar with were always dug by slaves.

"Is that a fact? So, if it ain't to learn something new, why would so fine a gentleman want to volunteer for such a detail?"

"Just to get some exercise and feel my feet on dry land for a few hours."

"Suit yerself; but I doubt you've got the stomach for it." The sergeant turned away chuckling, and in order to keep him happy, Morgan acted a little squeamish when the first bodies were brought up from the hold. The guards would undoubtedly report this and the sergeant would probably assign him to this detail permanently as a way of rubbing a gentleman's nose in the dirt.

Four prisoners, accompanied by two guards, loaded the bodies into the longboat and rowed to shore. From the landing they carried the bodies about fifty yards inland and buried them in the sand. The exercise and small amounts of food he could buy with gambling winnings were important to build his strength, something very necessary since the escape plan required good physical condition. After about ten days on the burial detail, Morgan became well enough acquainted with one of the guards to offer a proposition.

"Soldier, I know how both you and I can make a little extra money."

"So do I, Baines; you wear a skirt and I'll be your bloody pimp." To the prisoners he was a brash, cocky sort but would lickspittle his superiors like a spineless jellyfish.

"Very funny, about what I'd expect from a lobster. So go to hell; I'll tell my idea to someone else." Morgan pulled on his oar, trying to appear disinterested, knowing the soldier's avarice could not long be contained. He was right.

"All right then, what's your big scheme?"

"First we talk shares."

"No. First you tell me your great idea. Then if I think it's even worth considering, we might talk shares."

Morgan sighed resignedly, implying defeat. "You get some rope and timber and we'll make a fishnet. I'll ask around and find some fishermen to man the net, and you and Cranby will each get one tenth of all the fish we catch."

"I got a better idea."

"What's that?"

"You get one tenth." Morgan didn't answer. He and the guard both knew Sergeant Cranby would decide the split and take the lion's share himself.

It was two weeks before all the materials were assembled and seamen began to unbraid the rope and weave it into netting. The first net was a crude affair but produced enough fish to show promise of large catches in the future. Morgan, as supervisor of the fishing detail, along with his burial duties, was able to spend a lot of time on deck. The fresh air, pulling on oars, and a better diet did wonders to restore lost flesh and strength.

Soon the time came to take a couple of others into his confidence. He carefully observed how often different ones volunteered for the burial squad, for among those he would find the best candidates. These were men with enough spirit left to accept a distasteful task in return for a few hours of fresh air, who no doubt would be in better physical condition than most. Morgan moved cautiously, resisting the temptation to take unnecessary chances in order to move the big day closer. His self-discipline was amazing since it was a character trait he had never exercised before. It was doubly hard now since it wasn't only freedom he was fighting for but also the chance to see Keary again. There would be only one chance, and failure would mean certain death—the only question being whether it was from a hangman's rope or slowly in the dungeon.

"How would you like to escape this damn hulk, George?" The blond-haired youth stiffened and his shovel stopped in mid-stroke. The guard had wandered a few paces down the beach as the two prisoners dug in the sand.

"What'cha got in mind?" Hope and fear blended in his expression as he watched the guard carefully and resumed digging.

"Talk to your mate in the hold tonight. If you're both willing I'll tell you the plan later. Now keep right on digging so that damned lobster doesn't suspect anything."

Once the bodies were interred and the grave covered, Morgan noticed a new bounce in George's step and felt he had made a wise choice. The next day the youth reported his mate was willing and Morgan found time to give him a brief outline of the plan.

"I'll pick the day George, and the signal will be when I start talking to the guards about a new idea to fish from the longboat. Now remember if the conversation is only about the longboat, the plan is still on. But if I sense any last minute problem, I'll also suggest we build a raft. Any mention of a raft and the plan is off until further notice—understood?" George nodded and plunged his shovel into the sand all the way to the handle.

Morgan finally set the date but later had to cancel it. The day before he planned the attempt Jake, the other conspirator, came up from the hold in a different way than expected. He would be making the trip with them to the shore, but not the return. Jake was a victim of smallpox and had died during the night. The slow, painstaking process of finding a replacement began and it was a month before a new date could be set.

Chapter XII

The small boy smiled joyfully and, tucking the collar of his jacket under his chin, faced the raw December wind with a light heart as he headed south on Front Street. The sea captain had given him a whole shilling hard money just to run an errand of some six or seven blocks. After returning with the reply, he would head straight for the sweet shop and spend three pence.

His mind wrestled with the selection he would soon have to make and his smile gave way to a studious frown. The vision of taffy and chocolate caused him to go past the tinsmith's and he had to retrace his steps four or five doors. He entered the tinshop and found himself facing a pretty black-haired lady who smiled and invited him to the stove's warmth.

"No, thanks ma'am. I have a letter for Mr. Forner—or Flower—oh, I forget, but he's a tinsmith."

Her hands were folded in front of her as she waited with a patient smile for him to master the name. When he admitted he didn't remember, she helped him out by questioning softly, "Mr. Fowler?"

"That's it, ma'am. Is he here?" She sure was a pretty lady when she smiled like that.

"Yes, he's upstairs. If you give me the letter, I'll see he gets it." At the gentle touch on his shoulder, he would have gladly relinquished the letter had he not been given firm directions by the captain.

"Can't, ma'am. I'm supposed to wait for an answer to take back to the captain."

"Captain? Oh, that must be important! So that's why the captain sent such a grown lad to deliver it." As the lad's wind-kissed cheeks reddened even more, Keary took him by the arm and led him to the stairs. "Knock on the door at the top. Mr. Fowler will be in the common room."

"Thank you, ma'am." He ran lightly up the stairs and after a slight knock, entered the room.

A very short time later the lad ran back downstairs and out the door, leaving it open to swing in the wind. Walking over to the open door and smiling at the exuberance of youth, Keary heard the upstairs door open and Benjamin come out. It took him much longer to negotiate these same steps the lad had flown down just a few minutes before. She wanted to protest when she watched him carefully wrap the muffler around his face and step out into the cold, but whatever news the lad brought must have been important, and to try to stop Benjamin was fruitless. She only hoped it wasn't bad news.

Benjamin was extremely tired when he reached the White Dove Tavern and the warm fire was as inviting as the padded chair the tapster so thoughtfully provided.

"How about a hot buttered rum, Benjamin? It'll take

the chill out of your bones."

"No, Thaddeus, just a glass of port. It seems to be all my stomach will tolerate these days." When Benjamin entered the tavern, the tapster was about to congratulate him on a recovery but, noticing the gray pallor and heavy breathing, talked instead about the weather and quickly led him to the fire.

The door opened and a tall sea captain entered and stood just inside, giving his eyes a minute to adjust to the dim interior. Seeing the shrunken form sitting by the fire, he strode over and extended his hand. "Mr. Fowler?"

Benjamin ignored the outstretched hand. "Sit down, Captain. Your note said you had something important to discuss concerning my ward, Miss Cavanaugh."

Leaning toward the fire and wringing his large hands to stir the blood and chase the bite of cold from his fingers, the captain stared from under thick black brows at the little man across from him. "Yes, I would like to buy her indenture."

"Captain Shelby, you owned her indenture once and sold it. Why would you want to buy it back? Are you thinking of making another profit on an innocent maid?" Benjamin's cold stare and hard, biting voice took Captain Shelby by surprise. The cadaverous old man evidently had more strength than he portrayed.

"Now see here, Sir. I—"

Benjamin raised his hand and cut the captain short. "Please, Captain, spare me your bluster. If I were younger and enjoyed better health, I would welcome an excuse to call you out. But then, on the other hand, sticking pigs was never to my liking." The captain's hands clenched and he made ready to rise but Benjamin jabbed again. "Yes, Keary told me you and your aristocratic English whore kidnapped her. You see, you bastard, I wondered how an innocent maid as well-bred and educated as Keary could have become bound. I asked her about this several times and little by little dragged the story out of her."

Amos Shelby lowered his head and squirmed under Benjamin's hard stare. "What she told you is undoubtedly the truth and I'm not proud of it, Sir, but there is more to it than either you or Miss Cavanaugh know."

Benjamin snorted and waved a bony finger under the younger man's nose. "I know this much, Captain; such conduct is inexcusable and I don't care if your very life depended on it."

"I'm not here to make excuses, Sir, but to make amends." He was sprawled back in his chair now, looking down at his long fingers weaving in and out, the wind completely gone from his sails.

"And how do you propose to do that?" Benjamin pulled forward in the large chair, his ailing eyes hard and unfeeling, his clawlike hands holding onto the arms of the chair as though to keep the padded depths from swallowing him.

"By buying her indenture and turning her free. That way she could do whatever she wanted."

"Oh, I see. In other words, you would turn her out penniless in a strange country to shift the best way she could." Benjamin shook his head disgustedly and gulped at his wine. Jerking up, Captain Shelby's eyes were stormy as he shook his head.

"No. Actually I hadn't thought that far ahead. But now that you mention it, I'll make sure she has money and I'll arrange a decent home for her."

"I see. Do you know how much she sold for?"

"Of course. Discounting the auctioneer's commission, it would be fifty pounds." The tapster interrupted the conversation when he brought another glass of port to Benjamin and a bowl of flip for the captain.

Benjamin reached for a taper beside the fire and lit his pipe. "So you are willing to pay fifty pounds for her release and say—another fifty for her new start?"

"More, if that's what it takes."

Holding the pipe by the bowl and waving the stem up and down, punctuating his words, Benjamin challenged the captain. "And how do I know you won't buy her indenture, put her back aboard your ship, and throw her back in the hold with the rats and the stink until she agrees to become your whore?"

Amos winced at the truths hurled his way and bending forward, his elbows resting on his knees, said earnestly, "You can go with me to the magistrate; we'll sign the necessary papers and you can witness the money I give her and approve her new home."

"You almost sound sincere, Captain. Have you begun to fear death and the pains of hell at an early age, or is your sleep haunted by visions of the devil coming for you?" Benjamin's faded eyes began to twinkle as he sank back farther into the deep folds of the padded chair.

Captain Shelby wagged his head sorrowfully, remembering the trip with the indentured maid. "Yes, and the devil has black hair and stormy blue eyes and a quick Irish tongue. Since I last laid eyes on her, I've crossed the ocean and back and she hasn't been out of my thoughts for an hour."

Benjamin sat quiet, staring at the disconsolate man before him until Captain Shelby's eyes met his. "Well—

so you are suffering now worse than she suffered at your hands. Ordinarily I would say it's your just desert, Captain, but your pain seems too cruel for any crime. However, I must disappoint you further." He sipped his wine and carefully formulated his next words. "In the first place, I won't release her and am not at liberty to tell you why. And secondly, she is very much in love with another man if I'm any kind of an observer, and I think I am because that's all I do anymore."

"In love with a tradesman or another one of your station, I suppose. Surely, man, if you have a brain in your head, you know she deserves better than that." Captain Shelby was up on his feet, storming back and forth in front of the fire now but Benjamin's next words halted his stride.

"No, she's in love with a gentleman from a very wealthy family; someone I've known for a long time and greatly admire. Unfortunately, he is not here at present but I earnestly hope and pray for his return."

"Where is he, not in the rebel army I hope?" The captain's expression did not agree with his words.

"No, though I wish he were. Unfortunately, he was returning to England when the damned limeys seized his ship. At present he is probably a prisoner on the hulks. Captain, my life expectancy is about the same as a snowman's in April, but if there is one last wish the good Lord is in the right humor to grant me, I hope it's to see them united in marriage."

Dropping back into his chair and turning to Benjamin, Captain Shelby said, "Mr. Fowler, ordinarily I would like to see an old man's last wish come true, but in this case I will do everything I can to thwart it. If you won't allow me to buy her back, at least give me permission to call on her and ask forgiveness."

"Keary is free to see whomever she pleases, Captain, and has been since the first day she entered my home. However, I suggest you ask her yourself."

"Thank you, Sir. What hours would her duties permit me to call?"

"You'll find her in the shop all day, every day except Sunday." Benjamin tapped the dottle from the cold pipe and shoved it into the pocket of his long waistcoat as he pulled himself forward in the big chair.

"I take it you are quite confident I can't come between Keary and her love." Captain Shelby asked this hopefully but was disappointed in the grin that swept across the little man's face.

"Keary is a young lady of uncommon good sense, Captain, and that's where I place my confidence."

Amos Shelby rose and bowed. "Thank you, and good day, Sir."

"Good day, Captain." The tavern door closed and Benjamin decided to have one more glass of port before facing the cold again. Secretly he was happy Morgan owned Keary, taking the option of freeing her away from himself. Suppose the captain did find a good home for Keary? Would he be able to let her go—even if the situation was to her benefit?

Keary's eyes returned to the door every few minutes after Benjamin left, and after stewing for two hours, she grabbed a shawl and left to look for him. Turning toward Front Street, the direction he had taken, she hurried along the windswept street, holding tight to the shawl whipping around her shoulders and ignoring the snapping branches of the beaten trees. She had gone only a short way when she spied his weary form trudging around the corner. For a moment she stood irresolute, wondering if his pride would resent her concern. After observing him for a few minutes, however, she was more concerned with his safety than his pride. Running to meet him, his tired smile when he saw her showing gratitude, she grabbed his arm and tried to shift his weight as much as she could to her own sturdy body.

"You didn't have to check on me, Keary, I was doing fine." His labored voice wasn't at all convincing as it was caught up in the wind, and she patted his arm and slowed her steps.

"Check on you? Why, that was the furthest thing from my mind. I was just taking advantage of the opportunity to walk with a handsome escort."

He chuckled and turned his head around in the ring of the scarf covering most of his face, avoiding her scolding eyes. "Oh, whatever made me buy such a poor liar? I should have bought a good horse instead."

"Yes, and when you find a horse that can cook your supper too, that'll be something. Faith, if you don't stop worrying me to death like this, I'll not be around to be doing it either."

It turned out she didn't have to prepare supper for him that night. Keary helped him to his room and he fell into an exhausted sleep and didn't wake until morning. Before she left the room Keary made sure a large log was in the little fireplace, and after removing his boots and pulling the blankets up to his chin, she planted a gentle kiss on his forehead and returned to the shop with a sigh of relief.

* * *

Keary stood at the window absentmindedly watching a peddler go by in his large wagon pulled by a good horse. Most of the peddlers she had seen had old, broken-down wagons pulled by a packhorse, others pulled small handcarts, and still others carried packs on their backs. She had always admired the peddlers and tinkers, envying their free life, their constant travel and meeting new people everywhere. Although most of them had reputations of being so shrewd their practices bordered on dishonesty, she knew with their small volume and extensive travel, they had to operate on a wide margin of profit in order to survive.

Many made tinware among other things as a sideline and, although the workmanship was often shoddy, still managed to sell their wares in remote places where competition was at a minimum. They came to Philadelphia to restock and did most of their selling in remote farm areas. She smiled recalling some of the stories she had heard about peddlers. According to legend: Each of them had a girl in every village, could talk the horns off a bull, and could pick your pockets from ten feet away. The first thing a farmer's wife should do when a peddler arrived was lock her daughters in the attic and hide her purse in the cellar.

As the wagon drew abreast of the shop, Keary had an idea. Throwing a shawl over her head, she ran from the shop and hailed the peddler.

"Mornin', Miss, what can I do ye fer?"

"I would like to see your tinware."

His glance shot from her back to the shop quizzically. "Looks like you got all the tinware you need, Miss."

The wind whipped at her skirts and she pulled the shawl closer around her shoulders. "Not to buy. I may have a proposition for you."

"Well, tradin's my game." He climbed down from the high seat. "What'cha got in mind?"

She took a cream pitcher off the side of his wagon and asked, "How much do you charge for this?"

"Oh, anywhere from one and three to one and six, depending on how far out I am."

She turned the pitcher over in her hands and asked, "How much does it cost you to make?"

"Mebbe half that."

"Maybe I can show you a way to make more money, Mr. ah—"

"Jist Sam, Miss. Most people call me 'Honest Sam.'"

Keary choked back a laugh as she returned the cream pitcher to the wagon, wondering how anyone could keep a straight face and call a peddler "honest." "I'm Keary Cavanaugh, Sam. If you have a few minutes, I'd like to show you something." She took him on a tour of the shop, showing him the principle of each one doing a specified job which resulted in higher production.

Sam shook his head as Keary completed the tour. "I'm sure glad ye ain't sellin' in any of my territories, Miss. I sure can't compete with a system sich as this."

"No need to think about competition, Sam. How would you like to have a shop like this working for you?"

"I don't understand, Miss."

Keary led him back to the counter where she could talk to him out of earshot of the other lads. "We have what we call a 'to be sold again' discount. If you buy in quantity I can sell you merchandise as cheap, or maybe even cheaper, than you can make it yourself. That would leave you more free time for selling."

"Can ye give me a fr'instance?"

Keary lifted a sifter from beneath the counter and held

it up to Sam. "Take this flour sifter. If you buy a dozen, the price to you would be twelve pence each. Here's a price list I made up with every item a country housewife may want."

Glancing through the list, Sam was impressed. "Yer right, Miss. At these prices, I cain't afford to make 'em and I have to admit, the quality is better. O' course, I form everything by hand. If I give ye an order, how long would it take to make the stuff?"

"It's already made—just a matter of taking it off the shelves. Of course, it would have to be all cash—hard money."

"That's the only way to do business, Miss." His eyes wandered over to the painted pieces displayed on the shelf behind the counter. "How much extra fer painting?"

Keary turned and lifted a small teakettle from the shelf. "This is not painting, Sam. This is real 'japanning'; the artwork is done and then baked." She handed him the teakettle. "Try to scratch it with your fingernail."

After several attempts to scratch the surface, he handed it back, shaking his head. "I know a few women who would give a year's pin money fer one of those and never put it on the stove. N'sir, they'd put it on a shelf fer everyone to see."

Sam bought a large order, including a few pieces of japanned ware, and vowed to be back in less than a month. Keary added up the profit quickly in her head and tried to estimate how many more peddlers came to Philadelphia for stock. However many there were, they all came to Market Street and she would be waiting. With a new market opening up, it was more imperative than ever to talk Jamie into accepting more of her ideas for faster production. Perhaps it was time to give him another gentle nudge.

After the others left for the day, Keary rearranged the display as a way of passing time. She didn't enjoy cooking for herself, and this was a subconscious way to delay it. A tap sounded on the window and she looked up to see a familiar face with an unfamiliar expression. At first, she wasn't sure it was Captain Shelby because she couldn't remember seeing him without the arrogant smirk. Leaning forward and meekly tapping on the window, he cut an entirely different figure than the one she remembered strolling across the quarterdeck, his haughty head held high and his hands invariably clasped behind while everyone jumped to do his bidding. He gestured toward the front door and Keary reluctantly walked over and opened it.

"Miss Cavanaugh, it's good to see you again." He stood hesitantly in the doorway waiting for an invitation to enter, which was slow in coming.

Keary held the door and looked him up and down, scorn showing in her blue eyes. "Proprieties say I should answer in kind, Captain, but I'm not that much of a hypocrite. Do you need tinware, or is this a social call?"

"Actually, I've come to apologize and hopefully make amends for the way I treated you. I'm sure now, beyond a doubt, that you were telling the truth and Lady Fenleigh was lying. Looking back, I know it was churlish of me to treat you as I did. Now I want to find a way to make amends."

She dropped her hand from the door and walked back into the shop, still not inviting him in, but he meekly followed. "Your apology is accepted, Captain, but we can't change the past, can we?"

"No, but I was hoping our future relationship could be different."

She turned quickly, her stormy eyes flashing as she tried to keep her voice civil. "How interesting," she said sarcastically, "and what kind of relationship do you have in mind?"

"Well, Miss, my ship will be laid up here for repairs for at least three weeks and I was hoping for permission to call on you."

She chuckled, unable to believe what she was hearing. "I see. First you offer to share your cabin for a single voyage, only to sell me when we reached Philadelphia. Now you offer a three-week romance before you leave to go back to sea. Tell me, Captain, would you be here now if you were only in port for a few days or would you be visiting a bawdy house on Front Street where you wouldn't risk rejection?"

"To tell you the truth, I passed up a very lucrative cargo for Jamaica in order to come here, and I don't even have a guaranteed return cargo. I may have to sail in ballast to the Sugar Islands and wait there for a cargo. And even without taking such a gamble, do you think I would trade the balmy weather of the Sugar Islands this time of year to freeze in this cold country without a very compelling reason?"

"Please, Captain, spare me what little blarney you've managed to pick up in Ireland. It ill befits your English nature."

She had not lost the sharp tongue and Amos Shelby found himself working harder than ever before to impress a woman. "It's the truth, every word of it. And in addition, I postponed much-needed repairs on the ship so I could have them performed here. Being involved in trade, you certainly know wages are much higher here than in England, so the repairs are naturally more expensive."

"Aw tosh, and you'll be havin' me believe it's all this you're after doin' just to be seein' a bound wench?" She used the brogue deliberately as a way of emphasizing he once had the opportunity of treating her like a lady, and hadn't.

"Miss Cavanaugh, I should have known by your speech and manners that you were not what Lady Fenleigh claimed. But to answer your question—yes, I did all of that just to see you and make amends. And I'd sail to China if necessary. I hoped we could have dinner and you would give me an opportunity to prove my sincerity."

"Do I detect a human being under that rough exterior, Captain? If it were only my own case, I might be convinced, but I seem to remember you were about to sacrifice others to achieve your ends on the voyage."

"What a man threatens and what he does are sometimes quite different. It was just my way of making sure you wouldn't make accusations to the British officer. Had he known there were indentures aboard, he would have taken them for the Royal Navy and both the lads and I would have lost."

She wasn't convinced; her eyes locked his in a cold brilliance mirroring her scorn. "A likely story! And I suppose what you did to Barney was for his own good too?"

"That rascal! What I should have done to him was throw him overboard."

"And lose your precious profit?"

"What profit?"

"When you sell a free man as an indenture, that's all profit, isn't it?"

"Free man! What has that rogue been telling you?" He leaned over the counter; the flickering candlelight showed traces of a recent shave glowing faintly blue beneath his smooth cheeks.

"The truth of course; you allowed him to work for his passage and then sold him as an indenture."

"And you believed his tale?"

She didn't flinch from his black eyes blazing with anger. "Of course; why shouldn't I?"

"Because the man is a liar. He was a convicted felon and chose indenture over prison. Since the war broke out, the only place to send him was to the Sugar Islands, and since he had sailed with me once before, I told the authorities I was sailing to the islands as a favor to him. But my charity has come back to haunt me because he has robbed his new master and jumped ship. Now the captain is threatening to sue me for passing off a convicted felon as an indenture." He walked back and forth in front of the counter, his hands grasped behind his back, and Keary was reminded once again of his appearance on the quarterdeck sailing to Philadelphia. "I'll have to pay him, of course, since an investigation would show my original involvement."

Keary considered Barney a good friend; he wasn't uneducated and crude like the other sailors and she resented these accusations. Walking around the counter, she faced him squarely, halting his stride. "A very likely story, Captain, but I don't believe a word of it. Why would Barney lie to me?"

"There's no need to make up your mind right now. Captain Miles's ship is berthed beside mine. Why not talk to him or, better still, you can visit Barney at the city jail. He's there charged with robbery and assault."

Suddenly all argument was gone. Most of the reasons for which she hated him had vanished, and though she still remembered his harsh treatment aboard ship, Keary knew her fate under any other captain believing her to be a whore would have been much worse. "All right, Captain, we'll let bygones be bygones. Would you care to join me in a late supper? I've delayed starting it because my master is sleeping and I don't enjoy eating alone."

"I was hoping we could go out for supper." An unbearable burden had been removed from his conscience and he wanted to celebrate. He would enjoy accompanying her to a nice tavern where her beauty would be appreciated by the other patrons.

"My master is quite ill and I wouldn't want him waking to find me gone. It might worry him needlessly."

He reached for her hand and patted it gently, feeling for the first time the soft white skin he had wanted to touch so many times. His eyes focused on hers, picking up reflections of the candle in their depths. Smiling warmly, he said, "Very well, if you agree to let me reciprocate another night."

"On your ship?" She quickly withdrew her hand and he sensed her distrust.

"No, no"—he looked faintly amused—"in a tavern of your choosing."

"Agreed." She blew out the lamps and, reaching for

the candle, led the way up the dark stairwell.

For the next three weeks, Amos Shelby was an ardent suitor and Keary's social life took on a new phase. He was the perfect gentleman now, holding his advances to a simple kiss of the hand, but he was persistent. Each night when he brought her home the conversation at the door was the same.

"Thank you, Captain, for a lovely evening."

"The pleasure was all mine, Miss Keary. May I call tomorrow evening?"

"I'm afraid not; with Mr. Fowler so ill, I dislike leaving him alone."

"I insist on the following evening then."

She would invariably answer, "Very well, I'll expect you about seven." This evening, however, the parting conversation was slightly different as she offered her hand and said, "Thank you, Amos, this was a beautiful evening and you are a wonderful dancer."

"Until now, I never enjoyed dancing; it was always a chore." His arm slid around her waist and she stiffened as he tried to draw her close and whispered, "But then, I never danced with an angel before." There was an unfamiliar softness in his voice but she still held him at arm's length with both hands pressing against his chest. "Keary, tomorrow will be our last night together and I want it to be something special—something to cherish on my return voyage."

Her curiosity was tinged with suspicion. "That depends on what 'something special' means."

"Well, I thought we would go to supper and afterward we could take advantage of this snow by taking a sleigh ride along the river."

His hands tightened on her waist and tugged as his lips sought hers. Rather than struggle she turned her cheek to accept his kiss, then took advantage of his astonishment by stepping backwards. "Amos, I accepted your apology and offer of friendship, but that is all. If I go on a sleigh ride with you, you must promise there will be no more advances." Searching her eyes he could see her determination, and reluctantly agreed to her terms.

That night as Keary donned her long woolen nightgown and climbed into a bed partially warmed by heated bricks, she began dreaming of tomorrow's sleigh ride. She was snuggled up with her tall companion under a fur robe on a lonely country road. The moonlit night was perfectly still except for the musical jingling of the horse's bell, and the trip was one of unending ecstasy. The situation was altered in one respect, however; the man sharing her robe in the dream was Morgan Baines.

Chapter XIII

Nothing outwardly distinguished this gray December morning from several others just like it. But to Morgan this was a very special day, one he had long planned for. He hadn't closed his eyes all night, going over each detail and wondering if he had considered every possibility. He tried unsuccessfully to sleep, knowing it might not be possible for the next several nights, but every time he managed to push the escape details from his mind thoughts of Keary would creep in and fill the void. He had given up trying to figure how she could fit into his life but, try as he may, he couldn't forget her. Many a long, cold night he had relived those few amorous embraces and every word she had spoken. The warmth of her smile, which completely disarmed him, was with him always.

Morgan crawled into the longboat with the two guards, three other prisoners, and two bodies. On the surface this morning's burial detail was no different from any of the countless others in which this group had participated. The guards were now accustomed to the same prisoners volunteering on a regular basis and this contributed to a relaxed atmosphere, the atmosphere Morgan had so carefully developed over a long period.

By way of further distracting the guards, Morgan immediately launched into a long harangue over the split of the fish. There were now two crews working large nets and the daily catch was enormous compared to the initial efforts with one small makeshift net.

"Damn it, the original agreement was for an equal split and now Sergeant Cranby takes half for himself and after you guards steal most of the other half, we're lucky to get a fifth of the total." He pretended anger and hoped his tirade was convincing. The guards ignored him, continuing to stare out over the water as if there were something of great interest to be seen. "Why should we break our backs hauling nets and cleaning fish every day when our share keeps getting smaller and smaller?"

The tall guard turned and said disdainfully, "You better keep your mouth shut, Baines, or the sergeant may hear about your bellyaching and cut out your share altogether. The trouble with you Yankees is you never know when you're well off. We give you a share out of the goodness of our hearts when we don't have to."

"Heart, hell you Limeys don't have one, and no brains either. How many fish do you think we can haul up without the extra nourishment? That's the trouble with Cranby, he never thinks ahead. If he'd share more equally, everyone would benefit in the long run. I was even working on an idea to rig nets from the longboat and fish farther from the hulk, where we could take advantage of the currents, but what incentive is there for us to work harder if all the extra fish are going to go to you and Cranby anyway?"

"I'd say staying alive and keeping your back lily-white is a pretty good incentive. And unless you want red stripes all over yours, I'd say you better keep your mouth shut." At the mention of fishing from the longboat George and the other accomplice stiffened, drawing quick breaths in wide-eyed unison, but pulled on their oars steadily enough so the guards didn't notice. Only Morgan noticed the excitement lurking behind apathetic expressions and knew his message had been received.

The boat went silent except for the rhythmic dipping of oars and Morgan was satisfied he had set the guards to thinking. He could almost see the visions they were forming of more fish to trade for more rum and thought, *So far so good.*

As the longboat scraped to a sudden stop, Morgan shot the guards a hateful glance and received a few snickers in return. The guards knew he had no bargaining power and could be replaced at any time by another prisoner. They would already be making plans to approach Sergeant Cranby with their new idea of net fishing from the longboat and, at the same time, figuring how much of the prisoner's share they could steal in addition to their own.

Of the four prisoners, all but one knew the escape plan and Morgan wanted that man with himself. He was a slender, athletic-looking lad of about eighteen. He looked as though he could run, and that was all Morgan cared about.

George and his accomplice, accompanied by the shorter guard, dragged one body out and started carrying it inland. Morgan handed two shovels to the other prisoner and turned back to the tall guard in a conspiratorial manner. "Net fishing from a longboat isn't as simple as you may think; you need to know where and when to fish at different times of the day and year. It requires knowledge of the tides and currents. I can show you how to make big catches, but I want some kind of guarantee of a fair share."

"And what's your idea of a fair share?" The guard was ready to humor Morgan for a while, knowing he could double-cross him later with impunity. Once the operation was successful and others had learned how to catch the most fish, he would put this insolent prisoner in the hold for a few weeks.

Morgan began the bargaining with outlandish demands, expecting the guard to counter with something just as unreasonable in the other extreme. The bargaining became as heated as if they were haggling over a real commodity with hard cash. Morgan saw the prisoner who had carried the shovels to George returning and, still talking, climbed into the boat to haul out the other body. He poised with one foot on the seat and the other on the gunwale, a position from which he could see his two accomplices digging the grave as their guard watched, bored with this routine detail. George removed his hat, scratched his forehead, and replaced the hat to signal he was ready. Morgan could only hope he wouldn't lose his nerve at the last minute. Everything was exactly as planned and there was no reason to wait longer. He had had very few opportunities to talk to his accomplices without the guards overhearing and had to be patient until he was sure they thoroughly understood the plan and had ample time to reflect on it. Now the time for planning and reflection was over; the time for action had arrived. Morgan reached down as if to secure a better hold on the body, then sprang.

The force of his hurling body and the suddenness of

his attack sent the guard reeling flat on his back in the sand with the musket landing a few feet away. Morgan landed on all fours but was up immediately, and in two steps had the musket. The stunned guard had no time to regain his senses before the cold steel of his own bayonet plunged into his chest. Looking over to the grave, Morgan saw the other guard lying prostrate while George delivered another heavy blow with the business end of the shovel. The plan had been for him to wait for Morgan's attack, then throw a shovelful of sand into the guard's face, followed immediately with a blow from the shovel. Both of these actions had probably already taken place and what Morgan was now witnessing was one for good measure.

Morgan, turning back to the boat, saw the young prisoner staring as if fascinated at the guard's body oozing blood. "You better start running, lad. Your best chance is to take a different route than anyone else. The agreement was we all take different directions."

"But I haven't done anything wrong. Why should I run?"

"To freedom you jackass. If you stay here you'll either be hanged or rot in that hulk." The lad evidently thought that because he hadn't known of the plot he would not be blamed.

"Then take me with you; I don't want to go alone."

"Look, the more we spread out, the better chance each of us has. See those others have already split up." Morgan gestured to where George and the other prisoner were running in opposite directions, then removed the bayonet and threw down the musket. He pulled the cartouche box loose from the dead soldier and, after checking to be sure it had extra flints, slung it over his shoulder and turned to the longboat. Under the seat lay a long-handled pick, which was seldom needed because of the softness of the sand. Morgan raised it over his head and drove it repeatedly through the bottom of the boat until he was satisfied the damage was beyond repair. Then, jumping clear he drove his shoulder against the bow and pushed with every ounce of strength he had until the clumsy craft grudgingly gave way and slid out into the water. The lad started to pick up the musket when Morgan stopped him. "Don't bother with that; if they corner you, that musket won't do you any good and it's awful heavy to carry all day."

"But we can use it to hunt."

"We'll not be discharging firearms behind enemy lines; that's the surest way I know to tell them where we are." As Morgan headed for the woods the youth remained frozen until Morgan called back disgustedly, "All right, you can follow me for a while."

When they reached the woods, Morgan stopped and looked back at the hulk. He knew the action would have been observed from the deck, but without another longboat, they would be powerless to pursue. Seeing no unusual amount of activity and no other boats near, he grinned—in spite of his fear and excitement over the recent action—when he thought of the expression Cranby would be wearing.

"I'd give my front seat in hell to see Cranby's face right now." He turned to check the lad's reaction and found nothing but fear mirrored there.

Their thin coats gave little protection against the raw December wind and Morgan was already dreading the night, knowing it was necessary to keep moving at least until dawn. Setting a course he believed would take them directly inland, he began a steady, unhurried pace he felt they could continue all night, which would place them as far from the coast as possible. He had no idea how much the British would search for four escaped prisoners in this biting wind and powdery snow, but at this time he was not in a gambling mood. He would stay off the road and avoid all farmhouses. The biggest danger would come from accidentally running into a British patrol.

The sleigh bounced and glided over the rough, newly frozen road behind a high-stepping sorrel. Keary had learned that such horses were imported from Narragansett Bay in New England. She had looked with admiration at these beautiful animals every time one passed the shop. They were wonderful saddle as well as buggy horses, and she secretly dreamed of owning one some day.

They reached a stretch of smooth road; fluffy white snow drifted down, softening the glow of the street lamps. Keary sat contentedly, leaning her back against the cushioned seat, her feet enclosed in a big fur robe. She was ill-prepared for the thunderbolt with which Amos broke the silence.

"Keary, I would like you to accompany me on my return voyage."

She was startled by his suggestion, waiting for the crooked smile that would betray the joke. Seeing he was in earnest she asked, "Can I expect the same comfortable accommodations you provided on the ship or have you assumed that, by now, I will have changed my mind and agree to share your quarters?"

"Of course I assume you will share my quarters but

think of what I'm offering you in return. You have never been anywhere other than Ireland and Philadelphia and I'm offering you a chance to see the whole world. I'll buy you a slave in the Sugar Islands and you will live a life of luxury."

"For how long—until you tire of me? Really Amos, you never seem to learn. I spent an entire voyage in a revolting hellhole rather than share your cabin, and you assume now, because of a few weeks of courting, I've changed my standards completely." Disgusted to the point of irritation, she stared unseeing at the soft snowflakes pirouetting like ballerinas dancing on the breeze.

"But Keary, my love, things are different now. Can't you see how much you mean to me? I want to make you queen of my ship and shower you with gifts. I could procure a cargo slated for India or China and you could enjoy exotic places you never dreamed of. Wouldn't you like that?"

"I would love to see those countries but not as the mistress of you—or any other man." Her words trailed off when one notable exception came to mind.

Exasperated with her stubbornness, a mocking note sounded in his voice. "Then what will it take to get you to say yes—a proposal of marriage?" She was really upset now at his implication she would be reaching above her station to expect a proposal of marriage and whirling around, her temples pounding thickly, her throat tight, she spat, "No! That proposal would be refused exactly as all the others. I have no intentions of sailing with you even if I were free."

"You would be free. I thought you understood that. Even though Mr. Fowler refused to allow me to buy back your indenture, I'm sure he would look on things differently if he thought it was your wish too."

"Mr. Fowler refused to sell my indenture? When did all of this take place?"

"I met him at the tavern before I ever called on you."

So that was why Mr. Fowler had left his sickbed and ventured out on that raw winter day. "Did he give you a reason for refusing?"

He turned to her with a slanted smile, a faint bitterness in his heavily browed eyes. "Many of them. It boiled down to the fact he doesn't believe I'm worthy of you, and lately I tend to agree with him."

"So—first you attempt to buy me as you would a slave and when that failed, you think I'll assist you. Really, Amos, your gall amazes me."

"It was not like that at all! I offered to buy your papers to set you free. Mr. Fowler will attest to that and the offer is still good. I'll give you your freedom in writing before you give me a final answer."

"No need. I would be beholden to you, and it would be dishonest for me to accept your generosity knowing in advance I would reject what you expected in return."

"There would be no need for you to feel beholden to me because all I would be doing is returning the profit I made on you—rather dishonestly, I admit, in the first place. Please believe me, my conscience won't rest until you're free—whether or not you accept my proposals."

His touching words struck a responsive chord and the hard knot inside her began to dissolve. "Thank you, Amos, for the kind thoughts and if I were cursed with a cruel master, I might accept. But Mr. Fowler is like a father to me and even if I were free I would remain to look after him during his illness."

"And be here in case his Virginia friend returns?" An interior dig of jealousy forced the words.

"How did you know about him?"

"Mr. Fowler told me." He was assailed by a terrible sense of bitterness and his next words were meant to be hurtful. "Now tell me, do you really expect him to marry you—a Virginia aristocrat? Compared to some of those southern planters I've met, many British noblemen are quite democratic."

She followed the icy moon rolling between thick, fleecy clouds while she pondered her answer. "Morgan isn't like that but to answer your question, I wouldn't expect him to marry me even if he did return—which is very unlikely."

"I'm afraid I don't understand."

"Neither do I; I've never had feelings like this before. The only way I can explain it is—had he been the captain of your ship and made the same offer you did, I seriously doubt I would have spent the voyage in the hold."

He gave a weary shrug and flicked the reins, heading the carriage back to town. Limbs of snow-laden trees cracked the silence as the sleigh glided smoothly over the icy road. After bidding her good night, Amos made his way to the nearest tavern. Shunning conversation he found a corner table and sought solace in bowl after bowl of flip while Keary, lying awake, stared at the ceiling and prayed, as she did every night, for the safety of a prisoner in a floating cell.

Chapter XIV

Morgan had been wandering, half-frozen, through woods for a week, sleeping on snow-covered ground or sneaking into barns at night. The second day out, his companion had insisted on stopping at a farmhouse to beg food and Morgan, not wanting to risk contact with the Tories, went on without him.

For the last several days Morgan had been exploring the north coast of Long Island, hoping to meet some friendly faces. From prisoners on the hulk he had heard stories of Americans raiding this coast in an attempt to keep supplies from the British. He suspected these raids were motivated more by profit than patriotism, but this mattered little to him so long as they offered a way off the island.

First it was the smell of smoke and then the rosy glow on the dark sky that drew him cautiously closer. Moving slowly, deliberately, he came to a clearing where the leaping flames manifested a sturdy white clapboard house and a half-stone gambrel-roofed barn losing an unequal battle to the raider's torch. A steady file of seamen worked feverishly transporting plunder down the hill to a waiting sloop. By the very nature of their efforts he could tell they were patriots, since the Tories would have no reason to conduct such an operation in British-controlled territory.

"Who's in charge here?" Morgan walked boldly up to a group of three men in seamen's togs. One of them, a broad-shouldered man in an oilskin coat, turned abruptly. His voice was as sharp as the knife he deftly slid from his belt.

"And who wants to know?"

"Morgan Baines of Virginia, and a recent guest on His Majesty's hulk, *Jersey*."

"You escaped from the *Jersey?*" The man's eyes narrowed suspiciously. "Why, that's impossible; no one ever escaped from that floating cesspool."

"That was true until last week, but four of us made it."

"Four? What happened to the other three?"

"We split up on the beach and each went his separate way. I don't know how the others fared."

A seaman approached the group looking nervously down the road from which British troops would come if alerted. "All loaded, Cap'n, and the men are fer gitten' ter hell outen here 'bout as fast as a bare-assed man sittin' on a hot stove."

"All right, Toby, cast off; we're right on your heels." Turning to Morgan he added, "I suppose you want off this island about as much as we do?"

"Yes. Probably a hell of a lot more so."

"Very well, get aboard. In a very short time a group of British Dragoons will come down that road and I 'spect they'll be none too friendly when they get here."

The voyage across Long Island Sound was rough, the

angry sea tossing the small sloop around like a ball and dowsing the crew with cold spray. However, the warmth of an oilskin, a generous tankard of rum, and the exhilarating feeling of freedom made it seem like a pleasure voyage to Morgan. With each swell he savored the taste of freedom and found it as intoxicating as the rum he gulped in prodigious quantities.

Morgan told of his adventures and learned of their operation. They were one of several Connecticut-based small boats, which regularly raided the Tory-infested, British-controlled Long Island coast on what the captain referred to as "educational visits." "We try to teach these Tories along here that selling their produce to the lobsters is not good business."

Shortly after dawn the sloop anchored in a small cove on the Connecticut side and for the first time in several months, Morgan planted his feet on American-held soil. He walked up to a small village, realizing this was only the first step in another long journey back to Philadelphia where he hoped to find a raven-haired Irish lass waiting.

He pushed the mug away and sighed. Sitting in this comfortable tavern and staring into the fire, it suddenly seemed that everything had changed. During captivity it was easy to plan an escape that would take him back to the eternal bliss of a life with Keary, but now it was time to face reality. Most of his money had gone for the *Banetree Princess*'s cargo, which he had planned to sell in London for a handsome profit. Now his entire wealth was less than twenty pounds. How could he marry Keary with no income other than his meager allowance to support her? Lacking professional or commercial experience there was no way, and he refused to subject her to a life of poverty.

No, it had been a beautiful dream during long nights on the dark hulk but now in the cold light of freedom it was time to face reality. He had only one option: go back to Virginia and find a woman with a decent dowry or a widow with a plantation. Since knowing Keary, the thought of marrying another woman was nauseating but what else could he do? Whatever the future held he could not ask Keary to marry a pauper, nor would he entice her into an illicit love affair—a situation in which a woman could derive nothing but pain.

Amos left a lonely void in Keary's life when he departed, with nothing to break the tedium except the time she spent in the shop. Benjamin's condition remained unchanged for the most part. Occasionally he could muster enough strength to come down to the shop for a short time, but most days he was content to stay in his big chair by the fire, or in bed.

She enjoyed breakfast each morning with Jamie and used these meetings to carefully instill new shop procedures in his mind. After an unrelenting barrage of subtle hints, two new apprentices had been hired, each performing a separate task. Since Tom had graduated to the forming and assembly bench, she felt they were well on their way to the assembly line she had envisioned several months ago. She always approached Jamie very cautiously as he could only digest a limited amount of change at one time, the very nature of change going against his grain.

This morning when they finished breakfast she accompanied Jamie to his workbench, and as he slipped the apron over his head and proceeded to tie the strings around his waist she screwed up her nose questioningly.

"Jamie, it boggles my mind how you know what your finished product will look like from all those little scratch marks you put on the metal." She held a small piece of tinplate in her hands while her head wagged from side to side in wonder.

"Well, some of it's mathematics and some of it's triangulation. Now starting with the size of the circle I set my dividers and—"

Waving her hand in an offhanded manner she protested. "Oh, don't try to explain it to me; women couldn't begin to understand anything that complicated." Noticing the expansion of his chest, she confidently continued, "I've been wondering about something though, and I hope you won't think me silly. It's probably a stupid idea."

"Well maybe, but some of your ideas are not that bad. Remember it was your idea to repair that damaged stuff and we sold every bit of it for good hard money."

Holding her breath and sending up a silent prayer asking for the power to present the idea in a way that would not offend him, she melted him with an innocent smile before asking, "Promise you won't laugh if the idea sounds preposterous?" His eyes promised but before his mouth could corroborate, she plunged ahead. "I was wondering why you make a pattern for a flour scoop or teakettle, for instance, and do all that layout work for one item. Wouldn't it save a lot of work if you kept the patterns so that later you could make as many products from the same pattern as you wanted? They would still be James Stuart originals."

While Keary made earnest supplications to the Holy Mother, Jamie leaned back against the workbench, his lame foot crossed over the strong one, his arms folded across his chest, studying the floor. Finally he offered, "It might work for some things, Miss, but people want different sizes and usually different designs."

"Couldn't you make five or six at a time? We could stock them on the shelves until they were all sold and then you could just give the lads the pattern and they could cut and form more."

"I dunno. This is the way we have always done it and I like tried and true methods. None of the other shops do it that way."

"None of the other shops sell James Stuart originals either. We are the only one and that's why we're so successful."

"I don't get the connection, Miss."

Neither did she. But she had started running this race and now must finish. "Ah, Jamie, remember how you first started initialing your work?"

"Sure." He responded with an absent stare, not showing the faintest flicker of interest.

"No other tinsmith had done that before, had they?"

"I guess not, dunno for sure." He was persistent in this foolish vagary and she curbed her irritability, careful not to alienate him.

"Well, that was something new and it's beginning to make you famous."

"So?"

"Don't you see, this system will get ten times as many originals in the hands of people and will make you famous ten times as fast. Why, I can see the time we'll be shipping your work to New York, Boston, and maybe even to Europe."

This caught his attention. "You really think so?"

"Why not? What woman would accept less when she could have a James Stuart original?"

Fearful at the thought of such an undertaking, Jamie faced her, stammering, "What if we can't sell that many?"

She sensed victory and squeezed his arm. "Can't sell James Stuart originals? Why Jamie, anyone who couldn't sell your work couldn't sell rum to a sailor."

For a moment he was lost in thought, then suddenly enthused, "I could make a rack on the wall and hang all the patterns there. Then anytime we need more of a certain item we'll know right where to find it."

"I knew you would figure something out. From now on when I have a problem I'm going to come straight to you; would that be all right?"

"Sure Miss, you just come straight to me. Like I said, tinsmithing takes years to learn, and it don't make sense you struggling with problems when I'm here to help."

As the sound of a customer entering summoned Keary to the front, a voice from out of her past admonished her. It was Father O'Connell saying sternly, "That will be five Our Fathers and five Hail Marys."

Keary was poring over ledgers, at the same time trying to think of something good for dinner, when the bell over the door penetrated the stillness. Looking up, her mind still on the ledgers, a cry of joy bubbled from her lips at the sight of Morgan framed in the doorway. She was unaware of her squeal of delight, as in a maze of swirling skirts she jumped from the stool and ran to him with outstretched arms. But everyone in the shop and half of Philadelphia should have heard it plainly.

Throwing her arms around his neck and holding him close, she murmured, "Morgan, you're alive!" and burrowing her face in his shoulder she whispered in his ear, "You're alive—you're alive." She pulled back to reassure herself it was really him and his mouth bore down crushing her lips in bruising passion. They held each other as if they would never let go, giving voice to the pent-up emotions they had suppressed through the long, lonely months. The late afternoon sun gilded the window panes illuminating flecks of settling dust as the silence in the tinshop, more deafening to the shop's inhabitants than the clamor of their now-silent hammers, carried the gentle words of love to the outsider's ears.

When Keary finally slumped in Morgan's arms, emotionally drained, his voice, still quavering from the tumult of his emotions, penetrated the quiet shop. "Ah, Keary, I had to wait a long time for my chance to escape, but if I had known this sort of welcome awaited me I would have jumped overboard and swum back to Philadelphia."

She pulled back in his arms, studying his rugged features and pleading for reassurance, "You are all right, aren't you? You aren't wounded or anything?"

"No. I'm a little the worse for wear and could stand some clean clothes and—"

Before he could continue she interrupted, "And a bath—you smell terrible."

Laughing, he released her. "You always know the right thing to say."

"It's a habit I seem to be developing in this land of free speech—a luxury we couldn't afford in Ireland. Come now, and I'll have one of the lads bring water for a bath."

As they ascended the narrow stairs, their arms

entwined, her head possessively leaning against his shoulder, the din in the shop resumed. At first just a single hammer touched the metal softly as if unsure the general mood would yet tolerate an interruption. Soon others joined the rhythm and, although they didn't exchange sly glances, a man and woman demonstrating affection in such an ardent manner was something none of them had been witness to before. Some of the older men would relive the scene as the adolescent aching in their own groins awakened, but even eleven-year-old Andrew, the youngest apprentice, would no longer view the beautiful lady as a cold authority symbol.

An hour later Morgan emerged from the spare bedroom clad in Benjamin's robe, which hit him just below the knees, the sleeves extending barely past his elbows. Keary had washed his clothes, hanging them by the fire to dry, and was busy turning them when Morgan entered the large common room.

"I'm sorry it's so hot in here but Uncle Benjamin is always so cold, I have to keep the fires high and I wanted to dry your clothes. I went to tell him you were here but he's sound asleep. He's so dissipated I don't dare open the window for fear the breeze may blow him out. He never eats anymore and hasn't been out of bed in a week."

Keary lifted the lid from a pot, releasing delicious aromas into the room. Morgan joined her at the fire and, dropping into the rocking chair and stretching his long legs toward the blaze, pulled her down to his lap, pressing his lips against the damp tendrils framing her face. He leaned back contentedly sniffing the fragrance of home-cooked stew. "After the winter I've just been through I'll never be too warm again—or have too much to eat."

"Where did you spend the winter, and how did you

get back?"

While the stew simmered and the clothes dried he told her of his bizarre capture, the thrilling escape, and the long trip back to Philadelphia. At times he would rise and, leaning over her shoulder, enfold her in his arms. When she raised her face to his, his mouth would close on hers hungrily, his tongue searching hers in minute detail sending shivers of desire racing through her eager body. His account was long in unfolding as each embrace threatened to outlast eternity. As the story drew to a close, only the smell of scorched stew prevented him from lifting her in his arms and making a rapid retreat to the bedchamber.

The appetite he thought would be with him the rest of his life after the short rations of the hulks had vanished and was replaced by a different hunger. They both nibbled at the stew, unmindful of its charred taste. Had it been cooked to perfection by the best chef in the world neither of them would have noticed or cared. Time passed in a wave of bliss. To Morgan, all his sexual conquests combined couldn't equal the desire he felt for Keary in the innermost depths of his soul. He thought of asking her to marry him. He would borrow a few hundred pounds from his brother, Simon, and they could move to the frontier to start their new life. It never occurred to him that he might find better opportunities in the city despite his recent plans to seek his fortune in London drawing rooms. His all-consuming love for Keary went hand in hand with his love for the land—two passions, born of the same emotion, neither of which he understood.

Reluctantly, Keary rose to clear the table, and as their eyes met she came to him. Her fingers moved over his face with the tenderness of a blind person trying to recognize a long, lost loved one. "Oh, Morgan, I've never been so happy. Hold me."

He pulled her gently to his lap and she snuggled her face against his throat, breathing a kiss and nibbling his earlobe. Parting her lips, she raised her mouth to his. His slow, drugging kisses set her aflame and she returned them with reckless abandon. She wound her arms inside his robe and around his back and her passion was further fueled by the touch of his warm flesh. His heartbeat throbbed against her ear while he possessed her body in a series of tantalizing caresses. Eventually the lamp wick sputtered and slowly died, leaving the room shadowed in the dying embers of the fireplace. In the deep recesses of his mind an alien voice, born of conscience and reared by practicality, told him this intimacy, if continued, could lead only to the bedchamber.

Morgan forced his hands to release her and his voice, thick and unsteady, contradicted his eyes. "I'm sorry, my sweet, I seem to have deterred you from your domestic chores."

Reluctantly, with a puzzled frown creasing her forehead, Keary rose to complete her tasks and Morgan coaxed the dying fire back to life. Leaning against the warm stone wall that sheltered the leaping flames, he watched Keary. The renewed firelight glowed on the wealth of dark hair as she moved her head and happily tapped a tiny foot while humming a rollicking Irish ballad over the steaming dishpan. The scene before him and the dark-paneled, comfortable old room represented a haven from all his problems.

Yes, this was the life for him. What would a hard day's work in the fields matter if he could return to a warm cabin and this soul-satisfying beauty every night? He began to envision their life together, rising before dawn to leave for the fields while Keary fed the stock, carried water, milked the cows, cared for the children, handled all the usual household chores, and finally joined him to tend the row upon row of newly turned soil. Suddenly the romantic flames were quenched by the water of practicality. His dreams of tranquility took on the stark nature of cold reality. What would the hard farm life do to her beauty? How long would her eyes sparkle through days of backbreaking chores and sleepless nights of nursing a sick child? The raven hair would soon be gray-streaked, framing a face of premature wrinkles. A small farmer seldom found leisure in his own lifetime; he built for his children and his children's children but he inevitably wore out at least one woman in the process.

No—he couldn't marry her without the means to support her in style. It was a beautiful dream but not feasible and he must tell her now. The longer he waited, the more difficult it would be. Resting his hands on the mantel, he looked long into the flames before saying, "In a few days, I must return to Virginia."

Keary's head shot around, disappointment evidenced by her open mouth and slack chin. "Why ever would you want to go back to Virginia?" Then teasingly she asked, "Do you have another young lady back there?"

"Well—no. That is, not a particular lady. However, my modest fortune is gone and if I'm to marry a rich lady, preferably a widow with a large plantation, I must first approach my brother for a loan to replenish my wardrobe."

She searched his eyes for the twinkle telling her he was joking, but the usual carefree eyes were grim, unwavering, passing a shock through her body that was reflected in her pained expression. "You've just professed your love for me; do you still plan to marry for wealth? I thought your values had changed."

Angry with himself for all his recent wrong decisions and the hurt he had dealt her, he paced the floor. Avoiding her accusing stare, he said defensively, "Don't look so horrified. I'm twenty-six years old and have no assets, no profession—no prospects of any kind, really. How can I accumulate wealth or even make a comfortable living? Had I been educated differently my prospects wouldn't be so dim. I have no desire to live the life of a pauper, so I must pursue wealth in the only way I know how."

She studied her folded hands and without looking up, said, "I'd rather be a pauper than spend the rest of my days with someone I didn't love."

"Perhaps I would feel the same if I hadn't been born to wealth, but I can think of nothing worse than having a rich man's taste and a poor man's purse." He plumped on the chair studying the fire, wishing he could be completely honest with her. He knew she would agree to marry him even though he was penniless, but his aristocratic heritage would not allow this. To marry one of his own kind for avaricious reasons was simply playing the game, but a gentleman did not marry for love below his station unless it was to elevate his intended to a better life.

Keary silently mulled over this new situation. The sight of Morgan today left no doubt in her mind she loved him, and if her competition were another woman, she would be more than ready to do battle. But how does one compete with money? Looking across the room at his hunched form before the fire, she asked, "Before you left, after the first amorous embrace, you avoided another romantic encounter. Why was that?"

"At the time, my plans were to go to England and find a rich wife. I knew if there was one person in this whole world who had the power to disrupt those plans it was you." Gathering his dry clothes in his arms, he continued, "I must have wealth and you deserve a man with a future in his own right—a professional man or a good, solid merchant."

A small flicker of hope took form as she pondered this. If he had passed up the opportunity for a romantic interlude because of his concern for her, he must have loved her even then. Or, if not love, it was a very close relative.

As Morgan headed down the hall to the bedroom, he called over his shoulder, "Do you think Benjamin is awake? I would like to pay my respects before leaving."

"If he's not, I better wake him and try to get some nourishment into him." The words were hollow, mechanical, for her thoughts were still on the heart-wrenching developments of the last few minutes. Knowing he had not taken advantage of her vulnerability but instead had openly admitted his concern for her virtue helped some, but couldn't erase the desolation she felt. She moved down the hall, despair enveloping her, wanting to scream out that he had no right making her love him, while at the same time she told herself this was to be expected. He was a gentleman and she, as a bound girl, should not aspire to his social station. She was grateful he had enough respect for her not to make a proposition such as Amos had. *But,* she thought, tears welling in her eyes, *respect isn't all I want from him.*

When Benjamin didn't answer the knock her trembling hands fumbled with the doorknob to no avail. Morgan's closeness to her physically only emphasized the enormous gulf between them in actuality and added to her inability to function. Finally seizing the knob with both hands, she uttered a Gaelic curse and kicked the door full force. It swung open and she swayed, almost losing her balance but quickly regaining her footing. Walking quietly toward the bed she called softly, "Uncle Benjamin, see who has come to visit."

Benjamin's head, the few remaining white hairs standing on end, lay in an unnatural position, his nightcap at his side, lifeless eyes staring off into space. She turned to Morgan for assurance as a premonition of disaster crawled through her brain, but his quizzical stare told her nothing. She lifted the cold hand and urgently called, "Wake up, Uncle Benjamin, wake up."

By the time Morgan realized the situation and reached her side she was shaking the lifeless body and screaming hysterically, "Oh my God, he's dead, he's dead." Grief gripped her heart like a cold hand and she threw herself over the still form, weeping with desolation and sorrow. Morgan stood by overwhelmed with sadness, permitting her anguish to pour forth in an agonizing flood. When she finally raised her tear-sodden face, biting her lips to control the sobs, he gently lifted her and carried her back to the common room.

He placed her on the old settee and brushing his lips lightly to her brow said, "You try to relax a few minutes while I run to the Hogshead Tavern on Second Street. I will inquire as to who prepares the dead for burial in this neighborhood."

When Morgan returned with an old woman, evidence

of her displeasure at being aroused from a sound sleep written plainly on her face, Keary still lay where he had placed her, tearfully fondling an old pipe Benjamin had always kept close by. He directed the old woman to Benjamin's room and returned to Keary. He enfolded her in his arms and carried her down the hall, past the room that held the remains of one who had not only become her dearest friend but a father too. Morgan lowered her to the bed and, after kissing her forehead, lifted her face to his. "I'll leave now but promise you'll try to get some rest." She said nothing but her eyes pleaded with him to stay. He lowered himself to the side of the bed and removed his boots. Then, stretching his long form beside hers he cradled her head in his arms until the sobs became less frequent and were finally replaced by slow, steady breathing. When the first bleak rays of another winter day cast dim shadows over the city, Keary opened her eyes. She tried to disengage herself from Morgan's arm without waking him. His voice told her she hadn't succeeded. "There's no need to rise yet, Keary. You'll need your rest." He fondled the curl tickling his neck.

Thrusting her body away from the warmth of him she said, "Yes, I must; there's much to be done."

Morgan propped himself on his elbow blinking at the calm, cool composure of one who had recently been through so much. "What can I do to help?"

"Right now you can leave so I can get dressed."

The next few days Morgan was constantly at her side helping with the funeral arrangements and seeing to the comfort of an endless stream of callers. The day they returned to the flat after the funeral, she felt empty and afraid. This was even a more painful experience than her father's death. Only fourteen when her father died, she had been taken to Fenleigh Manor as a governess, where her mistress made all the decisions. Though she had loved her father very much his death didn't leave the void Benjamin's did, probably because Benjamin had needed almost constant care. He also came to her at a time in her life when she was better able to appreciate a close, loving relationship. After suffering Bruce's counterfeit affection, Lady Fenleigh's treachery, Amos Shelby's cruelty, and a narrow escape from Mr. Wentworth's slavery, Uncle Benjamin had become a father and savior combined. It seemed impossible she had only known him eight months; he was so dear to her and had become such an important part of her life.

Apprehension gripped her as she pushed the sorrow of Benjamin's passing out of her mind long enough to contemplate the immediate future. "Morgan what will happen to me? I still have more than six years to serve on my indenture. Will I be sold as part of the estate?"

He reached for her hand and she sank to her knees in front of him. "You won't be sold as part of the estate or any other way. I'm sure I can raise enough money to buy your freedom." There was no legal record of the fact Benjamin never really owned her papers but it was too late to worry about that. "We'll find a good home for you until a proper marriage can be arranged."

She drew back like a cat ready to spring, her blue-violet eyes raking him furiously. "Don't talk about an arranged marriage for me. For a man to marry wealth or position is one thing; men are free to shape their own life outside the home. But with a woman it is an entirely different matter. Everything belongs to the husband and he has the power to make her a virtual slave. For me to be fulfilled, I must have a man's love and there can be no substitutes."

The knock on the door startled them since her vehement outburst had drowned out the footsteps on the stairs. Opening the door, Keary appraised the tall, distinguished looking gentleman with a tricorn under one arm and a briefcase in the other hand.

"Miss Cavanaugh? I'm Charles Willoughby, Mr. Fowler's lawyer. May I come in?"

Stepping aside she said, "Of course," and pointed her arm in the direction of Morgan, who had risen. "Mr. Willoughby, this is Mr. Baines, an old friend of Mr. Fowler." She bade him to sit and brought a bottle of wine from the tall sideboard, pouring three small glasses before seating herself across from the immaculately dressed solicitor. He sipped his wine almost ceremoniously, all the while admiring the raven-haired maid across from him who was beautiful even in the black bombazine. After another appreciative sip he settled back, unwound a sheaf of papers from the briefcase and, clearing his throat professionally, began.

"Miss Cavanaugh, two months ago Mr. Fowler amended his will leaving his entire estate to you."

The shuffling of his papers didn't muffle Keary's astounded gasp as she sat wide-eyed and open-mouthed. When her voice returned, she blurted, "How could that be? He hasn't been out of the house in months." Her mind whirled, unable to believe such good fortune. "Besides, I'm a bound girl."

"True, he wasn't out. He sent for me one day when you were out and you haven't been bound since that day. He freed you."

Tears smarted her eyes and she leaned forward, searching his face. "Does that mean I own the shop?"

"You own considerably more than that, Miss. I have everything here and will go over it in detail, but basically you own this building, the one next door that the blacksmith rents, and the two small lots back on the alley. But before you get too excited, let me warn you the debts are considerable also."

Morgan drew his chair closer and for the next two hours the three of them waded through the stack of papers, Morgan and the lawyer poring over each one while Keary made careful notes on a sheet of paper. When they finished, she quickly added two columns of figures and said, "As near as I can evaluate this, the estate is worth almost two thousand pounds and the debts are about nine hundred."

Glancing admiringly at her, his gray eyes twinkling, Mr. Willoughby said, "That was quick, Miss, especially when some of the items were listed in pounds and some in dollars."

She rose to pour more wine. "Oh, when I think of money I just automatically convert everything to pounds. To me that's real money."

"Well, assuming your figures are accurate, there's still a problem. Most of the debt is payable immediately and Mr. Wentworth wants his money now. He has already contacted me."

Keary stopped pouring and whirled, looking in Morgan's direction. "Wentworth? Does he have a son named Jason?"

Mr. Willoughby shook his head affirmatively. "Yes. Do you know him?"

"Mr. Baines and I both know him all too well, I'm

afraid. If he has demanded immediate payment, how much time will I have?"

"I could get you a month maybe, six weeks at the most."

She paced the room, her mind racing. Suddenly a smile chased concern and she faced the lawyer. "I'll be able to handle the debt then."

"That's what Benjamin thought you would say." He chuckled and began picking up his papers preparing to leave. "Will you need my assistance dealing with Mr. Wentworth or the other creditors? Perhaps I could arrange more liberal terms. Mr. Wentworth will probably be extremely difficult to deal with, but I'm willing to try."

"Thank you, Sir, but I don't expect him to be all that difficult to deal with. Besides, my methods may put a strain on your legal ethics." Her confident smile brought a puzzled frown to the lawyer's face as he mumbled his "good days."

When the lawyer's footsteps died away and the little bell above the shop door announced his exit Morgan stirred and, stretching his six-foot frame to its full height, said, "Well, it's been a long day and I have other business to attend to so I, too, will bid you good day, but I'll stop by to see you again before I leave." He reached out and tenderly brushed a curl from her cheek.

Keary's heart quickened at the realization they were alone and now they had the means to get married. Morgan could learn to run the shop and she could help him. She knew it could become a very prosperous business in time and she could explain some of her ideas for expansion and branching into other fields. Her heart raced at the prospect and she smiled her first genuine smile in three days as she reached her arms out to him, anxious to share her ideas. But he turned quickly, grabbed his tricorn from the table, and started for the door. Hiding her disappointment at his obvious haste to leave, she asked flippantly, "When will you be leaving for Virginia?"

"In about a week. I had planned on leaving earlier but I wanted to be sure you were all right. Now that you are free and a woman of means, I am sure you'll do fine." He bowed slightly, opened the door, and hurried down the steps.

Suddenly the black bombazine was heavy on her frame, smothering her in the high-buttoned bodice and voluminous skirts. She ran to her room clawing at the buttons, completely overcome with the pent-up grief of the last few days. Despite having attained her freedom and inheriting property as well, she hadn't felt so forlorn since the day Lady Fenleigh had abandoned her to Amos Shelby. Dropping the heavy black dress to the floor, she threw herself across the bed and cried uncontrollably. Later, when all that was left of her sorrow was dry, burning eyes and spasmodic hiccoughs, she vowed she would not be dependent on anyone again. She was free, independent and, for the first time in her life, owned something of value. There was a thriving, pulsating commercial world out there beckoning and she welcomed its challenge. True, it was a man's world but a few other women had penetrated it and Keary felt there was room for one more.

She would smother her love for Morgan and, in time, maybe she could forget the crooked smile and sparkling topaz eyes. Strangely, she did not feel bitterness toward him. He had been honest, never speaking of marriage, and as a tradeswoman it was still a large jump to his social stratum.

Perhaps she would marry someone like Amos after all. He professed to love her dearly and though he was not as handsome as Morgan, he still cut a striking figure in a manly way that had no doubt accelerated the heartbeat of many a maid. And, if not Amos, perhaps a fat old merchant with lots of money and one foot in the grave. She would soon be a woman of property, once she attended to old Wentworth, and she could marry whomever she chose—well, not quite. Pondering this, she said to herself, *Perhaps I'll put off thinking of marriage as long as Morgan remains unwed.*

The day following the funeral was Saturday and Keary decided to keep the shop closed. It had been closed for three days following Benjamin's death and since they always closed on Sundays, she told Jamie and the lads to stay home another day. They would reopen on Monday.

It was a beautiful day and she had dressed hurriedly, wanting to enjoy the sunshine and fresh river breeze. She decided to forego breakfast at home and have coffee and hot pastries at the coffee shop. By now coffee had replaced tea as her favorite beverage to such an extent that she never gave it a thought. After breakfast she would wander down to the riverfront and watch the ships, riverboats, and dock life for which she had such a fascination.

At the foot of the stairs she couldn't resist a quick glance into the shop, still trying to adjust her consciousness to the fact this was all hers. The determined knock on the door startled her and turning, she stooped to see the squat form of Silas Wentworth through the small pane. She opened the door a crack to tell him the shop was closed for the day, but he rudely brushed her aside and entered. His failure to remove his hat demonstrated disdain for one below his station as he fastened narrow eyes on her and announced, "Miss Cavanaugh, I'm Silas Wentworth, and I'm here to discuss the disposition of certain debts."

"Yes, I know who you are, Mr. Wentworth; I'll not soon forget our first meeting. It seems I owe you some seven hundred pounds."

Holding a dainty handkerchief to his long nose, he said mockingly, "Nine hundred would be more accurate since I've purchased the other debts of Mr. Fowler. I thought since foreclosure was imminent, it would be much simpler that way." She faced him squarely, her face impassive. "In the event you don't understand what I'm saying, Miss, perhaps I can put it a little plainer. You owe me nine hundred pounds and I'm calling the notes now." His satisfied leer demanded she recoil in horror, setting up the proposition he intended forcing on her.

"Mr. Wentworth, the shop is prospering and can meet the obligation on a systematic basis. Since you are collecting a good rate of interest, why do you want to call the notes?" Her steady composure threw him off balance for a moment.

"That's neither here nor there. I'm calling the notes and that's all there is to it." He paused, expecting her to beg for time, but after an uncomfortable silence was forced to continue. "There is, however, one option I can offer since it is evident you don't have the money."

"And that is?"

"For some reason I fail to understand my son, Jason,

is taken with you. I believe he has made a proposal of marriage?"

Keary began to see where the conversation was heading and her eyes narrowed while an angry flush crept over her features. "Oh, is that what he was offering? I thought, like his father, he was trying to buy a slave."

"Come, come, Miss. You must understand the need for conditions considering the difference in station. Why he wants to marry so far below his station, I'll never know; but I've decided to indulge him."

"Did it ever occur to you that having refused him once I would probably do it again?"

"Please be realistic. You stand to lose your property and have no choice in the matter. But I'm offering you the opportunity of a lifetime; you can have your cake and eat it too, so to speak. You can not only marry into one of the first families of Philadelphia, but as a wedding present I would forgive the debt. Now what could be more generous than that?"

Keary threw her head back and laughed at this charlatan practicing his chicanery on a verdant, penniless maid. "Your generosity overwhelms me, Sir. Your son would acquire a slave and an estate valued at over two thousand pounds and you would magnanimously forgive a nine-hundred-pound debt. It seems to me that would constitute a very handsome dowry from a bound girl. But make no mistake, Sir, I will not marry your son, regardless of the financial arrangements." Scorn fairly dripped from her words and unused to being chastised by a mere maid, he raised one fist above his head and bellowed.

"But the property is already mine for the taking. Of course a woman can't be expected to understand these little subtleties in business."

Opening the door she gestured him out, saying, "I'll settle up with you in less than a week."

Used to bluffs in the business world, he cackled and his avaricious eyes sought hers. "Since you have no real choice, why not settle the matter here and now?"

Keary lifted her hand indicating the door and dropped a modified curtsy. "Good day, Sir."

As a confused Mr. Wentworth left the shop, Keary bolted the door, thinking, *I'll handle you shortly, you old miser, and now if I only knew how to handle a certain Virginia gentleman, I'd be happy.*

Chapter XV

Monday morning over breakfast Keary faced the issue of telling Jamie she had inherited the shop. As long as Benjamin was alive there had been no problem because, theoretically at least, Jamie was working for him. But she wasn't sure how he would take working for a woman. Deciding the best way was to tackle the situation head-on, she ventured, "Jamie, Mr. Fowler left me the shop and I don't know what I'm going to do. After all, I don't know anything about tinsmithing."

Surprised, he raised his eyes from his bowl of gruel. "But I know tinsmithing and I've told you before if you have any problems just come to me."

She reached across the table and squeezed the rough fingers. The tears of gratitude shining in her eyes caused him to gulp coffee that was much hotter than he realized and he lowered his head to keep her from seeing his own watery eyes as she continued. "Oh, if you will agree to run the whole thing I won't have to be frightened; I could stay up front and sell. Of course, as foreman you would get a raise in pay."

She breathed a sigh of relief when Jamie returned to the shop, thankful that concern was out of the way. That left only one more thing to do before confronting Mr. Wentworth.

Keary disliked leaving the shop during the day since Jamie lacked much as a salesman and didn't like to be disturbed to talk to customers, but if she were successful today that would cease to be a problem. She hurried along at a good clip, enjoying the fresh smell of spring air. Turning left from Second Street on to Walnut, she deftly dodged an oncoming freight wagon and crossed the street diagonally to the bakery. A delicious aroma assailed her nostrils as she opened the door and gazed lovingly at the displays of pastries stacked on tiered shelves. Mr. Penrose, wiping his hands on his apron, greeted her.

"Good day, Miss Cavanaugh. I was sorry to hear of Benjamin's passing." The fair-skinned man with his white hair and perpetual covering of flour reminded her of a ghost.

"Thank you, Mr. Penrose. He had been ill for some time and I'll miss him sorely. He was a lovely man. I came here today to discuss some business if you can spare a few minutes."

"Wait here and I'll be right with you." He opened the oven door and began sliding the wooden peel in and out, each stroke producing three loaves of bread and adding to the mouth-watering aroma already filling the old brick building. He grabbed a horn from the wall and, stepping out on the street, blew three quick blasts to inform the neighborhood his fresh hot bread was ready. Returning to the shop he guided her gently by the elbow to a small office in the rear of the bakery.

"Sorry to keep you waiting; now, you mentioned business?"

"Yes, I would like to buy Molly."

"You what!"

"I would like to buy Molly's indenture. I have employment for her and am willing to offer you a profit. I'll give you ten pounds hard money. You will realize a profit and have had eight months of her service free."

"I don't deny I could use some hard money, but Molly's such a help to me I sometimes wonder how I ever managed without her."

Keary studied the baker, wondering if this was a ruse to up the price. When he didn't elaborate further she said, "I'll give you twelve and that's as high as I can go."

He pondered for a while, then shook his head negatively. Keary instantly regretted saying this was her final offer, since a couple of pounds more might have swung it and she was prepared to go much higher for Molly. Not only would Molly be a tremendous asset to the business but a welcome companion as well. Feeling stupid for such a hasty blunder, she turned to the door and was stopped halfway by his call.

"There is some other business I would like to do with you though, Miss. I like that new sign you just put up. How much would you charge to cut out a piece of tin in the shape of a baker holding up a loaf of bread?"

"For Molly's papers I'll give you twelve pounds and throw in the sign." As he seemed to be considering the offer she quickly added, "and the painting."

"Fifteen." He said this tentatively, looking for a thirteen or a fourteen counter. Keary figured this but was not about to leave him an out at this time.

"Done." She held out her hand to shake with the surprised but happy baker.

Later as the two girls left the bakery, Keary explained Molly's duties. "You'll be doing what you like best, painting tinware. When I have to leave the shop you'll work behind the counter selling. You'll have your own room and we'll see what we can do about getting you a few decent dresses." She glanced out of the corner of her eye at her buxom companion and with an accusing grin, said, "Of course you won't have all that delicious pastry to eat anymore."

Molly laughed as she hurried along beside her new mistress. "Ye know, 'tis funny ye be sayin' sech a thing. The farst week I was after eatin' evr'thing in the place. Now it's starvin' I'd have t'be afore I'd sink me teeth into pastry." As they neared the shop Molly squeezed Keary's arm and again, for the fourth or fifth time, said, "Oh Keary, 'tis so happy I be, it's hard ter be thankin' ye enough."

"There's nothing to be thanking me for; I just recognize talent when I see it. Everyone likes your painting and I want to get all the business I can. Of course having my old friend to share the evenings with is very nice too. That flat is awfully lonely without Uncle Benjamin, especially with Morgan leaving in a few days."

"Morgan! And pray tell who might he be?"

"Remember the tall, handsome gentleman who came to my rescue the day we were sold?"

"The one who be liftin' the farst mate by the shirt and lookin' like he be about to hurl 'im clear across the river? The saints be praised, Keary, I swear I niver seen such a handsome man in me whole life. Is he a friend of yours, now?"

"More than a friend I thought, but I thought wrong."

"Ye mean ye be settin' yer cap fer 'im? Oh Keary, it scares me, ye aimin' so high." She clucked like an old mother hen, shaking her blond head in a negative manner.

Keary smiled ruefully at her concern and, squeezing her friend's arm, sighed as she said sadly, "No need to worry, Molly. His plans don't include me."

Molly was settled in her new room, and after a little training from Keary she could sell like a seasoned merchant. Helping Mr. Penrose in the bakery had given her some experience handling money and dealing with people, but it was her plain, outgoing nature that helped the most.

It was Thursday afternoon before Keary felt she could leave Molly alone—and then only after she got Jamie's promise to keep an eye on things. As it turned out, this took little persuasion on her part. From the time Molly first walked into the shop Jamie seemed to be underfoot a lot. He recognized the name from Keary's discussion of her painting and accepted her immediately as a fellow artist, but Keary was sure he admired more than her work.

Keary was forced to sit on an old wooden bench in the outer office for what seemed an eternity in these distasteful surroundings. The wizened old clerk practically drowned out the sound of his scratching quill with clucking noises, using his tongue to adjust poor-fitting wooden teeth to sore gums. Everything about the place reeked of stale gloom. The office was on the second floor of a large warehouse, and even the beautiful view of the waterfront was forbidden to enter by a heavy coat of grime on the one small window. Evidently beauty was unimportant in this sullen atmosphere, which had probably not seen a smile in years.

"Ah, Miss Cavanaugh, I'm happy to see you. I gather this visit means you have come to your senses." Silas Wentworth fumbled among the papers scattered around his desk, but his gesture was largely to convince his visitor her business was not all that important to him. He knew exactly which paper was which and had been looking at them all the time he had made her wait in the outer office. Silas liked the feeling of power he got from making other people wait, and he had learned humbled people did not drive hard bargains.

"Since we are going to be family, I suppose I should call you Keary."

The revulsion from such a suggestion could not have been extracted from her voice with a pair of pliers. "You may call me Miss Cavanaugh, as all other tradesmen do. And before you make any more foolish assumptions, let me advise you. I have no intentions of becoming part of your family—not if debtor's prison were the only alternative. Nor have I come here for sympathy or charity. I have come to pay my debt."

Shocked, he scrutinized her through narrowing eyes, wondering how she could have acquired that much money. He sat uncomfortably on the edge of his chair, his retort being half demand and half question. "Pay? Where did you get that much money?"

"That, Sir, is none of your affair." She opened her drawstring bag and brought out a stack of Continental paper money. As she started to count the notes he sprang from his chair and leaned across the desk, sneering.

"What kind of a fool do you take me for? That Continental paper is practically worthless and I won't accept it."

All innocence, she stopped counting and the dark-blue eyes never wavered as she appraised her antagonist, her voice dripping scorn. "You have no choice. According to the laws of Pennsylvania, Continental currency is legal tender in the payment of debts."

"But for your information there is a gentleman's agreement in this town that long-standing debts can only be discharged with hard money or an acceptable equivalent. That paper is only good for day-to-day transactions and both parties have to agree on the amount. Anyone with an ounce of business sense would see the necessity, since paper money fluctuates so much and lately has fluctuated in only one direction—down."

"That's interesting, gentlemen forming agreements to flaunt the laws of their own government. But, at any rate, I fail to see how such a gentleman's agreement could affect me. Have you not noticed, Sir, I wear skirts?"

Scoffing at her feminine ineptitude, he waved her off. "Regardless, I refuse to accept anything but hard money."

"Then we shall have to put the matter before the courts. Or better still, before the Committee of Safety." As the color drained from his cheeks she struggled to keep her inner excitement hidden behind a complacent mask. "According to my Uncle Benjamin you had to make a public apology for your earlier criticism of The Declaration of Independence and there are a few members of the Committee who would dearly love to find a good excuse to escort you out of town in a suit of tar and feathers."

Silas slumped in the chair, chin on his chest and shoulders limp. *If she only knew*, he thought, *there are at least six on that hateful Committee who would give the shirts off their back to convict me of a crime—any crime. Why they would jump at any opportunity.* Beads of perspiration formed on his forehead and he offered feebly, "Perhaps we can work out more liberal terms?"

"And perhaps it would be better if you took the money and gave me a receipt marked 'paid in full.'"

"But, Miss, you could buy that whole stack of paper for twenty pounds gold."

"Seventeen pounds ten to be exact, Sir."

Dropping back in his chair, Silas racked his brain for an answer to this dilemma but could find none. Though there was not another person in Philadelphia accepting paper money, this little Irish baggage was forcing him— one of the most astute merchants on the whole continent—to take it. It was bad enough she was stealing all that property right out from under his nose, but only last week he had paid hard money to buy the rest of Benjamin's debts. Oh, the contemptible wench, she had haunted his dreams for months after he had so narrowly missed buying her indenture that day. Now she had not only denied him those lovely visions of her naked body, but had cheated him out of nine hundred pounds as well.

"The documents, please."

Silas glowered at her outstretched hand. He started scribbling on the notes, broke his quill, and in his fury opened and slammed drawers in search of another. When finished he hurled them across the desk and sat back hard. Without redirecting her stare, Keary said simply,

"You didn't sign them."

After Silas repeated the routine with the same anger, Keary carefully sanded the notes, folded them, and placed them in her bag. Turning to leave she heard him sputtering, "I'll not forget this, wench."

"I certainly hope not, you old bastard, it should contribute greatly to your education. The trouble with men is they just don't understand those little subtleties in business."

Once outside in the fresh air she heaved a sigh of relief and, as Father O'Connell's cherubic face tried to enter the backdoor of her mind, she mentally pointed a finger at him. *It's yerself what said it, Fath'r, killin' a snake's no sin.*

Chapter XVI

Holding the teakettle up to the light and turning it in her hands, Keary was disappointed to see it lacked the usual lustre of Molly's work. She walked over to the bench where Molly sat splashing lovely, bright designs on a metal tray. "Molly, I love the design on this teakettle but it doesn't have the hard finish your other work had."

"'Tis because they sh'd be baked in the oven. When I be workin' fer Mr. Penrose, the good man was after lettin' me bake me work in his oven, 'til we be findin' it ruined the taste of the pastries." Molly slowed down her speech, trying to eliminate the brogue. "After that I had to tell the ladies to bake them in their own ovens. I've been telling them the same here."

"No, I'd rather have them see and feel the finish before they buy. I'm sure Jamie could make you an oven." That was all the excuse Molly needed to hurry to Jamie's bench, and as she stood making her request known to the tousle-haired, abashed Jamie, Keary pretended interest in some of Molly's other creations. She was aware of the growing attraction between these two and, studying a unique design Molly had painted on a coffin tray, congratulated herself again on the foresight of buying her friend's indenture.

The bell above the door called her back to the front to find Morgan standing there. His hair in disarray gave evidence to the beautiful spring day, and the twinkle in his eye gave evidence of his desire to live it to the fullest.

"I was wondering if you could tear yourself away from the world of commerce for an afternoon of sailing on the river?" Despite his apparent nonchalance, there was a slight hesitancy indicating anxiety over how well she would receive him.

Convention told her that since he had made one romantic overture and later told her he intended marrying for wealth, she should refuse. But then, Keary was not one to allow proprieties to stand in the way of romance. *Besides,* she thought, *a refusal now would only confirm how much he has hurt me.* And if he wanted to play the carefree game, she knew the rules. "I would be delighted, Sir, provided you don't sail too close to the British blockade. I understand the last time you did that, you lived to regret it."

"On the contrary; I got several months room and board at His Majesty's expense."

Laughing, she called over her shoulder on the way to the stairs, "Give me a few minutes to change; not even an Irish wench goes sailing in a mobcap and work apron."

She reappeared in a few minutes in the same outfit she wore the day of the auction, even to the scarf holding back the curls. As she flung the shawl carelessly over her shoulders, he marveled that this carefree, secure businesswoman was the same frightened, woebegone child he had befriended such a short time ago. They walked to the river wharf, reveling in being young, being free, and being together. She resolved to enjoy the day and not dwell on his departure or the void she knew it would leave in her heart. The wild, warm breeze whipped at her skirts, almost rolling her down the cobblestone walk leading to the wharf. Morgan flung his arm around her shoulders in a comradery fashion but, pulling her close to his chest, their bodies stiffened in shock. Their outward attempts at carefree companionship belied the hunger that welded them together in a surge of devouring yearning.

The brisk wind caught the sails of the small, sleek boat immediately and it heeled over, slicing through the choppy river. Keary, who had never sailed in a small boat before, gasped, grabbing the gunwale for support; then her nervous smile gradually changed to pure delight with the thrill of sailing. Leaning back against the gunwale with her jet tresses blowing out of the scarf, she allowed all her problems to float off on the wind on this first day of May, 1777.

"You look like a born sailor, Morgan."

"Our plantation is on the Potomac River and I was sailing almost as soon as I was walking." A strong arm of the wind slapped and fluttered the sails as Morgan worked to keep the boat on course.

"When will you be leaving for Virginia?" The question popped out despite her determination not to think or talk about his leaving.

"I had planned to be there by now, but an old friend loaned me some clothes and a little money to tide me over so I decided to see if my favorite Irish maid would spend a day sailing with me before I left." A flock of migratory birds flapped overhead and Keary brushed a cloud of hair from her eyes as she watched their flight.

"I'm glad you did. I've watched small sailboats often and always wanted to sail in one. But I wish now that I had put my hair in a bag and worn breeches."

"Breeches! My dear lady, you are bound and determined to ruin your reputation, aren't you?"

"What little reputation I had left is probably gone anyway after the way I handled Mr. Wentworth the other day."

"Jason's father? Now pray tell me what you did to that miserly old gentleman." She told him the whole story beginning with Jason's proposal. He was fascinated by her gestures and mimicry, and was laughing heartily by the time she finished.

"So you are now the proprietor of a thriving tinsmith shop and own all that property outright. Be careful not to accumulate too much wealth or I may have to add your name to my list of prospects."

"Why, Mr. Baines, if I thought a handsome gentleman like you could be lured into my trap with wealth, I'd own half of Philadelphia by this time next year." She made the remark sound lighthearted, still fervently wishing he would grasp its sincerity.

"Haven't I told you many times my ambition is to marry wealth? It's just that I never expected the box of gold to be so beautifully wrapped." She was sitting close to him now, his vitality so palpable it reached out and touched her. She moved away slightly, unwilling to be rebuffed again.

"Actually if it's a woman of wealth you are looking for, I'm afraid you'll have to look elsewhere. What I did to Mr. Wentworth gave me a lot of satisfaction and was what he deserved, but I'm beginning to think it wasn't too smart."

"Why? Has he threatened you?"

"No. Still, to carry out my future plans will require a lot of money and securing it would have been difficult under the best of circumstances—what with me being a woman, and a young one at that. Now that I have practically reneged on a debt it will probably be impossible."

"Why would you need credit? It seems to me your business is producing enough to meet expenses."

"The business is doing fine, especially since Molly came to work. But there are so many other opportunities, if only I had the capital to develop them. You heard the will and know of my other assets."

"Yes, I remember there was other property involved."

"For instance the building next door, which is occupied by Mr. Wykoff, the blacksmith. He only uses one small part of it profitably, and since he is a widower uses only one room for living quarters. If I had the money to develop the rest of the building it would produce a lot of income. His rent is only half what it should be and, as near as I can figure out, he is six months behind."

"So, is the hardhearted businesswoman going to evict him?"

"No. I've seen enough of that in Ireland. But I'm going to help him use his space better, and when I have the money I'll remodel the rest."

"Why don't you sell the lots?"

"Because I want to build on them. If I combine the lots, I can build a six-flat tenement on them."

"Hmm, you are an enterprising young lady. Maybe I could get you the money."

"Where?"

"From my brother. Being the eldest, he inherited the bulk of my father's estate and may be looking for a good investment. I'll explain your plans to him." Morgan seemed deep in thought for a moment, then added, "Perhaps you should make a list of how much you need, what it's to be used for, and what kind of return he may expect. Too bad you can't go to Virginia and explain it yourself. I have a feeling you could do it better than I."

"Why can't I go to Virginia?" Her question caught him by surprise and he quickly groped for answers.

"Well, for one thing, I don't have a calash, or even a cart. All I have is one borrowed saddle horse."

"I could rent a horse, and that would be faster than a calash anyway."

"Keary, it would be four days hard riding and, with a woman to slow me down, maybe five or six."

"And what makes you think I would slow you down?"

"Women can't ride hard all day like men."

"This one can." She sat erect and pointed to herself with her thumb.

He studied her, still skeptical. "We'd have to leave day after tomorrow."

"I'll be ready." She was excited and forgot to keep her feelings in check as she reached over to kiss his cheek, but as their eyes met he slipped his arm around her waist and turned his lips instead. At first the kiss was no more than a friendly seal to a bargain, but as she pulled back with her hair blowing wildly his eyes showed desire and he crushed her to his chest, his mouth searching hungrily for hers. Her fingers combed through his tousled locks as his tongue pressed between her soft red lips and the touch of her breasts spread fire across his hard chest. Her common sense cried out to end this scene before her passion rendered this impossible, but her need for him ran roughshod over common sense.

"Keary, you are so beautiful, you don't know how many times I dreamed about you during those long, cold nights in prison."

"But I do; I have dreams of my own." Sitting with one hand on the tiller, he pulled her over on his lap. As the wind grew and the river roughened she clung to him and her mouth roved up and down his neck, alternately nibbling at his earlobe and drawing a line with her tongue down to the hollow of his throat. The wind gained energy, gathering a few dark clouds and pushing them into a tumbling mixture of gray and white, a harbinger of things to come.

"We've got to come about, Lass."

"What's that?"

"Turn the boat around and head back—look." His eyes pointed to the west and she raised her head from its snug harbor to see the oncoming dark clouds gobbling up blue in large chunks. Her wide eyes stared fascinated at the threatening weather and he felt her soft breasts heaving against him. All thoughts of rich widows suddenly took wings as his mouth could not resist the inviting red lips and closed savagely on hers. Her writhing torso felt like it would explode in his arms as he momentarily forgot he was steering a boat. A large wave hit the small craft broadside with authority and sent them both tumbling against the gunwale. A heavy spray followed and Keary came up sputtering. They were both tangled in her skirts and as she reached to tug them around her legs to protect her modesty, he laughed.

"I didn't know a kiss could turn a boat around, but if it

can, I'm afraid we'd never reach our destination if we went on a long trip." He was half lying and half sitting with one hand still holding the tiller and her sprawled on top of him. "First you drown me with your beauty and if you don't get up you'll drown us both in a very cold river." He helped her to a seat by the tiller and pointed a direction to steer by while he brought the boom around. At first the boat didn't want to answer, but as she got the feel of it she was able to stay on course even while he changed the boom and the jib luffed. He finished trimming the sails and turned, hands on hips and feet wide apart, staring admiringly at her. Shaking his head he flashed a grin in her direction. "You're not only a shrewd businesswoman, but a born sailor as well."

She returned the grin, watching the wind whip his hair and said to herself, *And someday this natural born sailor is going to be your wife, Mr. Baines.* The thought startled her since she had all but convinced herself this could never be. Then, as he stumbled back to her holding the gunwale for support, a small voice told her, *Anything's possible, Keary.*

Daylight was slow in breaking as low clouds made the night reluctant to leave. It foretold a gloomy day but Keary refused to let this dampen her spirits. She felt vibrant despite a night without sleep. With Molly's help she thought the riding skirt would be finished before midnight, but she wasn't pleased with the results and had to rip out the seams and start over. It was almost time to leave before they finally finished and even now Keary was dubious about wearing it. Turning in front of the mirror she perused the tight fit across the hips which, coupled with the daring design, made her feel the skirt was better suited to wearing along the waterfront to lure sailors into dark rooms than to wear riding with a Virginia aristocrat. Actually it was a cross between a skirt and trousers, having the fullness of a riding skirt but divided into two legs to allow her to ride astride once they were out of town. She was unsure of Morgan's reaction but had resolved not to ride sidesaddle all the way to Virginia.

Frowning into the mirror she was now more concerned with the fit than the design. Attempting to keep it from hiking up as she rode, she had made it more shockingly snug than anticipated. The tamny material would be durable and not show the dust, but the deep crimson sheen accented every movement of her hips in a way she had not foreseen. If only she had a longer coat it would not be so shocking, but the short Spanish-style jacket was the only one she had that would match the color. Well, it was too late to worry about it now as she heard hoofbeats on the cobblestones below and knew it would be the livery boy bringing her horse. She tied a ruffled stock around her throat and gathered her streaming locks back in a crimson band. A cocked hat, its large white plumes swaying gently as she crossed the room, completed the costume.

Molly beamed at her reassuringly and to Keary's misgivings, said, "Keary if I looked like that I would walk down Market Street at noon on Wednesday and watch every woman in Philadelphia turn green with envy."

Keary, still unsure, answered, "That's easy for you to say, but if I'm back in five minutes you'll know Morgan refused to ride with me."

When she reached the street Morgan didn't notice the

skirt immediately, being too concerned watching the big chestnut shy nervously while the stable boy tried to soothe him. "Keary, that is an awful lot of horse; I think we should go back to the livery and get a gentler one."

"Aw tosh, you sound just like the livery owner. He tried to give me an old mare with a back shaped like a rocking chair." She gave the horse an apple and got a nuzzle in thanks. "I rode Rebel here for two hours yesterday and now we're old friends, aren't we, Rebel?" She stroked the horse's long neck.

"My God, Keary, what are you wearing?"

"Do you like it?" She turned completely around in a circle and tried to sound casual. "It's my own little creation for traveling—actually no Irish wench should be without one."

The appreciation showing in his eyes was his answer as he made ready to help her mount. Closing his hands around her waist, his thumbs probed sensually and he sucked in a quick breath at the lack of undergarments and the realization those curves were all hers.

She rode sidesaddle, keeping up a gay conversation as they left the city. Once in the countryside, Keary reached down and untied the thong holding up the other stirrup. Swinging her leg over the saddle she clucked her tongue and Rebel broke into a trot.

"Come on." She called back over her shoulder, "I don't want you slowing me down." As her tightly clad rear moved rhythmically up and down to the horse's gait, Morgan swallowed hard and spurred his horse. Riding behind her all day with that view, he would lose his sanity. His horse came abreast of hers and his gaze wandered down to the snugly clad hips moving in an undulating motion. Suddenly his own breeches were too tight. It became a task keeping his eyes straight ahead, and Keary smiled. *Perhaps I haven't been using the right tactics,* she thought.

By mid-afternoon Keary was exhausted. Though she was an excellent horsewoman, it had been a long time since she and Bruce had ridden the moors of Fenleigh Manor together. Each time Morgan would ask if she wanted to rest she stubbornly refused, but as they approached a chattering, pebbled stream with a huge shadowy walnut tree, its cool tranquility creating a snug retreat, he used a different tact.

"Keary, I think it's time we watered the horses and gave them a little rest."

She offered no objections. Throwing her leg over the horse's neck she jumped to the ground and, leaning against the ancient walnut, slid down to the welcoming, fragrant new grass.

After watering the horses, Morgan removed the bits and allowed them to graze on the first sprigs of spring. He stretched and was inclined to rub his sore buttocks but thought better of the gesture, instead easing himself down beside Keary. Grinning, he said, "If you'll admit to being just a little bit tired so will I."

"I didn't slow you down?"

"No. You didn't slow me down."

"Then I'll admit to being very, very tired."

"How long would you have gone on before asking for a rest?"

"Until I fell out of the saddle."

"Why?" His perplexed eyes engaged hers with frank interest.

"Because I promised not to slow you down."

He picked up her small hand and, placing it in the palm

of his own, tenderly stroked the slender fingers. "How do you keep your hands so beautiful, working as you do?"

"My hands aren't beautiful; they are rough and worn. A real lady's hands are smooth and white."

"A few little callouses here and there don't matter in the least, so if I say they are beautiful, they're beautiful. It's strange, I used to judge ladies by their families, education, and social graces. Now I find myself comparing all women to you. If they compare favorably they are ladies and if they don't they're not. Of course I seem to find them all wanting in some respects." As he spoke he raised each finger and laced it between his own. Then, raising the hand to his mouth he kissed each finger in turn before turning it over and tracing the lines with the tip of his tongue.

She tried to withdraw the hand, having promised herself there would be no romantic interludes on this trip so long as he intended searching for a wealthy woman to wed. She loved him dearly but was reluctant to allow his advances without a commitment. She felt she should withdraw her hand but not only did it stay put but her fingers, with a mind of their own, began a slow massage of his cheek and chin. His arm climbed over her shoulder, caressing her neck and reaching under the long black tresses to slowly and methodically fondle her ear. He gently pulled her into the snug harbor of his embrace, and as her head tilted back her eyes searched his face, reaching into his thoughts for the promise of wedlock he refused to verbalize.

"I love you, Keary." Their lips met, threatening to devour each other but, as he slowly released her lips and continued to nuzzle her throat, she heard him murmur, "I wish things were different, that I had some prospects, something we could build on."

"But we can love. We could—"

Morgan stiffened at the loud snapping sound interrupting his idyllic mood. Quietly he pulled Keary's arms from around his neck and slowly turned in the direction of the sound. The width of the giant walnut hid them completely, and as Morgan peered around the massive trunk he spotted two rough-looking men intent on making away with their horses. One man was trying to hold Rebel by the mane while the other tried to force the bit in his reluctant mouth. Morgan held up his hand warning Keary to be silent. His only weapon was a pistol and that was in his saddlebags—unloaded. Looking around he spotted a small stick and managed to pick it up without moving out of the path of the tree's shelter. He stepped out with the sun behind him, knowing it would be impossible for the thieves to be sure of what he held in his hand. His sharp voice caught them off guard. "Release that horse or I'll blow your head off."

Both men stood frozen at the apparition that had suddenly appeared from out of nowhere and before they could react, Morgan continued in a much calmer voice. "I only have one shot in this pistol so the rogue who runs first is the least likely to get a ball in his back. Now make up your minds, scum, which of you is going to stay and get the ball." They turned at the same instant and took off at a pace that would put a rabbit to shame. When Keary peeked around the tree Morgan was convulsed with laughter.

"Did you see that fat one run? He hit that tree, bounced back three feet, and was going full speed again as soon as his feet touched the ground. I bet he'll have a lump on his head the size of an egg."

Keary failed to see the humor in a situation that caused her worry over his safety, but finally the contagion of his mood and the relief she felt now that he was safe made her join in his laughter. He grabbed her and spun her around until they tripped over a protruding root, landing in a heap on the green apron of the freshly awakened earth. They rolled over and he found himself looking down into the deep blue eyes that offered him a pass to paradise if only he would accept the invitation.

"Oh, my sweet, it seems the only safe place I'll find to pour out my love will be in the comfort of our own room at an inn. There's one about two miles down the road and I suggest we stop there for the night."

Keary wished to continue the conversation they had started before the untimely interruption but didn't know quite how to bring it up again. It was one thing to offer a solution to a problem when it was already the focal point of a conversation—and he had practically said he'd marry her if there was a way for them to live comfortably—but she found it awkward trying to reintroduce the subject.

As she pondered the problem he continued to make other references to their room, and from what she gathered from his allusions it seemed their sleeping together had been a foregone conclusion in his mind from the time the trip was first planned. She couldn't deny the thought had been on her mind most of the day and there was nothing she would rather do than share his bed. Trying to analyze the situation from a practical standpoint she found herself unable to be analytical, preferring instead to think of the warm blankets that would form a defensive privacy for their bodies snuggled together on soft down feathers. She would lay her head on his muscular chest and listen to the beat of his heart as she silently prayed for a fierce rainstorm that would keep them together for days on end. Yes, she wanted to share a bed as much as he did—but not for a night. It must be 'til death do us part.

They rode on in silence, each deep in thought, until they reached the path leading to the inn. Resolving to share his bed even without the plain gold ring if he would make a commitment, Keary tried to resume the conversation. "Morgan, just before those horse thieves arrived you said something and I was about to answer."

"Yes, I said we would wait and discuss it in the privacy of our own room."

"Before that."

"Before what?"

"Morgan, you're making this very difficult for me. We were having a serious discussion about our future and I believe I have a solution to our most pressing problem."

"I'm sure your solution is a fine one but we're both very tired. We can discuss it at length after we're settled." Despite his resolve not to take advantage of her, his self-control had reached its limits. As interested as he was in discussing their future, the aching in his loins demanded precedence.

Keary began to do a slow burn. How could he treat their future so offhandedly? If he would only listen and agree to her suggestion she would be more than happy to have the honeymoon commence immediately. But she was damned if she would share a room with a man who had informed her of his intention to search Virginia's social fields for the wealth a rich woman could bring him.

It was not much in the way of an inn by Philadelphia standards but, having six guest rooms and a regular menu, was much better than an ordinary where travelers shared the regular meal with the family and also shared their beds. The common room, or combination dining and taproom, was a welcome sight as Keary stretched tired muscles unused to riding.

Morgan approached the short, fat Dutchman wearing a once-white apron over leather breeches and a loose-fitting homespun shirt.

"We would like a room, please."

"Ja, ve got nice room oopstairs."

Stepping up quickly beside Morgan, Keary interrupted, "What my brother meant was, we need two rooms. We haven't shared a room since we were small children."

The Dutchman laughed but looked at her strangely, evidently wondering whether their mother had a black or a sandy-haired lover. He found it hard to believe the same man fathered such opposites. "Ja, ve gott two rooms on da top floor side by side togetter. In da summertime iss hot, but now iss nice."

"That will be fine, Sir." She looked straight ahead, not wanting to meet Morgan's eyes. All the way up the stairs she braced herself for a sarcastic remark, but he walked in silence. Then at her door, he bowed.

"I'll see you at supper, sister dear."

Keary entered the common room to find a noisy group freely imbibing the innkeeper's special concoction of rum, molasses, water, and vinegar. In Philadelphia it was known as "Switchel," but the Dutchman called it by a name she couldn't pronounce. Morgan was enjoying himself with a small group, guzzling the brew with relish.

She first smiled at the jovial group but the corners of her mouth reversed direction when she noticed the blond serving girl brazenly brush her breasts against Morgan in passing, then bend over giving him a bird's-eye view of her ample bosom.

At the sight of Keary the girl became more subdued, but she quickly resumed her flirtatious ways after hearing the term "sister." Keary's appetite suddenly disappeared as the girl continued to rub herself against Morgan at every opportunity and fawned over him as if he were royalty. She excused herself quickly after supper and walked to the steps, noticing Morgan holding a very confidential conversation with the blonde. She paced the room angrily as time passed slowly and Morgan did not return to his room. Finally, after she heard his tread on the stairs and his door open and close, she relaxed.

Morgan strode to the window, hoping for signs of good traveling weather tomorrow. Kneeling to hold his head out the low window, which was adjacent to the wall separating his room from Keary's, he heard her lay a hairbrush on the table as plainly as if it were in his own room. Glancing to his left he saw her open window was so close to his that he could almost lean out and stick his head in her room. He listened intently and could identify her every action, even to pouring water. Morgan rested back on his haunches, his eyes giving off an unholy gleam. If he could hear her that plainly, the reverse would also be true. He removed his boots and tiptoed down to the landing. Then making just a little more noise than absolutely necessary, he ran back up the stairs, closed the door firmly, and did his best imitation of a high-pitched giggle.

Keary's head snapped around and her cheeks flushed

with anger. Tiptoeing to the wall, she laid her cheek against it and listened. She could hear movement and yes—she was sure—very heavy breathing. Was that a shoe being dropped to the floor—glasses clinking? The giggling was unmistakable but what was that other sound? At first she refused to believe it, but now there was no doubt—the bed was shaking. She ran to her own bed, threw herself face down, and pulled the covers over her ears.

Chapter XVII

The next morning at breakfast Morgan was in a joyful mood and the blond girl resumed her flirtations, making sure he enjoyed the choicest morsels and his coffee mug was always full. Keary's eyes were red and slightly swollen. She was long of face and short of temper.

The sky broke clear after the emerging sun had painted an orange-red glow on the eastern sky. Morgan's lips formed a whistle and Keary's a scowl as they turned on to the main road to begin the second day of their journey. That night they stayed at an ordinary since there were no inns close by. Mrs. Sindler, a woman in her thirties who looked to be sixty, made them feel as welcome as possible under the circumstances. The small house was already crowded with her husband and five children but the woman received them gracefully, happy to earn the extra cash. Neither Morgan nor Keary were accustomed to eating from wooden trenchers or using spoons made from horns but tried to fit in with the primitive conditions of the simple farm folk. Keary was reminded of her early childhood in Ireland as the three small children stood at the end of the serving board eating with their fingers from a common trencher.

She didn't have to invent a ruse to have a separate room this night, however, as she slept with three small girls in a straw covered rope bed in a loft over the common room. Ordinarily it would have been difficult sleeping under such conditions but Keary had been introduced to the popular drink of farmers—cider. She thought it was a non-alcoholic beverage after seeing Mrs. Sindler and the children freely imbibing and, after a long day in the saddle, welcomed several glasses of the refreshing liquid. By the time she stripped down to the special pantaloons she had designed for wear under the unusual riding skirt, the bed came up to meet her and she slept soundly, oblivious to the crowded conditions. Morgan, curled up on the common room floor, found sleep a little more difficult.

The following night they found an inn, but it was so crowded Keary had to share a room with two other women and three small children while Morgan was put up with two gentlemen. After a long day of following a narrow, winding road that didn't seem to know where it was going, they reached the Potomac River and waited for the ferry, which was on the other side.

Morgan wore a contented smile as he gazed out across the wide expanse of water. "We will not make Banetree tonight but at least we will enjoy some southern hospitality."

True to his prediction, they approached a great plantation; the huge white mansion loomed gracefully at the convex end of a long tree-lined oyster-shell drive. Black slaves anticipated her every wish and she was treated to a hot scented bath, the loan of a beautiful gown, and a two-hour supper preceded by mint juleps and followed by a fine Madeira. Though the squire was off to war, his wife was an excellent hostess, and after a comfortable night in a large down four-poster, a gigantic breakfast, and a firm promise to return, they were off to Banetree.

Spring adorned the countryside with lavish profusion and Keary was awed by it all as they followed the river road on the last leg of their journey. Had it not been for Morgan's little escapade the other night she would have been ecstatic, but not even the bright, fresh foliage could dispel the emptiness enveloping her since that night at the inn.

Realizing he had hurt her deeply, Morgan paced his horse to hers. The dark pines, which temporarily blotted out the rolling, sunlit countryside, patterned her face with changing light and shadow.

"Keary, I owe you an apology. I played a prank on you the other night and though it seemed funny then, it doesn't now. When I came to my room that first night I could hear every sound from yours, so I sneaked down to the landing and ran back up. I made all those noises to convince you there was a girl in my room. I guess I did it to get back at you for that ridiculous brother-sister story." He glanced over to see if she was still angry and her eyes, the color of a dark, stormy sea, mocked him.

"You owe me no apology; you've made it very clear I have no place in your future. Bed or wed whomever you like." She dug her heels into the large chestnut and galloped off into the immense quiet of open country.

Morgan caught up to her in a large, shadowy grove on the summit of a hillock overlooking the great river below, alive with feeding birds. She had swung her leg over the saddle and was sitting crosswise on the horse, facing him with tears rimming the long, thick lashes. She held her arms out to him and he lifted her over and sat her on his own saddle, kissing the tears away.

"I'm sorry, love, it was a dumb thing to do."

"Don't talk, Morgan; just hold me." She wanted to enjoy the look of love in his eyes and feel those powerful arms around her. She snuggled her head against his shoulder and hung on tightly as he reached for the reins of her horse. Long after he had tied the reins to his own saddle she continued to hold on, relishing the delicious feeling of closeness. The trailing feathers of her cocked hat tickled his face and he gently removed the hat, allowing a few wispy curls to fall over her forehead. Crushing her against his chest, he repeated over and over, "I'm sorry, Keary, it was thoughtless and cruel." The horse, unused to two riders, shied nervously and Morgan, with the hat in one hand and the reins in the other, said, "As much as I enjoy your company, my love, this horse doesn't seem to share my pleasure."

They rode in silence for a while under trees stretching tall against the sky. The dark, damp fields smelled of freshly turned loam and as they trotted their horses beneath the dark pine shadows, Keary broke the silence. "Let's get down and walk for a while; your Virginia is beautiful and I want to enjoy it." They walked leisurely and she turned often to devour as much of the scenery as possible. Her determination to make Virginia her permanent home grew with each step.

She was amazed when they passed one great plantation after another. One in particular caught her eye. The mansion was a wooden structure of Georgian design, two and a half stories high with a broad, columned portico;

the stark whiteness was softened by wide green lawns and fine gardens.

"Oh, what a beautiful mansion! I wonder who lives there?"

"That's Mount Vernon, the home of General Washington himself."

"He must be extremely wealthy."

"Yes, I guess he is now, but that was not always so. My father was wealthy when he had very little. But it didn't matter then and it doesn't now. In the south people are judged on many things and wealth is not as important as in the north. If you can stay an extra day we can call on Mrs. Washington."

"Oh, I'd be scared to death. What would I say to such a great lady?"

"She would laugh if she heard you say that. She's a very down-to-earth person and a charming hostess. Plantation life can be lonely and people around here love company. All it takes to be accepted in this society is proper clothes and manners. Often in the afternoon you will see darkies standing at the gates of the plantations. If any gentlefolk pass they are invited to stay for supper and spend the night. And hopefully, if the guests are amicable, they can be persuaded to spend several nights."

"If General Washington was not rich how did he manage to build a mansion like that in one lifetime?"

"He didn't build it; he inherited it. In fact, his circumstances were very much like my own. When their father died, Lawrence, the eldest son of his first wife, inherited the estate. He added land and improvements and named it Mount Vernon after a British officer he had served under and greatly admired. George, along with his mother, sister, and brothers, moved to a smaller farm the family owned and I believe his mother still lives there. George spent much of his early life as a surveyor and a militia officer during the war with the French. Martha came from a family of moderate means, but she married Mr. Custis who was very wealthy. When Lawrence died, George inherited Mount Vernon and when Mr. Custis died, some say George was calling on Martha before the last bit of dirt was shoveled on her husband's grave."

"Do all Virginia gentlemen marry without love? What constitutes a belle in this country—the size of her purse, how many acres she has, or does love enter in occasionally?"

"Well, in their case I can't say; I guess only George and Martha know for sure. Whether or not it's what some call love I don't know, but they seem to get along better than most. Of course she's a very great lady; I've never known anyone to dislike her. A lot of marriages around here are arranged or are marriages of convenience, and it doesn't seem to present any more problems than ordinary."

He began to lift her to the saddle but as her eyes reached the level of his, his lips impulsively brushed the tip of her nose. Her pensive blue eyes locked with the gold glint of his and lowered as he moved to lightly kiss the long, black lashes. He continued to hold her suspended as he grinned at her predicament and said, "Now you see what I meant by slowing me down."

"Sorry to be such a burden, Sir." She made an effort to free herself from his grasp.

"Well, I guess a few more minutes wouldn't hold me up too long." His lips met hers and the almost imperceptible rotation of his head seemed to draw her closer. By now his hands elevating her ribs were beginning to hurt but it was the kind of pain she felt she could endure forever.

He slowly lowered her to the saddle and they rode silently for a while past green fields, through slowly changing patterns of sunlight and shadow. "Where does the name Banetree come from? Is there really a tree by that name?"

"Well, there is and there isn't. At one time there were lots of them around here, but it's hard to find one anymore. The name comes from markings on trees put there by my great-great-grandfather, Roger Baines."

"But the spelling's not the same."

"You'll find that's true about a lot of things that mean the same. When this country was first settled there weren't many people around who could write their own names let alone spell."

Keary relaxed in the saddle, already becoming accustomed to the easygoing southern ways. He would tell her the story, but at his own pace.

"Roger Baines was in the service of the king for some twenty years and was given a large tract of land for meritorious service. He landed at Williamsburg with seven sons and two daughters, built a raft, and came here by the water route. On arrival, the sons were put to work building a shelter and planting a crop while old Roger went out to survey his land. In those days patents were vaguely written because of ignorance of the country and a dearth of competent surveyors. So Roger set out with a legal description in his pocket, a hatchet in one hand, and a blunderbuss in the other. It seems he paid little attention to the legal description, preferring to mark boundaries by his fancy. A spring, a good stand of timber, fertile land, river frontage, or anything else of value just seems to have naturally fallen within the boundaries of his notches. As other settlers came up the river with patents of their own, several disputes developed when boundaries overlapped."

"You mean a lot of the land he claimed was not rightfully his?"

"Yes, that's how legend has it. Now, I don't know how many of the old stories are true, but it has been said that anyone who contested any of Roger's land ended up buried on it, and it became common knowledge anyone trespassing on Baines's land had better be ready to fight. Does this seem barbaric to you?"

"No. Not when it comes to land. In my mind a man who won't fight for land is not worth a grain of salt. Had I been Roger's wife and saw this beautiful land for the taking, I'd have shouldered a blunderbuss right beside him. Then your great-grandfather was Roger's eldest son?"

"No, I believe he was about the fourth but was the only one to live to a ripe old age. Between the Indians and others contesting the land he was the only one, including Roger himself, to die a natural death."

"Was Roger killed by Indians?"

"No, as the story goes, one of his neighbors took his dispute to the courts in Williamsburg. The judge found in his favor and the governor sent a bailiff along with an armed guard to enforce the decision. When the boat pulled in Roger and a couple of his sons were waiting on the dock with drawn swords. A fierce battle ensued in which the bailiff and a couple of the guards were killed and more wounded. The rest, having had enough, returned to Williamsburg. As their boat pulled out Roger yelled after them in his thick Scottish brogue. Though posterity has never agreed on the exact translation of his speech, legend has it that the message clearly inferred the governor's parents were not married at the time of his birth, and his mother was a female dog. This left the governor in a quandary. He had to completely ignore the remarks or publicly challenge Roger to a duel. The governor evidently considered discretion the better part of valor because no more was ever heard of him."

"But there must have been other fights after that; you said he was killed."

"No. That was Roger's last fight. He walked back to the cabin afterwards and collapsed from a bad wound in his side. He died several weeks later but the sons managed to keep it a secret for a couple of years. By that time Roger's reputation was the best defense the plantation had. At any rate the notched trees became the legal boundary of the plantation and new settlers were warned to stay clear of 'Baines's trees' and over a period of time it became simply 'Banetree.'"

"Morgan Baines of Banetree, it has a nice ring to it." Then to herself she said, *Keary Baines of Banetree also has a nice ring.*

They traveled in soft quiet, the river on one side and the forest on the other. She was contented, the silence broken only by the tread of horses hooves on a road dappled by sunlight streaming through the new foliage of ancient forests. Her trance was broken as Morgan stopped and examined a tall elm, showing her several old notches that time had attempted to blend into the contour of new bark.

"I'll have to cut a fresh notch. Although there is no longer a need for markings, it's tradition to keep fresh notches in a few of the more prominent old trees. At any rate this is the start of Banetree."

From the road endless rows of cultivated small green plants broke through the rich black soil. "That's tobacco, and once produced a large income. There's great demand for it in Europe now but the trouble is getting it past the blockade."

"You mean you grow all that tobacco and are not even sure you can sell it?"

"On a plantation it's necessary to plan far ahead. Much different from a shop where you can make something and sell it the same day. Thankfully, tobacco can be stored a long time and the first shipments to reach Europe will bring a very high price. But I don't envy my brother having to sweat out too many years of waiting with all that expense and no income."

The size and splendor of Banetree was a shock to Keary despite her years at Fenleigh Manor, the main difference being one of warmth and hospitality. The white clapboard of Banetree was as inviting as the cold stone of Fenleigh was forbidding.

A dozen black faces ran out to greet them, shouting and dancing as they rode up the oyster-shell drive. None of the horrible conditions she had heard regarding slavery were in evidence here. Grinning faces greeted Morgan on all sides as young boys competed for the honor of caring for the horses.

"Mista Mogan, why y'all comin' home like dis an' don't be tellin' no one? An' why is you mekkin' that young lady sit a hoss like a gen'lman? She should come a-callin' proper like in a carriage." Keary blushed realizing she had forgotten to revert back to sidesaddle before approaching the house. The old Negress was ramrod straight, of slight build, and from her wrinkled skin and snow-white hair her age could be easily pegged at somewhere between fifty and a hundred and fifty. Keary knew at a glance who the real master of Banetree was. Morgan lifted the old woman in his arms and she never quit talking as he swung her around in a bear hug. "Lawd A'mighty, you just goes off an' we don't know iffen you is alive or dead an' den you just pops up like a bad apple."

"Now Mammy, you know I couldn't stay away from you for very long." Then eyeing the serious old black woman, he said, "Mammy, there's something wrong here. What is it?"

"It's li'l Massa Simon an li'l Massa George. They gets the smallpox an' both pass away two weeks ago."

Morgan gasped and the color drained from his face. His expression was that of one who had just caught a miniball in the stomach. "My God, Mammy, no. Not those two little devils; they were much too full of life." Rubbing his hand over his forehead, he asked, "How is Simon taking it?"

"That's the wust part of it, Mista Mogan. He just goes to his room an' gits drunk an' he stay that way ever since. Mista Mogan, he don't eat nuff t'keep his bones apart an' he don't never leave dat room."

"I'll go see him as soon as I change, Mammy. In the meantime will you have someone take Miss Keary to her room and see to her needs?"

"Cissy, you no count gal, why you just standin' there like your feet was stuck to the floor? Git yo'self movin' an' take Miss Kah'y to the best guest room an' see she get hot bath watah. Den get some of Miss Mah'lynn's clothes for her to wear."

"Is Marilynn here, Mammy?"

273

"Land-a-Goshen! Ain't you heard, Mista Mogan? Miss Mah'lynn, she be gettin' herseff mah'ied to Mista Smiff an' they be sailin' off to England."

Death was written on Simon's face; the hollow cheeks partly covered with a growth of bristle were the color of dried mud. When Morgan entered his room, he looked up through bloodshot eyes and, recognizing his sibling, unsuccessfully attempted a weak smile. "Morgan, it's good to see you. Come have a drink with me." The words had to struggle through a congested throat and sounded stutteringly hollow in the process. "They say it's not good to drink alone, but I find I can get just as drunk alone as with someone."

Morgan was astounded at Simon's appearance. His skeletal frame seemed on the verge of breaking through gray, withered skin. The elegant, once-clean clothes hung on him like a well-dressed scarecrow down on his luck. Dissipation was evident in the puffy eyes and drooping jowls, the shaking hands and shuffling walk. Trying to conceal his alarm Morgan greeted his brother.

"I'm sorry to hear about Simon and George; it must have been a terrible blow."

"Yes. But just another of many lately: first my wife, then mother, then father, Marilynn running off, then the boys—all in a couple of years. It's become damned lonely around here. The ones who aren't dead are off to war. You wouldn't believe how few showed up for the boys' funeral." His voice faded off and he studied the ever-present drink in his hand. Then, drifting back to reality and realizing Morgan was with him, he asked, "What are you doing back here? What happened to your trip to England?"

"I'm afraid I have more bad news; the British seized my ship and took it to New York to be sold as a prize."

"I'm not surprised." Simon lacked the will to care one way or the other about the ship. He had never had the zest for life his younger brother had, and the little he had was gone now. "They'll probably take the others too if I support this damned revolution. I doubt they'll stop until they take all the family holdings in England. And if I support the Crown, the Committee of Safety will confiscate Banetree." Sighing deeply, he slowly turned the glass in his hand, studying the bronze liquid. "There's no way to win. What am I going to do, Morgan?"

"Save Banetree, and to hell with the rest."

"That sounds good, but how? We haven't been able to ship tobacco for more than a year. Our warehouses are overflowing and God only knows when this war will ever end so we can trade again." His pessimism and self-pity played on Morgan's nerves.

"There has to be something to do, or at least try. You can't immure yourself in this room and drink yourself to death. Dammit, Simon, it took four generations to build Banetree; are you just going to sit here and let them take it from you without even putting up a fight?"

"If you can figure out something, go ahead. The keys to my desk and the safe are on that table. All I ask is to keep this room and an ample supply of spirits. It's not that I've given up; it's just that I never learned how to fight. Everything was given to me—even my marriage was arranged. Now, I just don't care anymore, one way or the other."

"And if I can get Banetree back on its feet, then what?"

"Banetree will be yours. I'll make a new will just in case, but that's not really necessary; father's will already covers the situation."

"You mean you are just going to step aside and turn Banetree over to me?" Morgan trusted his brother and loved him despite the older one's weakness; still, he was a little skeptical that anyone could simply give up so great a plantation.

"Yes, that's exactly what I mean. And not just for you to manage. Since it will be yours eventually I may as well deed it over to you now. From this moment on I want nothing to do with responsibility of any kind. I'm going to stay in this room and stay drunk until I die—which hopefully will be very soon." He sat heavily at his desk, picked up a pen, and added, "Now I'll perform my last constructive act. I'll put this in writing in order to help you in dealing with the many creditors. If you'll be so kind as to summon Mr. Benson as a witness, Banetree will be yours within the hour."

It was well past midnight when Keary climbed the stairs to the guest room and Morgan had an opportunity to retire to the study. After a cursory inspection of the books, he could see why Simon had been so generous. Cash was critically short and the debt was heavy. All the liquid assets were in England since Simon had foolishly sent most of the cash to the mother country thinking it would be safer there. He had made no provision for operating capital at Banetree in the event of a long war. At least with summer coming on, food would be plentiful and the plantation was self-sufficient in many other things as well. If he could smuggle one shipload of tobacco past the blockade, all expenses could be met for a year or so. It would not be enough to provide the lavish life-style of bygone years but would keep Banetree off the auction block.

Keary wanted five hundred pounds and there was barely a thousand in the safe. Of course if he told her the situation she would understand. Still, he didn't want to disappoint her. Leaning back in the overstuffed chair he visualized those beautiful blue eyes widening in delight when he handed her the money. Why she was so intent on making money when most women of her beauty would simply marry it, he didn't know. But then he thought, *She's no ordinary woman; she's one of a kind.*

With Banetree his, he began to dream of a future and the "his" became "ours." A smile crossed his face as he thought of Mammy meeting her match in Keary. There was one little lady the old termagant would not dominate.

It was well past three in the morning when Morgan finally pushed the books aside and headed up the stairs. Despite having stared at the neat rows of figures all that time, little of the content registered. Most of the time he had been dreaming of a life with Keary on his beloved plantation. Only a few days ago he couldn't see even the remotest possibility of ever having her, and now the way was wide open. All he had to do was put Banetree in the black.

It would be a herculean task but the rewards would be more than he had ever dreamed of. And as much as he wanted to enjoy the thought of owning the family plantation the thought of sharing it with Keary took prominence in his dreams.

The following morning Keary appeared at breakfast in

one of Marilynn's riding dresses. "And how did you know I was going to take you on a tour of Banetree today?"

"I didn't. But if you weren't, I was going to go myself. In Ireland I always lived close to the land and this feels almost like going home. The city is all right for making money but I could never be permanently happy there."

"Speaking of money, my brother was much impressed with your plans and has agreed to a loan. I'll give it to you before you leave."

A terrifying cloud of unknown origin temporarily blotted the sunny, promising morning and she fought to keep her voice steady. "Before I leave? But aren't you coming along? I know you plan to settle here permanently now, but I took it for granted you would escort me back first."

He felt a sudden tension within her and reached across the table for her hand. "I had intended to, but now it's impossible. With my brother's bad health I'll be needed here for a while. But I'll send an escort with you and you can take the calash; it will be much more comfortable."

Something died inside her and her voice barely reached a whisper. "Then I guess tomorrow will be goodbye."

Her hollow look of despair produced a knot in his chest. "No. Philadelphia is not that far away." And hoping to relieve the tension he quickly added, "Especially without a woman to slow me down." Her answering look was a blend of hope and anxiety.

To further ease the tension, he said kiddingly as they walked out to the waiting horses, "It will be nice to have a lady to ride with for a change instead of an Irish wench who rides astride like a man."

Struggling to overcome the dark shadows he so

recently cast over her bright morning, she answered with an artificial sauciness. "Don't be so sure I won't ride astride even in a skirt. I may have forgotten how to ride sidesaddle."

"Go ahead if you want, but if I don't turn you over my knee, Mammy will."

They spent most of the day riding around Banetree. With the fragrance of spring in the air and the slow, easy life permeating her inner being, Keary's spirits rose despite tomorrow's dark clouds hanging heavily over today's sunshine. They rode past the slave quarters and she noticed something else the growing number of abolitionists never mentioned. The old people remained part of the community and were given tasks they could perform at their own pace and still feel useful.

"Do you keep all the old people until they die?"

"Yes, and it's one of the main problems in trying to abolish slavery."

"Abolish slavery! Don't tell me you are in favor of that?"

"Yes, I am. Although it may sound strange coming from a southern planter, there are a lot of southerners who agree with me. We know the system can't last forever and eventually they must be freed, but how to accomplish it is the problem. For instance, what happens to the old people? And, since agriculture is a very seasonal business, what do they do for employment in the winter? For a peaceful transition it would take fifty years, and where do you find politicians and planters willing to plan that far ahead?"

"I believe slavery is an evil institution and have always been against it. But why do you say it can't last?"

"Because one person has no right owning another.

Some say that slaves are no better than animals but I was raised with slave children and know them as feeling people with hopes and dreams just like we have. But to free them without a lot of preparation would make their lot much worse than it is now, not to mention the total disruption of the southern society." She began to realize how little she really knew about Morgan.

A barefoot, chocolate-colored woman in a coarse woolen skirt and brawlis shirt stood in the doorway of a small cabin. Despite the plain clothes and lack of adornment, Keary was struck by the beauty of the woman. Morgan's nod and the girl's wave were the only greeting that passed between them but Keary didn't miss the message in the girl's large, doelike eyes. It was evident she was in love with Morgan and for once Keary was thankful for southern customs forbidding such a union.

"Who is that woman? Even in those clothes she looks more like a queen than a slave."

"Her name is Pearl and she was born here. She is very talented at spinning, weaving, sewing, and just about anything to do with cloth." Keary thought Pearl probably had other talents of which Morgan was well aware. Realizing she would be leaving soon and Morgan would remain, she wondered if he would soon visit Pearl's cabin and suddenly wished she had not pulled that ridiculous brother-sister routine.

That evening, gliding slowly back and forth on the garden swing, Morgan was on the verge of asking Keary to remain at Banetree and become his wife; but caution warned that if other means to save the plantation weren't forthcoming, his only alternative was to marry a woman of wealth. If it came to that, this time the cause would be a noble one for, rather than marrying wealth to secure his own comfortable future, he would be doing it to save the family heritage. Until yesterday he hadn't thought much about Banetree because it belonged to his brother and would eventually revert to his brother's eldest son, Simon. Now it was his own. Suddenly the sweat and sacrifice of all his ancestors who had put the plantation above all personal desires flooded his mind. Could he do less? And there was more to it than that. Some hundred and forty people called Banetree home. What would happen to Mammy, Pearl, Cato, Cissy, Bishop, and the rest? Families would be split, children taken from their mothers, husbands separated from wives, and he was the only one who could prevent this disaster.

What a difference a day makes; in one day the carefree man who had nothing to worry about except to care for himself now had the responsibility of one hundred forty souls. More than anything in the world he wanted Keary for his wife, but the day he could make that decision based only on their own wants had passed. *Yes*, he thought, *one day makes a hell of a lot of difference*.

The night was filled with crickets singing and frogs croaking in some damp place, and the bulbs of fireflies winked on and off across the lawn. A wondrous fragrance of spring fields and early honeysuckle surrounded them.

"Are things as bad as all that, Morgan?" Keary asked, noting the line furrowing his brow that added a harshness to his features.

"What do you mean?"

"You are sad; I can see it in your eyes."

"I feel bad for Simon. He's lost everything including those two wonderful boys. You would have liked them. I've often wondered how Simon, as proper and as straightlaced as he always was, could have fathered such hellions. I tell you, Keary, those two could get into more mischief than I could as a boy and that's saying something. If you'd have known Mammy before, you would be able to appreciate the loss she feels. When I was a child my own father was afraid to upbraid me when she was around but I swear she loved those boys even more than she did me. The difference is that Mammy's strong. She'll do her crying at night in the privacy of her own room and during the day she'll run the house with the same martinet style she always has. But for Simon this was the last straw in a long list of disappointments, and he was none too strong to begin with." He leaned forward and rested his elbows on his knees. Clasping his hands, he stared at everything, seeing nothing.

"I'm sorry, Morgan. I see your family was much closer than I originally thought. Do you miss Marilynn?"

"Yes. We were very close. But I know the man she married and he's a good sort. A lot older than she is but I'm sure from the household gossip she was in love with him. Had I been successful in reaching England I would have made it a point to find her."

"Are you sorry then you didn't get to England?"

"No. Of course not. Had I gone to England I would have never had the opportunity to really know you. In fact I was no sooner on the *Banetree Princess* than I wanted to sell both ship and cargo and return to you."

"Well I'm glad you did but it seems the loss of a ship, cargo, and several months in prison is a pretty steep price to pay."

"Maybe, but somehow when I saw you again the ship and the prison term didn't seem that important."

Keary's chest threatened to explode, her heart was

pounding so hard. If that wasn't a declaration of love she had never heard one. The long months in prison and the loss of his ship seemed to mean little to him in comparison to losing her. Yet as the thrill of his words soared through her it was tempered by a sense of irritation. Why couldn't he say those few simple words, "Keary, I want to marry you."

"Keary?"

"Yes."

"I wasn't going to tell you this but an awful lot has happened since we arrived here." He stood and paced back and forth in front of her as if uncertain how to begin. Her heart was in her mouth, fearing it was something that could adversely affect their relationship. She waited. "It's something that I suppose was always a possibility since the day I was born a Baines, but something I never even considered since I was the second son and Simon had two sons of his own. Keary, Banetree is mine. I mean I own it outright. Simon signed the papers relinquishing his rights completely."

"Why, Morgan, that's wonderful! Ah—isn't it?" She was unsure why he sounded so remorseful after such a great stroke of fortune.

"Yes, I guess it is. I love Banetree with all my heart. It just seems the price has been the total devastation of my family."

"But, darling, now you won't have to marry for wealth." The words were out before she realized the thought had even entered her mind. She began fumbling for an apology then decided against it. The cards were on the table and it was his turn to play.

"You know, my love, though I'm ashamed to admit it, those were my very thoughts as Simon was signing the papers." He reached out for her hands and she rose to meet him. Their lips met more tenderly than usual. Somehow the moment was above passion and was devoted to a much deeper feeling. He stepped back and she could see his smile of fulfillment despite the meager light of a half-moon three-fourths covered by lazy silvery clouds. He slipped his arm around her waist and they strolled Banetree's gardens, neither of them feeling a need to speak.

Finally as they entered the house he turned and asked, "Since I can't accompany you back to Philadelphia now, can you stay a few more days?"

She felt the sorrow again that had hit her like a blunt arrow that morning. Until his earlier announcement that he could not accompany her, she had been looking forward to the return trip. Being alone with him all day she had been sure he would propose and this time she would enjoy watching the Dutchman's face at the inn when she told him Morgan was her husband rather than her brother. Of course now she better understood why he couldn't accompany her and she no longer had the desolute feeling that this would be good-bye.

"You mean I have to return to Philadelphia all alone?" Her put-on expression of horror was a little overdone and he couldn't contain his laughter.

"No, of course not. I told you I'll send you in the calash with an escort. But I'll be needed here at Banetree because it will be touch and go until I can figure out a way to get this plantation on a paying basis. After looking at the books I'm not sure Simon gave me anything more than a giant headache. Right now there's no income and the debts are staggering. If I can raise enough money to see it through the war, Banetree can again be what it once was."

"Morgan—"

"Yes?"

"It wasn't Simon who agreed to my loan, was it? It was you and I'm sorry—I can't take the money."

He tilted his brow, looking at her uncertainly. "And why not?"

"Because you can't afford it and I know you're doing it because you don't want to disappoint me."

"That may be true but Banetree needs good investments now more than ever before and I've seen ample evidence of your business acumen."

The massive crystal chandelier that dominated the entrance hall snatched at the candlelight, causing vivid prism lights to dance in her hair. Morgan's breath caught and he stepped to her side, his arms eager to capture the beauty before him, but she held up her hand warding off his advance. "We haven't agreed on a rate of return."

"Let's say one fourth of whatever you make on it." His arms raised again, settling on her elbows as she moved back.

"Let's say one half."

"How about a third?"

"You realize, Sir, we are bargaining in reverse."

"And do you realize, Miss, this isn't an ordinary business deal?"

"How so?" The soft tone coupled with beseeching eyes begged him to explain the statement in more romantic terms.

"Because I expect to get all of your profits."

Her heart quickened, anticipating his answer to her next question. "And how would you accomplish that?"

"I thought such an astute business woman would

know how to interpret that." He pulled her closer, eager to end the bantering.

She wanted him to spell it out more plainly, feeling there was no longer the slightest barrier to their betrothal. "Is that a promise, love—the kind to keep a maid warm on a cold winter night?"

"I wish I were free to make promises, my love. But as of today, I am master of a great plantation and it has to come before my happiness or my very life. And, from this day forward, every decision I make has to be with the full knowledge that Banetree comes first. But I will say this, if I could have one wish in life, it would be that you could share Banetree with me as my wife."

She stood on tiptoe and kissed the tip of his nose, sliding her mouth down to bear on his. His passion couldn't stand another postponement and he lifted her, carrying her quickly in the direction of his room. When they reached the doorway she said simply, "Put me down." He hesitated but at the determined look in her eyes, he instinctively obliged. As her feet touched the floor she continued, "Now is not the time, love."

"But why, Keary?" Frustration smoldered in his gold-flecked eyes. "Soon I'll have Banetree on a paying basis and then we'll—"

Her index finger pressed against his lips, silencing him. "Yes, I know, but if something came between you and your goal you would have to run roughshod over it and that includes me. I didn't realize that until now, but it's true." When he started to protest she wound her arms around his waist and rested her head on his chest. "Do you remember when you told me the story about your great-great-grandfather Roger?"

"Yes."

"I told you then if I had been his wife I would have shouldered a blunderbuss and been at his side. Morgan, save your beloved Banetree and then come for me. Four generations of ancestors are counting on you to do that."

"But I'm afraid I may lose you."

"You'll not lose me, my love. I fell in love with the boy and now find myself more in love with the man."

Chapter XVIII

Keary's return to Philadelphia in a grand calash drawn by a pair of matched sorrels and accompanied by two tall black escorts caused quite a stir. Long into the night she talked to Molly of the splendor of Banetree and, without intending to, told of her love for Morgan.

She was pleasantly surprised the following morning to find the shop had done so well in her absence, and Keary complimented a beaming Molly over and over. Turning to replace a ledger, she spotted a row of cannisters, each one a little larger than the next.

"What are these, Molly? She was intrigued by the matching designs of the paint and the more she studied them the more her wonder grew. Each one had the exact same pattern but in progressive miniature. "How in the world did you do this, and what are they?"

Molly took a deep breath, speaking slowly to eliminate the brogue. "They are cannisters and come in sets of six. A lady can buy a full set or one or two at a time and add more later. We have three basic color patterns and plan to add more later. Ladies line them on a shelf and fill them with flour, coffee, salt, grains, spices, or whatever. They are really handy and decorative at the same time."

"Have you sold any of them?"

"Oh yes, loads of them. And we have so many orders, I don't know when we'll get caught up, especially with the painting."

"But how do you maintain the proportions and the exact same pattern regardless of size?" Keary studied first one and then another, shaking her head in wonder.

"Well, that's a long story. I got the idea of making the cannisters from the bins Mr. Penrose had at the bakery. I started painting them freehand, like I always do, but Jamie said he had a better way. He took the length and girth of each one then divided it up into equal spaces before the metal was put in the roller. This pattern showed me where to start each flower and stem or bird or whatever, but I was still falling far behind the lads forming them. Then Jasper gets the idea of putting even more marks on them so about all I had to do was follow the lines. The next day he went a step further and started painting the background color and all I had to do was add the designs. And the best part is that it's almost impossible to make a mistake."

"And Jamie went along with all this?"

"Well, of course. After all, look at all the other changes he made to improve production after old Mr. Fowler got sick. You know he told me that before he took over they didn't even save patterns, just made one thing at a time. Then he hired all these lads and taught each of them how to do a single task. He says it's unbelievable how much more work gets done now."

Keary smiled. "I just meant that he was usually more cautious." At Molly's cocked head and dubious eyes, she quickly added, "You know Jamie's so thorough—he—ah—always adds up the pros and cons before acting."

"Now that you mention it, he did hold back at first. Then I told him if he didn't make me a set of cannisters that very day I wouldn't go to the dance with him on Saturday."

"Dance! Do I smell a romance here?"

Molly blushed. "He ain't kissed me or nothing yet, but we do have an understanding."

"I see. What sort of understanding?"

"Well he's going to save as much of his wages as he can to buy my freedom and then we're going to wed."

"Will you be leaving me then?"

"Oh no, Keary. We'd never do a thing like that. I may have to leave for a little while if I get in a family way, but I'd still paint at home."

Keary studied Molly's animated features; the pale eyes sparkled with happiness, making the round peasant face almost pretty. Putting her arm around Molly's shoulder, she said, "I think you're going about this all wrong. When it comes to romance I would be more devious than you."

"Oh, Keary, I couldn't be devious with you after all you've done for me."

"Not with me, with Jamie. Now, if our roles were reversed, I would say, 'Since you hold my indenture, I would like to make you an offer. If you release me right now and pay me wages, my intended and I would pay you so much each week until the debt is paid off.'"

"You would do that so we could marry right away? How kind of you; I have to tell Jamie right now."

"Wait; now comes the devious part. You can quit early tonight and fix a nice supper for the two of you. I will just happen to have a lot of work to do down here on the ledgers. Wear your new dress and hint—just hint mind you—that maybe I might accept an offer like I just explained. With enough encouragement Jamie will decide it's best to get married right away."

"You really think so?"

"I'm sure of it if you can manage one little thing."

"What's that?"

"You must convince him it was his idea from the start. And Molly—"

"Yes?"

"Tomorrow I don't want to hear that he still hasn't kissed you." Keary stifled a giggle. Molly had said it was impossible to make a mistake painting the cannisters under their new system, but watching her work as they talked, Keary was sure one half of that bird wasn't supposed to be red and the other half yellow.

With the loan from Morgan, Keary was ready to put more of her plans into operation. She had left Banetree harboring feelings of guilt over accepting the money but was certain now she had done the right thing. With her ideas the money would multiply so much faster and, as Morgan had said, it would all be his someday anyway.

She began drawing up her plans but before long her mind was drifting off, returning again to the final parting with Morgan. She relived the ride to the river in the calash, feeling his muscular arms about her, his lips warm against hers. Morgan had instructed the escorts to ride ahead to the ferry and once the calash turned on the main road, he tied off the reins and allowed the horse to set its own pace. The six-hour drive to the ferry, past whispering fields and green covered pastures, was spent in passionate outpourings of their love. A warm glow enveloped her as she recalled his embraces and demanding kisses as they fought to suppress their desire.

Abruptly she snapped out of her daydreams. Keary had more incentive now to make money than ever before and she set her mind to do just that. She jumped down from the stool and hurried next door.

Entering the blacksmith's shop she smiled to put the proprietor at ease. The old man barely looked up from the anvil. "Mr. Wykoff, as you have probably already heard, Mr. Fowler left me this building in his will." He continued pounding on the cherry-red metal held with large tongs, his mumbling barely audible above the clanging.

"If it's the rent you're after, Miss, I ain't got it." He thrust the tongs back into the hot coals, turned his back indifferently, and pumped the bellows.

"Do you know when you will have it?"

"Nope."

"Mr. Wykoff, do you want me to evict you?"

"Course not; no one wants to get evicted."

"Then will you please stop working long enough to discuss the matter?"

He laid the hammer down and walked toward her. "All right, Miss, but what's the good of talking when I can't pay?" He wiped his brow with an old rag and tucked it in the drawstring of his apron.

"Well, we could begin by asking why you can't pay."

"Cause business is bad, that's why."

"But business is generally very good right now; most blacksmiths have more work than they can handle."

"Maybe they're luckier than me."

"And maybe I can bring some of that work to you."

"How could a woman get blacksmith work?"

"Need I remind you that I'm already doing quite well in the tinsmith business?"

"Sure, with Jamie to help you. I heard about all the changes he made after Benjamin took sick." She wanted to explode but held her raging resentment in check, realizing this was business and to be successful she must learn to control her temper.

"That's what I meant, of course; I asked Jamie before I came over here."

"That's different. Jamie's a right smart lad and I sure would like to hear his ideas."

"That's better. According to Jamie, you have too much space and he suggested turning the upstairs into two flats. Your shop could be partitioned off and the front could be turned into a store like the tinsmith shop. A door could be cut through and, in effect, we would have one big store. I'll buy things from you and resell them. But it will not be one at a time as you have been used to; all orders will be for at least a dozen of each item."

"Now, don't go figuring on all my space. Don't forget I need a lot of room for shoeing horses."

She frowned in annoyance. What right did he have making demands when he hadn't paid his rent in months? "How many horses have you shod in the last month?"

"I dunno, maybe one or two."

"Then why not use the space for something more profitable?"

"Dunno, never thought of it that way."

"All right, Mr. Wykoff, starting today I'll reduce your rent by half and continue it at that rate for six months. After that the rent will remain the same, but I will take ten percent of all the business I give you. For the back rent, I'll prepare a note at seven-percent interest, payable so much a month until the principal has been paid off."

"But even if my rent is reduced, how can I pay on another note and ever get caught up?"

"Don't worry, you'll be making more money than you ever did before. Now, I've seen the gate hardware you make and it's beautiful, so I'm going to give you an order for some of it right now. Later we'll get to fireplace tools, wagon hardware, and other things. Here is the list of what I want now and the prices I will pay."

"Land sakes, this is robbery! I usually get a lot more for hinges than this."

"Mr. Wykoff, you don't usually sell a dozen of each item at a time, or have a customer who will buy everything you can produce—and pay cash in the bargain. Don't forget I have to resell everything at a profit." She flashed her prettiest smile and added, "Do we have an agreement?"

"Guess I don't have much choice." His vexatious attitude was hard to tolerate, but Keary had a goal and he would play an important part in her reaching it.

"Don't worry, Sir, in two months you'll be hiring more help to handle your increased business and making more money than you ever did before." She noticed his skeptical expression and added, "At least that's what Jamie says."

Morgan strode nervously back and forth across the dock, raising the glass to his eye then collapsing it and trying to will the incoming ship to make better time against the river's current. The light breeze was barely sufficient to balloon the sails and with each tack the ship was fortunate to gain a hundred yards. Having sailed these waters since childhood, Morgan could see the captain knew his business and was gaining every inch possible, but this did little to salve his impatience.

It was a stroke of luck finding a man such as Captain Hardy who would chance such a dangerous mission. Morgan had heard of this enterprising seaman through a chance remark in Mr. Brown's office where he had gone to buy time on some of his debts. He had already been in the saddle all day on his journey to Fredericksburg when Mr. Brown had kiddingly said, "Morgan, what you need is a man like Captain Hardy to ship your tobacco."

"And who is Captain Hardy?"

"I don't know for sure but I hear he's been bragging in Baltimore he will ship tobacco past the blockade for half the cargo."

"Where can I find him?" Morgan was out of his seat and leaning over the desk separating them.

"In Baltimore, I guess. But why? Fifty percent is not very fair."

"Hell, half a loaf is better than none. What good is that tobacco rotting in a warehouse? Besides, if the price in Europe is as high as I think it is right now, my share could still be close to what it would be under normal conditions." Morgan paced nervously back and forth across the large walnut-paneled office, his brain racing. Suddenly he turned to the startled lawyer. "Do you have a horse I could borrow? Mine is spent from a long day's travel."

"I suppose so, but you can't leave before morning and I'm sure yours will be rested by then."

"I want to leave tonight. Who knows when someone

else will suddenly realize that what the captain is offering is a fair arrangement." It took a little arguing to get the horse but Morgan arrived in Baltimore the next day after an all-night ride. He found Captain Hardy in a tavern and it took only fifteen minutes to arrive at an agreement. The captain would attempt to smuggle the tobacco to Europe and they would divide the proceeds evenly. Morgan rode back to Banetree and began making preparations so that Hardy's ship could be loaded in the least amount of time. A large British fleet had left New York for an unknown destination, and Morgan felt there never was a better time to attempt the gamble than right now.

Every hogshead to be shipped was already loaded on carts or lined up on the docks. Fifty slaves were standing by ready to set record time loading the ship, having received their detailed instructions so many times they knew them by heart. Every hour counted and Morgan had planned the loading the day before when the ship had been sighted off the point. But then came the contrary winds and now hardly any wind at all.

The last word he had heard of the British they were off the Delaware Capes and this was the most propitious time the Gods of war would ever give him.

"Mr. Benson, is the longboat near?" The overseer jumped, unused to the younger Baines being so crisp.

"Yes, Sir, it's at the next wharf."

"Put twelve men in it and meet the ship at the end of the starboard tack. Take a speaking trumpet and advise the captain you'll help tow when he's ready."

As Mr. Benson began rounding up his crew Morgan turned to Cato, the field foreman. "Cato, hitch up as many mule teams as you've got in tandem and back them up on the dock; we'll help pull her when she's close enough."

"Yas suh."

The ship reached the far side of the river and began coming about for a run at the dock. Despite his anxiety, Morgan couldn't help admiring the skill of both captain and crew as she came about with very little loss of headway. Through his glass he could see the crew paying out a line followed by the slaves leaning into their oars. He was further encouraged when the ship lowered its own longboat and another crew began towing. On this tack the ship made much more headway than previously and Morgan held his breath as the captain sailed dangerously close to shore before issuing the command to come about. Only when the ship was again heading out into the current without scraping bottom could Morgan relax. The next tack could do it if he could bring the mules into play.

He jumped into the small skiff with two paddlers and set out for the ship. Traveling downstream he overtook it easily and, raising his hands to the side of his mouth, shouted, "Captain, on your next port tack I'll send a skiff out with a heavy line. When you secure it I'll have thirty men and fourteen mules help pull you in. If the angle looks good to you, wave a red flag, if not wave a white one—all right?"

"Good, Morgan, but have your mules pull upstream along that road rather than straight for the dock."

"I understand, Captain; good luck." The two paddlers had a hard time getting back against the current, and by the time Morgan was again on the dock the ship was on the far side of the river about to start what was hopefully its final tack. Once the two fresh paddlers were perched on their knees in the skiff it was again time to wait. The wind gave no signs of freshening and at times the ship seemed to stand still.

Each minute seemed like an hour as Morgan nervously paced the dock opening his glass, studying the ship's position, and then closing the glass with a loud report. As the vessel came closer his heart leapt at the sight of a sailor waving a red flag from the bow. At Morgan's order the skiff shot out into the river. A few moments later a sailor threw a line over the side and one slave tied them together while the other one paddled furiously to keep the skiff from floating downstream.

"Giddap mules, and pull like yo means it." Cato's whip cracked over their heads and fourteen mules pawed the ground, nostrils snorting and ears standing up. The first longboat came alongside the dock and eight men jumped out and began pulling on the line while the other four rowed clear. A few minutes later the ship's boat arrived and repeated the procedure.

Captain Hardy stood calmly at the rail as the ship hit the wharf a glancing blow and for a dreadful second Morgan thought the wharf, tobacco, and several men were going to end up in the river. The next bump was not as hard and each one after that diminished in force.

The lines were made secure and the captain called to Morgan, "That was pretty good thinking for a landlubber. Perhaps you missed your calling and should have been a sailor."

Morgan laughed. "No thanks; the last time I tried your trade I ended up in prison."

Chapter XIX

Keary picked up the few dishes and put them in a large pan simmering in front of the fire. Eating alone wasn't to her liking and it was such a waste of time to cook and clean up for one person. Molly and Jamie worked on their house every night now and she ate supper by herself most of the time. She was beginning to entertain the idea of hiring a housekeeper, since her time could be spent more profitably in her growing business enterprises and it would relieve her from household chores, which she found boring compared to the excitement of the business world. She dropped a glob of soap in the steaming dishpan and carried it to the cupboard to cool a little before dipping her hands into the scalding water. Just then she heard the knock at the door. Descending the steps, she wondered who could be calling at this time of night.

At the sight of the dust-covered traveler, her hand flew to her throat. "Amos, whatever are you doing in Philadelphia?"

Before the shock wore off he drew her into his arms and his hard lips pressed hers. Keary stood quietly, feeling her coolness would dampen his ardor quicker than resisting. Her mind fluttered like a trapped bird as she groped for an easy way to tell him she was promised now and he could no longer call on her. Holding her at arm's length, a broad smile creased his weathered face and his eyes glowed with pleasure. "Keary, it's been so long. That ocean seemed five times as wide as it ever did before."

"But how did you get through? I didn't think any ships could get up the river now."

He led her toward the stairs, his arm on her shoulder holding her close. "My ship is still cruising off the Delaware Capes. I turned command over to my first officer and bought a horse so I could reach Philadelphia as fast as I could."

"Wasn't that dangerous with the American patrols?"

"Maybe. I never thought much about it. At any rate, no one bothered me." As they entered the common room he took her in his arms again. "Keary, before I left I know I bungled things badly. I would like a chance to start over. It seems when I'm with you I do everything wrong. This time I'm not going to be a bungling fool. If you only knew how much I've missed—"

"Don't say it, Amos." She pulled from his arms and walked across the room. Her heart was heavy with what she must do and, searching for the right words, she gazed into the flames of the small fire she had lit to ward off the night chill from the large common room. He walked to her side and slipped his arm around her waist, unable to resist the urge to touch her. She raised her head and focused on his eyes, which reflected the tiny flames of the fire in their depths. "I'm sorry, Amos, I have been dreading this meeting as much as you seem to have been looking forward to it. I've tried to find an easy way to tell you this, but there isn't any."

He pulled her around to face him and read pity in her eyes. "You mean you won't have me? Is there—someone else?"

"Yes. The gentleman I told you about. He escaped from prison and has come back. He's in Virginia but will return soon."

His usual resonant voice was dull and flat. "And then you will be married?"

"I don't know for sure; I think so."

"You mean he hasn't asked you! The man must be an idiot." He strode across the room and pulled the heavy drape apart, looking down to the street, quiet now in the spring night.

"No, Amos, he isn't an idiot. I'm sure he loves me and wants to marry me but he has heavy responsibilities. The family plantation is heavily in debt and it's up to him to save it. If he is successful, I'm sure we'll wed."

"He is an idiot. In his place I, too, would try to save my property but it wouldn't stand in the way of marrying you. What is he, one of those aristocratic snobs who places family and fortune in front of everything else?" The eruption of angry words could no longer be held back; he couldn't conceal his resentment.

The old clock on the mantel tolled the hour and the shadows on the walls danced to a macabre rhythm as Keary sunk in Benjamin's chair with a deep sigh. "No, Amos, he comes from a very old family by American standards, but even if he tells himself that, I don't think that's the overriding reason he has to put the plantation first. I was there and saw over a hundred people dependent on that plantation for their livelihood; most of them were born there. If it went on the auction block those people would be sent in several different directions. Husbands would be separated from wives, mothers from children, whole families torn apart, and he would have to live with that for the rest of his life."

"Slaves? That's an immoral institution to begin with and I can't imagine you wanting to marry a man who owns other human beings. I could have made a fortune hauling slaves in my ship but I'll have naught to do with the filthy business." He had returned to the fire, his hands clasped behind his back in the old Captain Shelby stance, and was glaring moodily under heavy brows into the fire.

"I know how you feel, Amos, and strange as it seems, Morgan would agree with you. I felt the same way before I visited there."

He slapped the bricks of the fireplace as he turned stiffly, his eyes like two cold flints. He wanted to hurt her as she had hurt him and his voice mocked her. "Ho now, that's rich. Then why doesn't he free them?"

Struggling to hold her temper she said quietly, "It's not that simple." She rose from the chair and turning to the sideboard, continued, "Let's not argue any longer, Amos. I've tried to be honest with you so let's have a glass of wine and talk of other things. How long will you be in Philadelphia?"

"It's hard to say now. Originally I'd planned on staying a month; that would have given us time to have the banns read and I thought you could accompany me on the return voyage. You see, I found a beautiful little farm in Cornwall and took an option on it."

"Banns read! And you bought a farm!" She didn't want to upbraid him now so soon after the blow she had already dealt, but his presumptions went against her grain. "Why would you buy a farm in Cornwall?"

"Because you said you liked the country and there's no quainter place on the face of the earth. If you could see the farm and village, I'm sure you would fall in love with it."

"Even if I wanted to marry you I wouldn't live in England. I don't wish to return to Ireland, much less England. You're right in saying I eventually want to live in the country, but in Virginia—not Cornwall. You see, Amos, I'm an American now."

Frustration crept up his neck like a hot hand, and intent on vexing her, he said, "I see. Has old Fowler been pumping you full of all this liberty nonsense?"

"Mr. Fowler is dead." Her voice was husky and sudden tears threatened to mist her eyes.

"Dead! Then what are you doing here? Didn't your new master inherit your indenture with the business?" The anguished tone that had come into her voice wrenched his heart and he pulled his chair closer to hers, reaching to hold her hand that was fondly rubbing the arm of the worn chair where the dear man had spent so many hours. "I'll see your new master immediately and buy your freedom."

"No need; I'm free now. In fact, I own this business and his other property as well. Dear Uncle Benjamin made me his sole heir."

"Then if you are a woman of property, why doesn't this Morgan chap marry you and use your property to save his beloved plantation?"

She ignored his sarcasm, too spent to argue further. "What his debts are, or what his needs are for operating capital the next few years, I have no idea. Maybe he thinks my inheritance isn't enough. He is hoping to ship some tobacco and if that's successful, my property may make the difference. At least that's my hope."

Amos swirled the remaining wine in his glass, tossed it off, and rose. Keary walked him to the door. He tilted her chin, looked into the face that had haunted him for months, and with an amused smile playing on his lips, said, "Then you're not really betrothed and maybe the contest is still not over." His smile showed a row of strong white teeth set in rugged features, shadowed by the flickering firelight. She nodded in admiration at his persistence.

"No, but surely you wouldn't want me after I've already told you I love another man."

"It doesn't matter, Keary. It would seem proper to just walk away and wish you happiness, but this flame within me will not easily be extinguished."

She took his hands in hers. "I know how you feel, Amos, and I wish with all my heart there was some way to ease the hurt, but I can never love you. I hope we can at least be friends."

"Well, you can ease the hurt some by going with me on a picnic tomorrow. I'll rent a calash and we can ride up the river."

Laughing, she shook her head in disbelief. "You don't give up easily, do you?"

"Not where you're concerned."

"I really don't think it would be proper. Although I'm not officially betrothed, I feel that I am."

"I promise you there will be no talk of romance; I'll keep my distance. It's been a very long, hard voyage and I would enjoy a day of relaxation."

"If you come for me about noon, I'll pack a basket."

Shoving him to the open door she continued, "Now go. It's late, and if I'm to take tomorrow afternoon off, I'll have to start my day early in the morning so now I'm off to bed."

Though Morgan had made the trip from Banetree to Philadelphia many times, he had never made it this fast. Only concern for the horse kept him from making it in even less time. He couldn't actually ask Keary to marry him—that would have to await Captain Hardy's return—but he could tell her about the tobacco shipment and watch the deep-blue eyes dance with excitement. Unlike most women he knew, Keary never masked her emotions. When she was sad, tears formed easily and when she was happy, she was like a young puppy, her whole body laughing. In the last three days of hard riding he had pictured her happy smile when he told her the news—and tonight he would see it.

His first inclination was to go straight to her shop, but as he noticed the stallion's head begin to lower he decided to take the tired animal to the livery first. Once the horse was stabled and munching grain contentedly, Morgan threw the saddlebags over his shoulder and walked the three blocks to the shop.

"Why, Mr. Baines, what a surprise."

"Hello, Molly. Is your beautiful mistress here?"

Caught in a spider-tangle of uncertainty, Molly lapsed into her Irish brogue. "No, Sir. That is—she—'tis on a picnic she be goin', Sir." She fidgeted, unsure of how to continue, then blurted, "'Twas Cap'n Shelby, himself, she went with."

"And who is Captain Shelby?"

"He be—" She stopped herself, trying to eliminate the Irish from her speech. "He is the captain of the ship we came over on."

"Hmm, is this the same man who treated her so cruelly? I seem to remember she was not very fond of him."

"Yes, Sir. And why she went with him, I'll never know."

"Well, if I know Keary, the captain better watch his step or she'll own his ship before the day is done. When she returns, tell her I'll be back later this evening." He turned to the door, attempting to make light of the fact Keary was with another man, but an interior dig of jealousy pricked his consciousness as he stepped out into the sunshine of the early summer day. Perhaps he should have awaited their return. Remembering Keary telling of how the captain conspired in her kidnapping and the harsh treatment she had suffered at his hands, he would like nothing better than to give the bloke a lesson in manners. But then, if Keary left with him socially, it must mean they had settled their differences and any interference on his part would be thought of as pure jealousy. Knowing the truth of that, he decided to wait.

With time to kill and a green monster to drown, Morgan entered the first tavern he came to. He recognized a few faces seated around a large table and strode over to the group. By the expensive cut of clothes and the quick hush that descended when he approached, he judged most of the group were Tories. He still carried a grudge against the British and would have retreated had it not been for his years of training in proper manners. He decided to have one drink and leave.

"Good afternoon, gentlemen."

The return greeting was followed by an uncomfortable silence and he was sure now he had interrupted a Tory political meeting. On his way into town he had heard the British fleet was anchored at the mouth of the Delaware and figured he had intruded on this very subject being discussed. "Is it true the British fleet has arrived?"

Several in the group nodded but no one offered to elaborate. Suddenly Morgan thought of a way to repay the British for taking his ship and throwing him in prison. He knew the British spy system would already be functioning and anything said, amidst this group, would surely find its way to General Howe. "I hear Washington's men are fortifying Mud Island and putting che-val-de-frise in the river."

"What in hell is che-val-de-frise?" a portly gentleman asked.

"They're pointed spikes that are either driven into the river bottom or mounted on sunken platforms. They are pointed at an angle so they'll tear the bottom out of any ship sailing by." Morgan knew any real intelligence gathered here would get to the British by the fastest means possible. He sipped his drink, allowing the information to be digested then, glancing over his shoulder to make sure there was no one eavesdropping, he said, "That's not all they're doing." And as the group hunched their shoulders forward and pulled their heads together conspiratorially, he continued, "I hear they are rigging underwater explosives set in some way to go off if a ship hits them."

There wasn't a man in America who hadn't heard of David Bushnell's submersible boat. His attempts to attach underwater explosives to British ships in the Hudson River weren't very successful but the psychological effect of his efforts was devastating. He proved explosives could be detonated under water by a timing device and this set the stage that convinced the British more scientific innovations were possible.

"And you have all heard of the chain?" They nodded gravely. Both the Delaware and the Hudson were known to have huge chains spread across to block the passage of ships. "Well, there's more than one. Once the British ships get close enough to the first one to try to break it, the other one can be floated up from the bottom and the British will be caught in a trap. And that's when the big gun will open up from the shore."

"What big gun?" It was a chorus from a group of wide-eyed, anxious Tory citizens.

"Why, the one they're hauling across New Jersey right now. I thought everyone had heard about it. Haven't you people in Philadelphia heard of it?"

Heads began to wag from side to side and puzzled, questioning looks were passed from one to another. Morgan saw he had a captive, frightened audience. "Now, I didn't actually see it, mind you. The fellows who were going ahead smoothing the road and removing rocks and trees were the ones who told me about it. They said the cart had thirty-two wheels and it took a whole herd of oxen to pull it. From the directions they were headed, I gather they'll mount it on some high point across from Mud Island. According to those fellows, the balls are so big it takes a ship's crane to load them into the muzzle. They said one ball would break a ship in half."

Anxious glances darted back and forth along the table and Morgan fought to keep a straight face, wondering who would be first to convey this vital information to spies who, in turn, would carry it to the British fleet on a sloop. He made as if to leave, then turned as if other important bit of information had just come to mind. "Of course, if there's a thunderstorm, the British will have no chance at all."

"Why's that, Sir?" Several voices made up the choir this time.

"You've heard of Dr. Franklin's lightning rod?" They nodded in unison. "Well, some enterprising gentlemen have devised a way to use it to conduct lightning into the water. During last week's storm, they caught a bolt of lightning and killed every fish for five miles in each direction. Three hours later, you could touch the river with a sword and sparks would jump out of the water. Can you imagine what would happen to a ship sitting in that water? Why, it would burn to a crisp in minutes."

Suddenly every member of the group remembered important business and the room cleared quickly. For the remainder of the afternoon Morgan drifted from tavern to tavern revelling in telling the same story, each time letting his fertile imagination embellish it a little more.

He had time for one more stop before going back to Keary's shop. Entering the Pirate's Cove on Front Street, he saw a sailor making elaborate gestures as he retold Morgan's tale.

"An' I be tellin' ye lads, when that rod catches a bolt a lightnin' and sends it inter the waters ye'd think there was a million lanterns burnin' underwater. Why the whole river turns red and the water starts to boil. Flames jump right outen the water and all the rocks on the shore melt. Now lads, just think what it would be like on a ship out there."

The British wouldn't believe the entire story but they wouldn't totally discount any part of it either. They held

Americans in contempt on military matters but were in awe of them when it came to engineering and mechanics. All too often the redcoats had expected to catch the Americans in open terrain where the dreaded British bayonet could make short work of amateur shopkeepers and farmers. Then, by the time plodding English generals could place their precise ranks in battle formation, the Yankees would have erected fortifications. And many a time the redcoats would march for weeks to trap Washington against a river only to see his troops build a bridge before the British attack could be launched.

If the British did try to ascend the Delaware River, Morgan was sure they would do it very cautiously. He laughed stepping out into the warm sunlight, *And now, my dear General Howe, perhaps it was not such a good idea to steal my ship and put me in prison after all.*

He turned toward Spruce Street and almost collided with Deborah Thornton. Morgan barely recognized the blond beauty dressed entirely in black, rather than the bright, gay colors she usually wore.

"Deborah, what a pleasant surprise."

"Hello Morgan. I heard you escaped and were back in Philadelphia. But you never came to call." Her lower lip protruded in a practiced pout.

"Well, I—a—at first I didn't have decent clothes to come calling. Then I had to go back to Virginia to attend to some urgent business, and I've just returned this very afternoon." Checking to see how well his fabricated story was being received, he brought attention to her black attire. "Deborah, are you in mourning?"

"Yes, my father passed away last week. Oh, Morgan, I've been so dreadfully afraid; I don't know what to do. Will you come home with me now, just for an hour or so?

I desperately need someone to talk to."

"I'm sorry, I have a very urgent engagement right now, but I can come by tomorrow."

"Please? I'm so completely alone. Father always protected me before, and now I feel so insecure. Please?"

Morgan didn't know how to say no to her plea and twenty minutes later he and Deborah entered her beautiful home on Third Street. The "hour or so" led to another urgent plea—this time to stay for supper. He scratched his head wondering why the slightest refusal of her wishes came out sounding like disrespect for the dead.

"I just feel so helpless with father gone. A woman needs a man to protect her and manage her affairs—and money. Don't you agree, Morgan dear?" Holding both his hands, she stood close, allowing her breasts to barely touch his chest.

"Yes, I'm sure you will have to find someone to handle your affairs." He had been parrying her overtures for an hour and was searching for an opportunity to break off the conversation and leave. Keary would be expecting him and he was anxious to tell her his good news.

"Perhaps if I could just get out of town for a while, out in the country. You are so lucky having a place like Banetree. Although I was born and raised in the city, my lifelong dream has been to live on a country estate."

"Yes, I agree the country is a better place to relax and forget your cares, but I think you should give yourself more time before making a permanent decision. After a few months, you may think differently. But if you are still in the same frame of mind, maybe you could buy a country place close to Philadelphia and still come to the city when you wanted."

This was not the answer Deborah wanted and she was

not one to give up easily. "Perhaps after your business here is finished, we could plan a visit to Banetree."

"Yes, well—ah—I'm not sure how long I'll be tied up, but we can talk about it later."

He glanced at the clock and saw it was too late to visit Keary. Noticing his slight frown when he raised his eyes to the clock, Deborah quickly said, "Now don't start thinking of going to an inn tonight. I've already had Robinson prepare a guest room for you. You'll stay here as long as you're in Philadelphia, and I'll not take no for an answer. Why, Father would turn over in his grave if he thought I failed to extend hospitality to such an old friend."

Damn her, he thought, *there she goes with that sympathy stuff again. If I refuse, it'll be like refusing her dead father.* He would just have to wait until morning to see Keary. "Thank you, Deborah, that's very kind of you; now if Robinson will show me to my room, it's been a very long day." It was evident he could have shared her room without too much persuasion, and a few months ago he would have jumped at the chance. But since meeting Keary, a subtle change had come over him and other women lacked the appeal they once held, regardless of their riches.

The following morning Deborah used all her womanly wiles to keep him there, but he skillfully convinced her his other business was urgent.

The heat was stifling and the front door of the shop was standing wide open, allowing Morgan to enter without tripping the bell over the door. For a moment he stood there watching Keary chew on the end of a quill with her mouth all screwed up in one of the many expressions he had repeatedly pictured in his dreams. She glanced up and the expression quickly changed to one of pure delight as the quill fell, spilling ink on the paper. She ran to him with her arms outstretched and fell into his loving embrace, caring little that all work in the shop had ceased as she caressed his face with her lips.

The feel of her in his arms was better even than his almost-constant dreams since he had parted with her at the ferry and had fought the overpowering desire to take her back to Banetree immediately as his wife. The eagerness of her body made him reluctant to pull away, but he was bursting with his news and finally eased her grasp and held her at arm's length.

"Keary, I found a captain willing to risk the blockade and he has already sailed for Europe with a cargo of my tobacco."

"Oh, Morgan, what do you think his chances are of getting through?"

"Well, it's a light, fast vessel and the captain seems daring enough. If anyone can get through, I believe he can."

"Will one shipload bring enough mon—er—I mean will this save Banetree?"

"No. But it's a start. At least it's something to build hopes on." He marveled at her ability to detect even the slightest change in his mood, usually before he was aware of it himself.

"Let's go for a walk Morgan; you look troubled." Once out on the street, she asked, "What is bothering you, love? You looked so strained for one bringing such good news."

"Nothing is bothering me except the worry of whether or not the ship will get through the blockade. Maybe I'm so thrilled with the wonderful prospects in store for us if the trip is successful that I'm almost afraid to believe it."

"I pray that it will." She squeezed his arm, hugging the happiness of being with him so close again. "Will you be staying long?"

"No, just a few days and then I'll be going back to Banetree to begin learning my new profession as plantation manager. But if and when the captain returns, I'll be coming back here as fast as my horse can make it." It wasn't exactly the promise she had hoped for, but since his eyes seemed to pledge more than his words, she was content for now.

The air was sticky and sweat reappeared on bodies as fast as it was wiped off. It was the kind of day to sit back, enjoy a cool drink, and wave a fan steadily. But even the heat and humidity had taken second place as a topic of conversation since the British fleet had been sighted. Millions of flies and other insects buzzed over the offal and garbage lining the gutters, while the quiet populace stared at the river as if expecting dragons to appear. From the moment the first rider had thundered into town with news of the British arrival, Philadelphia had assumed a mood somewhere between a funeral and silent panic. A few hours after the first sighting, the enemy fleet had dropped anchor in the Delaware Capes and their objective was no longer in doubt.

Morgan had been walking deep in thought and after a while broke the silence. "Maybe you should come to Banetree with me?"

"Don't be silly, love. I'll be perfectly safe; after all, the British haven't come to make war on women. Go back to your land and don't worry about me."

"Are you trying to get rid of me?"

"You know better than that. But when a man's land is at stake, nothing should stand in his way. The Irish understand this since we haven't been allowed to own land for hundreds of years."

The following night was Morgan's last. He intended leaving Keary early to get a good night's sleep and be ready for a fresh start at dawn. But leaving her seemed to get more difficult each time. His arms slipped around her waist and pulled gently; his lips brushed hers tenderly, becoming more insistent as her body molded to his. She trembled under his hand traveling slowly down her back.

"I love you; I love you." His husky voice murmured in her ear as his lips seared a path down her neck and he gathered her closer, exploring her waist, hips, and buttocks while instinctively her body arched toward him. He kissed her again with a savage intensity, forcing her mouth open with his thrusting tongue, leaving it burning in the aftermath of his fiery possession.

Lifting his mouth from hers, he gazed into the stormy pools of her eyes and saw his own love mirrored there. He knew there could be no turning back; this time he had to possess her completely. Ever since the morning she left Banetree he had fought the urge to follow, knowing it would be impossible to hold her again and not take her. He lifted her with powerful arms and she yielded to the overwhelming need that had been building for months. Her whole being cried out to be fulfilled as he carried her to the bedroom. Her breast pressed into his shoulder as she snuggled her head along his neck and nibbled tantalizingly on his earlobe. She gloried briefly in a passionate dream of nakedness, Morgan always at her side, their life happy and carefree, and she whispered, "Morgan, darling, take me and love me—let's never stop."

The lone candle in her chamber flickered, casting an uneven glow over her body as Morgan gently eased her to the bed. He unlaced the crisscrossed ribbons of the bodice and her breasts surged at the intimacy of his touch, her nipples taut beneath the thin fabric of the chemise. As his hands lifted her waist to untie the skirt, she arched her back and currents of desire surged through her body as he slipped the skirt from her ankles and moved his hands under the chemise, lightly caressing her thighs and hips as he slowly drew it up and over her head.

He paused to kiss her, whispering his love for each part of her body as his hands began a lust-arousing exploration of her soft flesh. His fingers roamed intimately over her breasts and the rosy peaks grew to pebble hardness as his lips caressed each nipple. She massaged the strong tendons in the back of his neck, writhing and moaning as slowly his hands moved downward, skimming either side of her body. His stroking fingers stopped just short of the furry mound, sending pleasant jolts through her unsated body, and his lips traced a sensuous path up her ribs to her breasts, bringing the pink tips to crested peaks. She desperately needed more of him and began to tear at his clothing, wanting flesh against flesh—man against woman.

He rose and she watched transfixed, the soft light dancing over his hard-muscled body, his slim waist seeming barely adequate to support the broad shoulders and firm chest. He quickly drew the shirt from his head and with unsteady fingers fumbled with the laces of his breeches. His naked torso advanced slowly to the bed and her lusty desire reached out for him as he lowered his body beside her.

"My God, Keary, I've never seen anything so beautiful; I can't ever let you go. I'm going to hold you and love you all night."

"Oh, Morgan, hold me close, darling. I've never loved anyone before."

Gently his hand outlined the circles of her breasts and they surged at his touch. His mouth teased the buds that had swollen to their fullest and his lips seared a path down her abdomen. Keary threw her arms back beside her twisting head, moaning in ecstasy as her hips raised to meet this scorching tormentor. Morgan searched for pleasure points, his touch light and painfully teasing. His tormented groan and raw sensuousness carried her to greater heights and she seized his head and pressed seared lips against his burning mouth. Taking her hand, he guided it to himself and his hardness electrified her; she felt the heat of his body course down the full length of her own. Her breath came in long, surrendering moans, and passion flamed through her veins as Morgan lowered his body over hers and gently probed the deep, warm recess of her womanhood.

An electric shock of pain coursed through her body, but a tremor inside her heated thighs and groin began to vibrate with a liquid fire and moans of ecstasy slipped through her lips. A flaming passion rose in Keary, clouding her brain, and she abandoned herself to the whirl of sensations as she soared to an awesome, shuddering height feeling the hysteria of delight rising inside her. Finally, in a burst of tremors, a deep feeling of peace entered her being, and as Morgan leaned back she drew his face to hers in a renewed embrace.

"That was worth waiting for all this time, my love," she murmured as he looked questioningly into her eyes.

He kissed her tenderly, brushing small damp tendrils from her face. Raising his body from hers, he chuckled as he drew her close. "I thought I knew everything there was to know about lovemaking but you, my sweet Irish Miss, awakened flames within me I never knew existed." A golden wave of passion and love flowed between them and she was too emotion-filled to speak. Morgan left a little later than planned the next morning. Though leaving Keary was now more painful than ever, he was relieved in one respect. Reports coming into the city said the British fleet had weighed anchor and sailed out over the horizon.

Chapter XX

Morgan had been at his desk for hours writing to his creditors. Once the last grain of sand had been spread on the neat script and the blob of wax had been stamped with his seal, he stretched his tired back and rubbing his eyes, reached for another sheet of paper. This was the letter he wanted to write first but was afraid if he started it, he might not get to his less interesting correspondence. Dipping the pen he began:

My dearest Keary,
   I have been very busy learning plantation management, but there hasn't been an hour since we parted that I haven't thought of you. You are on my mind when I open my eyes at early dawn and a vision of your beauty is with me when I close my eyes at night. I love you more than I . . .

He hesitated at the sound of hooves pounding up the driveway. Replacing the quill in the ivory inkwell, he hoped the rider wasn't bringing dire news. The front door slammed, the echo of riding boots crossed the tiled floor, and the angular form of Lester Benson, the overseer's son, filled the doorway.

"Mr. Baines?"

"Yes, Lester, what is it?"

"It's the *Pelican*, Sir. She's been sighted rounding the point like a fox with the dogs on his tail."

"The *Pelican!* What the devil is Hardy doing coming back?"

"Dunno, Sir, but a rider just came up from Yorktown on a horse blowing smoke out his ass. Says British sails are in the lower bay thicker'n porcupine quills."

"What's the *Pelican*'s position now?"

"Can't say, but the lookout says she rounded the point heeled over so far her sails were almost scooping water."

"Tell your father to break out every man on the plantation with axes and saws and everything he can find that will cut a tree. We'll put that ship in the north cove and cover her with trees and bushes. Tell him to—oh hell—just tell him the plan; he'll know what to do."

As the ship came up river and headed for the cove, dozens of black men swarmed aboard her. First she was dragged into shelter 'til her bottom settled into a soft mud anchorage then, even before captain or crew knew what was happening, bushes seemed to be growing out of her decks and trees sprouted from the water in front of her. Crewmen were sent aloft alongside black slaves, and fresh cut branches were sent up to them on lines. These were lashed to the masts and within two hours any ship sailing by would never know there was anything in that woods except trees.

Morgan poured two glasses of brandy and, handing one to the Captain, held back his question waiting for the man's story.

"Dammit, Morgan, we came so close; first we had a rudder problem and had to put into Yorktown for repairs. That took eight days, but as soon as the repairs were finished I rounded my crew up from the taverns and made sail. Even then we would have made it but the tide and wind were both against us. We were right off Norfolk when we spotted the British fleet. I tell you there was more canvas out there than water. Believe me, if the sun would have been coming up we wouldn't have been able to see it. We hauled close to study the situation but two frigates came after us like a bull at a baiting, and there was no time to do anything but get the hell out of there as fast as we could. We crowded on every stitch of canvas and the whole crew stood on deck and held their coats open. The only good thing we learned is that we can outrun any vessel in that whole fleet."

"You mean Howe's whole fleet is in the bay?"

"Howe's fleet! Hells bells, Morgan, I think every ship in the British Empire is there and the rest of the European navies besides. I swear they will all have to travel in the same direction because there won't be enough room in the whole Chesapeake Bay for them to come about."

"What the hell is a fleet that size doing in the bay?"

"My guess is the objective is still Philadelphia."

"Philadelphia! Hell, why didn't they go by way of China?"

"You've got me. All I know is the best way to outsmart the British is figure what a person with brains would do and then figure them to do the opposite."

"So what's the next step?"

"Get drunk tonight and figure it out tomorrow; got any more of that brandy?"

"I think so."

"Then get it out. I think a lot better with a hangover."

The following morning a rider came from the point with news that made Morgan and the captain return to the bottle. The word he brought was that the whole northern part of the bay was so thick with ships it resembled a forest in winter. The situation looked hopeless, but after a little morning "hair of the dog" they began to analyze the situation rationally.

"What will you do now, John?"

"I have no choice; wait it out or lose my ship. What worries me most right now is how long this crew will stay."

"Is there any way to get them to stay long enough to wait out the British?"

"Rum. And possibly fear of the British. They know if they are caught roaming the countryside the lobsters will press them into the Royal Navy. But even fear and rum will keep them here only so long. Let's assume Philadelphia is the British objective. It's a certainty they can't supply an army that size overland for very long. Soon they'll have to move their fleet to the Delaware and then maybe I can get out of here."

"Well, I'll scrounge every barrel of rum I can. Then I'll be heading back to Philadelphia."

"Why Philadelphia?"

"Banetree is in trouble. I have a lot of debt and all the cash and liquid assets are in England, so I have to raise money the only way I know—marry it."

"And you have prospects in Philadelphia?"

"Yes."

"I wish I could go with you, but it looks like I'm stuck here until General Howe decides what he's going to do. And that idiot may try to attack Boston by way of Georgia."

"I hope you can get out soon. The plantation can supply all the food you need and I'll get as much rum as I can. In the meantime, consider Banetree your home."

"Thanks. When the time comes to get out of here, I hope I still have a crew."

"If necessary, Mr. Benson can supply you with a few blacks who have had experience on small craft and would make good sailors with a little help from your crew. I'll leave instructions for him to provide you with as much help as he can."

"In the meantime how do I go about meeting the fairer sex around here?" The captain was an amiable man with a perpetual smile and was accustomed to dividing his shore time between women and taverns.

"No trouble at all. Just ride along past the plantations and you'll find yourself invited to stay for as long as you wish. Of course it helps to know which ones are the best prospects so I'll leave you a list. On second thought, I'll omit a few of the choice ones because you may decide to leave the ship there until the tobacco rots."

Morgan wondered how much those ridiculous rumors he had started in Philadelphia had dissuaded General Howe from entering the Delaware River. If they were a factor, his own cleverness was now the reason his tobacco could not get out. *When will I ever learn to keep my big mouth shut?* he admonished himself.

Only a few days ago he was studying a calendar, trying to determine how soon he could reasonably expect the *Pelican*'s return. Once the money was in his hands he had planned a trip of his own, returning with a black-haired bride. It had been a beautiful dream—but only a dream.

The letters he had sent to his creditors had promised payment within six months. Now, with the ship tucked away in the cove, he wasn't even sure it could sail within that time. And with contrary winds the two crossings would surely take six to eight months. His chances of making both crossings without being captured were no better than even.

No, the odds were too heavy to risk Banetree. As desperately as he wanted to marry Keary, his duty was clear. Deborah Thornton was worth a fortune and once they were wed, it would all belong to him. He could pay off the debts of Banetree and never have a financial worry the rest of his life.

He tried to convince himself that a life free of financial worries, even with Deborah, wouldn't be that bad but he knew deep down, regardless of whom he married, his mind would never be free of Keary.

Even with Morgan gone Keary was in high spirits. She had only to close her eyes and remember that beautiful night to understand the meaning of heaven. Now, more than ever, she had a purpose in life. She would make as much money as possible and when Morgan asked her to marry him, she would surprise him with a handsome dowry.

She was not the only one in high spirits today. All Philadelphia was in a holiday mood, looking forward to their first view of General Washington and his army. As soon as the British fleet was sighted in the Chesapeake Bay, Washington had marched south to get between them and Philadelphia. This day his entire army would march through the city and the excitement was contagious.

Keary was planning to attend the parade, but rather than leave early like the others to get a spot on Front Street, she intended viewing it at a point farther along the route of march. This plan gave her a few hours alone to review her finances and business affairs. So far, everything was succeeding better than anticipated.

"Good morning, Miss." Keary looked up to see Mr. Wykoff facing her. With the door standing open to take advantage of a fresh river breeze, he had entered silently.

"Good morning, Mr. Wykoff, aren't you going to the parade today?"

"Yes, I'm on my way there now, but first I wanted to pay my rent and what's due on the note." He set a small stack of coins on the counter.

"Thank you. I assume business is good then?"

"Oh yes. Next week I'm going to hire another apprentice." The blacksmith left and she made a mental note to pay him a visit within the next few days to show him more of "Jamie's ideas."

The two flats over the blacksmith shop were nearing completion and she had a steady stream of prospective tenants. Even when she mentioned a rent of two guineas a month and a year's rent in advance, she did not scare all of them off. She decided to wait until the flats were finished and ready for occupancy before committing herself, since prices were climbing every month. With the war believed to be heading this way, one army or the other would occupy Philadelphia and the demand for housing would be fantastic.

With this in mind she had sold the two lots on the alley and with an additional one hundred pounds bought a building across the street. It had been owned by a cordwainer who ran a shop on the ground floor and divided the second and third floors into flats. When the cordwainer died, his widow was anxious to sell the property and move to her sister's house in the country.

Keary planned to turn the shop into flats and add partitions on the other floors to make more units. This, along with healthy rent increases, would make the building a virtual gold mine. It was also the kind of investment that could be quickly converted into cash in the event Morgan needed it.

The next visitor startled her, even though she knew he would not stay away long. Still, it was a meeting she dreaded.

"Good morning, Amos; it's nice to see you."

"That's a nice polite greeting but not what I'd hoped for."

"Why do you insist on making things difficult for me? I've tried to explain there could never be anything between us except friendship."

"The remark was made in jest. Besides, I didn't come here to argue; I thought you might want to accompany me to the big parade. I am most anxious to see this tobacco planter and his ragtag army which feels it can stand up to the might of the British Empire."

"It would be a pleasure, Sir, both to see General Washington's army and the expression on your English face when you see an army of men who are not afraid to stand up to big, bad John Bull."

Keary, who had never seen any army except for a few redcoats in Cork, was not sure what to expect, but it was something entirely different from this disorganized mob now passing in review. Except for an occasional uniform or part of one, there was no way other than the muskets to tell these men from artisans or farmers. The only badge of uniformity other than the muskets was the sprig of greenery each soldier wore in his hat. General Washington, wanting a sign of uniformity to impress the civilians, had ordered each man to wear this little adornment. It was a far cry from British cockades but did give the troops a look of freshness and life. Though most of the higher officers had cockades of sorts, most junior officers still wore the feather, which had prompted the British to compose a verse for the popular song "Yankee Doodle."

> Yankee Doodle went to town
> Riding on a pony
> Stuck a feather in his hat
> And called it macaroni.

The crowd cheered loudest for the Pennsylvania regiments but had warm greetings for the others as well, even the Yorkers. Keary remembered the redcoats from Cork and now contrasted those smart-looking scarlet uniforms with this ragged group. Then on further study she began to see differences other than dress; there was also a difference in bearing. Each man walked with a resolution and spirit she had not seen in Cork. These men would think for themselves and endure hardships, not through discipline but because they themselves had willingly decided to sacrifice for a cause they believed in. She watched fascinated as freckle-faced lads marched alongside ancient, wrinkled old men, their white manes flowing behind. Yes, this was not a well-disciplined army, but the men knew why they were there and it was not because a far-off prince or king had ordered them.

She began studying the officers as the crowd speculated on their identity. Everyone recognized General Washington when the statuesque Virginian rode by on a prancing white horse, and she knew immediately she was seeing greatness. Now some of the other generals caught her attention as the crowd identified them.

"That's General Knox," someone behind her said as a huge two hundred seventy-five pound baby-faced young man rode by on an overworked horse. It was hard for her to picture this young man as chief of artillery.

A constant roar traveled along the crowd and Keary stood on tiptoe searching for its cause. "Here he comes, Mad Anthony himself." This from a well-dressed man beside her. Interspersed with the cheers were a sprinkling of feminine shrieks, and Keary remembered hearing General Wayne had quite a reputation with the ladies. Two women whispered behind her.

"My dear, did you hear what is being said about him and Peggy Shippen?" Keary had met Peggy Shippen and craned to hear more, but the woman held one hand to her friend's ear and whispered while the words threatened to escape through her friend's open mouth.

As General Muhlenberg approached, a short man beside her decided to share his knowledge with the rest. "Before the war he was a preacher, and one Sunday after finishing his sermon he stood right there in the pulpit and took his robes off. And do you know what he had on underneath? A Continental uniform, that's what."

But of all the generals other than Washington, Keary's careful scrutiny picked out Nathanael Greene of Rhode Island as a man she would want on her side in a fight. The former Quaker with one stiff leg sticking out in the stirrup didn't have the dash of Wayne or some of the others, but for an instant his eyes met hers with a look of determination she knew would never admit defeat. Suddenly the principles these men were fighting for became important to Keary as well.

All the way home they walked in silence. Until now she hadn't really given the Americans much of a chance, despite her earlier protests to Amos. How could thirteen

vidual colonies without formal organization, other
a weak Congress, stand up to the might of the
ld's foremost empire? After the parade most of the
pulace returned with lower opinions of American
ances than before, but Keary's reaction was just the
opposite. She was not as easily impressed with flashy
uniforms and well-dressed ranks as the others. Actually, she could not put her finger on the exact reasons for her change of heart, but she was much more of a rebel on her way home than she had been that morning, and she pondered the best way to contribute to the revolution.

When they returned, Amos was intent on maintaining his former derisive attitude. "Was that the army you believed could stand up to British regulars?"

"Yes, I believe they will. Although they don't have the pretty uniforms and maybe don't march as well as the redcoats, I saw a determination there today. And you know, I had a strong feeling watching them. Wouldn't it be wonderful to have a country run by men such as these, rather than by lords and dukes and such?"

"Keary, you're beginning to sound like a traitor. Don't get involved with revolutionaries or you'll lose everything you have once this war's over."

"You are assuming a British victory." Her impertinent smirk challenged him.

"Assuming? Don't be ridiculous! I'll admit the rebel army was larger than I thought and a little better organized, but ultimate British victory is a foregone conclusion."

"If you were impressed with the size of Washington's army, what about the others? There is another American army in the north fighting Burgoyne, and when the British tried to take Charleston they were repulsed by another American army there. For a long time I thought the rebels had no chance, but now I'm not so sure."

"I don't care how many armies they have; the king [cut] send as many troops as necessary." His manner la[cut] conviction.

"Where will he get them? He's already had to h[cut] foreign troops."

Amos's face turned red. England's need to hire foreig[cut] mercenaries to restore its rule over the colonies wa[cut] embarrassing to loyalists. "Regardless, the king will not give up until the war has been won and his rule in America has been established for all time."

"Amos, I recently took a trip to Virginia and thought I had crossed half of America. Then after looking at a map I found it was like taking one step in a walk across this entire city. Once I left the coast I met people who have never seen a redcoat and are hardly aware there is a war going on. That's how much effect the whole British army is having on this huge continent."

His eyes studied the floor, seeking an answer. Like most Englishmen he was confident the Crown would win the war, but like most Englishmen he had no idea how.

As Washington marched south to meet the British, Keary waited anxiously along with the rest of the city for news. A major battle was in the offing and she studied a map trying to figure out whether or not it would likely occur on terrain she and Morgan had traveled on their way to Banetree. General Howe's troops were said to have landed at a place called Head of Elk on the northernmost part of the Chesapeake Bay. Many people had questioned Washington's strategy of bringing his army this far south while Howe's troops were still on board ship and could be taken back to New York faster than the Americans could march overland. But Washington's severest critics had to eat humble pie now, admitting the old fox had been right again.

Chapter XXI

Morgan had made the trip from Banetree to Philadelphia many times but never under these conditions. Every inn, ordinary, and farmhouse was filled to capacity with army officers and camp followers, and he finally had to sleep under a tree on an empty stomach. The following day he was fortunate to find a little bread but had to pay more for it than he would normally pay for an entire meal. He was offered a barn to sleep in that night at a price comparable to a first-class inn, but unwilling to share quarters overcrowded with animals, people, and lice, he again chose the outdoors.

As the morning sun sent its first rays of light through the towering forests and rolling meadows, Morgan was awakened by what he judged to be the beginning of a thunderstorm. He rose cursing his luck at being caught in a storm with no place to seek shelter, but the clear sky gave no evidence of foul weather. Chasing the fog of sleep from his brain, he listened intently to the growing roar and slowly realized the incessant din was not induced by nature. It was the thunder of cannon.

The next two hours as he rode warily along the lonely road, the sound alternately grew then subsided. It seemed to be moving from right to left, indicating a running battle.

A regiment of militia hurried by and couriers frequently passed as he traveled north, closer and closer to the angry guns echoing across the morning air. In a clearing ahead, several marquee tents bustled with military activity. He reined in to inquire about the battle and was stopped short by a booming voice with an unmistakable New England twang.

"You there. Are you a courier?" Morgan turned to see a squat colonel, hands on hips and feet spread wide.

"No Colonel, I'm a civilian on my way to Philadelphia."

"Where are you coming from?" Eyes like cold flints probed suspiciously.

"Virginia. Just over the Potomac."

"See any redcoats along the way?"

"No, I haven't seen any troops except one regiment of militia about a mile back."

The colonel studied him closely. "Hmm, you're real sure there're no lobsters back there?"

"Redcoats are not that hard to see in this green country. If there had been any I'd have seen them."

"Or you could be a Tory and not tell what you've seen." Any travelers foolish enough to be on the road this day would naturally draw suspicion so Morgan didn't take offense. "That's a fine-looking horse you have there; I think the army could use an animal like that. Go into that tent and the lieutenant will give you a receipt for him. And if you know what's good for you, you'll get the hell out of here before the British come. The report we have say they are heading this way and you might find yourself right smack in the middle of a battle."

"But this is my horse; you have no right taking him."

"Sorry, that horse just joined the army, and if you can't stand to be separated from him you can do the same. I can swear you in right now."

"Now see here"—Morgan bristled and started for the colonel, but two soldiers with fixed bayonets came to their officer's assistance and Morgan quickly changed his mind—"how am I going to get to Philadelphia? I have urgent business there."

The colonel laughed. "Well, we have a method in the army which is so simple I think even a Virginian could learn it. You put your left foot out in front of you, then your right, and just keep repeating the procedure. Soldiers call it marching and civilians call it walking. But with practice anyone can learn it." A round of snickers spread through the onlookers as the colonel went back into his tent and a soldier led off the prize Arabian stallion.

As Morgan plodded along, the road became more crowded. The roar of guns slackened to sporadic musket fire and the forests and fields issued a steady stream of stragglers. They came singly, in pairs, and in small groups to join the swell of humanity trudging along the road. They were the refugees of a defeated army but not a beaten one. There was no panic and Morgan heard more jokes than complaints. Listening to conversations around him he came to the conclusion the American army had not been beaten decisively but had certainly been outmaneuvered.

Each time a new group would emerge from the woods to join the mob plodding along the road they would be greeted with good-natured ridicule. "Why, we thought you lads were back fighting the lobsters all by yourselves, and here you've been skedaddlin'."

"Look who's talking; I see you boys got here ahead of us."

"You got it all wrong. General Washington, himself, ordered us back to protect stragglers such as yourself from the redcoats."

The lighthearted banter continued as groups formed into companies and companies into regiments. By nightfall, as the campsite was laid out, the mob was once again an army; rations were issued, cookfires were lit, and the men were already bragging about how they would defeat the British in the next battle.

"Have you set the date yet, Molly?" Keary looked up from the column of figures she had been studying.

"Sometime in the spring. Jamie wants to make it sooner but he's letting the itch in his britches get the better of his thinking. We need to finish our house and get some proper furniture."

"What are you doing, completely rebuilding the house?"

"Practically, but it will be awfully nice when we finish, considering it was only a coach house to begin with. We figure it will take 'til spring just working a few hours a night."

"You could live here—at least for a while. I have much more room than I need." Molly turned from placing more of her wares on the shelf behind the counter and squeezed Keary's arm.

"Thanks, love, but I know Jamie. So long as he knows I

won't marry him 'til it's finished, he'll stay with it. If I married him first, it would never get done."

Keary began immediately to think of ways to hasten Molly's wedding. If Jamie were to pay her for the material and pay the apprentices for their extra time, he could make more tinware for Molly to paint and sell. They could make enough money in a few weeks to hire the remodeling. While the idea seemed a good one, her conscience told her to mind her own business. Molly and Jamie were happy finishing the house in their own way. She walked over to where Molly was dabbing a spot here and a spot there on a small cannister.

"Molly, I want to buy your gown and Jamie's suit for a wedding present. A white satin with lots of lace for you and a deep blue velvet suit for Jamie."

For a moment Molly's eyes were dreamy and she was deep in some faraway fantasy land, then she shook her head and laughed. "Keary, I know you mean well, but as big as I am and with lots of lace I'd look like Mr. Griffin's cow all dressed up for Christmas. And what would I do with a dress like that? Pack it away for my daughter's wedding? For a lot less money I could get a dress and keep it for my good dress to wear to parties or something special for a long time. As for Jamie, if I came at him with a velvet suit, he would run so fast I would never catch him again."

Suddenly Keary realized Molly had never had a really good dress her whole life and she made a silent vow this one would be of the finest material, designed by one of the best dressmakers in Philadelphia. "All right, Molly, you and I will pick out the material for both the dress and suit and I'll pay for them. Business has been really good lately. People are spending money like water and the entire town seems to have caught the fever. They can't get rid of their money fast enough."

"I know. The best part is that no one haggles anymore. I tell them a price and they pay it. We're selling more japanned ware than plain—and that reminds me, on the blacksmith side of the shop we need more stock of every kind; Mr. Wykoff just can't produce enough."

"Since we can't keep up with the demand, I'm going to start buying a lot of things for resale. I'll hire two more girls and you can train one for sales and teach one to paint."

"One will be enough, Keary. We don't need the expense of two right now."

"I'm not thinking of now. I'm thinking of the future and I have big plans."

Morgan was invited to share mess with the group he had marched with all day and by now he had learned they were the First Maryland, a regiment already rich in laurels and destined for a lot more before the war was over. For three more days they marched north, poorly shod feet kicking up huge clouds of dust on roads dried out by the late summer sun. The army was now concentrated around the Warwick Tavern and Morgan knew he was within twenty miles of Philadelphia. At first light he would leave the army and complete the last leg of his journey. For a while that evening, sitting by the fire, he wished his responsibilities would take wings, leaving him free to join this army. Fighting a war would not be so bad if he could dream of returning to Keary at the end. After gazing into the dancing flames for a while he jerked himself back to reality. He had responsibilities and tomorrow he must return to Philadelphia and do what he must do.

The following morning, however, the army was not given the luxury of sleeping until dawn. At three bells drumrolls broke the stillness of the night and grumbling soldiers rose, munched on cold rations, and formed ranks. Morgan was about to bid his comrades good-bye when he saw a horse being hitched to an ambulance cart. He walked over to where a crew was carefully loading a wounded man.

"Sergeant, does that man have a musket and powder he won't be using?"

"'Spect so, why?"

"Well if this early morning formation means what I think it does, there'll be fighting before this day's over and I thought maybe I'd give you boys a hand."

"Now that's interesting. The rest of us is gonna git our rears shot at 'cause we ain't got no choice in the matter, but you have. So why would you willingly decide to chance making this your last day on earth?"

"It's a long story; let's just say the lobsters did me a wrong turn once and this is my way of getting even."

"All right, Mister"—he handed Morgan the musket and cartouche box—"you just go with these here fellers you been sharing mess with and they'll show you what to do. But I'm warning you this ain't gonna be no turkey shoot. General Howe's got himself one hell of an army out there and afore this day's history there's gonna be a lot of dead sojers on that field."

"I know, Sergeant, but I still want to go."

"Then I 'spect you got some pretty good reasons, but a word of advice."

"Yes?"

"If you're a praying man, this ain't a bad time to start."

By first light the regiment had already covered three miles and were deploying in battle formation. Morgan joined the others in an age-old military maneuver—hurry up and wait.

The sun painted a fiery red glow on the eastern horizon, which turned into a soft orange before the entire sky faded into a brilliant blue—and still they waited. A few gray-white clouds ambled in from the west and within an hour the whole western sky was a mixture of gray and black. The command to advance was given and immediately rescinded, and again they waited. Millions of leaves on trees and bushes shivered in a freshening breeze as small cones of dust rose from the nearby road and disappeared over the rolling hills and forests.

A courier galloped up, talked to the colonel a few moments, and continued on. The drums rolled, ranks again formed, and the advance was renewed.

A long shadow spread across the field as onrushing dark clouds tumbled over each other in a race to blot out the sun and erase the last vestige of blue from the lowering sky. Each new gust of wind was stronger than its predecessor and trees lowered their branches cowardly before the oncoming gale. Other drums were heard between the wind gusts, and on a slight rise across a wheat field, Morgan watched in awe as long scarlet lines began to form in a manner so precise as to put the Americans to shame. Without sunlight to dance off polished steel, the glistening British bayonets could not be seen at that distance, but every veteran soldier on the field knew they were there. The first raindrops were so large and scattered, each could be identified by its loud spat as it struck the earth. The angry clouds sent long black tendrils down to the tops of trees, and in the distance the oncoming rain appeared as an airborne waterfall.

As the distance between the two armies narrowed to four hundred yards, they couldn't see each other through the blinding rain nor could any one soldier see more than a dozen of his comrades. Soldiers began wrapping rags and holding hats over flintlocks, trying to keep their powder dry. Morgan followed suit but within moments his cartouche box was soaked through. Not only was the leather pouch worn badly, but it seemed its designer envisioned a war fought entirely in fair weather. Soon the command was given to withdraw and the regiment trudged north again. This time as they reached the same crossroads, Morgan turned right and resumed his journey to Philadelphia. As the mud deepened and each step became a chore, he gained a deeper appreciation of a soldier's life.

After two and a half days of tugging mud-heavy boots out of a clinging earth unwilling to release them, Morgan was a weary traveler when he arrived in Philadelphia. The forlorn figure entering the tinshop on Spruce Street bore little resemblance to the Virginia gentleman who left four weeks before, but this mattered little to Keary. She loved the man beneath the dirt and grime and her warm embrace said this eloquently.

"Morgan, I didn't expect you back so soon. Is everything all right?"

"Yes. At least there's nothing wrong a good hot bath won't cure." Seeing her again he cursed the cruel fate that dictated he marry Deborah.

After a hot bath and a welcome meal, he told Keary of

his problems at Banetree and his subsequent adventure. He was thankful that Molly's presence precluded a romantic interlude with Keary since he would soon have to tell her of his intentions. His plans to tell her immediately had gone by the wayside the moment her arms closed around his neck and he looked into her dancing blue eyes. He told himself it was because of the possibility Deborah might refuse but knew this to be a lame excuse.

Molly rose and grabbed her shawl as the lumbering feet on the stairs announced Jamie, arriving to escort her home. As the door closed behind them, Keary quickly pounced on Morgan's lap and winding her arms about his neck, smothered his lips, drinking in his kiss as a dusty desert flower drinks in the first refreshing drops of rain. Despite all his resolutions to the contrary, Morgan responded immediately, caressing her and pouring out his love in a torrent of tender words. He fondled the curves of her lithe body, his hands roaming intimately over her breast, his manhood threatening to burst through the thin summer breeches. As she writhed in his arms, he rose and carried her to the bedroom, his lips locked to hers. Not until he began to untie the laces of her stomacher did he realize his intent and he suddenly froze. *This isn't fair*, he thought, *making love to her when I'm planning to wed another*. Pulling back from her willing body, he said, "Keary, will you get me a glass of wine?"

"A glass of wine?" She stared at him in disbelief but thinking he wanted to prolong the ecstasy, she shrugged her shoulders and bounded out of bed. When she returned, after struggling for what seemed like hours with the stubborn cork, his deep, even breathing and slack mouth fooled her into thinking he was sound asleep.

Morgan slept soundly until late the next morning when he was awakened to the sound of Keary singing her old Irish ballad in the kitchen. The night before, after the initial shock of her disappointment wore off, she had removed his boots and folded the faded quilt gently around his prone body. She realized he must be exhausted after trudging through miles of sucking mud, but tomorrow he would be well rested and they would resume where they left off. She had undressed and slipped noiselessly in beside him.

Morgan lay awake, maintaining the slow, steady breathing as he valiantly fought the almost unsurmountable urge to turn to the warm, vibrant body curled up to his. She held his upper arm snugly between her breasts and the back of his knuckles reposed against soft, warm thighs. He summoned tremendous willpower to hold his arm still. Once he was sure she was sleeping, he gave in to exhaustion and slept soundly.

He rose quickly when he woke to her lilting voice, not trusting his behavior a second time if she realized he was awake. When he entered the common room calling a cheery good morning, she flew to his arms raising her face for the searing kiss that always sent currents of desire racing up her spine. Instead his kiss was a gentle pressure to her lips before he placed his arm around her waist and walked to the table. Puzzled, she placed the hot food on his plate and sat down quietly opposite him. The breakfast of hot gruel, johnnycake, and cold pork was a banquet after army fare, and he was relaxing over several cups of black coffee when the sound of drums rolled through the open window. Keary hurried to the window and, seeing rows of British soldiers coming up the street, ran back and pulled on Morgan's arm.

"Let's go down to the street. I want to get closer." They hurried over to Walnut Street and watched as a regiment of redcoats swung smartly by, in perfect time to the cadence of drums. A large segment of the crowd was cheering and here and there Union Jacks already fluttered from windows.

"Are they ready to change sides so suddenly?" Keary asked in disbelief.

"I'm afraid many of them will always be on the side of whoever's winning at the time." He spat disgustedly. "There was a time I would have been cheering myself, but I believe that time has passed forever."

"What changed your mind, the prison hulks?"

"That had a lot to do with it, but those few days with the American army has made me look at things in a different way. I can't forget those men risking everything they have, including their lives, for a cause they believe in. For the right of self-determination, they endure every kind of hardship and privation imaginable. I'm beginning to see what a great country men like these could build, and once Banetree is secure I'm thinking seriously of joining the American army."

"I know what you mean." She squeezed his arm, studying the rugged features, happy his plans of becoming a British citizen were behind him. "Jamie is an avowed rebel but can't serve in the army because of his leg. But strange as it may seem, Molly is more devoted to the cause than Jamie. Of course her revolutionary spirit and hatred of everything British had fertile ground to grow on in Ireland. I understand some of her family were very much involved in the Irish rebellion."

"If that's the case, I'm surprised you're not an ardent rebel too."

"Perhaps I would have been had the British attacked Philadelphia when I first arrived. But with the war so far away I was more interested in making money. It may be just as well though. When I watched the American army march through the city I felt they would give the redcoats a good battle, but it seems I was wrong." The crowds watching the entrance of the British troops began breaking up and Keary and Morgan picked their way through clustered groups. Guiding her past the last knot of excited loyalists, Morgan waited until they were out of earshot before continuing the conversation.

"It wasn't their lack of courage that caused the loss of the capitol. It was a rainstorm."

She turned to him in disbelief. "A rainstorm! I don't understand."

"It's the truth. Washington was ready to attack when a sudden rainstorm came up and all of the powder was soaked and useless. Had he proceeded with the battle, it would have been fought with the bayonet and Americans are not trained in that kind of warfare, while the British are the best in the world. Americans are at their best when they can take advantage of their superior marksmanship. Washington had to decide between giving up a city or suffering serious damage to his army and I believe he made the right choice."

They had arrived at a grassy parkland leading down to the river. Trees were filled with silver-white glints of sun and wild flowers opened wide on slender green stems.

Morgan stretched under a tree and pulled Keary down beside him.

She had been puzzled by his coolness and so felt an extra thrill at being close to him again. She was prepared for his tender words but was instead surprised when he said, "Yes, the fortunes of war turn on strange things and this time it was wet powder."

A slight pout crossed her lips as she asked, "Don't they have some way to keep the powder dry?"

"They have cartouche boxes but most of them are homemade from anything they can get their hands on, including wood and leather. They wear out, crack, and break from hard use."

"I thought they kept powder in those little horns. Some of the ones I've seen were beautiful and looked as if they had been made by artists."

"Only the riflemen from the frontier use powder horns. They hunt for most of their meat and have years of experience fighting Indians. They are the best marksmen in the world but in close combat their rifles are no match for muskets. They take too long to load and can't be fitted for bayonets."

He glanced over at her long, shimmering black tresses, soft, creamy complexion, and that small but square chin that could show such determination at one time, yet blend so easily with her soft femininity at others. He wanted to forget discussions of war and take her in his arms. It was a beautiful day and she seemed in a very romantic mood, yet his conscience would not allow him to exploit her. Heaving a sigh, he continued, "Regulars carry muskets and long before a battle, the powder is measured, rolled in paper called a cartouche, and stored in a box. Under fire, the soldiers bite off the end of a cartouche and pour the powder in the barrel of a musket. They drop in a lead bullet, ram it home, prime the pan, and it's ready to fire. A well-trained soldier can do it in a third of the time it takes to load a rifle."

"How is a rifle loaded differently?"

"They're much longer with spiral grooves in the barrel. A ball fits much tighter and has to be driven down the long barrel. This gives them greater accuracy than a looser fitting ball in a short smoothbore musket. I doubt it's very comfortable standing there measuring powder from one of those horns and drivng the ball home with bullets flying past your ears."

"Why don't they make the boxes out of tin?"

"Most of them make their own and don't have tin, or wouldn't know how to work it if they did."

"Morgan, let's go back to the shop and talk to Jamie. I'll bet he could make a box that could be submerged in water and still keep the powder dry."

Within hours, Jamie had a cartouche box designed to hold thirty rounds and which would stay dry in a hurricane. They exclaimed over the exactness of his work and Jamie, flustered, said, "I saved the pattern, Miss Keary. I thought you would want to make more of them."

"Yes, Jamie, we'll have to continue our regular production, but we'll devote some time each day to these. Can we trust the lads not to mention this outside of the shop?"

"I dunno, Miss, that may be a problem."

Morgan, studying the box approvingly, said, "I see no problem with secrecy regarding the manufacture of spice boxes. Being practically airtight, these will keep spices fresh and should sell like hotcakes." He sat the box on

345

the bench and grinning at Jamie's bewildered look continued, "Yes, I foresee ladies wanting spice boxes in every state on the continent."

A slight frown knitted Keary's brow as she looked from Jamie to Morgan. "The boxes are fine, but I think we have overlooked one small detail. Now that the British occupy Philadelphia, how are we going to get these to Washington?"

"You make them; I'll get them to Washington." Anxiety gnawed at Keary at the thought of Morgan smuggling contraband past the British lines but she said nothing.

As Morgan left the shop mulling over a plan to smuggle the "spice boxes" to the rebels he told himself it would not be wise to ask for Deborah's hand until he had completed the plan in his mind and tested it in action. Actually, though he didn't put it into words, his reasoning was that if he didn't propose to Deborah immediately then it naturally followed he was under no moral obligation to tell Keary now. Of course he would have to avoid serious lovemaking and make no further mention of a future together at Banetree. But at least he could see her, feel her closeness, and allow her entrance into his dreams.

A few days later Sam, one of the peddlers who regularly replenished his stock at the shop, stopped for merchandise. He was nosing around the shelves and tables wanting to be sure he didn't miss new items while Keary filled his order, when she casually asked, "Sam, how do you get by the sentries to peddle your wares?" She had thought for the duration of the British occupation that the peddler trade would be lost because most of them worked territories held by rebels.

"The sentries don't bother me none, Miss, since I'm an honest merchant going about my business. It seems the British are interested in keeping things as close to normal as possible. And then, o'course, there are these." He reached into one of the long flapping pockets of the tattered, collarless waistcoat and unfolded a broadside, the propaganda sheet used by both sides to influence the populace. Keary studied the paper and saw it was an invitation to all persons outside the city to come in and swear allegiance to the king.

Sam tapped the paper with a long, dirty finger. "As long as I agree to give one o' these to people I meet on my travels, I'm free to come and go as I please." He grinned his crooked yellow-toothed grin and dropped a pale-lashed eyelid in a mocking wink, "O'course, the whole stack seems to catch on fire accidentally as soon as I'm past the sentries."

Later that day Keary told Morgan of the peddler's tale and was puzzled by the sprightly gleam in his eyes. Several days later another peddler in slouched hat and homespun lazily unwound his tall frame and leaped to the sidewalk. He tethered his horse and sauntered into the shop.

"Morgan! Whatever are you doing in that ridiculous outfit?"

He doffed his hat, and except for the dancing eyes, his face was serious. "Why, starting my spice box delivery service, of course. I found an old peddler who lost his desire to tour a countryside infested with soldiers and decided to retire to the safety of His Majesty's troops." Keary's face was filled with concern and to allay her fears, he said, "On my first trip I'll only carry a few boxes to show to some American officers. I'll stop at one of the outlying towns and have a carpenter build a false bottom in the wagon so, on later trips, I can haul them in quantity." When her eyes remained bleak and unsure, he said, "After a few trips, I'll have the American officers find someone to take my place so I can leave for Banetree. I'll have to attempt to put off my creditors for a few more months." He knew his recent actions were deceitful and the decent thing to do would be to tell her everything. But not even his recent adventure of facing the British across that field struck so much terror in his heart. He vowed to tell her after the trip and snapped the reins.

Keary puzzled over Morgan's strange behavior as she watched him drive off. When he first came back she was sure it was to ask for her hand. Since then he had acted more like a friend than a lover and was now talking of returning to Banetree. Something had changed since that beautiful night he poured out his love but she didn't have the slightest hint of what it was.

Tears welled up in her large blue eyes as he left. Why didn't he find excuses to be alone with her? Why didn't he call in the evening when Molly was away working with Jamie on their house? Every night Keary had donned a pretty dress, arranged her hair, put enough food for both of them in the kettle, and then sat and waited—and waited. He came around fairly often but always during the day when it was awkward for them to slip away. Where did he spend his evenings and why didn't he come to see her then? He must know she was ready to take up where they left off his first night back. She remembered his passion that night and knew he couldn't have suddenly lost all that desire. Should she confront him and ask for an explanation? It seemed the sensible thing to do but somehow her pride wouldn't allow it.

Keary wasn't the only one who watched Morgan drive off. Across the street a well-dressed figure stood hidden behind a parked carriage and studied the scene with a puzzled frown. *What the devil is Morgan Baines doing dressed like that? And what is he doing driving a peddler's wagon?* As he watched the wagon disappear around the corner, Jason Wentworth's gaze went back to the tinshop. Something strange was going on here and he vowed to get to the bottom of it.

"Halt! State your name and business, tinker."

The arrogant sentry reminded Morgan of his days on the hulks and he restrained himself from saying "My business is cheating the British at any cost." But he had mentally rehearsed his part well and said, "Tinkerin' Tim's the name and tradin's my game." The sentry's eyes traveled from the disheveled hair to a three-day's growth of beard covering a cheek swollen with a wad of tobacco. They continued down the dirty linsey-woolsey shirt, leather breeches, and muddy farm boots, then back again to the sweat-stained, broad-brimmed hat.

"Are you carrying any broadsides?"

"Yes Sir, Sergeant, and I aim to spread the news far and wide that good King George is ready to forgive and forget. 'Spect you'll see lots of loyal subjects headin' into town once I spread the word." After poking through the wagon, the sentry accepted a bottle of rum without bothering to thank the donor. The tinker snapped the reins, spitting dangerously close to the sentry's foot, and drove off whistling "The Grenadier's March."

Morgan parked the wagon at a small tavern and entered the dimly lit interior. So far the trip had been uneventful and his disguise was so authentic that he actually made a couple of sales. Adjusting his eyes to the shadowed room, he saw a colonel and a major at a table and made his way toward them. Nodding his head in greeting he said, "Colonel, I was wondering if the American army could make use of a cartouche box like this." He set the box on the table and watched as the wide-eyed officers examined it in detail.

"Where did you get this, tinker?"

"I'm afraid I'm not at liberty to discuss that right now, Sir, but I can get a lot more of them. If you can put me in touch with an officer empowered to deal with me, I'll be much obliged."

"General Greene has just been made quartermaster for the whole army and his headquarters are only a mile down the road. Come along; I'm sure he will be very interested."

They traveled along a winding ribbon of dusty road to a small white clapboard house. Morgan remained outside as the colonel passed the single sentry guarding the door. In a few minutes the colonel signalled for Morgan to enter. General Greene sat at a badly scarred wooden table, his pen scratching, and the colonel quietly motioned Morgan to a chair. The general was in shirt sleeves, his collar open and the stock shifted to the side. Morgan saw the stiff leg held out at an angle under the table and noticed the way the general held his head slightly sideways as he wrote. When he finally looked up, Morgan could see why. The right eye was blemished and watered heavily and no doubt the general had been favoring it. He dusted sand on the letter and set it aside.

"Did you make this cartouche box, tinker?" Morgan was startled by the directness of his approach. His soft, cultured voice seemed out of place with his businesslike countenance.

"I'm not a tinker, general, and couldn't make such a box if my life depended on it."

"Where did you get it?"

"In Philadelphia. I know the smith who made it."

"I see. Did you just come from Philadelphia?"

Morgan had been sitting in the chair, holding the battered hat between his knees. At the general's question he rose and walked slowly to the desk. "Yes. Do you want information on British troops there? I can't tell you very much other than what regiments I have personally seen."

"I'll want to talk to you about that later. Now you say you can get more of these? How much will they cost?"

"The smith would have to be paid for the tin, but there would be no charge for the labor and no profit."

"Then we'll be happy to get as many as we can. How many can you deliver?"

"I intend to find a carpenter to build a false bottom in the wagon and will be able to deliver about two hundred at a time."

"There will be a reliable carpenter at the tavern in the morning. Now tell me, how are things in Philadelphia?"

Morgan told him of the large segments of the population who had immediately swung to the British. The general frowned as if he had heard the story before. He asked a few pointed questions and finding Morgan was unable to provide vital information he didn't already know, he changed the subject.

"You say you are not a tinker, Mr.—"

"Baines, Sir. Morgan Baines."

He motioned for Morgan to sit again. "What is your

trade, Mr. Baines?"

"I'm a planter, Sir, from Virginia."

The amiable general laughed as he adjusted his stiff leg. "It seems we are both out of our element then. I'm an iron forger turned soldier—and now quartermaster against my will; but then, orders are orders." He reached for the pen again and Morgan sensed the interview was over.

He rose to leave and called from the door, "There's an old friend of the family serving in this army. If you should happen to see him, I would appreciate it if you would convey my respects."

"I'll be glad to. What is his name?"

"George Washington. His plantation is very near mine."

The general smiled briefly and slanted his head to the paper, saying, "Yes, I seem to recall someone by that name."

A week later, using a different road, Morgan hauled the first full load of cartouche boxes through the British lines. The trip went without incident and he returned the next day. It would be another week before Jamie had enough boxes for another trip, so Morgan set out to search for a place to keep the horse and wagon. It would be difficult explaining to the stable owner how he could make a living on one brief trip a week, and Morgan decided it would be better to keep the wagon outside the city between trips. He secured Quaker clothes and made arrangements to enter and leave the city on different produce wagons that made the trip daily.

For the first time in several months time became

Morgan's enemy. In the old days he had no trouble finding ways to fill idle time but lately he was becoming somewhat of a recluse. It was necessary to make a few social calls on Deborah in order that his proposal would seem more honest. During these visits he tried valiantly to develop some affection for her but her peevish ways compared to Keary's open and honest personality made this impossible. Everything she said or did found him analyzing it critically and then remembering opposite reactions of Keary's.

He would hold off seeing Keary as long as he could stand it and then his visits were confined to daytime hours, when it would be impossible to be alone with her.

Morgan had rented a small room when he found it impossible to stay at Deborah's constantly, explaining he had to leave town for a few days and then, on his return, making the excuse he had come back late at night and didn't want to disturb her. Each day he had to make up another excuse but this was preferable to being with her continuously.

Everything in his plans said the time was ripe to ask for Deborah's hand and to tell Keary that it was all over between them forever. Still, he always managed to convince himself that it would do no harm to wait one more day.

Chapter XXII

Finally the cartouche box operation was running smoothly and Morgan had trained two other men that General Greene had sent for the purpose. He could find no more excuses to postpone the inevitable.

After changing clothes in his small room, Morgan walked the six blocks to Deborah Thornton's house as if he were going to a funeral. He could no longer put off asking Deborah to be his wife but something within him hoped she would refuse. Upon being ushered into the parlor, he was surprised to find a British captain waiting there.

"I'm Captain Ellsworth." The immaculately attired officer bowed stiffly.

"Morgan Baines at your service, Sir."

The captain made clear at once that he and Deborah had plans for the evening. "Miss Thornton is attending the theatre with me."

"Good evening, Captain—Morgan! What a pleasant surprise! When did you arrive?" The surprise was feigned as Deborah swept into the parlor. Morgan was sure the servant had lost no time informing his mistress of the identity of another gentleman caller.

"Just this very minute, Deborah." He enjoyed seeing the captain's discomfort at his use of her given name.

She had been holding onto his arm, gazing adoringly into his face. At his reply, she playfully slapped his wrist with her folded fan. "You know very well what I mean. When did you get back to Philadelphia?"

"Today. I only took time to change and came right over, but the captain tells me you're going to the theatre; it seems my timing was bad. I was concerned how you were faring. You know I hate to leave you alone since your father's death. It's a relief to see you are bearing up well enough to resume some social life."

"Actually, I've been very lonely sitting here night after night by myself so I finally decided to accept an invitation." She avoided looking at the captain, sure his mouth had dropped open, knowing he had seen her out almost every night since the British arrived.

"Well, now that I know you're over your grief, I feel much relieved. I'll be going now; you don't want to be late for the theatre."

"Why don't you come with us? I'm sure the captain wouldn't mind, would you Captain Ellsworth?" Her fluttering lashes beseeched him so imploringly, Morgan almost felt sorry for the poor fellow.

The officer began stammering and Morgan came to his rescue. "I'm sorry, Deborah, it would be impossible this evening since I have already made other plans. I only stopped to see how you were doing."

She turned to the captain, the snap of her opening fan cracking across the stillness of the room. Waving it furiously in an attempt to cool her ire, she said, "Excuse us, Captain, I'll see Mr. Baines to the door." Once out of earshot, she whispered behind the fan, "Surely you don't think there is anything between the captain and myself, Morgan—something that would keep you from calling?"

"Of course not, Deborah."

"Good, but just to prove it, I'll expect you for supper tomorrow night at seven—just the two of us."

"That would be fine." He stepped out into the early fall air feeling like a condemned man. Until tonight there was always a chance she would refuse him but her adoring eyes this evening banished all hope.

Keary checked the table setting one more time, moving the napkins and adjusting the flame on the whale oil lamp. Why she was so nervous, she didn't know. She and Morgan had dined together often but it had always been impromptu. When she invited him he was very reluctant to accept, offering a number of weak excuses, but she had refused to take no for an answer. She vowed to find the reason for his recent change of attitude even if it meant confronting him with direct questions.

Whether or not the six hundred pounds she intended giving him would make a difference in his situation, she had no way of knowing, but it provided fodder for fond dreams and she expected this evening would be something special. If his attitude had to do with his worries over Banetree, maybe this money would help.

She heard slow, deliberate treads on the steps and wondered who could be calling. Morgan was the only one she was expecting but he always bounded up the steps two at a time. She opened the door and, seeing his serious expression, knew immediately something was very wrong. "Come in, Morgan. You look as though you're carrying the world on your shoulders."

He grinned halfheartedly and removed his tricorn. "No, just North America."

"Well—I have something here which might help cheer you." She handed him the small drawstring bag full of gold coins. "There is six hundred pounds to repay my debt."

"But the debt was only five hundred." He eyed her warily. Had Benjamin told her the source of the funds used to purchase her indenture?

"The amount includes profit and since I did very well with the money, it's only fair. There will be more as I collect it."

"Don't you still need operating capital?"

"Not since I decided against building. Both shops are doing very well and all my tenements are rented at exorbitant prices. Some of the tenants have paid as much as a year in advance to insure their accommodations. If you need more money, I'm in a position now to loan you some."

"No, thanks, I'll send this off to Banetree immediately. It will buy a few necessities." He turned away, refusing to meet her eyes. "And now I must tell you something I've been dreading. I won't ever have to borrow money again; I'm going to marry Deborah Thornton."

Keary dropped into a chair. The room was spinning and she fought to regain her breath while his words pounded in her brain like some maddening chant. Finally, after an awful silence, she addressed his back. "Why? I know you don't love her."

"No, Keary. I can't lie to you, I don't love her. But I

need her money to save Banetree."

"But, I can raise money. I can—" She had risen and was walking unsteadily to his side.

He wheeled around, his voice strained and harsher than he intended. He hated himself for what he was doing to her. "Do you have any idea of the enormous expense of that place? And with no income the situation gets worse every day this damned war goes on."

She wanted to argue with him, make him see what he was doing was wrong, but she realized the truth of what he said. When she pictured Deborah sharing his life and Banetree, tears she had held back came to her eyes, magnifying and distorting the scene into a hazy blur, and she ran from the room. Throwing herself on the bed, she sobbed uncontrollably, unaware of the slow, heavy footsteps descending the stairs. She cried until there were no tears left and spent the remainder of the night staring out at the few flickering street lamps until the windows of nearby buildings gave off the fire of the morning sun.

She had fought visions of Morgan and Deborah all night. The two of them walking down the aisle of Christ Church in white satin and black velvet, standing side by side greeting guests at the huge reception, whirling in each other's arms in the large ballroom as violinists wove their haunting tunes for dancing feet, and finally, the worst vision of all—Deborah in Morgan's powerful arms with only his sandy hair and her blond tresses showing above the blankets of the large bed.

Her only comfort was her certain knowledge that the marriage was one of convenience. Morgan didn't love Deborah. The knowledge that many gentlemen married for wealth soothed the ache in her head, but nothing could ease the pain in her heart. She feared the wedding would take place soon if things at Banetree were as desperate as Morgan's tone indicated. Still, he couldn't be foreclosed on without due process and she prayed he would hold out as long as possible. And not even one as brazen as Deborah would marry this soon after her father's death. A small flicker of hope emerged and Keary's mind began functioning again. If she could make enough money to save Banetree, even for a little while, maybe he would call off the wedding.

She splashed water from the pitcher to the basin and refreshed herself. After changing into work clothes, she repaired her hair and went out to stare dully at the beautifully arranged table. With a deep sigh, she cleared the table and set the blackened whale oil lamp in the kitchen. The charred pans of burnt food were removed from the cranes and oven of the cold fireplace and placed on the cupboard to soak before she went down to the shop to begin another day's work.

For the next several weeks Keary worked night and day. She paid little heed when the city reeled in shocked disbelief at the audacity of Washington attacking Howe's entire army at Germantown, a little village only a few miles from Philadelphia. The sound of guns had been heard plainly in the city, beginning before dawn and lasting some three hours. After an all-day wait for news the battle was hailed as a British victory, but knowledgeable people were cognizant of Howe's forces pulling back closer to the city and digging fortifications. But even limited British celebrations were short-lived as the next news jolted Philadelphia to its very foundations.

Lieutenant Boyle, a British officer, told her of this defeat when he came to the shop one day with a face longer than a frontiersman's rifle. He dropped in almost every day on some pretense, usually an invitation for Keary to accompany him to some social event. Usually he wore a broad smile on his well-arranged features and began his conversations with lighthearted, well-rehearsed banter enriched by a broad array of compliments. His dejected mood this day didn't concern her too much as British troubles were usually welcome to her.

"Good morning, Lieutenant. You look as if you have just been demoted to private."

"It's worse than that, Miss Cavanaugh. Our army has suffered a humiliating defeat."

"How could that be? Surely we would have heard the sound of guns if there was another battle." She lowered her eyes to the counter to conceal her hopeful excitement.

"Not around here, Miss. At a place called Saratoga, way up in the woods of New York along the Hudson River."

Remembering discussions with Morgan, she said, "That's where Burgoyne's army is, isn't it? Did he retreat?" She managed to keep her face grave even though her heart was racing.

"Worse. He surrendered his entire army. It's probably the most decisive action of the whole damned war and we lost."

Keary wanted to throw up her arms and cheer and Molly, sitting at her table just inside the door of the shop, was making clucking noises as if she were choking. Keary glanced in at Molly and asked warily, "How many—that is, he must have saved something."

Lieutenant Boyle shook his head, strutting back and forth in front of the counter in his irritation. "I'm not sure; some say as high as seven thousand of the best troops in the world! And, of course, all his guns, powder, wagons—everything he had."

Keary saw Molly rise from her chair, grinning from ear to ear, and retreat farther into the shop. A minute later, loud laughter erupting from the shop indicated Molly had told Jamie. Keary tried to concentrate on what Lieutenant Boyle was saying while her mind raced happily, assimilating the tremendous impact this victory would have on American independence.

"I was on my way here to invite you to a ball this Saturday when I heard the news, so you'll have to forgive me if the invitation doesn't sound as enthusiastic as I planned."

She was about to couch her refusal as pleasantly as possible when she was reminded of Morgan's forthcoming wedding. "What ball, Lieutenant?"

"It's to be held at the City Tavern by the officers of the Forty-seventh Foot. There's to be a lavish dinner and dancing afterward. I was very fortunate to get two tickets, since every officer in the city wants to go."

Keary wondered how popular the tickets would have been if the Saratoga news had been known at the time. Such news could dampen the party spirit of even the imperturbable British. The thought amused her and contributed to her decision to attend. But the deciding factor was a resolution that she was not going to let Morgan's impending wedding turn her into a social hermit, and Lieutenant Boyle was the perfect escort. He was the type she could handle easily, and since he was British, she had no qualms about using him. "I'd be delighted, Lieutenant. What time will you call for me?"

His face brightened for a second but it was evident his mind had not left that remote battlefield in New York. "Will eight of the clock be satisfactory to you?"

"Fine. I'm looking forward to a gala evening." She watched his subdued figure retreat through the doorway as Molly and Jamie hurried to her side and the three of them laughed and talked over the defeat of the mighty British.

Morgan dressed slowly, not looking forward to the evening's activities. At Deborah's insistence, he was living again in her house but had evaded her subtle hints to share her bedroom. Deborah was a beautiful woman and he couldn't explain, even to himself, how he was able to resist her charms. He had always thought of women as something to be exploited and his conquests were much the same as any sporting event, but that was before he met Keary. Since then, all other women paled in comparison and every moment without her was agony. Since the night he had told her of his wedding plans and saw her grief, he couldn't forgive himself nor think of another woman romantically. He fought a constant urge to ask her forgiveness and take his chances on saving Banetree, but when faced with hard facts he knew he mustn't do it.

A slight knock on the door interrupted his musings. The butler bowed stiffly and announced, "A messenger to see you, Sir. From Virginia, he said."

"Thank you, Robinson. Show him up here, please." Shortly afterwards Lester, the son of Banetree's overseer, entered the room. He was long of bone and lean of flesh. His suntanned complexion would take on an altogether different appearance when a lack of summer sun turned the tan to freckle-dotted paleness. He held a broad-brimmed hat and brushed back a crop of unruly blond hair.

"Pa said to thank you for the money, Mr. Baines, and to let you know it got through all right. But he says he needs an awful lot more." He advanced and handed Morgan a packet of letters.

"Tell your pa not to worry, Lester. I'll soon have plenty." Morgan began thumbing through the letters, sighing as one after another were duns from creditors. "How is my brother these days?"

"Mister Simon? Why—ah—haven't you heard? Your brother passed away, Sir."

"When?" Morgan's shock startled the youngster and he groped for words.

"Why—ah—last week, Sir. He left a note there was to be no funeral and not even the neighbors were to be told. But we thought someone would write you. Maybe there's something in that letter I brought you."

Morgan opened the letter from Mr. Benson explaining the circumstances of Simon's death due to an overdose of medication. The letter avoided the word "suicide" but Morgan knew, in reading between the lines, that Simon's death was planned. After the initial shock wore off, Morgan had to admit his brother was better off. He looked at the fidgeting lad and asked, "Is Captain Hardy still hanging around, or has he decided to leave and return when the British pull out of the bay?"

"You ain't heard about him either, Mr. Baines?"

"Heard what? Don't tell me the British found the ship?"

363

"No, Sir. When the whole British fleet was there, the captain called all his men together for a meeting. He had an idea to slip out and anchor right in the middle of the British ships. Then as some of the British ships were unloaded and started to leave, he would just leave with them. He warned his men if they were caught, they would probably be pressed into the British Navy or taken to the hulks in New York, but if they got through, there would be a big share for every last one of them. He passed out a lot of rum and they talked about it a long time. When they finally got under way, I didn't think there was one of them sober enough to climb the rigging to set sails, but somehow they did and the next morning the ship was anchored right smack in the middle of the British fleet. Last time I saw the ship, it was sailing proud as could be down the bay. She was part of a British convoy and carried a Union Jack on her mast."

Morgan couldn't believe what he was hearing. So there was a chance of selling the tobacco after all! His first thought was to call off the wedding and tell Keary immediately, but cool reasoning took over. First the captain had to sail the entire length of the Chesapeake Bay with a British convoy and not be questioned. Once out in the Atlantic Ocean he would have watch for an opportunity to slip away from them at night and slip by another British blockade off the French coast. After selling the tobacco, he would have to elude the same blockades a second time and return. The odds were long and if the ship was captured by the British, there would be the agony of hurting Keary a second time. And to face the pain in her eyes again was more than he could bear. The ray of hope did, however, convince him to delay the wedding as long as possible. Looking at the stack o letters, he decided to answer them all tomorrow and buy every day he could.

"Did you have any trouble getting through the British lines? I understand they have tightened up security all around the city."

"No, Sir. I saw a farmer bringing in a load of produce and just sort of fell in beside the wagon. I guess I look enough like a farmer no one bothered to question me, but they did seem to be checking some others awful close."

Morgan was thinking of the next load of cartouche boxes. Perhaps it was time to disassociate himself from the operation. He couldn't save Banetree locked up in a British prison and he didn't want to face Keary when he had to pick up a load.

"Morgan, we're going to be late. Please hurry, darling." Deborah's voice came through the closed door loud and clear.

"Yes, I'll be ready in a minute." Turning to Lester he said in a lower voice, "The butler will get you some supper and find a place for you to sleep. In a few days I'll have some letters for your return journey."

He donned the coat and strode over to the mirror. Deborah had purchased the clothes and it bothered him to have to accept her charity. *Oh well*, he thought as he tied the cravat, *soon I won't have to accept her small favors. Her entire estate will be mine or, better yet, I'll be taking Keary to Banetree and leaving Deborah and the rest of her miserable social crowd behind.*

Chapter XXIII

Morgan was amused by the subdued atmosphere that greeted Deborah and him when they entered the City Tavern. Only a week ago the British had been ridiculing the American army and predicting an early end to the war. General Howe was being hailed as a genius for the manner in which he had captured Philadelphia and Burgoyne was expected hourly to capture Albany. Now with Burgoyne's entire army prisoners, Washington would not only have more troops available to encircle the city but would have the use of those captured guns as well.

One group of officers' spirits, as they vied for someone's attention, didn't seem as dampened as the others. Their appearance was that of a standard bootlicking group and Morgan was curious which general was receiving all the attention. Deborah always insisted on dragging him to every British social function to which she could secure an invitation, and at each one there was inevitably such a group. Sir William Howe was not scheduled to attend this evening's affair, so Morgan figured from the size of the attentive group it had to be either Clinton or Cornwallis, the next two in rank. It was strange there were no ladies in this group, as generals usually were accompanied by women who had "scarlet fever," the label patriots hung on all women who were romantically involved with redcoats.

Deborah was also very much interested in the tight-knit group and Morgan was sure it wouldn't take her long to wrangle an introduction to whichever general was holding court. Her seemingly aimless path was leading in that direction as she exchanged greetings with acquaintances along the way. As Deborah and Morgan neared the group, a captain stepped aside leaving a clear, unobstructed view to the center of the circle. They both froze, dumbstruck when they saw the person holding court was not a general but a beautiful raven-haired maid.

Keary's periwinkle blue gown emphasized her brilliant blue eyes, and the fashionably, very low-cut bodice rimmed in tiny seed pearls revealed an expanse of snowy-white bosom. The tiny waist rose above yards of pearl-seeded overskirt and white satin petticoat that billowed over oblong hoops. She had tied her natural hair up from her face allowing long ringlets to fall in back. She stared impassively at the new arrivals and the crowd opened a little as officers turned to learn the object of her attention.

"Good evening, Miss Cavanaugh." Morgan managed a stiff bow, his embarrassment apparent.

"Good evening, Mr. Baines and—Miss Thornton, I believe." The hesitation was deliberate. Deborah's normally fair skin turned crimson from her powdered wig to the low-cut bodice of her pink satin gown.

"Morgan dear, can this be an auction? Do you think Miss Cavanaugh is to be sold again?" Morgan's eyes glinted with disgust and he reached for Deborah's arm to pull her away from the group.

"An auction! How exciting." Keary reached over and touched Deborah's wrist playfully with her folded fan. "Did you come to buy a husband, dear? No, of course not. I forgot, you've already bought one."

Deborah was livid and her bosom, above the expansive décolletage, was heaving with the effort to breathe in the confines of the tightly laced corset. "I'm afraid, my dear, the Irish mentality is incapable of understanding the subtleties of marriage agreements among gentlefolk. Were I a tradeswoman, I might refer to it as grossly myself."

"Yes, I see your point, Miss Thornton. Forgive me. You see, my trading experience has mostly to do with tin; I've never dealt in humans." Although Morgan was not particularly fond of being referred to as merchandise, his admiration for Keary's spunk brought forth a poorly concealed chuckle, which was not lost on Deborah.

The band struck up a waltz, the current rage in London but new to America, and several officers argued over prior claims to the first dance with Keary. But she turned to Lieutenant Boyle and held out her hand. "I'm sorry, gentlemen, but my escort has first claim."

Lieutenant Boyle of the Fortieth Regiment of Foot, resplendent in his scarlet coat lapelled to the waist with buff satin, stammered sheepishly, "I'm afraid I don't know the dance, Miss Cavanaugh."

A tall captain quickly took her outstretched hand. "Allow me, Miss."

Keary had never attempted the dance before but ladies

had discussed it in the shop one day and demonstrated the step for her. Dancing came naturally to Keary, and hearing the rhythm of the music she felt confident as the captain led her to the floor. He was extremely graceful, and after a few turns the couple whirled with reckless abandon.

Morgan turned to Deborah and asked, "Would you like to try it, dear?"

She watched Keary whirling around the floor, her long black tresses and billowing skirts fanning gracefully around her lithe form. "I'm afraid I don't know the dance," she answered curtly.

Since none of the other ladies could muster the courage to try it either, Keary and the captain were the only ones on the floor. When the dance ended, the hall erupted in applause and shouts for more. Deborah, who had been standing on the sideline shooting Keary venomous stares as fiery as the coals in Mr. Wykoff's forge, was relieved when the band finally played a cotillion. Her joy was short-lived, however, when the officers continued to flirt outrageously with Keary as partners changed at the end of each promenade. There was no shortage of men eager to dance with Deborah, and ordinarily she would have considered this a successful evening. But there was no doubt as to who the belle of this ball was, and second fiddle was not the role for Deborah.

Later in the evening the band struck up a country reel but the floor stood empty. The dance was strange to the British, and those Americans who knew it well abstained, considering it a dance of the common people and therefore beneath them. Keary stood close to the band clapping her hands and tapping her toe to the lilting air, which reminded her so much of Irish folk music. She was torn from her trance when Morgan bowed in front of her and offered his hand.

"I'm afraid I don't know the dance," she protested feebly.

"I've watched you, and there was never a dance invented you couldn't do. We're very familiar with the reel in my part of the country and it's a dance you would enjoy. A dance for honest people—people unafraid to show emotion." He lifted her hand, placing it on his shoulder as his own found her waist. His hand burned like a hot iron and Keary was thankful she had been left breathless from the last dance so her excitement would be less apparent. Morgan demonstrated the basic step carefully and after a few misses, they were prancing around the floor with all of the exaggerated gestures suggested by the earthy music. His closeness seared her, transmitting pulsating thrills through her body, and as the dance ended and he reluctantly released her, she saw longing in his tormented eyes.

Immediately after the reel Deborah developed a sudden headache and asked to be taken home. Keary watched them leave with a familiar, dull ache in her heart. She tried to keep up the festive spirit for Lieutenant Boyle's sake but it was an uphill battle. She had little time to rest, however, as a steady stream of officers continued to pester for dances. Finally, in desperation, she protested. "I'm sorry, gentlemen. I'm going to enjoy a glass of punch and rest for a while."

"Then allow me to get your punch, Keary." She turned at the familiar voice and faced Amos Shelby.

"Amos, I didn't know you were in Philadelphia."

"I have been sailing off the coast waiting for the island

forts to be cleared so we could land our cargo. It seems the rebels put up a rather stubborn fight but now the river is entirely in the hands of His Majesty's navy and commerce is normal again. Thank God."

"When did you arrive and how did you know I was here?"

"I arrived this afternoon and didn't know you were here. I went to the shop and when no one answered my knock, I came here for dinner. I heard the music and foot stomping and decided to investigate, which was a very fortunate decision, it seems." He grinned as he flipped the tails of his waistcoat and sat delicately on the dainty chair beside her. "Is your Virginia planter here? I would like to meet him."

"He has already left and he's not my Virginia planter." Amos raised an eyebrow at the accent on "my."

"May I assume this means you're not going to fulfill your former plans?"

"You may."

"And may I also assume my advances will be more welcome now?"

"You have my permission to call if you wish." Lieutenant Boyle appeared at her side and she rose to meet him, placing her hand on his arm. "Captain Shelby, this is my escort, Lieutenant Boyle." As the men acknowledged each other Keary was thinking, *This is the way it should be. I can let gentlemen vie for my attention instead of pining for Morgan.*

Later as she lay in bed reliving the evening, she was determined to enjoy and become part of the gayest social season in Philadelphia's history. The English officers she had met were not the snobs of Deborah Thornton's crowd. She would invest in a really nice wardrobe and attend all the best social functions and later, when Miss Thornton realized she had a rival, Keary would truly enjoy watching Deborah's frustration. The blond witch would no doubt whisper the story of Keary's former indenture to every officer in the British army but it would have no effect. British officers away from home weren't as interested in ladies' backgrounds as they were in their faces and figures. After all, Sir William paraded his mistress, Mrs. Loring, around town unashamedly and Keary doubted that blond whore could trace her ancestry back further than a tumble in a hayloft. She didn't fool herself into thinking she could get serious about anyone else, but when the redcoats left, she intended sending a few of them off with heavy hearts.

January 2, 1778 broke clear and cold and Keary was relieved to settle down to a regular routine after the holidays. With the British army providing fuel for the economy, business was booming and money poured into the shop at an unprecedented rate. *But,* Keary thought, *money in itself is meaningless if it can't be used to bring Morgan and myself together.* She still saw the longing look as he released her after the reel and knew deep down in her heart he loved her. But what to do about it was another question. If money were the only criteria then Deborah, with her inherited empire of ships and counting houses, would win hands down. But was Morgan aware of how much wealth she, herself, had accumulated since inheriting Uncle Benjamin's meager holdings, and would this be enough to operate Banetree until he was able to sell a crop? At any rate he would not find out without asking; her pride would not allow her to make the overture.

She wanted to believe that were it his happiness alone at stake, he would be more apt to gamble. But with the unthinkable prospect of Banetree's population being sold indiscriminately, he could not afford this luxury. She had been over this many times in her mind and the answer was still just as elusive.

In an attempt to fulfill her resolve to sample Philadelphia's social life, she had accepted invitations almost every night. Amos Shelby and Lieutenant Brad Boyle were constantly competing for her attention; becoming bored with the social whirl, she probably should decide between them but didn't love either. Of the two, Keary enjoyed Amos's company more. He had proposed giving up the idea of the Cornwall farm, offering to settle in America instead. Since he was due to leave soon, he would no doubt press for an understanding. He often hinted at marriage without making an outright proposal. He was handsome, a good conversationalist, and at times quite witty, but even if she could consider him romantically, a recent discussion had manifested a deep difference between them. She recalled when it had surfaced and wondered if he had any grasp at all of the American situation.

"Keary, I wouldn't mind settling in America but I believe we should go to England until this damned rebellion is over and the king's troops have restored order."

"Amos, I have told you repeatedly I won't go anywhere with you. So deciding where you will live is entirely up to you. And what gives you the ridiculous idea the king's troops will ever win this war?" She was perturbed at him for taking things for granted and her voice was edgy.

Amos Shelby was used to giving commands and being obeyed, so her sharp tone fell on deaf ears. "Well, I admit it's taking longer than I thought, but be serious, love. The rebels can't hold out against the might of the British Empire much longer. If necessary, the king will only send more and more troops."

"And if they all end up getting captured, as General Burgoyne's troops did, eventually the Americans will have the biggest army in the world—in a cage."

"That was just an isolated incident. Don't forget how easily Sir William took your very city here."

"And what good did it do him? The British are afraid to leave the city now for fear they will end up like Burgoyne."

"By that gleam in your eye, I think you want this to happen."

"I enjoy it any time John Bull's tail gets twitched, especially when the Americans do it. The longer I live here, the more American I feel."

A worried frown puckered Amos's forehead. "But Keary, you are talking sedition. Certainly you are not in sympathy with these traitors?"

"You seem to forget I'm Irish and don't have the same opinion of the Crown as you."

"Why not? Ireland has been part of the empire for hundreds of years."

"Never by consent of the Irish people. But tell me, Amos, where would you want to live in America? Where would this farm be?"

"It would have to be in an area controlled by British troops."

"Well, if you can find a farm area controlled by British

troops, I'll go with you tomorrow."

"Why there's—a—there must be a lot of them. Other than seaports, I don't know the geography too well, but I'm sure there must be several."

"The truth is, Amos, the British hold Philadelphia and New York, I believe they have a few troops in Rhode Island, and that's it—after more than three years of war. If you ever saw a map of this continent, you would realize it would take a million troops to occupy it."

His mood had turned solemn after the conversation and he had never broached the subject again. Another thing that bothered Keary was how he could shout his loyalty from the rooftops after trading with the rebels, but then she never could understand the British mind anyway.

Keary cursed the laws which, as soon as the marriage vows were spoken, transferred all the wife's wealth to the husband. Not so much because she might one day lose all of her own property, but because they offered Morgan an easy way out of a problem that they could be sharing and working on together. She pushed these thoughts from her mind and returned to the ledgers.

After a fantastic business season, it was time to total the receipts. Her advertising had resulted in rich dividends, bringing British in by the score to buy gifts for their ladies. But the British weren't the only ones spending money like drunken sailors; it seemed the whole town was lining up to see who would be the first to enter debtor's prison. Philadelphia was going through a radical change, which even as recent an arrival as herself could discern. Social spending, drinking, dress, and sexual standards were rapidly changing, and it appeared as one mammoth race to see who could get there first.

The whole city was on one gigantic binge with no care for the future.

Inflation was becoming a serious problem as prices climbed to dizzying heights. Keary had given a lot of thought to this phenomenon and decided the best hedge was to buy commodities that were easy to store and hold until the prices rose. The best way was to buy from incoming ships before captains became familiar with the local prices.

Today she walked along the wharf, bitter winds whipping her cape and skirts as she pondered the best way to contact unsuspecting captains whose ships would most likely be carrying goods of interest.

She stopped at the gangplank of a large new vessel, wondering how best to approach a captain about something of which she knew little. After shivering in the cold for a few minutes, she shrugged and ascended the gangplank, deciding a direct approach was best. Still holding the hoisted skirts in her clenched hands, she asked the surprised sailor, "Can you direct me to the captain, Sir?"

"Why—uh—" He quickly snatched the round sailor hat from his head and stood crumpling it in his hands. "That is—I dunno, Miss."

"You do know where his quarters are, don't you?"

"Quarters? Why yes, I know, Miss."

"Then if you can't take me there can you at least give me directions?"

"Yes ma'am. You go right down that passageway and—" Seeming to gather courage, he slammed the hat back on his head and motioned, "Come this way, Miss."

Keary followed through a series of passages and across a deck until he finally stopped in front of a door at the far end of the passageway.

"Right here, Miss."

She smiled sweetly saying, "Thank you." The sailor, flustered, turned so quickly he bumped his head on a hanging lantern and reeled back into Keary. Regaining his balance, he made a quick retreat.

A gruff command to enter answered Keary's knock, and a hanging lantern over a small table revealed a heavyset bald-headed man with a very prominent nose. His small, beady eyes grew appreciably when they settled on the visitor and his gruff voice rose in a slight squeak.

"Come in, Miss. Captain Meyers at your service." Jumping up, he smoothed the wrinkled waistcoat and added, "What can I do for you?"

"Captain Meyers, I'm Miss Cavanaugh. My master owns a draper's shop on Spruce Street. He has heard captains often carry articles for their own personal trade and has sent me to inquire."

"Your master's correct, Miss, but I have a merchant who always buys whatever I bring him. Since I haven't been in these parts for four years, I'm not sure he is still around."

"Perhaps I can be of help. What is his name?"

"George Spencer."

"I'm sorry, Captain. He left when the king's troops came; I guess he was a rebel sympathizer. Many of them left, you know." To herself she said, *I wonder who the devil George Spencer is?*

"That's too bad; he was a likeable chap. Well, Miss, I do have several bolts of fine cloth your master may be interested in if he'd like to stop by and take a look at them."

"That won't be necessary, Sir. Since I do most of the

sewing, he allows me to make decisions on such purchases." Keary had been in business too long now to guiltily call up Father O'Connell's image when she told barefaced lies.

The captain showed her a dozen rolls of fine silks, satins, and brocades. There were shades and hues she had never seen before and she was sure the Philadelphia ladies would pay dearly for such materials. When the captain began quoting her prices, she was sure he wasn't aware of the inflation running rampant in the city. Hoping not to appear too anxious, she asked, "Would you give me a discount if I bought the whole lot—hard money, of course."

The captain began scratching on a piece of paper and she wandered among other merchandise and tilted the lid of a slightly damaged box. Her eyes widened and she stifled a gasp at the sight of two dozen of the latest fashion dolls. Lifting one after another and examining them, she tried to keep her growing excitement from showing. "What are you going to do with these dolls, Captain?"

"I'm not sure, Miss. With the crate damaged like that, I can't make out who it was consigned to and I'm sure not going to check all over Philadelphia in this weather to find out. Do you have use for them?"

"Not immediately, but I would like to make a window display sometime when I'm not so busy and I was thinking I could use some of these."

"Well, if you take all the cloth, I'll give you a five-percent discount and throw in the dolls—on one condition."

"And that is?"

"You will have to arrange for a carter to haul the goods. I have no way of delivering."

"Done." She counted a stack of gold coins and added, "I will pay you half now and the rest when I come with the carter. Now, may I have a receipt?"

The captain laughed as he turned back to the cabin. "I see now why your master trusts you so much."

That night after the goods were safely stowed in the common room, Keary was so excited that instead of preparing supper, she gnawed on a chunk of cheese and a cold biscuit. All during the slow ride home on the wagon her mind had been hatching a plan that promised huge profits. After thoroughly examining the dolls, her earlier suspicions were confirmed beyond a doubt. The dolls, which were shipped from France each year to display the latest fashions to the rest of the world, were never much different from the previous year. The necklines might be more daring, the waists higher or lower, or a couple of yards more in the skirt, but these dolls initiated a new, drastic change. Every doll displayed the new "false rump" and narrower, more pliable hoops. The false rump was a small roll of cork which, when tied by string to the waist, lay just above the buttocks. The fullness of the skirt was drawn back and lay over the cork roll. From what these dolls told Keary, every highborn lady in London had probably already discarded her old wardrobe and was clamoring for gowns such as these. At least that's what the rumors would circulate—once she started them.

With hundreds of wealthy ladies in Philadelphia demanding new styles and material, someone could make a fortune and Keary decided it might as well be her. She didn't have enough ready capital to corner the entire market—and even without the dolls others could copy fashions—but she had enough to make a killing and vowed to press her advantage to the utmost.

For the next few days Keary combed the waterfront for the newest and best quality materials, and with what money she had and by fierce haggling, she managed to obtain a large supply. She selected a doll with the style she liked best, wrapped it carefully in a beautiful piece of material, and left the shop.

Mrs. Swinehart maintained a very exclusive shop on the first floor of her elegant manor. Her clientele were the elite of Philadelphia. Entering the spacious room, Keary called, "Good morning, Mrs. Swinehart. I have a very special job for you." As the grand lady approached her, Keary continued, "I have my own material and would like this dress made." She produced the doll and Mrs. Swinehart gasped.

"Where did you get this, Miss Keary?"

"Why, from Paris, of course. I had them shipped as soon as I heard of the new fashion sweeping Paris and London. I wanted them in case the French ports are closed if the rumors of war between England and France are true."

The dressmaker studied the doll and then said, "Well, I'm sure it's authentic from everything I've heard of the style changes, but no dolls have arrived since last year. Did I understand you to infer you had more of these?"

"Yes, and they all confirm the style change is complete in respect to many major details."

"Could I borrow some of the dolls for a while, Miss Keary? I'm sure most of my customers would love to see them."

"Yes, I'm sure they would—and they can for a price. I'll need this gown for the General's Ball, Saturday a week. Many ladies will want to know who made it and I'll send them to you. Of course, in payment for this reference, you will have to promise to make my gown without charge." Mrs. Swinehart looked dubious and Keary continued, "Unless you'd rather I took it somewhere else."

"No, no, Miss Keary. It's just that—well, how can I make other dresses without the dolls?"

"For a short time my common room will be used to display the dolls and the new material I've already purchased. After the lady buys the material and selects the doll, one of your girls may come over and study the style. But the doll itself will never leave my room. Of course there will be a slight charge for this."

"But if you sell the material and charge me a fee for the use of the doll, how can I make any money?"

"Mrs. Swinehart, you will be the only dressmaker I will allow to study the dolls in detail at first. After a short period in which you will gain an advantage over your competitors, I will allow others the same privilege—at the same, or a higher fee. You must charge accordingly—and remember, rich ladies will want the price high enough so that few others can afford similar gowns."

"You want the dress for Saturday a week?"

"Yes. I'll come by a few days before for a fitting—and, Mrs. Swinehart?"

"Yes?"

"Not a word about this to anyone."

"Oh no, Miss. My lips are sealed." Keary left, satisfied. She knew that telling the talkative dressmaker was cheaper than placing an advertisement in the newspaper—and much more effective.

Chapter XXIV

In less than two days women were coming to the shop in droves, begging to see the dolls. Keary adamantly denied having the dolls at first, but later whispered to a few choice gossips that they would be in her possession by the middle of the following week. At that time she would claim the dolls had been delayed. The clamor would be loud but in the long run would raise the excitement to a fever pitch the night before the ball. The more the rumor of the dolls circulated the more excitement would generate, and all of this would add impact to her entrance.

She made frequent trips to the waterfront and warehouse district and to each merchant she posed the same questions: "How much cork do you have on hand, and what is the price?" Eventually, she bought up every pound of cork in Philadelphia, agreeing to pay on delivery. The delivery schedule had been carefully set up so that she could sell enough material beforehand to raise the money.

She had made another purchase in which, for the first

time in her life, she had asked for credit. The merchant was happy to be relieved of several bolts of muslin even though Keary had dickered until the price was ridiculously low. The most difficult part of her plan was finding five girls reasonably good with a needle and thread, but before the week was out this was accomplished, and the very next day Keary's flat was turned into a thriving factory.

Keary made her entrance at the General's Ball on the arm of a proud Lieutenant Boyle. Her gown was a "polonaise" fashion never before seen in the colonies. The décolletage of the soft, dusky rose taffeta gown was cut in a daringly low square, barely covering the shoulders, and the ruffle of the sleeves ended at the elbow. Yards of overskirt were pulled back and flounced over the bustle or "false rump," revealing an almost straight petticoat of silver-gray satin embroidered in small dusky roses. Another shocking feature of the gown was the length, which ended about six inches above the floor displaying dainty ankles and gray satin dancing slippers. Taking a cue from the fashion doll, Keary had smoothed all of her hair high on her head except for one long curl over her shoulder, tucking several pink feathers amidst the jet mass.

For the first time since attending social affairs, she found herself surrounded by women instead of men. She had barely reached the center of the large entrance hall when the cackling females descended. Their questions came in rapid-fire succession from so many different directions, the entire hall resounded in a cacophony of feminine screeching. The more they pressed for information, the more evasive she became.

"The gown was sent as a gift from a friend in Paris. I know nothing of the dolls you are speaking of." Then she would turn to parry another question. They all knew the dress had been made by Mrs. Swinehart, and the material and style were so beautiful the women wanted to stamp their feet in consternation.

Later in the evening after everyone had observed the freedom of her swaying skirt, unencumbered by hoops, and the dainty feet twirling unconfined across the dance floor, she whispered the truth to a few chosen gossips. They, in turn, told a few more and Monday morning Keary was deluged with throngs of curious, impatient women. The excitement, when the dolls were unveiled, was unbridled until the talk turned to price.

"But, Miss Keary, two pound ten a yard is a very steep price for a brocade even so fine as this. And the dressmaker's fee on top of that will make it almost prohibitive."

"Yes, that's true but very few women will be able to afford the price and that will insure yours will be exclusive. This material and the hues were never attainable before and the styles are just now reaching London from France. I had great difficulty in obtaining both the materials and the dolls, and they didn't come cheap. That is why the price is higher. I'm sure you wouldn't want a gown like every other one in town."

"Well—how many yards will this style take?" While Keary referred to a chart she had made showing material requirements for each doll, the woman was already selecting another one. The higher she raised prices, the more eager the women were to buy, and early Wednesday Molly was at the wharf searching for new ship arrivals. In a little over a week they had sold all of the material and the new shades were impossible to find.

Keary was calmly adding up her profits the day Mrs. Swinehart hurried into the shop wringing her hands. "Miss Keary, I don't know what I'm going to do. I have several ladies' dresses nearly finished and can't find an ounce of cork in Philadelphia to pad the rumps."

"Oh, that is a problem, Mrs. Swinehart. Let me think. . . . It wouldn't be sensible to sew padding in each dress. A single false rump would do to wear under all their new-style gowns."

"I had thought of that too. The padding could be worn separately but I can't find a single ounce of cork anywhere in town. Everything else I've thought of would be too heavy. If I only knew where the merchants order their cork from, I could go there direct."

Keary looked woefully at the distraught woman. "I'm afraid that would be impossible, Mrs. Swinehart. Cork comes from warm climates, mostly from the Mediterranean countries, so there probably won't be any available for several months at least."

"Dear me, what can I do? The ladies will be so disappointed and they will blame me. Several of them are counting on wearing these gowns to General Cornwallis's ball next Saturday."

Keary came around the counter and patted the anxious woman's arm. "I may have a solution."

"Oh please, Miss Keary, tell me what it is."

"I have cork and several girls are busy right now sewing it into muslin coverings for false rumps. The ladies can purchase them from me."

Mrs. Swinehart's eyebrows raised but she smothered her astonishment. "That's wonderful. How much will the rumps cost?"

"I will have to decide on the price. Just tell your customers I only have a limited amount and if they want one, they had better hurry. Once these are gone, I really don't know what they'll do because Philadelphia probably won't see another ounce of cork for months."

Keary knew exactly what they would do but had no intention of telling Mrs. Swinehart at this time. She had tried on one of the wire frames Mr. Wykoff had made in his shop and, after a few revisions, preferred it over the cork. Even women who couldn't afford a new gown would redesign older ones and would naturally want the false rump. If they didn't arrive at the idea themselves, a small advertisement in the newspaper would steer them that way.

Keary and Molly were relaxing over a cup of coffee at the painting table after a particularly hard day when the bell above the door tinkled, announcing a late caller. A short, heavyset gentleman in a finely tailored surtout lost no time in making the reason for his visit clear after acknowledging Keary's greeting. "I understand you have fashion dolls from Paris, Miss."

"Yes?"

"How many?" His words were clipped, giving the impression he had not the time or patience to waste on a tradeswoman.

"Two dozen, Sir."

"I'll give you one hundred pounds for them."

Keary looked boldly into the pompous fellow's eyes,

wondering why she had bothered to address him as sir and allowing it was probably because of being an Irish native on English soil for so long. "You realize, of course, that these are only copies."

"That doesn't matter. Do we have a deal?"

"One hundred fifty."

"One hundred twenty-five."

"Hard money?"

The man waved offhandedly. "Yes."

Keary walked behind the counter. "We have a deal." She wrote up a sales agreement stating the dolls were copies of originals from Paris.

After he counted out the money and left hurriedly with the box of dolls under his arm, Molly said, "I didn't think you'd ever sell those dolls. There is still profit to be made from them. If I keep going to the wharves, I'm sure I'll find some more material. At least enough to sell a few more dresses."

"Maybe, but by now every dressmaker in town has seen enough to make reasonably good copies. Besides, you heard me tell the gentleman and even put it in writing that those dolls were only copies. Now if he interprets that to mean he owns the only set in Philadelphia, I can't help it."

Keary threw the bolt on the door of the shop to discourage further late callers and continued, "You know Sarah, the dark-haired girl I had sewing on the false rumps?"

"Yes."

"She is a very intelligent girl and very talented with a needle. I had her scour every draper shop in town and buy all the old dolls. I gave her five pounds and enough material to make copies of these current styles on the old dolls. I still have two complete sets for that pompous gentleman's competitors. After all, how can dressmakers survive now without the dolls?"

Molly dropped down in her chair and shook her head slowly, a grimace pulling her mouth downward. "Keary, does your mind ever stop for a rest? It seems to me you keep it working overtime."

"I'll never rest if I can help it. In fact, I've just been thinking of a way you can earn enough money to furnish your new home." Molly's eyes lit up knowing Keary's ideas always bore fruit. "There are several dolls left over and we can quietly accumulate more. As artistic as you are, you could be a good designer. Now that we know the trend, I'm sure summer dresses will generally be the same. We'll buy up large supplies of barragon, dimity, lustring, erminetta, and whatever other summer materials we can get our hands on and after you fashion a dress for the doll, I'll make a visit with the doll and material to Mrs. Swinehart. I'll swear the doll didn't come from Paris but I won't be too convincing. After a few days we'll start a rumor the dolls were smuggled in by way of Africa or some other place and that summer fashions are enough different from winter that a discerning woman could easily see the difference. Once the rumors get a strong foothold, I'll categorically deny the dolls came from Paris but no one will believe me. In fact, the more I deny it, the more people will be sure I'm lying and the more determined they will be to have the new summer fashions."

"The idea sounds good but I'm not sure I can design clothes."

"You've seen the new fashions and I know you can do it. It'll be a lot of work on your own time, but I'll give you a share of the profits and I can assure you they will be large. If you're interested, I'll get Sarah to help you. She can do the sewing but I'll trust your artistic instincts for the basic designs. It will be a lot better way for you to spend your evenings than working on that house, and a lot more profitable."

After Molly and Jamie left for their house, Keary had cleared off the counter and turned to leave the shop when the outside door to the building opened and Jason Wentworth hurried in. "Miss Keary, I've been wanting to apologize for a long time for both my father's and my behavior. Our conduct was unforgivable."

"Your apology is accepted, Mr. Wentworth, but if you'll excuse me, I was just closing; I have a lot of work to do." Since their last conversation, she had seen Jason at social events but had always managed to avoid his advances.

"But don't you see what I'm saying, Miss Keary. I'll marry you without any conditions whatever. As equals, so to speak."

Keary's temper flared but she brought it quickly under control. "Jason, I don't know how to explain to you that I wouldn't marry you with or without conditions."

"There's someone else, isn't there?" His voice was shrill and demanding. "Is it Morgan Baines? He sure seems to spend a lot of time around here in that ridiculous peddler's cart. No, you can't have him, he's marrying Deborah. It must be Lieutenant Boyle."

"It's none of your business who it is. I owe you no accounting."

"But, Miss Keary, you don't know how much I want

you—how much I need you."

"Please go, Sir. We have no more to talk about." She continued into the shop, hoping to discourage him while she pretended interest in some of the products Molly had just painted. He followed, staying right on her heels. Finally, in exasperation she said, "Mr. Wentworth, there's no point in pursuing this further. I won't marry you under any conditions or even so much as allow you to call. Now please leave." Her words went unheeded as his eyes rested on a large pile of newly made boxes under a bench.

"My, my, what have we here? The last time I watched Morgan load that cart of his, he must have packed two hundred of these in the false bottom and smuggled them out past the lines." He turned a box over and over in his hands, examining it closely. "I'm not sure what these are or whether or not they were empty at the time, but they must have tremendous value to the rebels for him to take such chances."

"Don't be silly; what would Morgan be doing with spice boxes?"

"It's hard to say what he would be doing with any kind of tinware, but you can't deny he came here on a regular basis and loaded up before sneaking through the lines. And for some reason these were always kept hidden." His eyes searched the shop further, unsure of what he was searching for.

"Mr. Wentworth, you have been spying on me. If I were a man, I would call you out." She was shaking visibly as he laid the box down and turned to her with outstretched arms.

"And now, Miss, what do you say to my offer of marriage?"

"I say get out of this shop and stay out. How long have

you been standing around spying on me?" He ignored her question and grabbed at her, pulling her toward him. She pushed with all her strength and they fell toward the bench. She heard a thump, his arms suddenly releasing their hold, and as she pushed his weight from her trembling body she saw Morgan's crouching form standing over Jason.

"Morgan, where did you come from?"

"I've noticed Jason hanging around here a lot and had a feeling he was up to no good. I was coming down Second Street and saw him heading this way so I decided to follow him. Then when I got here and saw the front door standing open in the middle of winter, I knew something was wrong."

"Did you hear what he said?"

"Yes. I only hope he hasn't mentioned his suspicions to anyone else." Then bending over Jason's prostrate form, he added, "I must have hit him harder than I thought; he doesn't seem very anxious to get up." He bent closer, and seeing a pool of blood on the floor and noticing no movement, he said, "My God, Keary, I think he's dead!" Closer examination proved this to be true. "He must have hit his head on this." He pointed to a conical stake dripping blood. "We better get him out of here and figure out an alibi."

Keary was standing rigidly, her face bone-white. He looked up at her horrified expression. "Hurry and change into something suitable for dining out. Once I dispose of the body I'll come back for you and we'll go out to dinner. We'll go to several taverns and coffee shops, if necessary, until we've been seen by enough people who know us." Rising, he pulled her into his arms. "It was an accident and not our fault. Now get dressed while I dispose of the body." He relaxed, expecting her to pull back, but her boneless body sagged against him. He fought the all-consuming desire to hold her close and instead took her shoulders gently in his hands and held her at arm's length. "You must hurry, my love." Despite the tragic event she had just witnessed, Keary would long remember the endearment and his accompanying look.

She tried to hurry but her fumbling fingers couldn't do anything right; by the time Morgan returned she was dressed but not satisfied. "Oh, Morgan, I can't go out looking like this; my hair is a mess, there is no color in my cheeks, and this dress feels like an oilskin sack. I look like a witch."

"Most women would die happy if they could look like this just once in their entire life." He reached out his hands and she melted in his arms. "I'm sorry to put you through this. I probably hit him harder than necessary, but when I saw him mauling you something inside me exploded."

"Sorry? You probably saved my life."

"Oh, I doubt he would have hurt you. He wanted you too much."

"Well if he had gotten what he wanted from me, that would have been worse than death."

"Don't say that—or even think it. If I had seen him trying anything like that I could have killed him in cold blood."

She continued to lie against his hard chest, feeling the comfort of both his words and nearness. "Do you think anyone saw him come here, or will we be connected with this in any way?"

"I doubt it since he had his collar pulled up against the wind. I wouldn't have recognized him if I hadn't almost bumped into him. But just by way of pointing the finger of suspicion in a different direction, I planted a few messages on his body."

"Messages?"

"Yes. I scribbled some unintelligible numbers and letters upside down and backwards and wrinkled the paper after rubbing it in dirt, to make it appear as though it had seen hard use. When his body is found it will appear he was an agent of some kind. The British will know he wasn't working for them and will figure he was working for the rebels and got his just deserts." He tried to maintain a level voice, but the shock of having killed a man, her warm breath on his throat, and the pressure of her breasts against his chest produced an alien shaky tone to his usual casual southern drawl.

"What do we do now?"

He knew the next answer would make her release her hold and unconsciously tightened his own grip in anticipation. "We go out to supper."

"If you can't eat, at least push the food around on your plate, pretend to chew, and cut your meat." Morgan said this in a helpful but urgent way. It was impossible for Keary to eat this soon after such a tragic accident but she knew his reason for insisting she put on appearances. She touched a morsel to her mouth and almost retched. "All right, if it's impossible, bat your eyes at me, flirt coyly behind your fan, and laugh demurely. Pretend we are lovers and that's the reason you can't eat."

Pretend we're lovers, she thought. *That shouldn't be too difficult.* She cast longing appeals from wide eyes over a spread fan and hung on his every word with adoration fairly oozing from her. It worked. The waiter was convinced, patrons at nearby tables were convinced, and suddenly Morgan lost what little appetite he had. To deny himself her attention under ordinary circumstances was bad enough, but to resist so blatant an invitation from those beautiful eyes was impossible. Once they had been seen by several acquaintances he suggested they leave.

They were halfway home, walking hand in hand, oblivious to the raging wind whipping small, hard pellets of snow in their faces, before Keary thought to ask, "What did you do with his body?"

"I started to get my horse, then changed my mind since a horse is more easily recognizable on a night like this than a man. I just carried him like a drunk down to a waterfront alley and laid him beside a building where the drifting snow would cover him quickly. Hopefully he won't be found until this snow melts. I laid him face down so, with that wound on the back of his head, it would appear someone hit him from behind and just left him where he fell."

When they reached her door, Keary fumbled for the key and was happy to hear him say, "Do you mind if I come up for a while? I want to unwind and feel a few drops of brandy would be in order."

To Keary, who was not used to anything stronger than wine or punch, the fiery liquid jolted her system but left a soothing effect afterwards. They sat facing each other awkwardly, their valiant attempts at small talk trailing off futilely. She wished he would leave now and at the same time wished he would stay forever. One drink led to another and by the time he did make ready to leave, the room reeled as she stood.

"Will you be all right?"

She wasn't sure whether his chief concern was for her nerves after the night's events or for her unsteadiness after too much brandy on an empty stomach. "Yes, I'll be all right; you go ahead and I'll try to get some sleep." He took her hands in his and pulled gently. She wanted to protest but was powerless to do so as his body came closer and closer. For a second they stood hands clasped, her head resting on his chest. He released her hands and his powerful arms enveloped her, his fingers digging into her flesh before a change of pressure altered the mood from urgency to tenderness. His hand moved possessively down her back until it reached her waist, forcing her pliable body to melt against his.

"Please don't, Morgan, it's not right." As she pulled her head back to meet his eyes the pressure of his hand on her back levered her thighs against his. Her resolution vanished and her hands crept around his neck, molding gentle curves against lean, hard muscles.

"Then tell me what is right. Is it right I have to give up the woman I love for the family heritage?" She felt his body contort in a slight spasm, sending a quiver down his arms, and he gripped tighter. She responded by squeezing and burrowing her cheek deeper into the softness of his neck.

"It's more than just heritage. I try to understand this and not be bitter. Your ancestors would be proud of you."

"Then why am I not proud of myself? Why do I sleep under the same roof as her and, instead of visiting her chambers, lie awake dreaming of you?" Suddenly the horrible memories of the evening vanished and all her cares took wings. He could not have professed his love more eloquently or found a better way to remove the shadows from her heart.

"Keary, my love, I'm not sure I can go through with this."

"Shh." She pressed her index finger over his lips. "You can't jeopardize Banetree. If you lost it because of me, you'd hate me the rest of our lives."

"But—"

"Don't say anything right now. Come back after we've both settled down from this horrible experience and we'll talk." He didn't say anything more but his lips met hers tenderly, lingering and yearning for that which could not be. This was not a moment of raw passion such as they had shared once, but the feeling of pure love passing between them was more satisfying than the most erotic pleasures they had experienced. She cried out for his love. "Oh, Morgan, hold me—hold me forever." The security of his embrace, the brandy, and an overwhelming feeling of tenderness erased the shadows of the night's horror. His lips brushed hers with a series of slow shivery kisses and she floated on a soft, wispy cloud.

He surrendered the torment that had plagued him for weeks and his hand, resting on the mass of tangled curls, pulled her head back roughly. His eyes met hers with savage fire and the tortured words escaped in strangled breaths. "Keary, my love. If you only knew the hell I've been through, staying away from you. I haven't had an hour's peace since our last night at Banetree."

Against her will her arms crept around his neck, locking under the sandy queue. She could feel his uneven breathing on her cheek and gave herself freely to the passion of his kiss. His tongue, urgent and exploring, forced through to the depths of her mouth while his hands massaged the soft curves that molded the contour of her body. All of the pent-up desire of the last week sought release and she didn't care if he was free, promised, or married. He was the man she loved—the only man she'd ever love.

Chapter XXV

The following day Brad came by. He had rented a calash and, with the weather unusually temperate for this early in the spring, invited Keary for a ride along the river. After a little thought she consented to go, hoping the fresh air would alleviate the pounding in her head from yesterday's celebration.

"Keary, I have just learned General Howe is to be replaced and will be leaving for England soon."

"Is that official or just another of those endless rumors?" She wasn't interested in British politics one way or the other and was simply making conversation.

"It's only a rumor now but usually when a rumor is this persistent and widespread, it's true. There is also a rumor we will be giving up Philadelphia."

Now she was interested. "You mean you would just leave after all the trouble of taking this city?"

"Well, I understand the other generals were against this campaign from the start and only Sir William wanted it. The others wanted to go up the Hudson River and unite with Burgoyne at Albany. Looking back on things that would have been the wise choice, but Howe was too stubborn to listen to anyone else and it seems to have led to his downfall. At any rate, what I wanted to tell you was that even if the army leaves, I think I'll stay behind."

"You mean you are going to desert?"

"I don't like the sound of that word; let's just say resign. As an officer I have that right but would be expected to go back to England rather than stay in enemy territory. So I think I'll resign by letter after the army has left. What I'm trying to say is that I'd like to stay behind and marry you." Keary looked away; this was not the first time he had proposed and it was embarrassing trying to find ways to refuse without hurting him.

"What do you intend to do then, join the Continental army? Have your loyalties changed that much?"

"No, I would like to manage your business and you could stay home and raise children like other women." At first she was dumbstruck but then began to see a parallel between Brad and Morgan. She was amused wondering if Morgan had been so blunt when he proposed to Deborah.

No wonder I'm so successful in business, she thought wryly. *I'm certainly not much good at attracting the right kind of man. First there was Bruce, who wasn't interested enough to risk his position as stableboy for me; next Jason wanted to send me to school to make me worthy of him; Amos proposed taking me to England as his mistress; and now Brad wants to step in and manage my business without the slightest care of whether or not he is qualified to do so.*

After a while, in which he seemed to be rehearsing a speech in his mind, Brad continued, "Keary, I'm Irish too and only took a British commission because I had no other prospects at the time. My sympathies in this revolution do not run very deep one way or the other. If I really looked at things closely I would probably favor the rebels. What I'm trying to say is that I could be quite happy living in America."

"What do you know about managing a tinshop?"

"Probably as much as you knew when you started. But I'm willing to work hard and learn."

She rode in silence, wondering if she were going to become a target for every ambitious bachelor in Philadelphia. Would she end up in a business-type marriage as so many others seemed to be doing, or would she become an old maid? It was hard for her to visualize ever loving anyone other than Morgan. She chuckled to herself, thinking if it were to be a business arrangement, she might as well marry a wealthy man. She glanced at Brad, who wore a look of childish hope, and realized he didn't have the slightest idea of what true love was. But how to refuse him without hurting him was a problem. As an officer without family connections or independent wealth to purchase higher commissions, he could not hope to attain rank higher than captain and would look to other pursuits if he had ambition. She admired ambition in a man and would help him in any way she could short of sharing his name and bed.

"Brad, I am fond of you but not with the depth necessary to make a happy marriage. And even if my feelings for you were stronger, what makes you think running a tinshop is the life for you? No one knows whether or not they are qualified to manage a business until they've had some experience. And the way to get that is by learning the work from the bottom up; work with the metal and spend full days confined to the shop."

"Oh, I know I can do it, Keary. And once I prove it,

that'll put a different light on things. When can I start?"

"Well, if you want to come into the shop whenever you have free time, I have no objections."

"I can get all the free time I want; I just give the sergeant more duties. Now to show you how sincere I am, I'm going to come in early and work full days and learn the business in no time at all. Then we can talk more about marriage."

"Just a minute—" She started to say there would be no further talk of marriage, regardless of how well he learned the business, but then hesitated. Why crush him now, when all that would be necessary was to let him work in the shop for a few days and learn for himself what hard work really was? Yes, Brad was not the most industrious person she knew and a few days in the shop would convince him it would be a mistake to give up the soft life of an army officer.

All the way home Brad had visions of owning a thriving business and being married to the most beautiful woman he had ever met. Sitting beside him Keary chuckled, picturing him trying to straighten out his back after bending over a workbench all day.

After leaving Keary, Brad was in a mood to celebrate. Stopping at a tavern, he treated the dozen or so customers, announcing he had just become engaged. And as far as he was concerned, he had. It would only take a few months to convince Keary he was serious about learning the business and then it would be no problem getting her to say yes. Toasts, backslapping, and well-wishing became the order of things as the announcement —and a free spender—triggered a party atmosphere.

Brad looked over in the corner where a tall solitary figure leaned back against the wall oblivious to the rest of the room.

"Morgan Baines, just the man I wanted to see. Since we are both getting married we can celebrate together."

"Married? Congratulations, and who is the lucky lady?"

"Why, Miss Cavanaugh, of course; surely you must have been aware of my suit." Morgan looked as if he had just been hit with a musket butt as Brad handed him a glass of port. He stared unseeing past the glass, then drained it in one gulp.

Brad beamed. "Now that's the way I like to see a man toast my good fortune; have another."

"No thanks, I'll have rum instead." He drained the mug and ordered another round. As a euphoric Brad circulated around the room accepting the good wishes and laughing at the ribald jokes, Morgan returned to the table in the corner. Though he drank one tankard of rum after another, nothing seemed to relieve the lump in his chest.

Common sense told him Keary had the right to find her own happiness since he was getting married, but common sense has little to do with love. He felt an overwhelming urge to ask Keary to call off her wedding if he would do the same. There was still a chance Captain Hardy would get through with the tobacco, bringing him enough money to sustain Banetree for another year. But if the ship was captured, then what? His creditors could not reasonably be expected to hold off much longer.

Marriage to Deborah was something creditors had faith in; ships running the blockade was something they did not. Why, Captain Hardy had not even been able to buy insurance for his ship or cargo. No, one word of the cancellation of his wedding and creditors would swoop down on him like vultures. The rum made him sick enough to add to the filth in the gutters on the way home; but he wasn't swipsey nor could he escape for one minute that awful vision of Keary in Brad's arms.

"Morgan dear, I'm afraid we'll have to postpone our wedding for a few weeks. I'm to be one of the 'fair ladies' in the Meschianza and it wouldn't look right if I was the only married lady in the group. You do understand, don't you dear? Major Andre has selected the ladies as representing the flower of Philadelphia society, so it's quite an honor, one I couldn't very well refuse."

"That will be quite all right; I wouldn't want you to miss such a grand opportunity." With the original wedding date only a week away, he was relieved by the reprieve. He was also aware Deborah didn't want her wedding overshadowed by the most extravagant celebration in the history of North America. The Meschianza, a farewell party for the departing General Sir William Howe, was all the women talked about lately.

"What is a fair lady exactly?" He asked this aimlessly, without looking up from the letter he was writing.

"What is it? Why it will be one of the most important roles in the whole affair. Though the whole city and every major ship in the river will be decorated and there will be balls everywhere, everyone knows the main festivities will be at Duke Wharton's estate. All the top officers and leading citizens of the city will be there. The entire grounds will be illuminated and there will be a mock combat of knights. There will be a fair lady for each knight and before the joust he will place her scarf over his lance. Of course each scarf will be a different color and—oh Morgan, you should see our costumes! We have gauze turbans with long veils trimmed in gold, silver, and ornamented tassels, and the turban is crested with beautiful feathers and jewels. The gown is a Grecian style made of white silk with yards and yards of free-flowing material. The sash worn around the waist is loose fitting and richly decorated with gold trim and spangles and is the same color as the scarf. Each lady will wear the color of her knight and mine is a rich wine color."

With Deborah so exuberant, Morgan was forced to lay his quill aside for a minute and pretend interest. "Do you have to speak lines or anything?"

"Oh yes. We are supposed to be captives from the Orient; that's why the Turkish costumes. Seven of the knights will be on each side: the Knights of the Blended Rose and the Knights of the Fiery Mountain. Each will claim that their captives surpass any ladies in the world in beauty, wit, and every accomplishment. Unable to convince each other, the knights will have a joust which will end in a draw. After the joust the ladies will join hands and proclaim all the knights are equal in valor and the ladies equal in beauty. It's a long speech and since we all have to say it together, it will require a lot of practice."

"Is that the end of it then?"

"Oh no, that's only the beginning. Next we parade onto the grounds and each knight comes back to his lady and asks her to accompany him to the ball. There will be a huge tent set up with a real polished wood floor for dancing. The knights and their ladies will lead the procession into the hall and perform a special dance before the regular dancing begins. I'm afraid I'll be neglecting you something terrible for a while, since we'll be practicing both the speech and the dance every day until the ball."

"Well, you run along and enjoy yourself; I don't see how a couple of weeks could make that much difference."

"Oh, thank you, Morgan; I knew you'd understand. And you'll be so proud of me when you see the costumes."

As Deborah ran out excitedly, Morgan sat back shaking his head in wonder at the British. They were in a life and death struggle to retain the richest and most important part of the whole empire, and its army officers and most influential citizens were more concerned with planning a going-away party for the general who had done the most to lose it.

Two more weeks of liberty, he thought jubilantly. With the pressure off for two weeks he thought briefly of a quick trip to Banetree. It had been several weeks since his last visit and the spring planting would be almost complete. The thought of getting away from Deborah and British-controlled Philadelphia gave him a quick lift, until he remembered it would mean leaving Keary too. Though he rarely saw her anymore it was still comforting to know she was near and he could hope for a chance meeting. He thought of stopping by to congratulate her on her betrothal; at least that was a good excuse for a visit. But it was torture each time he saw her and each time he vowed it would be the last. Once she was out of sight though, he began looking for excuses to see her again, regardless of how awkward the situation was.

*   *   *

Major Andre was quite pleased with himself these days. After all, the Meschianza was his idea, and though it had started out modestly enough, it had mushroomed into the most extravagant event ever held outside of London itself. Now other officers were trying to outdo each other in an attempt to incur favor with the high brass. "Good, let them try to gather some of the credit; the more others contribute, the larger the celebration will become and in the long run will still revert to my credit. At this point not even a general can usurp my position as director of the pageant, nor dilute the glory that will come from it. Regardless of the contributions of others it will always be remembered that I conceived the idea, organized and directed the whole affair, and showed remarkable administrative talents in the process. This will be the perfect recommendation for a headquarters assignment, which will save me from duty in a line regiment with all that marching in mud and snow. Yes, during the summer campaign, while those other poor chaps are sweltering in tents and eating dust, I'll be entertaining the ladies back at headquarters."

Now for the coup de grace. He had heard of this artisan named James Stuart, who was reported to be a tinsmith of extraordinary talent. Ladies constantly boasted of having some of this fellow's tinware in their possession. They would show a candle sconce proudly and say "It's a James Stuart original," much in the same manner a European would show off some fine silver or a rare painting. Strange people, these Americans, who could take such pride in something so common as tinware, but Andre now had his own reason to visit the famous tinsmith. If this Stuart fellow was such a genius with tin, he could probably make a knight's costume that would make the other officers' costumes pale in comparison. Andre adjusted his saber belt, tucked the tinsmith's address in his coat pocket, and smiled. As the director of the Meschianza, he would not only make the opening address sitting astride a great white horse, he would do it in the most elegant costume of the whole affair.

His already buoyant spirits were to receive yet another lift as he entered the shop. Rather than an old humpbacked tinsmith, which he expected, he was greeted by a black-haired beauty who made his chest contract.

"Perhaps I have the wrong place, Miss. I was looking for a tinsmith named James Stuart."

"You have the right place, Major, but Jamie doesn't talk to customers unless the job requires special instructions which I can't relay to him."

"Well this job certainly does, Miss—er—I don't believe I caught your name." He smiled in that arrogant way that suggested ladies usually gave him more than their name.

"I hadn't mentioned it, Sir."

"Will you?"

"For what purpose?"

"So that I may know what to call you. You have already addressed me as Major, which places me at a disadvantage."

"And you have addressed me as 'Miss,' which seems adequate for doing business."

Helen, the girl Keary had hired to help Molly with the painting, entered with an armload of finished work. "Where do you want me to put these, Miss Cavanaugh?"

"Miss Cavanaugh; I should have known. You're the one who stood all Philadelphia on its ear with the fashion dolls. I've heard of your great beauty and should have

406

known there couldn't be two such beautiful creatures on this continent."

"Thank you. Now, you mentioned business, Major. What is it you need?"

"Well, originally I had only one thing in mind, but now there are two. You have heard of the Meschianza no doubt?"

"I've heard of little else lately."

"One of the main presentations will be a mock joust between knights. I, as well as the other knights, have experienced difficulty fabricating a costume, though I have done extensive experimenting. After hearing of this Stuart fellow, I decided he would probably be able to make a very authentic costume."

"I'm sure he could, but it would have to be handmade and would therefore be very expensive."

"Hang the expense, Miss Cavanaugh; this will be the greatest event this city has ever seen, and I intend having the best costume in the whole pageant."

"Very well, you can explain to Jamie exactly what you want. Now, I believe you mentioned one other thing?"

"Yes. Each knight will have his own fair lady who will be attired as a goddess and will wear his colors. All of these ladies have already been selected, but the most important role of all has not. Neither myself nor the other members of the committee have been able to agree on a single candidate."

He grinned knowingly, expecting to see excitement in her eyes like all other women when the great event was being discussed. Her eyes remained impassive and he continued, bewildered by her attitude. "There will be a huge pavilion of food and drink hidden behind sliding doors. At the proper time a trumpet will sound and the doors will be rolled back, exposing an illuminated platform serving as a pedestal for the queen of the ball. With a wave of her hand, she will summon a uniformed servant who will light a single candle from a torch she will be holding. With this he will light four more held by two other servants who, in turn, will light others as well as chandeliers and standing sconces. It's hard to describe, but everything is so well synchronized it appears that a single wave of light is proceeding from the queen and lighting the entire pavilion. The effect is really breathtaking and it appears the light is traveling on its own power. As soon as the light reaches the back of the pavilion, the knights and their ladies will parade by, pay homage to the queen, perform a dance for her, and then the feasting will begin. Ever since the final plans have been settled, we have been searching Philadelphia for a lady beautiful enough to be queen, and now I've found her. Miss Cavanaugh, I'd like you to be queen of the Meschianza."

"I'm sorry, Major, but I must decline."

"Decline! I don't understand. I know the costume is very expensive, but if you will accept I'm sure the committee will agree to provide it. I'll talk to them this very day."

"It has nothing to do with cost, Sir; I simply do not want to display myself to all those people." She felt like saying *British* instead of "people" but had learned not to antagonize the conquerors unnecessarily.

Andre was astonished. After weeks of every available female in Philadelphia throwing herself at him in an attempt to win this coveted role, the one he finally offered it to refused. After showing Jamie what he wanted in the way of a costume, he pleaded long and persuasively with her but to no avail. Her answer was, "Major, I will not do it and that's final."

After the major left, Keary walked back into the shop, interested in how Jamie would go about simulating armor out of tin. Jamie showed her the penciled sketch he had been working on and Keary studied it, finally asking, "Will you be able to do this, Jamie? Will they be able to move with all this stiff tin on?"

"Yes, Miss Keary, there's nothing to it. The secret is the pieces don't actually join together. They will all be sewed to a shirt and overlap—like this." He held up two pieces of metal, sliding one over the other to show her the effect of movement. "The helmet will be a little trickier but I think I've got it figured out. We'll have to come up with a shirt. I took his measurements but I ain't a seamstress."

"I'll take care of the shirt."

"Make it out of linsey-woolsey so the major can sweat and itch a little under his armor."

"Officers don't wear linsey-woolsey, Jamie." She laughed, picturing the arrogant Andre trying to scratch under his armor. "On second thought, linsey-woolsey it will be." She continued to study the drawing. "Maybe we should keep the patterns."

"What for, Miss Keary? We're only making one suit."

"Well, Lieutenant Boyle will be here in a little while. Let's be sure he sees the armor. He will be sure to mention it in front of other knights and once they hear the major is to have a better costume, they will come here in droves. Of course we'll keep the patterns hidden so they will each think their costume is special made—which will tend to justify the exorbitant price I'll charge them."

"How much did you charge the major?" Jamie asked this matter-of-factly, without looking up from the sketch he was making for the helmet.

"Twenty guineas."

Now he looked up, his eyes wide, disbelieving. "Why so much? We could make a fair profit at five."

"Yes, we could, but we can make a much better one at twenty. I figured the major wanted the price high to discourage others from copying his idea in the event they got wind of it. Of course the closer we get to the day of the pageant, the higher the price will go."

"Doesn't your conscience bother you when you rob people like that? Mine would."

"Why Jamie"—she leaned close to him so others couldn't hear—"I thought you were an ardent rebel. They are the enemy, you know."

"Yeah, I didn't think of it that way. But I still think if you raise the price the others will just forget it."

"That's because you don't know the British that well. I'll wager, regardless of price, at least ten of the fourteen will order armor as soon as they hear about it—and I'll make sure they hear about it."

Chapter XXVI

Deborah Thornton paced nervously up and down the room as a despondent Captain Barnes sipped brandy and avoided her venomous stares. "When did you first hear about these new tin costumes?" She spread her arms wide in supplication, indicating she was the innocent victim of a horrible plot.

"Four or five days ago."

"Four or five days! And you are just now telling me? You just sit there calmly telling me you plan to escort me into that hall in a costume of painted paper while every other knight in the place will be arrayed in shining metal?"

"What good would it do to tell you? I'm already so far in debt I don't know how I'll ever repay it. There's just no way I can afford more than twenty guineas for a new costume."

"And there's no way I'm going to let you escort me to that dance floor dressed in the cheapest costume in the whole place. Where is this tinsmith?"

"On Spruce Street."

She wheeled and screamed so loud the captain almost jumped out of his chair. "You mean the shop that Irish witch owns?"

"Yes. I understand Major Andre wants her to be queen, but she refused."

"Her? Queen?" Deborah was livid. "She doesn't deserve to be queen of a pigsty. What did the others say?"

"Oh, they're all in favor of it. Ever since her name was mentioned, they haven't been able to agree on anyone else. The committee has even had her costume made, hoping she will reconsider if she doesn't have to pay that exorbitant price for a costume."

"What does the gown look like?"

"I understand it's white silk similar to the others, but the style is different enough to set her off from the rest and instead of a turban she's to wear a jeweled crown and carry a jeweled scepter."

Deborah set the decanter down so hard it tipped, spilling wine over the polished table top. Turning to the captain, she snatched her shawl from the back of a chair and snapped, "I'm not going to walk with you dressed in paper; you must have a proper costume. We'll go down and order it this very minute." Dragging at his arm, she added sarcastically, "Don't worry about the price; consider it a gift from me."

"Good morning, Miss Thornton. I can't imagine what would bring Your Ladyship to Spruce Street to mingle with common tradespeople. Are you lost?"

"No, I'm with the captain; he is interested in the armor you have made for other officers." Deborah looked straight ahead, trying to avoid Keary's amused smile.

"For what purpose, Captain?"

"So I can have a set made, Miss."

Keary looked condescendingly from Deborah to the captain. *So,* she thought, *this is the last knight, and he must be Deborah's escort.* She deliberately took a long time answering, allowing Deborah an opportunity to stew. "I'm afraid it's too late to order armor and have it finished in time for the Meschianza." Her words were addressed to the captain but her mocking gaze never left Deborah.

"But I need—that is, the captain needs it badly."

So, Keary thought wryly, *the haughty Deborah Thornton could be the only fair lady without a knight in shining armor.* Her mock sympathy was played to the hilt. "Well, Miss—er—ah, Captain, I'm sorry but the only way we could have your armor in time is if I could induce Mr. Stuart to stay evenings and make it for you. Of course he would expect to be compensated at a higher rate of pay." Keary congratulated herself on having Jamie save the pattern even after the thirteenth sale. She had told him, "That's thirteen, but there are fourteen knights; let's save the pattern."

"But, Miss Keary, the pageant's Saturday."

"I know, Jamie, but the other officer will be in." Now she was especially glad she had insisted. Not only would she charge an exorbitant price, but the patterns could be formed into armor in a matter of hours.

"How much will it cost?" The captain asked this cautiously, shooting a furtive glance at Deborah, who stood tapping her toe impatiently.

"Forty guineas." Keary looked straight at Deborah

with a look of amusement, the fury unmistakable in those pale blue eyes. The captain looked questioningly at Deborah who nodded affirmatively, the color of her cheeks reaching a beet-red.

"Very well, Miss, what do I do now?"

"I will send a young lady in to take your measurements."

As Keary went to get Molly, Deborah and the captain inspected a suit of armor hanging on a rack. The metal plates were bent to different curvatures and had several tiny holes punched into them, allowing them to be sewn onto plain linsey-woolsey shirts and trousers. The plates overlapped, hiding every bit of the clothing and allowing unusual freedom of movement. The helmet looked remarkably authentic with a visor that could be raised and lowered. The captain took an interest watching a lad work a long-handled machine forming a hemmed edge around a helmet visor. Deborah was watching a girl sewing plates to a shirt when Major Andre entered.

"Deborah—Captain—what a surprise. I see you have also discovered my little secret."

"Yes, Major, and I think it was a devilish trick to play. It's just a good thing I didn't think of it first or I would have had the only shining knight at the ball." She tried to present a vivacious front she didn't feel and as soon as the major became engrossed trying on his armor, her scowl returned.

Captain Barnes was especially interested in shop operations and when his measurements were complete, he wandered around the shop asking all manner of questions. While trying to explain one of the functions, a lad took out a cartouche box and pointing to a seam, said, "You see, Captain, here is the hem I was talking about here on this spice box."

The captain nodded and went on to look at other products. Impatient to be on her way, Deborah went to the front room, hoping this would hurry him. She was already boiling inside and when she saw Keary behind the counter she fairly exploded.

"Forty guineas! What a blatant attempt at grand larceny. But then I guess one can't expect anything different from Irish trash."

Keary was about to answer in her usual caustic way when Major Andre entered the room.

"Major, do you still want me to be queen of your ball?"

"Certainly; in fact, I was just rehearsing persuasive arguments to entreat you one last time. Have you changed your mind?"

"Yes. On the conditions I don't have to wear a wig or powder my hair."

"Splendid! I'll have your costume sent over this very day so you can try it on. Your black hair will set off the white dress perfectly and if I may be presumptuous I'd suggest you wear it long so that—" His words were cut off by the loud slam of the door as Deborah left.

Captain Barnes was not very astute at reading women and, totally unaware of the war he had just witnessed, tried to make normal conversation. "It's funny, Miss Thornton, but that spice box that lad showed me was exactly like the ones we found on a couple of captured rebels."

"Don't be silly; the rebels are starving. What would they be doing carrying spice boxes?"

He was taken aback by the sharpness of her words as

she snapped at him without slackening her brisk pace. "I didn't mean they were using them for spices. They had converted them to cartouche boxes. You know, the rebels are very clever at things like that; in fact, they are very adept at a lot of things." He spoke of rebels as if they were a different race of people from loyalists.

"I'm sure they are, Captain." She was getting more irritated with him by the minute. The biggest pageant in history was only a few days away and he could find nothing more interesting to talk about than spice boxes. When she first learned she was to have a part in the pageant she was thrilled to have been assigned to such a tall, handsome partner. But with all the charming, witty officers in Philadelphia, she now wondered how she could have been so unfortunate as to draw such a dullard for a partner.

"Actually those spice boxes make better cartouche boxes than our army carries. They seal so tight the powder would never get wet."

"Yes, I'm sure they're fine spice boxes or cartouche boxes or whatever they are, but right now I'm more concerned with whether or not your costume will be ready on time. It would be just like that horrible she-devil to tell us at the last minute it won't be ready. Then what will we do? Can you tell me that?"

"Oh, it'll be ready on time, no fear. Did you notice how many of those pieces that lad formed in the short time we were there? Or how many the other lad cut out? Or how many that girl sewed to the shirt? There was a tinsmith near my home in England and I used to watch him work; he was a good craftsman, but this shop turns out work ten times as fast as he could if he had twenty helpers. Why, I bet there were more than a hundred spice boxes on the bottom of that bench."

"Spice boxes." She shook her head disgustedly, feeling there was no hope for him. It was impossible to carry on an interesting discussion with such a dolt, and the minute he was quiet a vision of Keary standing on the queen's pedestal haunted her. *Perhaps I can forget the Irish wench by thinking of spice boxes,* she thought wryly. *Let's see, my gallant escort said they were perfectly sealed, better than their English counterparts, and more than a hundred under one bench.* Regardless of how much she hated Keary she had to admit the Irish wench was no dumbbell: She had made a fortune out of the armor, had turned an old, run-down shop into a thriving enterprise, and had found markets to sell hundreds of spice boxes. Spice boxes?

Her gait slowed perceptively, but the wheels of her mind raced. With the British controlling Philadelphia, she could not ship merchandise out of the city. With only the local market available, how could anyone sell that many of any one item—especially a luxury item that the average woman wouldn't buy?

She walked on in silence, completely oblivious to the fainthearted attempts the captain occasionally made at conversation. Keary was Irish and as such would hate the British, and what's more she was the type to do something about it. She questioned the captain carefully and found out the lad in the shop had said one peddler picked up a load of the boxes almost every week. The more Deborah pondered the strange spice box situation, the more sure she became it was no accident the rebel prisoners had converted them into cartouche boxes. Her scowl turned into a satanic smile, and the captain was amazed to see her greet passersby with a warmth he had

417

never beheld in her before. He was never much good at figuring out women and now decided it was useless to even try.

"Captain, do you think I could get one of those spice boxes or whatever they are the prisoners were carrying?"

"I guess so, but why?"

"The comments you made about how clever the rebels are were very interesting. I'll be entertaining tomorrow night and believe the spice box story would be good conversation. Could you get me one before that?"

"Of course."

"And when you go for your armor fitting, I want to go with you." She squeezed his arm, flashed him a broad smile, and sauntered along happily.

She would not report Keary immediately. There might be those at headquarters who would cover the whole thing up in order to keep her available to be queen of the Meschianza. No, the arrest must be perfectly timed and by some officer not involved in the festivities, preferably by one not overly friendly with Major Andre. The perfect choice would be a junior officer who could arrange a surveillance of the shop and hopefully catch a shipment trying to cross the lines. Lieutenant Pearson would be perfect. She would agree to settle some of his gambling debts and in return he would conduct the investigation and time the arrest according to her instructions.

Then, she thought gleefully, *I'll have Captain Barnes escort me to her room and get the queen's dress. Robinson can bring it to the ball and after the joust and dance, I'll sneak off and change hurriedly. Let's see, as the time draws near to open the pavilion, Major Andre will start frantically searching for Keary. I'll whisper to Captain Barnes there has been a change in plans and that he is to switch partners with*

418

Major Andre. Then I'll change into the queen's costume and find the major. What can he do? As the queen I'll sit at Sir William's table and reign over the banquet. She snickered, *Oh I do hope the Irish wench enjoys ruling over a dark, damp prison cell while I am queen of the Meschianza.*

When the big day arrived, all Philadelphia breathed a collective sigh of relief as the first rays of the morning sun were greeted by a cloudless sky. If one element could have ruined the Meschianza it was the weather, since many of the events were scheduled to be held outdoors. The entire city buzzed with the activity of last-minute preparations, as even those not directly involved in official plans were arranging private parties.

Brad, who like most officers was off duty this day, had plans that were in a completely different vein than the others. When he first heard Keary was to be queen of the pageant and had not invited him to be her escort, he was devastated. Then after a little reflection, he viewed this as an opportunity. *I'll come to the shop*, he thought, *and pretend all this social nonsense is of complete indifference to me. When she leaves for the ball, I'll be hard at work in the shop. If that doesn't convince her I'm an industrious person with serious intentions, I don't know what will.* He felt exuberant this morning as he sauntered along Second Street, inhaling the fresh spring breeze from the river and dreaming of his wonderful prospects. Not only would he soon be marrying the most beautiful woman in Philadelphia but would gain a profitable business and other property as well. Once before he had received a small windfall and now congratulated himself on how well he had invested it. An uncle had left him a small inheritance and he had used it to purchase a commission in the British army. Without independent wealth or family connections promotions would be slow, but it was a better life than tilling the soil in Ireland.

Once the commission was secured, he was automatically on a different social level and his aspirations could reasonably be set a little higher. He, of course, could not hope to mingle with nobility or even the very wealthy, but he could socialize and be accepted by lesser merchants and well-to-do tradesmen. It might be necessary now to sacrifice his commission but that was a small price to pay for the opportunity presenting itself. Of course if the British continued to hold Philadelphia he could have the best of both worlds. Either way, once they were married, he would find a good businessman to manage her shop so that he could become a man of leisure. First he would buy a good horse and join the jockey club. Horse racing was the perfect sport for a gentleman, especially one who could afford respectable wagers. Next he would buy a good sporty sloop for yachting on the river and a suitable wardrobe for the Philadelphia social life. Until the wedding, however, he would be a model of assiduity.

Amos leaned over the rail as the morning sun began to peek through the city, washing the river with first light. The crew was in a surly mood after realizing he had duped them, but he would worry about that later. They had picked up a cargo in Philadelphia bound for New York and planned to pick up one there for England. Then after arrival in New York he had decided on one last attempt to get Keary to accept his proposal. Without telling the crew, he had contracted for a return trip to Philadelphia and they had not learned their true destination until the ship was at sea. Oh well, he had handled disgruntled crews before and right now there were more important matters to attend to. And if Keary accepted his proposal the ship would again be sailing to New York, and the crew would have still more to gripe about.

He climbed down the rope ladder to the longboat, ignoring the hateful stares of the rowers. The usual easy conversation of the crew was missing and the only sound was oars dipping into the water. Amos was relieved to bound out of the boat onto the wharf. Without a backward look, he headed straight for Keary's shop to pour out the story he had rehearsed over and over during the voyage.

"Keary, I've sold the ship and do you know what that means? All I have to do is deliver the ship to its new owners in New York and then we'll be free to buy that farm. I've decided to let you select the place whether it's in rebel-held territory or not. I love you so much I don't care where I live so long as it's with you. We can get married right away and the voyage to New York will be the first part of our honeymoon. Then once the new owners take possession of the ship, we'll be free to begin looking for that farm and settle down to a long, happy marriage."

Once they approached New York, the blockade ships would stop them for inspection, and he would tell Keary the Royal Navy had ordered all merchant ships to proceed directly to England to load military cargo for a new offensive the army was planning. He would, of course, promise she could make the return voyage with him but later tell her complications prevented this. With the French in the war, he would fear for her safety and decide she should stay in Cornwall until his return. For the first few years he would have to make excuses each voyage, but she would get accustomed to her new surroundings and have children to tie her down. Then he could resume his old routine and spend a couple of months each year with her at Cornwall, without giving up any of his other ladies in various ports around the world.

Yes, it would be wise to get her pregnant immediately. A broad smile creased his face as he sauntered along; that would be a job he wouldn't mind one bit.

Keary was up earlier than usual this Saturday morning. Though she had originally planned to keep the shop open a half day, she had changed her mind at the last minute and announced to a happy group in the shop they would have both Saturday and Sunday off. Though closing for a British "holiday" went against her grain, she felt there was no use antagonizing the English so long as her cartouche boxes were moving freely to the patriots.

She smiled knowing Molly would come over soon under the pretense of helping her dress for the Meschianza, when in reality she wanted mostly to sit and hold the dress again. Molly enjoyed holding the rich silk across her lap, stroking it lovingly for hours. She only hoped Molly didn't come too early, as she wanted to take advantage of the quiet to inventory supplies and prepare orders for materials.

Major Andre was sending a carriage for her at two, and though she had protested the time was too early he had insisted, saying, "Miss Cavanaugh, it's the only time an enclosed carriage will be available and we don't want anyone see your dress before the grand unveiling." What would happen when she arrived at the Wharton estate? Would they hide her in a room somewhere until the ball started? Again she wondered how Deborah could have made her angry enough to accept this stupid role.

The knock on the door surprised her since it was too early for Molly, and everyone else in Philadelphia was preparing for the day's festivities.

"Amos, I didn't expect you back for months. Oh dear God, I hope nothing happened to your ship!"

"No, at least nothing bad; I sold it."

"Sold it! Whatever for?"

"Well if you can manage a cup of coffee for a weary sailor, I'll tell you. Or better still, if you would like to accompany me to breakfast, I have a surprise for you."

"I'm sorry, but this promises to be a very hectic day. Sir William Howe is leaving and I somehow managed to get myself involved in his going-away party."

"So that's the reason for all the decorations and such. Even the ships in the river are more banners than sails. I couldn't get a berth at the dock and had to come in on a longboat. Well, at least I'm glad to see you participating like one of His Majesty's loyal subjects."

She felt like telling him nothing could be further from the truth but instead said simply, "I'll put the kettle on."

Amos took his time approaching his intended subject, indulging in small talk about his trip to New York but carefully planting details that would lend credulity to his story about selling the ship. Keary waited patiently, fearing the subject would again get around to marriage. She rose, poured more coffee, and was about to sit back down when she heard loud pounding on the door downstairs.

"Hold your shirt on, I'm coming." She yelled

impatiently as she went down the steps toward the insistent pounding. Amos, who had come to the top landing out of curiosity, now followed her wearing a concerned frown at the crossed white belt visible through the small doorpane.

"Miss Cavanaugh?"

"Yes, Lieutenant."

"I'm Lieutenant Pearson of the provost office; I would like a look at your shop."

"Of course, Lieutenant." She tried to appear relaxed as her heart picked up tempo and her stomach knotted.

The lieutenant headed straight for the right bench as if following directions, and stooping, picked up a spice box from the lower shelf. "Hmm, you seem to make an awful lot of these. What are they, Miss?"

"Spice boxes." Keary didn't recognize her own voice as the hoarse words struggled out.

"Spice boxes, how very interesting. Corporal, would you hand me that one you have?" The corporal handed him a small bag and the lieutenant reached in and pulled out an exact duplicate. "Very similar, in fact a twin. Wouldn't you agree, Miss?"

"Yes, why?"

"Would it seem likely both of these were made right here in this shop?"

She took the one the corporal had brought and went through the motions of studying it. "Yes, I would say this is one we made. Of course we sell so many of these it's possible someone could have copied it but I doubt that. I don't see what difference it would make anyway, since the town's probably full of them."

"Hmm, strange you should say that. In our investigation we have not found another like it in the city, yet you say you sell lots of them. But the strangest part of all is that we have now found three of these on captured rebels, all being used as cartouche boxes. Now I've been working on a theory that the rebels send thieves into the city at night to sneak from house to house and steal the ladies' spice boxes. Do you suppose that's possible, Miss?" He glanced at her condescendingly, with an expression only an Englishman could deliver after such an obvious tongue-in-cheek remark.

"Since I know nothing about cartouche boxes, I'll take your word for the fact our spice boxes could be used for that purpose. But how the rebels get them I have no idea; once we sell them we have no control over what happens to them. Perhaps rebel agents have been buying them from us and then smuggling them through the lines. Also, I would assume that if a spice box could be used for that purpose, any other type of tin box could as well."

"A very perceptive observation, Miss, and a thought that occurred to me as well. But perhaps you'll be so kind as to clear up one little matter that seems to indicate these boxes were made with other purposes in mind besides storing spices. Why do these—er—spice boxes have this little strip of metal riveted on the back?"

"Certainly. If you'll come up to the store section, I'll show you." She led him to the counter and produced a rack. "You see, most women have several of these for their different spices. They are all kept on these racks, which we also sell, and the strap holds them in place on the rack."

"I see. Very ingenious. In fact it's almost as ingenious as the way those rebels learned to modify the strap so easily. Now let's see if I can figure how they did it." He bent the double strap back and unfolded it then, tapping it with the butt of his pistol on the counter, produced a long strip of metal. "Now you see, Miss, if I had the proper tool I could fasten this strip to the bottom of the box and form a perfect belt loop. It almost seems the boxes were designed for the ladies to carry on their belts as they do sewing boxes, wouldn't you say?"

"I'm sure I don't know. And, besides, I have no control over what people do with them after I sell them."

"We realize that, but there is one other little matter. We've known about these for four days and have had your place watched. Yesterday a peddler loaded about two hundred of these into a false bottom of a wagon and was apprehended trying to smuggle them through the lines. What have you to say to that?"

Her first thought was to say, *Thank God Morgan wasn't in that wagon.* But she answered offhandedly, "Have you questioned the peddler?"

"Yes."

"And what did he say?"

"He claims to have been hired by a man who lives outside the city. Of course that's quite convenient since there's no way to check on his story. But our interrogation methods are very thorough and I expect the rogue to break very soon."

"Well, the peddler told me he wanted to buy tinware to resell in the country. I sell to several peddlers and had no reason to suspect this one. If he was working for another merchant I suppose he would hide that fact because he was not telling his employer the right price I charged and therefore could pocket a profit. It's a common practice."

"Hmm, why do I get the impression your answers are part of a well-rehearsed speech? I'm sorry, Miss, but you'll have to come along with me."

"What do you intend doing with me?"

"It's not my decision, Miss. My superiors will look into the matter once the Meschianza is over. In the meantime, I'll have to put you in the city jail since our military prison has no accommodations for women."

"My God, Keary, what have you done?" Amos's face was a horrified question mark.

"I've done nothing, Amos, except sell merchandise like any loyal merchant."

"But this isn't child's play; this is serious business if the rebels are actually using these as cartouche boxes."

Jamie and Molly came bursting through the door and stopped cold at the sight of the British soldiers. "Keary, what's happening?"

Keary was outwardly calm but inside she felt about as secure as a chicken in a barnyard full of weasels. "Nothing much. It's just the lieutenant suspects the rebels are using our spice boxes to carry powder in."

Jamie stepped in front of the lieutenant. "Sir, Miss Keary had nothing to do with those boxes. I made them; I've made them for years and was selling them long before she ever came here."

"Please, Jamie, don't get involved." Turning to the lieutenant, she added, "This man works for me and only carries out orders. He didn't know any better than I did there were other possible uses for the spice boxes."

The lieutenant dismissed Jamie as unimportant and then turned to Amos. "And what is your relationship to Miss Cavanaugh, Sir?"

Keary quickly answered, "Captain Shelby is an old friend and just stopped by for a social visit."

Amos stammered, "Lieutenant, Miss Cavanaugh has just recently come here from Ireland and probably doesn't realize the seriousness of all this. Couldn't some sort of arrangements be made?"

"What do you have in mind, Captain?"

"Perhaps I could take her to my ship and b responsible for her until your superiors decide her fate."

"You can talk to the provost if you want. That is, i you're sure you want to get involved in a situation which could ultimately bring a charge of high treason." Amo averted Keary's eyes as the lieutenant led her out.

As he turned onto Spruce Street, Brad's step slackene and his smile faded. Two soldiers stood in front of th shop and a provost wagon was at the hitching post Deborah Thornton sat in a carriage about a half bloc away, and somehow Brad knew there was a connectio between her presence and whatever was going on at th shop.

"Miss Thornton, what's happening?"

"Oh, Lieutenant Boyle, you are just in time to see wha a horrible mistake you almost made."

"Mistake! I don't understand."

"You were about to marry a rebel spy."

"Keary? Why that's preposterous."

"Do you think so? Come sit here beside me an watch."

Brad crawled into the carriage, his eyes glued to th front door of the shop. If what Deborah said were true, a his plans would be ruined. All the property of a convicte rebel spy would be forfeited to the Crown.

"It seems the Irish wench was producing cartouch boxes and smuggling them out to the rebels. Once she in jail I'm sure she'll break down and name he accomplices and we'll learn the full extent of th treason. If you recall, they found coded messages c

Jason Wentworth's body and I have already told the authorities how close she was to him." Sweat appeared suddenly on Brad's forehead as Keary appeared through the door in the custody of the lieutenant. If she were involved in both treason and murder would he be suspect also? Others had gone to the gallows simply from guilt by association.

"What will they do with her?"

"For the present she will be put in city jail. Then as soon as the Meschianza is over, a full investigation will be launched."

As the provost wagon drove by, Brad slouched down in the seat holding a hand over the side of his face. He needn't have bothered as Keary's eyes were only for a bemused Deborah who stared triumphantly back. Once the provost wagon turned onto Second Street, Captain Barnes appeared and he and Deborah entered the building together. The captain waived both Jamie's and Molly's objections aside in typical arrogant British style, and he and Deborah ascended the stairs to Keary's flat. When they reappeared, Deborah was clutching a package lovingly to her bosom and Brad was nowhere to be seen.

Brad walked sadly back to his room, unable to comprehend the quick turn of events. This morning his prospects had never been brighter but his whole world had changed in only a few minutes. Perhaps it would be better to move his belongings somewhere else, change into civilian clothes, and remain out of sight for a few days until he found out what course the investigation took. If his absence was questioned, he could claim an illness, but if he was implicated in any way, he would slip quietly out of town.

Chapter XXVII

The turnkey at city jail was a dirty, bald-headed man with a three-day growth of beard and an odor that blended perfectly with his rancid surroundings.

"What have we here, Lieutenant?" He smacked oversize lips over stubby yellow teeth while his lecherous eyes devoured every inch of Keary and his vivid imagination removed her clothes.

"A political prisoner, jailor; she's to be held incommunicado until further notice. A private cell if you have one."

"A private cell, says he." The jailor shook his head. "With a lot of your sojers in here and the usual scum we always gits, I be lucky to find a place fer the lady to put her pretty little fanny."

"Then do the best you can, but mind you, this lady may have valuable information so see that no harm comes to her or the provost will hold you personally responsible."

As the lieutenant left, the turnkey looked at Keary. "Now don't you be payin' no attention to what I be tellin' the lieutenant, pretty little miss. If you want nice, comfortable quarters all you gotta do is cooperate—if you get my drift."

Keary smiled sardonically. "Sir, you certainly aren't stupid enough to believe I'm here for political reasons. What would a woman know about politics? My worst crime was refusing to share General Clinton's bed. And if I refused him and all he has to offer, why would I accept a dirty old pig like you?"

"Maybe you don't have all that much choice."

"My dear Sir, the general sent me here in a fit of pique. His anger seldom lasts very long and he'll be coming for me soon. Why do you think the lieutenant left specific instructions no harm should come to me? Were I to tell him someone has mistreated me, the most humane treatment that man could hope for would be a quick death. But before I would agree to that, I would insist the man's private parts be removed with a dull knife. Now if you'll show me to my cell."

Keary was amazed to see both men and women confined together in common cells. Many of the women were prostitutes and petty thieves but several had committed no crime at all. They had simply induced the constable to arrest them so they could be united with their men.

The stench was overpowering and all the inmates were covered with vermin. The conditions were revolting to one of her stripe; still she paid scant heed, her mind on other things. How did Deborah find out about the cartouche boxes? But what bothered her most was the thought of lying here in jail while Deborah married Morgan. How long would it take him to find out about her plight and what would his reaction be? She knew he would help in any way he could, but he had no influence with the British and being an escaped prisoner himself would be wise not to get too deeply involved.

It was late afternoon before Morgan came home to dress for the ball. He didn't want to go at all, having become bored with both British and Tory company. But he had promised Deborah and knew she was very excited about the affair. He had recently heard Keary was to have the most important part and pondered Deborah's reaction. She made no secret of her dislike for Keary or her own desire for the part.

He chuckled thinking how stupid people were. Most thinking people had already come to the conclusion that with the French in the war on the American side, the presence of a French fleet off the American coast would make it impossible for the British to hold Philadelphia and supply it by sea. But rather than concentrate on a very precarious military situation, the British were planning the biggest party in history.

When Morgan arrived home the butler met him at the door. "Miss Thornton asks if you will stop by her room before dressing, Sir." Morgan walked resignedly up the stairs, wondering what new changes in plans the women had decided on. It seemed for the last week, every time two or more of them got together, they either made or proposed some new change of plans, then rescinded the changes an hour later.

Outside her room he could hear her singing and wondered what had changed her ugly mood in the last couple of days. It had been like magic: One day she was ready to bite everyone's head off and the next day she couldn't be sweeter. He knocked once and her cheerful voice bade him enter.

"How do I look?" She spun around allowing the yards of silk to swirl and then fall in soft folds around her. She set the turban on her head at a jaunty angle and smiled sweetly.

"It's beautiful, Deborah." The compliment sounded forced and brought a momentary frown to her heavily painted face.

"Of course this is only my first costume; later I'll be wearing this." She lifted the queen's costume from the bed and held it up to herself. "This is the one I'll be wearing as queen."

"Oh, is there to be more than one? I heard Keary is to be queen."

"Then you haven't heard the latest news. The Irish wench has been arrested and is in city jail this very minute." She lifted a brush and began stroking her hair as a satisfied smirk looked back at her from the mirror.

"Keary in jail! But why? What could she possibly have done?"

"Well, I don't know the whole story, but it seems she was making some sort of little boxes for the rebels to carry powder in. With her unavailable, Major Andre asked me to be queen as well as a fair lady. Won't you be proud of me, darling?"

"Yes, of course, now I better get dressed." He left as she stood humming in front of the mirror trying on the turban and then the crown.

As he turned toward his room he heard a commotion in the lower hall. He looked over the balcony and saw a couple of "knights" doing mock combat while their "fair ladies" cheered them on. Seeing him one of the ladies called up.

"Morgan, would you tell Deborah to hurry please; we

have a carriage waiting." He turned back to see Deborah, who had evidently heard the others, sail past in a whirl of trailing silk. He watched as the laughing group filed out the front door and was left pondering his first move as the butler came by carrying the queen's costume.

"Where are you going with that costume, Robinson?"

"Miss Thornton wants me to bring it to the ball later, Sir."

"Will you be needing the calash?"

"Yes, Sir."

"Hmm, we seem to have a problem here; she probably forgot I'll be needing the calash. Oh well, no problem; I'll take the costume with me."

"But Sir, Miss Thornton was very insistent about each detail: where I should meet her, what time, how I should wrap the costume. She was even very definite no one should see the costume or even know I had it."

"Since I'll be there all evening, I'm sure she'll get it in plenty of time."

"I don't know, Sir, if anything goes wrong I may lose my position here. She was that insistent. In fact she has even gone to the trouble of arranging for an officer to meet me at the gate to assure I get in."

Morgan had little respect for men who would work for years in the service of others in this land of opportunity, and he was not particularly fond of obsequious people anyway. "Robinson, I said I'll take the costume and that's final." The butler was still uncertain but knew that in a few weeks Morgan would own the Thornton fortune and would be his employer. He had no alternative but to comply.

"Very well, Sir, I'll wrap the costume." Then in a superior attitude, which indicated he had little faith in

Morgan's ability to carry out such an important assignment, he added, "I'll attach a note with the instructions plainly spelled out."

Morgan strode nervously back and forth in the parlor waiting for Robinson to return with the costume and the coachman to hitch the calash. Rescue plans whirled through his mind, and although he knew well-thought-out plans had more chance of success than hastily conceived ones, he nevertheless resolved not to let Keary spend the entire night in that hellhole.

"Morgan, it's good to see you." Captain Reynolds walked around his desk with outstretched hand. "This has been a very lonely place today with everyone already partying except me. I was unfortunate enough to draw the short straw which made me officer of the day." The captain was the only one in the usually busy provost headquarters except for one corporal sitting behind a desk in the outer room.

Morgan was relieved to find a familiar officer on duty today. "Well, Wade, at least you won't have a big head tomorrow like everyone else, and to tell you the truth, I'd rather be sitting in this office with a good book tonight than out there watching a bunch of grown men playing knight." Morgan was careful to maintain an attitude that would indicate his business was trivial.

"You may be right at that but I hate to miss out on all that free food and drink; it's an opportunity which doesn't come too often in a soldier's life. Now what can I do for you? I'm sure you didn't come over here to keep me company, regardless of how much you dislike soldiers playing games."

Morgan shook his head as if embarrassed. "I almost wish you hadn't asked that question; I feel like a fool presenting so ridiculous a request." He turned, looking out the window as if ashamed to face the captain.

"So ask away and let me be the judge of how ridiculous it is."

"Well, you know that Duke Wharton's estate will be completely cordoned off to keep out all those except the guests, the servants and workers, and those taking part in the festivities.

"Yes."

"Since Deborah and her friends are in the pageant, they didn't receive formal invitations and are afraid they will not be admitted. I argued until I was blue in the face trying to convince them there'd be officers there who would recognize them, but dammit, Wade, when women get some stupid notion like this in their heads they just won't listen to reason. I swear they have been sitting around all day trying to figure out things that could go wrong."

The captain leaned back, chuckling. "And how can I help?"

"They want you to write them a pass to show the guards."

"No wonder you were embarrassed; I would have been too, in your situation. Well, cheer up. Soon you'll be married and can say no to such nonsense. In the meantime take it from an old married man and humor them; it's a lot easier than fighting a battle you have no hopes of winning." He continued to chuckle as he reached in the drawer and pulled out a piece of provost office stationery. After a little scratching, he sanded the paper and handed it to Morgan.

"Wade, I have a flask with a little brandy if you have two glasses."

"Not here but I'm sure I can find some in the colonel's office." As he left to search for the glasses Morgan slid open the desk drawer and took one more sheet of the stationery. He folded this over the order the captain had given him and placed them both in his inner coat pocket.

The sun was losing its early warmth as Morgan pulled up in front of Keary's shop. He pounded several times on the door before a frightened Molly appeared.

"Oh, Mr. Baines, I was hoping you'd come; what are we going to do?"

"First pack some things for Keary in a carpetbag and then you and Jamie keep right on running the shop as if nothing had happened, at least until the British come and shut it down. And don't worry; I'll get Keary out of that jail one way or another. If anyone comes here looking for either Keary or myself, tell them you don't know a thing."

"What are you going to do?"

"It's better you don't know; then you won't be able to tell them anything. Now get some of her clothes, some food, and some money since I don't have much of my own." While Molly prepared the bag he wrote an order to the jail on provost stationery, using the captain's order as a model. Once finished he folded it carefully and tore the captain's order into small pieces.

His next stop was a tenement house on Walnut Street. Morgan knocked on Lieutenant Boyle's second-floor room but received no response. He looked up and down the hall and seeing no one, decided everyone had already left for the festivities. The lock was a flimsy affair and one lunge with his shoulder sent the door flying open.

Brad was gone and so were most of his belongings. The disarray of the room showed evidence he left in a hurry, and this was the only explanation Morgan could think of for the one dress uniform still hanging on a wall peg. He hoped Brad was not off trying some crazy stunt to rescue Keary, which would accomplish nothing more than to alert the guards. His original plans called for Brad to actually carry the order into the prison but now he would have to do it himself. In a way it was a relief since he was not sure whether Brad's love for Keary would overcome his loyalty to the Crown, or whether he had the nerve to pull it off anyway.

He tried the uniform on. The breeches and hat fit fine but the coat was much too small and there were no boots. His own riding boots would suffice since British officers did not stick to strict uniform codes in the selection of boots, the one area where a certain degree of individuality was allowed even among subalterns. But the boots were at Deborah's house and he would lose precious time driving the calash through the throngs, who were so intent on partying they gave little consideration to traffic. However he had no choice in the matter and stewed and fussed the whole six blocks as the horse snorted angrily at revelers who constantly blocked his path. After securing the boots he still needed a uniform coat. He parked the calash a couple of blocks away and walked to the Fox and Hound Tavern, feeling that if a fast getaway was necessary he would stand a better chance on foot.

The dim interior of the tavern revealed exactly what he had hoped for. Several British officers were drinking heartily in their shirtsleeves with their coats hanging on wall pegs. He ordered a mug of methleglin and as the tapster poured a healthy portion of rum into the mixture of fermented honey and herbs, his eyes roved up and down the pegs. He strode over to the wall and hung his coat next to a uniform coat that looked to be his size. None of the boisterous officers paid any attention as a dice game commanded most of their attention.

"Mr. Baines." Morgan looked straight ahead hoping whoever recognized him would not pursue the matter. "Mr. Baines." The voice sounded closer and Morgan turned to find a sea captain at his elbow. "You don't know me, Sir, but I'm Amos Shelby, a friend of Keary's. I've had someone point you out to me."

"Captain Shelby, good to see you, Sir." He thought, *This is just my luck; of Keary's two suitors, I have to run into the one who can't help.*

"Mr. Baines"—the captain's words were slurred and the smell of rum was overpowering—"this has been a dreadful day. I came back from New York especially to ask Keary to marry me and found out she's one of them— you know, a rebel. God, what a close call. What if I'd married her and then found out? Why, I could have been implicated and earned a rope collar."

"Keary a rebel! Where did you hear such a ridiculous rumor as that?"

"Hear it—hell I was there, all through the questioning and everything. Didn't Miss Thornton tell you about it?"

"No. Why do you ask?"

"Because she was there; came in only about a minute after the soldiers took Keary away. She was with an army officer and went straight upstairs and was still there when I left."

439

"Hmm." Morgan wanted to cut this conversation off as soon as possible, yet he wanted to know how Deborah was involved, or for that matter, how the captain knew Deborah. He studied Shelby closely and decided the captain made it his business to learn everything about Keary's acquaintances he could. But what was Deborah doing at Keary's shop? Suddenly he remembered hearing that Jamie was making armor for the "knights" and figured somehow Deborah had accompanied her knight to pick up his armor. At least that could explain how she got the costume. But there would be time to think about all that later. Right now he had to get rid of Shelby.

"Captain, I would like to hear more about all this. Could we go to that booth in the back?"

"Sure thing, Sir. I have nothing to do the rest of this day but get drunk—good and drunk."

As Amos stumbled toward the booth Morgan walked over to the wall, threw a captain's coat over his arm, and strolled casually out the door. Once outside he quickened his pace but didn't look around until he reached the calash. Donning the coat he jumped into the seat and drove toward the city jail.

Keary stood beside the wall hoping to keep as much space between herself and the other inmates as possible. So long as the light streamed through the one small window her spirits received some support, but with the coming of dusk all hope faded with the dying light. Only one small lantern in the hall between the cell blocks flickered faintly, a short stubby candle in an old smoke-streaked lantern.

The large cell was occupied by about a dozen men and

three other women. One of the women seemed like a decent sort and attempted conversation, but as she scratched continually, Keary tried to keep as much space between them as possible. Some of the men eyed her lecherously and the thought of their vermin-ridden bodies next to hers made her want to scratch, although she was sure she had not yet become infected. Her legs and feet ached from standing all day and she refused to sit for fear of picking up some of those horrible crawling things.

The jailor sat in his office patiently waiting for the pretty little Miss to call for his help. He had seen it before: Women could be very brave so long as the sun was up, but their courage vanished quickly in the dark. He had purposely put a very short candle in the lantern, knowing it would soon burn out leaving the cell block in total darkness. Then the spunky one would have to make a decision whether to spend the night with one man or a dozen. He strolled over to a small window looking into the cell block. The lone candle was flickering on its last legs and his smile was pure lust. He stayed close to the door waiting for her cries for help when another sound broke the stillness. It was a knock on the front door and from the sound of it the caller was insistent. Sighing disgustedly, he crossed the anteroom muttering, "Hold your horses, I'm coming." He unbolted the heavy door and a captain entered. The captain was tall, arrogant, and had typical British disdain for so common a person as the jailor.

"I've come to escort Miss Cavanaugh back to the ball, my good man." The officer held a perfumed handkerchief over his nose in a blatant display of contempt for the foul-smelling turnkey.

"Oh, ye be comin' in my jail an' takin' one o'me prisoners just as big as ye please. And who the hell do ye think ye are?"

"I, my good fellow, am Captain Winsley Feathergill of General Clinton's staff and here is the order." He handed over the fake order hoping the man was irritated enough not to examine it too carefully.

"This is crap, Captain, bringing a prisoner to me jail then comin' to git her the same day." The jailor rebelled at the thought of giving up a prisoner he had drooled over for hours in anticipation of her sharing his bed this night.

"Damn it, man, I don't care how irregular it is but Miss Cavanaugh is to be queen of the Meschianza tonight, and if she's not back in time I wouldn't give a farthing for your chances of living to see another sunrise."

"Hmm, first she's a political prisoner, then she's General Clinton's mistress, and now she's queen of the Meschianza. I swear I ain't never heard so many stories 'bout one woman in me whole dad-blamed life. Mayhaps I better send one of me own men over to the provost office and see iffen I can find out what the hell's goin' on." Morgan thought of knocking the jailor senseless and tying him up, but he knew he would still have to find the proper keys and pursuit would begin as soon as the jailor was found.

"First of all, jailor, I don't know where you got the idea the lady was General Clinton's mistress since the general doesn't have a mistress." Morgan stared directly at the nervous little man and tapped his index finger on the fellow's chest as a way of adding emphasis to his next words. "Anyone spreading malicious rumors to the contrary could find himself a prisoner in his own jail, or if the general was angry enough, the unfortunate rogue could even earn himself a rope collar. Do you understand?"

"Yes, Sir." The jailor was visibly shaken and Morgan decided to press his advantage.

"Just wait here a minute and I'll show you who your prisoner is." He went out to the calash and returned with the queen's costume. "Now take me to her." The jailor opened the door leading to the center hall between the two rows of cells and, carrying a large lantern that bounced light eerily off the ceiling and bars, stopped in front of the first cell.

"Hey, wench, come over here; this officer wants to see you." Before the words had completely left his mouth, the little man found himself spun around and held firmly in the grip of a large fist.

"Miss Cavanaugh to you, scum. Why you persist in making an enemy of so powerful a man as General Clinton, I don't know. But if you don't learn to mind your manners I'll teach you some with a sword." Keary knew instantly the gesture had been a deliberate attempt to hide her own wide-eyed expression at seeing him in a British officer's uniform. As the jailor looked on sullenly, Morgan held the dress up ostensibly for her inspection.

"The general's compliments, Miss Cavanaugh. He has ordered the alterations you demanded on the dress and hopes you will reconsider and be queen of the ball tonight." Keary, unaware of his strategy, simply nodded and he continued before a lull could develop. "Oh, I'm so relieved, Miss; you have no idea how miserable the general has made the life of everyone around headquarters since you refused to be queen unless the dress was altered. However, I certainly didn't expect him to put you in jail." Turning to the jailor he said simply, "Let her out." But the little man was still not entirely convinced. He looked at the shimmering silk dress and the half circle of prisoners staring in disbelief at its elegance.

"If the general wants her released, why didn't he sign the order himself?"

Morgan adopted his best disdainful pose, trying to buy time to think of a good answer. "Why, my good man—" Keary threw back her head and laughed. It surprised Morgan and at the same time gave him a sense of relief since he had no idea how he was going to finish the sentence. As both Morgan and the jailor looked on puzzled she stood, hands on hips, and nodded knowingly. "Yes, Captain, why don't you go back and get the general's signature on the order? Then I could blackmail him."

Morgan turned his best look of disgust at the man's ignorance and tapped his foot impatiently. The jailor looked sheepish as he took a key from his rope belt and unlocked the door while venting his wrath at the other prisoners who guffawed at his loss. He spat disgustedly as the lady left on the arm of the overbearing British snob.

Once outside Morgan said, "Just keep right on walking toward that calash as if it were familiar to you." As they rode slowly down the street the jailor watched disgustedly at a lady so stubborn she would spend a night in jail rather than wear a dress she didn't like. Then a horrible vision entered his mind. The lady was telling the captain how the jailor had forced her into his bed and the captain was leaving to report this to General Clinton. Beads of sweat suddenly appeared on his forehead and he quickly slammed the door, shutting out the vision of that black-haired she-devil who had almost tempted him into committing the most grievous mistake of his life.

"Where are we going, Morgan?" Her voice gave off nervous ripples as she tried to talk with a dry mouth.

"The shortest way out of Philadelphia and away from the British. I doubt they will take too kindly to my stealing a British officer's coat or releasing one of their prisoners. How did they find out about the cartouche boxes?"

It was on the tip of her tongue to say his betrothed had told them but she changed her mind and said, "One of the officers saw them when he was being fitted for his armor. He saw one exactly like it on an American prisoner and simply put two and two together. Perhaps we should have kept them better hidden but then there was the danger of one of the lads in the shop becoming suspicious and reporting to the British. So it seemed safer to follow your original suggestion and call them spice boxes and treat them like any of our other products."

"Well, I guess it's too late to worry about it now; I just hope you'll be able to salvage your property when the British leave Philadelphia. It would be just like them to destroy your shop before leaving as a way to pay you back for being a rebel."

Keary giggled and to Morgan's surprised look, answered, "I know I should be worried about my property but right now all I can think of is how that pompous Andre will fuss and stew when he finds out he has no queen for his ball and no costume for whatever substitute queen he decides on."

The street seemed to shake beneath them as a loud explosion sent the first of the fireworks shooting across the freshly darkened sky. Bursting rockets sent tendrils of multicolored flames crisscrossing each other in high arcs as the crowds stood staring in openmouthed wonder. After the last spark had died out, the crowd again came to life as if they had arisen from a mass coma. Morgan had to stop the horse as a crowd formed around a Hessian band playing in the street ahead. He wanted to turn the rig around but the throngs milling behind them made it impossible.

"We can't sit here or that captain I borrowed this uniform from or someone who knows one of us may come along." He got down and pulled out the carpetbag Molly had packed. As he reached to assist her, Keary picked up the package containing the queen's costume. "Why don't you leave that behind? I doubt we'll be going anywhere that you can wear a dress like that."

She smiled saying, "It won't slow me down and I have plans for this dress."

"Yes, knowing you," he chuckled, "you'll probably sell it somewhere at a good profit."

Her smile became pure innocence as she wagged her head mischievously, "No, that's not part of my plan."

Elbowing their way through the milling crowd they worked steadily toward the outskirts of town. Everywhere the populace was freely indulging in the generous British hospitality. Commissary wagons were parked on every street freely dispensing food and spirits to one and all. This night it was impossible to tell a rebel from a Tory as both enjoyed the British gifts with equal relish. Half the town had already reached the state which New Englanders called "swipsey," and the celebration was just getting started. Morgan chuckled, "If anyone would have told me there would be a day I would walk out on a party like this, I would have called them crazy."

Every half hour a new fireworks display erupted and

for a few moments the crowd would quiet down and watch. Then, as if on cue, the drinking, dancing, and singing would begin anew. Several military as well as civilian bands roamed the streets, and the music was interrupted only for the fireworks and for the musicians to slake their thirst.

When Morgan and Keary finally reached the outskirts the crowd had thinned out. The lights of the city behind them made the darkness ahead seem even more eerie as the quarter moon was mostly concealed behind low, dark clouds. Keary wasn't sure what her future held but so long as she was with Morgan it didn't seem to matter.

A small light flickered ahead and Morgan said, "I hope there's no sentry there who'll recognize me from my peddling days." The two sentries standing beside the lantern box stared sadly toward the lights of the city and cursed their luck at drawing duty on this, the most exciting night of the war. Comrades had smuggled a bottle to the men on duty and though they went through the motions of manning their post, their hearts were with the revelers in the city.

Chapter XXVIII

"Don't say a word when we reach the sentry; just play the part of a blushing maiden who has been primed with enough spirits to endanger her virtue." Keary shot him a quick glance wondering just how far he expected her to carry this play-acting.

"Halt! Who goes there?" There was enough slur in the soldier's voice to tell Morgan which approach to use.

"Captain Winsley Feathergill of the Forty-seventh Foot."

"State your business, Sir." All the *s*'s became *sh*'s in the sentries attempt to be very military.

"I'm escorting this young lady to her father's home about a mile past the lines. Her father is gravely ill and my colonel was kind enough to give his permission for the visit." Morgan turned his back on Keary and, facing the sentry, made an obscene gesture with his finger indicating he had other plans for the lady. His elaborate wink was intended to make the soldier feel part of the conspiracy.

"Do you have a pass, Sir?" The sentry seemed

undecided whether or not to let them through. Morgan gave him a disgusted look indicating the dolt hadn't caught his drift. "But, Sir, I would be in a lot of trouble if the officer of the day caught me letting you through without a pass."

"Not as much as you'd be in if I reported you drinking on duty. But come now, my good fellow, this is not a night to be worrying about regulations; this is a night to celebrate." Morgan's eyes wandered over to the other sentry who was barely able to stand. He began formulating a plan of attack; he could slug the near one and rush the other before his rum-soaked brain could react. Between the two of them he wouldn't expect much resistance, but he didn't think Keary could run very fast in those skirts in the event someone saw the escape and gave chase.

Keary stepped up to the one who raised objections and running one finger intimately down his cheek, whispered, "Now be a nice lad and I'll pay you a visit on my way back—at no charge." The sentry froze, unable to speak, and Keary reached out for Morgan's hand, saying calmly, "Come along, Captain."

Once they were out of sight he asked, "What did you say to him?"

"Why, just that I would bake him a cake and give it to him on our return." It was too dark to see her expression but he was sure he felt her body shaking with stifled laughter.

There was a small cabin set well off the road and even on this dark night Morgan was able to find it without too much difficulty. It was about a mile past the lines and he explained it was used regularly by agents waiting for the optimum time to slip through the lines. "I used to stop here during my spice box days. No one lives here for fear of being caught in the middle if Washington ever decides to attack the city. Come to think of it if I were Washington, I'd attack tonight; I doubt the British could field two sober regiments from their whole army to oppose him." He found a candle and tinder box on the mantel, and after striking the flint and blowing through the small hole several times, a faint flame flickered uncertainly and finally developed into a rosy glow from which he could light the candle.

As Keary's eyes adjusted to the growing light bouncing off the walls of the one-room cabin she asked, "What will we do now?"

"First we must find you a place to stay. Hopefully it won't be too difficult since Molly put some hard money in the bag for you. Out here in the farm country a little gold goes a long way since only those who trade with the British ever see any of it. In fact, most business is done by barter since no one will accept Continental currency anymore." He turned to tell her of a place where he thought she might be able to find lodgings but the words trailed off. Her coal-black hair reflected the candlelight and those violet eyes shone with desire. Even as he reached for her hands his mind said it was wrong. A man with character would not make love to a lady of her quality unless he was in a position to propose marriage. He had learned before he could not make love to her and then forget it. Those eyes were like a whirlpool into which he could be drawn and never escape. As their hands touched, however, reason took wings.

Keary looked hard into his eyes and hope began to swell within her. As his arms encircled her she knew his unfathomable love was as great as her own. Though at times in the past she seriously doubted he was capable of the kind of love that she had felt for him from the start, those uncertainties were now washed away in a flood of passion as his lips met hers and a voice within kept repeating, "I love you, Morgan."

The voice faded as his tongue parted her lips, searching her eager mouth, and her fingers laced his sandy hair and traced his neck and cheeks with a featherlike touch. Their bodies swayed gently, molded together as if they were one form. His lips were like fire against hers and then traveled the length of her throat until she could feel them tantalizing the hollow of her breastbone. Powerful hands massaged her waist and back and hard-muscled legs pressed against her lower body. His hot breath was labored and each gasp sent a thrill through her. She knew this was wrong. Morgan was betrothed to another and despite her certain knowledge Deborah was wrong for him, honor forbade him to make love to one woman while pledged to another. Resolving to push him away she placed both hands on his chest, but her arms were like jelly while the rest of her snuggled closer.

Hot lips were now burrowing into the cleft of her décolletage as his nose pushed the sheer fischu aside, and her breasts wanted to escape the tight bodice and reach out for his hungry mouth. It seemed at first her feet had left the floor and she was floating effortlessly in space, then she realized he was carrying her. Where, she neither knew nor cared. He lowered her to the rope bed, which was a crude affair with a skimpy covering of straw; but to her it was the softest down with a covering of rich satin, and the stark cabin was a cozy boudoir hung in lace and smelling of exquisite perfume.

After laying her across the bed Morgan knelt beside

her and his silent eyes spoke eloquently of her beauty. The soft candlelight danced off the barragon gown while his hand gently massaged her stomach and his fingertips traced the crisscross pattern of her laces, moving tantalizingly closer to her heaving breasts. Despite valiant efforts to stop, her hips moved in an undulating motion and her back arched against the bed. His mouth descended slowly to hers and then explored her chest all the way to those vibrant mounds exposed almost to the nipples, making her want to pull at the bodice and give him complete liberty. Both arms enclosed his head and pulled as his hand left her laces and, with a light touch, ventured down her body to stroke her writhing hips and thighs. With each movement he exerted more pressure and narrowed the circle, bringing his hand ever closer to its ultimate destination. His hand retreated and even as her hips rose in search of it she could feel her skirts being gently tugged. The probing fingers returned and this time only the thin pantaloons separated them from yearning hot flesh. Now each finger could be felt separately and each with its own distinctive movements sent ripples o pleasure through her loins. She closed her mouth on hi ear and began nibbling viciously as his hand found it destination and began revolving slowly over her aching softness. She closed her mouth hard on his ear trying t stifle a scream of ecstasy poised in her throat.

"Keary, I can't go through with this ridiculou marriage. I love you—and only you." She wanted t protest, to tell him his obligations were more importan than personal happiness, but the words wouldn't come. I was too beautiful to savor the words he had just spoken Was this the time to tell him how much money she ha and see if it was enough to help him in the event he di call off his wedding? She wanted to concentrate but his words and actions aroused such passion she could not make her mind function. All she could do was lie back and enjoy the ecstasy of the moment while her body demanded fulfillment.

"I love you. I love you." She could hear those beautiful words again and didn't want to think of anything else.

"Hold me, darling; love me and never stop." Was that her talking or was it all part of a dream? If it were only a dream, hopefully she would never wake up.

Exactly when she heard the first voice other than Morgan's she wasn't sure, but the air was filled with voices now as Morgan sprang to his feet, pulling her skirts down at the same time. She had barely reached a sitting position when the musket-wielding man with a flaming red beard came crashing through the door. Others followed and she soon found herself facing a half circle of ragged-looking men all carrying muskets.

"Well, lobster, it looks like you and your lady went to the wrong party tonight." He pronounced the word *lady* as if it was synonymous with whore and his derisive stare confirmed the appraisal.

"I'm not a lobster, Sergeant, I'm an American and just sort of borrowed this uniform to help this young lady escape from jail."

"Is that a fact, Captain? Well to tell you the truth, I'm not an American either. I'm a Turkish Sultan who has come over here to loan the Congress a couple million dollars so they can give these lads a raise in pay."

"It's true, Sergeant." Keary jumped to her feet and addressed the bearded one. "This is Morgan Baines from Virginia. I was put in prison for making cartouche boxes for the American army and he helped me escape."

"So ye be a tinsmith, eh, Miss? Ye sure warn't makin' no tin boxes when I be peekin' through that 'ere winder. We already know what your occupation is so be kind enough ter keep yer nose outa things."

Morgan lunged for the bearded one and when his hands clasped around the man's throat, another man raised his musket and brought it down over Morgan's head with a sickening thud. Morgan fell like a sack of potatoes and lay motionless as Keary rushed to him and, kneeling, cradled his head in her lap.

"Throw the bugger in the forage wagon and we be takin' him to the stockade." The sergeant gestured with his musket and then turning, strode out. Keary stood bewildered as the two soldiers picked up Morgan's limp form and carried it out the door. She grabbed the carpetbag in one hand, tucked the costume under her other arm, and followed. The two soldiers swung Morgan's inert figure unceremoniously up to land hard on the wagon floor. Then as one climbed to the driver's seat, Keary put the carpetbag and package on the wagon and started to crawl up herself.

"Where do ye think ye be goin', slut?" The bearded man stood facing her, hands on hips.

"Why to take care of him, of course, since he may be badly hurt." She wheeled, facing him defiantly, her own hands on her hips, and added, "And I'm not a slut."

"Well ain't ye full of spunk now." A grin spread over his face as he continued. "That 'ere horse has hisself enough to pull wit'out no more riders. Iffen I be ye, I'd trot me pretty little ass back to Philadelphia wit the rest of the lobsters and Tories. Ye be findin' lots more customers there who can afford your services."

"Sergeant, Mr. Baines is not a British officer. We are to be married and I want to stay with him."

Her eyes pleaded and the bearded one shrugged. "Suit yerself, Missy, but if we runs into a bunch of lobsters there may be fightin'. And once he gits to the stockade ye won't git in to see him nohow." The wagon started to pull away and she followed.

When the party reached a crossroads, the wagon with a driver and one other man continued on while the sergeant and rest of the patrol turned off. Once the rest were gone Keary reached for the carpetbag. Walking behind the wagon she opened the bag and managed to fumble through it until her fingers found a drawstring bag in the bottom. Deftly she felt the coins until she was sure she had two guineas. She held the coins in one hand as she removed the bag with the other and slid it through the slit in her skirt, depositing it in her wraparound under pockets. While searching, her hand had brushed a bottle and now she withdrew this also. One soldier was walking beside the wagon talking to the driver and she addressed him.

"Sir, would you like some wine?" The man reached eagerly for the bottle as his face lit up. Then holding out the coins, she said, "All I have is two guineas but you can have one each if you let me get in the wagon and tend Mr. Baines's wounds." The soldier's eyes widened, and the one walking snatched the coins and holding them up to the faint moonlight, said,

"For two guineas, Miss, I'll give you the wagon." Before the laughter had died down Keary was already in the wagon. Morgan hadn't stirred since he was hit, but his breathing was regular and this gave her some encouragement. Running her fingers tentatively around his head, she came to a large lump oozing blood. She found a white petticoat in the bag and ripped it into strips to make a bandage. After wrapping his head and maneuvering him into a more comfortable position, there was nothing to do but wait. The next several hours seemed like an eternity as she bounced along the rough road hoping he would wake up or at least continue breathing.

With the first rays of dawn she could see him better and his ashen color was not encouraging. The wagon stopped and one man came back and peered over the side of the wagon at Morgan while the other went off into the woods. "Got anything to eat in that bag of yours, Miss?" Keary rummaged through it and brought out a loaf of bread, a small crock of butter, a slab of cheese, some sweet wafers, and several pieces of cold fried chicken. She handed the food to him and even before the other one returned from the woods, the first one fell on the food with a vengeance. Soon the other joined him and her entire larder disappeared in a matter of minutes. Once the food was gone the one who had been driving approached her.

"Miss, my partner and me have been talking. Since you was willing to give your favors to that lobster we was sorta thinkin' maybe you would—that is—well you know what I mean. We could force you but we'd rather do it sort of friendly like."

"I know you wouldn't force me; you are not professional soldiers." Her eyes met his and his lowered. "Did you come from a farm, Sir?"

"Yes, Miss, in Connecticut."

"And do you have a mother, a sister, and maybe a sweetheart there?"

"Why yes, Miss."

"Then I hope no one is ravishing them while you're gone."

"But that's different; they ain't no whores."

"And neither am I. Your sergeant jumped to conclusions because he saw me making love to my intended. But I assure you I don't make love to other men and certainly not for money."

The soldier, still looking down, kicked the wheel and said, "Ain't that much difference between that and bedding a lobster."

"But he's not a lobster, he's a—"

"All right we'll leave you alone; just don't go thinking we're dumb enough to swallow a story like that." He bounded up into the driver's seat, snapped the reins, and they drove off in silence.

The stockade was no more than an old barn with an addition made of logs driven vertically into the ground. The lieutenant in charge strode around to the back of the wagon and, after a contemptuous look at Morgan's inert form, nodded to the two soldiers who hoisted the prisoner and carried him into the jail.

"Lieutenant, is there any way I can stay and look after him? I'll pay for my keep and tend other wounded or whatever else I can to help."

"There's no place in there for women, Miss. But if you really want to stay you can look after me."

Ignoring his suggestive remark, she asked, "But who will care for him? Is there a doctor in there?"

"No, but he'll come by tomorrow and I'll have him look at the captain."

"That doesn't seem to me a very humane way to treat prisoners."

"Humane! Have you heard of the way the lobsters treat our lads on the hulks?"

"Yes, in fact Mr. Baines was a prisoner on the hulks."

"Who is Mr. Baines?"

"The man you have just interred as a British officer. He is a planter from Virginia and was in that uniform only to help me escape from the British."

"Oh, I see." He looked at her as if she were a child making up an excuse to explain to her mother why she hadn't done her chores that day. "And if he's an American, why did he try to escape?"

"And who said he tried to escape?"

"How else would he have received that blow on the head? When gentlemen surrender gracefully to our army they're not mistreated."

"For your information, Lieutenant, the sergeant called me a filthy name and that's when Morgan—ah— Mr. Baines attacked him and a soldier hit him on the head with a musket."

"I see. And when did this take place?"

"Right after we left Philadelphia."

"And of course Mr. Baines, as you call him, always walks around Philadelphia in a British uniform without causing the least bit of suspicion."

"No, he just put it on last night to secure my release from prison."

"And all it took to achieve that was a British uniform of which I'm sure some British officer was kind enough to loan him. Then he just walked into the prison and ordered your release." The lieutenant was a gangly type with a prominent nose, high forehead, and a disdainful smirk he seemed to have been born with.

"No, there were certain papers he tricked the provost officer into issuing and I told the jailor I was General Clinton's mistress so he would be afraid not to release me, especially after Morgan told him I was to be queen of the Meschianza."

"Well, General Clinton's mistress and queen of the Meschianza; at least when you concoct a story you don't go halfway. A bit of advice, Miss. The next time you run off with a British officer, try to come up with a more believable story." Keary was about to tell him of the cartouche boxes but changed her mind. It would only tend to make her story more unbelievable than before.

"Lieutenant, do you know a place where I might find lodgings nearby?"

"There's an inn about a mile down the road, but I doubt your chances would be very good. With the army near, everything is crowded. What the officers are not using the sutlers are. But my offer still stands; I could use a housekeeper."

"And where would I sleep?"

"Well there's only one room and—"

"Thank you, Lieutenant, I'll try the inn."

By the time she reached the inn, Keary's arms ached from carrying the carpetbag and she was already tired from a night without sleep. But more than sleep she longed for some bath water. Not since the voyage from Ireland had she felt such need for a hot bath.

Her heart sank at the crowded conditions of the inn. It was a large three-story building with some fifteen or sixteen rooms in addition to the common room, but the hordes of people suggested every room would be filled. A short, half-bald man in threadbare breeches and dirty homespun shirt sat at a small rolltop desk just inside the door and Keary decided he must be the innkeeper.

"Good day, Sir; I would like a room if possible."

"So voot udder pipple, Fräulein, but ve ain't gott." He threw his hands out to his sides in despair.

"Do you know where I might find lodgings? I've been up all night and would like at least a few hours rest." The old man shook his head from side to side without looking up and she hoisted the carpetbag, preparing to leave.

"Von tink I coot offer, Fräulein, if you voot vant you coot help mit der serfing of der dinners und der cleanink up. A small room und meals voot be free und I pay some vages plus der pipples giff you a few coppers iff der service iss goot."

Keary thought about it for a moment and then said. "Sir, I'll work during the supper hour for just a room and meals. Whatever gratuities I get I'll give to the other girls, but I need time during the day for other things."

"Iss done." He called another girl over to show Keary her room. "Fife bells and you be here und der udder fräuleins show you vot for." A short brown-haired girl led Keary around the back to a small clapboard lean-to built onto the back of the house. It was probably a storeroom of some kind originally and contained nothing more than a rope cot covered with straw and a single blanket plus a homemade nightstand and an old clay bowl. A single short candle rested in an old wall sconce

With a few coppers, Keary induced a stableboy to bring her fresh straw and a broom. After sweeping out the room she hung the blanket over a line and beat it furiously with the broom. She could only manage a sponge bath with the small bowl before lying down in hopes of getting a few hours sleep before reporting for work. However, despite being awake for two days she still could not close her eyes without thinking of Morgan, and by the time five bells rolled around she had not had a wink of sleep. Would he recover from the blow on his head and, if so, would he be completely normal? And if and when he returned to normal would he be able to convince his captors he was not a British officer? Tomorrow she would try to find out where the nearest American headquarters was located. She would go there and tell the whole story right from the beginning. Perhaps she could find someone who knew about the cartouche boxes and would be willing to help. At any rate she would find a way to help Morgan if it meant seeing General Washington himself. She stretched out on the rope bed with conflicting thoughts fighting for attention in her mind. Mostly she worried about his physical condition but occasionally she recalled those words he had said just before the soldiers surprised them.

"Keary, I love you, I love you."

She was at the common room at five and put to work immediately. The Dutchman had failed to tell her the help had to be there early for their own supper. She had not eaten since the previous morning and felt shaky as well as tired. The place was a madhouse with everyone wanting to be fed at the same time and she did not stop a minute for three hours. Finally after everyone else had eaten, she went to the kitchen and made herself a quick meal of cold beef and johnnycake. From there she stumbled to her bed and slept fitfully until dawn.

Upon awakening she felt worse than before but wolfed down a quick breakfast and set out for the stockade. The road was filled with marching troops and military wagons. Most of the soldiers were in rags and she wondered how these men could have survived the winter without warm clothes. Some of them were better clothed and looked to be well fed and she finally figured out these were militia, or troops raised by the individual states and called up for short periods of service. They would be recent arrivals and had not spent the winter at Valley Forge with the regular army. Dressed mostly in civilian clothes, they resembled a mob more than an army, the only identifying features being the muskets and other military accoutrements. Though they did not form precise ranks like the British, she could see the same determination she had noticed in Philadelphia as well as the bounce in their step and their animated expressions. Their hearty countenances were in direct contrast to the somber, robotlike mannerisms of the British.

The lieutenant in charge of the stockade was not there when she arrived and for that she was thankful. The sentry was a more friendly-looking type and she approached him smiling. The lad became flustered and she stood very close to him, intending to keep him that way.

"Sergeant"—she figured him to be only a private but doubted he would correct her—"I would like to visit one of the prisoners with your gracious permission."

"Sorry Miss, my orders are not to let anyone in or out." Unlike the statuelike British, the lad stood easy with his musket leaning against the wall, and the only sign of a uniform was the two white belts crossed over his homespun shirt. He doffed his hat in an uncertain manner, knowing it was the proper thing for a man to do when addressing a lady but unsure whether or not it was proper for a soldier on duty.

Keary moved still closer and in a very seductive voice

said, "The prisoner is wounded and maybe I could help him; I would be very grateful." The last two words fairly dripped with supplication and produced beads of perspiration on his forehead.

"I wish I could, Miss, but the lieutenant said no visitors without his permission."

She laid her head on his shoulder and began sobbing. "Please Sergeant, I won't be long."

He swallowed hard and said, "All right, but hurry. The lieutenant will be back in a couple of hours. If your friend's wounded he'll be in the sick ward; go through this door and turn right." She seized his face in her hands, kissed his cheek, and went sailing through the door in a swirl of rustling skirts.

The barn was dark and still retained the odor of its former inhabitants, which was a blessing since animal smells could never be as foul as human when sanitary conditions were neglected. The sick ward was no more than two former box stalls in which prisoners were laid on foul-smelling straw. In the far one she found Morgan along with two others who were so pale and disease-ridden she had to avert her eyes to keep from vomiting. Morgan was turning and moaning but gave no sign of recognizing her. His soup bowl was empty but she had no way of knowing whether he had eaten it or spilled it.

"Morgan, it's me, Keary; speak to me, please?" His eyes opened but he said nothing, looking at her as if she were a stranger. After fruitless efforts trying to get him to speak, she finally gave up and went searching for water and cloths to clean him. She found a towheaded lad of about fourteen carrying water from a well in the stockade area where other prisoners could be seen wandering aimlessly about. Met by hungry stares she quickly stepped back out of sight of the inmates, fearing how men cooped up for long periods would react to a young woman.

Placing a couple of coppers in the lad's hand, she asked, "Do you take care of the prisoners in the sick ward?"

"Just take them vittles and fill their water buckets."

"Who cares for them?"

The lad put the bucket down and looking perplexed, answered, "Dunno, Ma'am; a surgeon looks in on them some days, but he's usually so drunk he can't see much. If you ask me I think he's afraid of catching something cause he never gets very close to them."

"Then really there's no one to care for them."

"Well, Ma'am, mostly there ain't no one in the sick ward. When a prisoner gets sick his mates take care of him out in the compound. They only bring him in here if they think he's dying and there's no more they can do for him, or if they think he's got something that's catching."

"But what about the new one that came in yesterday?"

"Spect if he gets strong enough and has got any sense he'll go out in the compound. If not he'll stay here and die like the rest of them."

Keary looked the lad over carefully; he didn't seem very bright, but she felt he was honest and anxious to please. "Do you live around here, lad?"

"I just live wherever I can find some work, Ma'am. My pa went off to war two years ago and my ma died right afterwards. I'm just staying close to the army 'til I'm old enough to join, then I'll have a place to stay. Here I get my vittles and a place to sleep and sometimes a chance to earn a few coins."

"How would you like to earn two coppers every day

and a chance to become a tinsmith apprentice?"

"Oh, I'd like that a lot, Ma'am."

"All right, I'll tell you how to have both—ah—what is your name?"

"Jethro."

"Well, Jethro, if you make sure the captain eats his food every day and always has clean straw and water, I'll be here each day and give you the money. When I come by I'll have things for the captain and you must see that he gets them. Once the captain's well I'll take you to Philadelphia and start your apprenticeship. Have we got a bargain, Jethro?"

"Oh, yes Ma'am."

"Very well, Jethro; I'll see you tomorrow."

The following morning the lieutenant was there when Keary arrived, but she was prepared. After returning from the prison yesterday she had taken stock of her situation with the Dutchman. He was no doubt congratulating himself on how well he had taken advantage of a poor, homeless Irish maid. In return for a few scraps of food and an animal shelter he had secured the services of a serving girl who was already increasing his drinking trade. The other girls told her that even on Saturday night they had never seen so many men stay in the taproom for so long. Her original intention of showing a little ankle and allowing a few pinches had been to gain familiarity with some American officers she hoped would be able to help Morgan. That plan hadn't materialized but the image of the Dutchman's taproom had changed in one night and he was reaping a handsome profit. So by taking a few things from both the kitchen and the wine cellar she had helped balance the scale. She would work hard every night and stay later than agreed. This would make her even more valuable to him and he would think twice before making an issue of her little indiscretions. That the other girls would report her she was sure; and that the Dutchman would do nothing about it she was just as sure.

"Lieutenant, how nice to see you again." She pulled a wine bottle out of her bag and handed it to him. "I've come to visit my intended." He looked the bottle over musingly and she quickly added, "There's more where that came from."

"You can visit for one hour, Miss." Keary did not hesitate and as she passed the sentry, said, "I'll leave a nice pastry just inside the door." He didn't reply with the lieutenant watching but she noticed the sides of his mouth raise slightly.

Jethro had done his best to clean the stall and Morgan was sitting up but did not recognize her. "Has he been eating, Jethro?"

"Yes, Ma'am, he ate soup last night and gruel this morning; that's all there was."

"Well, there will be more from now on." She handed him the bundle saying, "Here's some meat and cheese, bread, butter, and wine. Make sure he eats plenty and help yourself to what's left." She pressed two more coppers into his palm and smiled at his wide-eyed expression.

Morgan wore a puzzled expression as she washed his face, carefully combed his hair around the wound, and retied the queue. She found a razor and soap in the bag Molly had packed but, having no experience shaving a man, decided to leave the beard alone.

The hour passed quickly and once again she found herself outside the stockade with nothing to do before supper time. She wanted to find a high-ranking American officer to tell her story to, but even if she could secure Morgan's release now, she wasn't sure it would be advisable to move him. Right now finding a competent doctor to examine him seemed more urgent. The sentry told her the nearest doctor was about two miles down the road and though it was in the opposite direction of the inn, she started immediately.

The doctor, an elderly man, was reluctant to travel two miles to see a British officer, but when Keary placed two guineas hard money on the table his repugnance vanished quickly. While the doctor hitched up his buggy, Keary crossed the street to a tavern and bought a bottle of rum. This would be insurance in the event the lieutenant objected to the doctor seeing Morgan.

By the time they reached the stockade the lieutenant wore a rosy glow and she was sure the wine bottle was either empty or well on its way. She produced the rum before stating her request and, true to her expectations, he allowed them to enter the stockade.

The doctor spent considerable time making his examination, evidently feeling this was necessary to justify so high a fee. A cursory inspection was all that was necessary to see there was nothing he could do, but the show of concern and lengthy study was part of his professional demeanor and seemed to come naturally. After draining a couple of cupsful of blood he handed Jethro a small green bottle of foul-smelling liquid and, after carefully explaining the dosage, turned to Keary with a well-practiced frown. "It's hard to say, Miss, he could snap out of it tomorrow or he could be this way the rest of his life. At any rate I'll stop in and see him again the next time I'm out this way."

To Keary the walk back to the inn seemed longer this time with the realization there was no quick solution available and all she could do was wait.

For the next several days Morgan showed no change. Keary no longer had trouble gaining entrance to see him so long as she presented the lieutenant a bottle on her arrival. She had managed to get Morgan moved to a separate stall, which Jethro had cleaned thoroughly and lined with fresh straw. She felt he would be safer from contagion here and as comfortable as possible. Until he was up and around he was probably as well off here as anywhere with Jethro to care for him.

Each day she did more around the inn, both to help keep her mind off Morgan and to make herself more indispensable to the Dutchman. Long after supper she remained in the taproom serving drinks. The gratuities were now substantial and she began to keep them, not knowing how long she might have to pay board for Morgan if she could secure his release, or how many bribes it might take to get to see the right officers.

The taproom business increased and she rearranged the tables and had the Dutchman find more benches to accommodate more customers. With a pleasant word here and a small compliment there she kept an ever-increasing throng drinking, to the delight of the proprietor. She circulated freely among the tables carrying trays filled with glasses, tankards, and pitchers and, by close attention, was becoming well versed in the military situation. This was important to her now as most speculation centered on whether or not the British would leave Philadelphia. If they did she could return to the shop and load up a wagon with cartouche boxes. These should convince some ranking American officer which side she was on, making him more apt to believe the remainder of her story and release Morgan. She would take him with her to Philadelphia, raise as much money as possible, and try to hold off his creditors. She heard over and over Morgan saying he could not go through with his wedding and loved only her. But suppose he didn't recover? She quickly put this thought out of her mind and concentrated on ways to help him. With the French fleet now contesting the sea lanes, perhaps she could find another captain willing to run the blockade with a cargo of tobacco.

Keary was setting a glass of methleglin before a fat major when she overheard him mention General Greene. She listened closely when he explained to a gentleman across the table, "Most things are still in short supply but I do believe there has been an improvement since General Greene became quartermaster."

She remembered seeing General Greene when the American army marched through Philadelphia, but where had she heard the name since? Circulating around the room serving drinks and carrying on the usual banter with the boisterous customers, her mind chased an elusive memory. However, it wasn't until she had hung up her serving apron and retired to her room that the search ended. As usual, the minute she wasn't busy, her thoughts turned to Morgan lying on a bed of straw in an American prison. Morgan—that was it! Morgan had mentioned the general! She sat on her rope bed and closed her eyes, trying to remember. Morgan had returned from a cartouche box smuggling trip and was telling her about a meeting with an American officer he had said would be a pleasure to serve under. She remembered being amazed as he glowingly described the meeting, knowing how he held many American officers in contempt. Her heart raced with the realization she now had the name of an officer who could help Morgan. The general's high rank might make it more difficult to get an audience but he would be easy to find. She began pirouetting around the small room smiling broadly at the rough-lumbered walls. Major generals might be hard to approach but they were guarded by men and she knew many ways to influence men. A few minutes later she was hammering on the door of the innkeeper's room.

"Ja, Fräulein?"

"Mr. Voorhees, I have to leave the first thing in the morning and will be gone a couple of days. I will require a horse—the bay will be fine. I'll bring him back in good shape or compensate you if he is injured in any way."

"I'm not understant, Fräulein. Jou be doin' so goot I be vantin' jou ter stay all der time."

"We can discuss that when I return, Sir, but right now all I need is a horse and a few days provisions. When I return I'll probably be bringing another guest to your inn and will work as long as the British hold Philadelphia."

Running his hand through tousled hair, the Dutchman said worriedly, "I dun't know, Fräulein. Dat horse wort' lots of money."

"If you refuse I'll work somewhere else when I return and I'll tell all your customers how you mistreated me."

She finally wrangled a grudging agreement out of the innkeeper and hurried to the kitchen where she gathered a few days rations for Morgan and herself. She didn't like to run roughshod over people but this errand could help Morgan; beside that consideration, everything else paled.

Chapter XXIX

Shortly after dawn Keary was on the road. The big bay had not been out of the stable for a couple of weeks and was acting ornery at first but now realized who was in charge and trotted along obediently. With a possibly long ride ahead she was glad Molly had packed the riding outfit she had made for her trip to Banetree. She disliked riding sidesaddle now that she had become more accustomed to riding astride. She made a quick stop at the prison to leave food and instructions with Jethro and kissed Morgan tenderly before departing. Flinging herself over the big bay's back she said, "Now, you ornery critter, you've been snorting and stomping; let's see what you are made of."

She had directions to the nearest army headquarters about three miles away and let the horse stretch out. This headquarters was that of General Wayne, popularly known as "Mad Anthony," whose fame as a soldier was great but was easily surpassed by his reputation as a ladies' man. The general wasn't in but a tall colonel told her General Greene could probably be found about twenty miles north along the Delaware River.

With the freedom of her split-skirt riding habit, Keary swung up astride the horse and the surprised colonel turned to the subaltern. "When the general returns we'd better not tell him what he missed."

"No, Sir! I'm just as happy he wasn't here. It could have held up the war considerably."

All along the river road troops were marching, wagons were rolling, and the feeling of impending action was in the air. Each time she stopped to ask for information she was warned of danger and advised to leave the area. But thinking she at last had a chance to help Morgan she ignored the warnings.

By mid-afternoon she approached a large marquee tent, its colorful banners floating lazily in the breeze. The place buzzed with activity, and learning this was the headquarters of General Lafayette, Keary resolved to see him. The aide, sitting at a field desk just outside the tent, rose and bowed as she approached.

"Captain, I would like to see the general, please." She was well aware he was only an ensign by his epaulette but had learned to address soldiers by a higher rank, thus making them believe she was ignorant of designations and just assumed such an imposing figure would naturally be of higher rank. The ensign's shoulders squared a little more as he bowed and kissed her hand.

"Ensign Bishop, at your service, Miss. Do you have an appointment? The general's schedule is completely filled today."

Keary overheard a feminine voice from within the tent and wondered exactly what important business filled the general's busy schedule. "I have no appointment, Sir, but my business is very urgent."

"If you care to wait I'll ask the general when he might be available, although I don't know when that may be."

She began pacing back and forth pondering her next move when the ensign asked, "Would you like me to have a soldier look after your horse while you wait?"

"Yes, thank you. That is very considerate."

When the ensign left to see to her horse she walked boldly into the tent. To her amazement, Lafayette was a very young man, not much older than herself. Despite his surprise at her uninvited entrance he bowed and regained his composure quickly.

"And to what gift of the Gods do I owe this unexpected pleasure?"

"I'm sorry for barging in on you, General, and please don't blame the ensign since I slipped in while he was tending my horse. I must find General Greene immediately and I'm hoping you can help me."

The general's glance shot across the room and as Keary followed his gaze she saw the beautiful young woman with hair as black as her own.

"And who is it wants to see the general, may I ask?" the debonair, young Frenchman questioned as his amused eyes swept from one dark-haired beauty to the other.

"Oh, I'm sorry. My name is Keary Cavanaugh."

"Miss Cavanaugh, may I present—"

The other woman raised her palm and the general stopped in mid-sentence. In a commanding but gentle voice she said, "I believe I can help you find General Greene, Miss Cavanaugh, but I would like something in return."

Keary hurried to her side. "If it's in my power, Ma'am, you have it."

"I should like to find the dressmaker who designed your riding habit."

Keary blanched as she answered, "Some may think it fits too snug but it's perfect for riding."

"Yes, I'm sure my husband won't approve but then I have ways of getting around him. Now if you'll agree to join me at supper, I'll loan you a gown while my maid studies your habit in the hope she will be able to make a copy."

"I would love to come to supper but I must find General Greene immediately."

"You will see him at supper, Miss Cavanaugh. You see, I am Kitty Greene. General Greene is my husband."

A messenger stormed into the tent, babbled his apologies, and handed the Marquis a crumpled piece of paper. After reading the dispatch and rattling off some quick orders in French to an aide, the general turned to the ladies.

"The British are out in force so I'm afraid I must go." Turning to Kitty he continued, "Give my regards to Nathanael and have a safe journey home." He bowed to Keary, lamenting, "Never have the fortunes of war dealt me so cruel a blow as to call after so brief an encounter with one so lovely." He kissed the hands of each lady and left quickly. Shortly, the thunder of hooves echoed down the road.

Keary tied her horse behind Kitty's calash and climbed in beside the woman who could easily pass for her sister. Though nothing had been asked, she knew if the roles were reversed she would want to know why another young woman wanted to see her husband. "I've never met your husband, Mrs. Greene, though I saw him when the army marched through Philadelphia." She glanced sideways and noticed a look of relief on the other's face and slowly she began to tell the whole story to her sympathetic listener.

"I'm sure Nathanael can give you an order that will free your Morgan immediately. I only wish I could be here to see if he recovers but I'll be leaving for Rhode Island tomorrow."

"Rhode Island? That's in New England, isn't it?"

"Yes. It's further than the whole length of Ireland. It must be hard for you to get used to the enormous distances here. I dread the parting since Nathanael and I are separated so much but there is no point in my staying during the summer when the army is always on the move. Then too, I miss the children and will be anxious to get back."

"Do you come to camp every winter?"

"No. Every other winter since a baby seems to follow each visit and there will be another one this year." Kitty laughed gayly. "My only hope is that Nathanael will be close enough to come home for a short visit." They pulled into the drive of a small white clapboard house and Kitty said, "Well here we are. It's not much but compared to the living conditions of the soldiers this past winter, it's a palace."

A lone sentry bowed and opened the door as Kitty led the way past a junior officer's desk in the parlor to the common room where the general sat at a plain plank table scratching furiously with a long quill.

"Nathanael, this is Miss Cavanaugh. She has some important business to discuss with you." The general swung one stiff leg around as Keary bent her knee in a quick curtsy.

"My pleasure, Miss Cavanaugh." He had an engaging smile despite a blemished left eye and the beginning of an extra chin. He arranged a chair for her, and after pouring a glass of wine, he continued. "Would that all my business be so pleasant."

After bidding Keary to join her once the interview was over, Kitty excused herself to dress for dinner and admonishing her husband, said, "And Nathanael, we dine at eight so I expect you to halt work early so you will have time to dress properly." He looked sheepishly at his open shirt, becoming aware of his lack of coat, cravat, or waistcoat. He hurriedly reached for his coat but Keary's voice stopped him.

"Don't don your coat for me, General. You appear much too comfortable without it."

He grinned as he returned to his chair. "What can I do for you, Miss Cavanaugh?"

She told her story as concisely as possible and was happy to find out he remembered Morgan.

"Oh yes, the Virginia planter—and a neighbor of General Washington, if I remember correctly. I'll write an order for his release immediately and send a dispatch rider in the morning. There has been action in that area today and we only send couriers out after dark when it's an emergency. I'll also give you a copy of the order in case the courier runs into trouble. Do you have a place to take him after his release?"

"Yes, Sir. There's an inn close by and if the British leave Philadelphia, I can take him back there. If not, I'll try to get him back to his plantation."

"Hopefully then, it will be Philadelphia." He leaned back in his chair studying her as he added, "So you're the one who designed the cartouche boxes?"

"No, Sir. I only had the idea; an employee of mine designed them."

"Well, at any rate, I certainly hope we can get more once you return to Philadelphia."

"We'll turn out all we can and I'll send you a set of patterns so you can contract with other tinsmiths around the country."

The conversation drifted to shop procedures and she was amazed to learn the general's family had a forge and he had begun working there when he was nine years old. There was a wistfulness to his expression as he told her of certain innovations of his own. She described her system whereby each worker specialized in a certain phase and he laughed as he said, "Miss Cavanaugh, I think General Washington made a mistake when he enticed me to take on the duties of quartermaster. He should have appointed you instead."

She told him of her ideas for future products, and for a short while the former ironmonger forgot his war problems in the midst of a conversation that brought back fond memories of his life along Narragansett shores, a life that now seemed to have taken place a long time ago.

"Nathanael, Miss Cavanaugh has to dress for dinner." Kitty tried to maintain a stern countenance as she stood in the doorway, hands on hips.

"I'm sorry, dear, I didn't realize we had been talking so long."

As the two women ascended the steps, Keary said, "Forgive me for keeping your husband but he seemed so content recalling former days at his forge."

"Think nothing of it, Keary. When he protests about my riding habit I'll remind him he was very much engrossed with a certain lady in a similar one. He may be a general but let's see what defense he can put up against that."

Keary felt uneasy standing in the center of the room while both Kitty and the maid studied her riding outfit, but the look of horror on the maid's round face when Kitty made her announcement made her more uncomfortable.

"I want you to make me a riding dress just like this." Kitty took Keary's hand and slowly turned her around as she admired the cut of the snug slit skirt. The wide-eyed maid was so stunned, she only nodded in agreement.

Morgan stretched and turned over as the lad persistently shook him. "Please Sir, get up or the guard may try to wake you with his boot."

Morgan sat up, rubbing his eyes. "What's up, lad?"

"The redcoats attacked just a short ways away, Sir. They're moving all the prisoners out."

Morgan wasn't sure who this lad was but he seemed to always be around and trying to help. When he stood up the room spun and the lad reached out to support his weight. "Where am I, lad? Who might you be?"

"I'm Jethro, Sir. Miss Keary asked me to look after you. You're in a prison camp."

Morgan looked down at the coat he was wearing and a few dim memories of stealing it from a tavern wall drifted fleetingly through his mind. "Which way do I go?"

"Just stay with me, Sir. I told Miss Keary I wouldn't leave you."

"Miss Keary?" The name sounded familiar but he wasn't sure why. "Where is she?"

"Dunno, Sir. She left early this morning, sumpin'

'bout gettin' a general to release you."

Outside they fell in with about thirty British and Hessian prisoners and began marching down the road. Morgan's head throbbed and his whole body ached. He had the feeling of being on the hulk again and although the deck swayed just as much, he couldn't figure out why all the guards were now prisoners. As the day wore on he had fleeting memories of a black-haired girl in a prison cell and the two of them in a small cabin. But how did she get out of the jail and he get in? Although the pace seemed grueling to Morgan it was, in fact, very slow as some of the prisoners were in poor physical condition from extended idleness and the usual prison fevers. Some of the men ahead were talking about York, and after a while Morgan came to the conclusion that was their destination. That night they stopped at an old barn and while the others ate hardtack, Jethro produced cold meat, bread, and cheese from his pack.

"There's enough for one more meal in the morning, Sir, then that's the end of what Miss Keary left."

"Miss Keary?" Ah yes, she was the beautiful girl with long black hair. Morgan laid his head back on a pile of rushes Jethro had collected and tried to visualize her but the effort was too great and in seconds he was sound asleep.

General Greene and Kitty walked Keary out to the barn as an orderly led her saddled horse up to the block. Against her will both she and Kitty had lingered an extra day. With conflicting reports of British activity coming in hourly, the general didn't want either of them on the road. Yesterday afternoon the courier with Morgan's release returned saying the prisoners had been moved and General Greene sent another courier out looking for them. During breakfast this morning another courier arrived with the news the British had evacuated Philadelphia. General Greene didn't seem too surprised, saying he felt the British-increased activity the last few days was to screen such a move. Keary had immediately made ready to leave, knowing the general would have to depart too and would appreciate a few minutes alone with Kitty for a fond farewell.

Kitty grabbed her arm before she mounted the horse, whispering, "Be sure to ride sidesaddle until you're out of sight or Nathanael will never let me wear a habit like that. You know he was once a very strong Quaker and I'm not sure it's all out of his system yet."

After promising to write both of them, she waved and cantered down the road toward Philadelphia, remembering the general's advice. "Miss Cavanaugh, there's no point in going out to look for him. This is a large country and it would be like looking for a needle in a haystack, especially if he has been freed. You could spend years wandering around this country looking for each other. I can locate him much quicker through military channels and will be sure he gets word you are in Philadelphia. I know you'll feel like you're not doing enough but take it from an old soldier, this is the surest way of finding him."

Once back in Philadelphia she could hire someone who knew the country to search for him. There was also the need to return the Dutchman's horse so perhaps she could kill two birds with one stone.

Each day as they marched, Morgan's memory improved and the ache in his head lessened. The blank between the cabin where he was captured and the beginning of this march was filled in by the lad Jethro. So long as Keary knew the circumstances, he was confident she would not quit until he was released. At York they were herded into an old barn with only a few guards.

A tall sergeant addressed them. "All you prisoners will be free during the day and will report back here at night. Now if any of you have any foolish notions of trying to escape, let me warn you the woods around here are full of hostile Indians just waiting for the opportunity to lift a few scalps." A shudder went through the assembly and Morgan had trouble stifling a laugh. He noticed the few Hessians turn pale and remembered hearing how terrified they were of Indians and how Americans took a fiendish delight in enlarging on these fears. The sergeant continued, "You will be able to find work in town and whatever wages you make will be your own; if you don't work you'll starve since we will no longer be feeding you. So long as you behave there will be no trouble and you will have Sundays off to spend as you please. For the time being, you will report back here each night and later on, if none of you cause trouble, you may get permission to seek your own housing."

The following morning most of the prisoners headed into town looking for work. In the inland towns where escape was not considered feasible, prisoners seldom made the attempt and not only because of fear of Indians. Many of them were sick of the war and were earning much more than they ever did as either soldiers or working in England. Many of these would never return to their country but would eventually become American citizens.

Morgan's pockets were empty but that didn't surprise him. He had enough prison experience to know either the guards or other prisoners would have robbed him. "Well lad," he said to Jethro, "we better go into town and find out how to earn enough money for our return trip."

"Sir, Miss Keary left some money." He reached into the pack and pulled out a small bag. Morgan whistled as he counted out almost ten pounds. "She said this was to buy your vittles and such in case she didn't get back right away."

"Well lad, this puts a different light on things. We'll go to town, get a few provisions, and leave shortly after dark. That is if you want to come along."

"I'm for going as long as it's toward Philadelphia, Sir. Miss Keary promised to make me a tinsmith apprentice."

"Then stick with me, because that's where we're heading."

To Keary, the shop was a sight for sore eyes as she reined in the tired horse after a thirty-mile ride. Molly was the first to see her and came running out with outstretched arms, and after embracing happily, they entered the shop with their arms wound around each other's waist. Keary was overjoyed to see everything was running as smoothly as before she left.

She wandered through the shop unable to believe her eyes. "But Molly, I thought the British would have shut the shop down."

"After the big celebration they were all sick for a couple of days," Molly laughed. "Then they were too busy getting ready to leave to pay any attention to civilians. Business has been good but of course all your British tenants have moved out."

"That's wonderful, Molly, since I made them all pay six months or a year in advance."

Jamie and Molly agreed to stay for supper, anxious to

hear of Keary's adventures. Some of her future plans she withheld, however, feeling the time was not yet ripe to divulge them.

Morgan had little trouble trading the British uniform for a suit of civilian clothes and left the draper's, chuckling as he pictured the tailor telling his grandchildren how he either killed or captured a British captain during the big war. As a civilian he was able to rent two horses, telling the livery keeper he would have them back in three days. *I may miss the date by a month or so,* he thought, *but this is much better than stealing them, and one way or another I'll get the man's horses back or compensate him.* At any rate, by the time the fellow started to worry about his horses Morgan would be in Philadelphia.

"Jethro, we have a change of plans. With these clothes and mounts I see no reason to wait until night. We'll start back to Philadelphia immediately; there's a black-haired lady there I'm awfully anxious to see."

"Me too, Sir. But how do you know she'll be in Philadelphia?"

"Because it's the sensible thing to do. And there's only one thing I don't like about that woman: She's a lot smarter than me—or anyone else for that matter."

Keary picked up the quill, signed the first document, and pushed it back across the desk to Mr. Willoughby. She felt proud of herself, having accomplished all her plans in only four days. A rider had returned the Dutchman's horse and retrieved her bag from the inn. Through the peddlers' network she learned Morgan had marched to York with the other prisoners. This was a sign his health was improving and it also meant General Greene's couriers would have no trouble finding him and securing his release. The only thing she was unsure of was whether or not he would return to Philadelphia or Banetree.

But Keary didn't have a wait-and-see nature; she always felt better doing something. And his last words had been, "I can't go through with this wedding to Deborah; I love you." Perhaps most women wouldn't sacrifice every ounce of security they had in the world on such a thin thread of hope but she could not bear to think of a future without Morgan.

After renting all her empty tenements to the deluge of returning government officials, she had sold everything she owned.

"Before giving you Mr. Bartlett's draught, Miss Cavanaugh, I would like to ask you something."

"Yes, Mr. Willoughby?"

"Are you going to use the proceeds of this transaction to save Mr. Baines's plantation?"

"Every last farthing." She met his stare and added, "Why do you ask?"

He chuckled. "Don't get your Irish up, Miss. It's just that I feel obligated to violate my word and tell you something. Do you remember the day Mr. Fowler purchased your indenture?"

"Of course I remember. It was probably the most fortunate experience of my whole life."

"Did you ever wonder how he managed to pay fifty pounds for you at a time he couldn't even pay his employee's wages or buy a fresh loaf of bread?"

"Well, I always felt the reason he had no money was that he'd spent it all on me and for this reason I alway felt close to him and wanted to be worthy of his generosity. He was a very sweet man and I only wish that I could have come here sooner and made more of his last years easier."

"Harumph. Though your appraisal of him is accurate, you're not making this easy for me. He would have spent his last fifty pounds to keep a lovely young lady like you from a terrible fate but unfortunately he didn't have the fifty pounds or one pound for that matter."

"Then how did he buy me?"

"He didn't, Miss Cavanaugh—Morgan Baines did."

"Morgan!" She sat in stoney silence for a minute, then shaking her head she slowly added, "Then what I'm doing is really a servant serving her master."

"What you are doing is a very beautiful thing and I am happy to have been a part of it."

Keary tucked the draught in her under pocket and left. She would miss Philadelphia and people like Mr. Willoughby. She recalled every detail of her day on the auction block and the thought of Morgan putting up the money gave her a warm feeling.

It saddened her to sell the shop that she had worked so hard to develop and loved so much. But when it came to a showdown between the shop and Banetree there was no contest. And if it offered the slightest prospect of bringing her and Morgan together, all misgivings vanished immediately.

As Morgan rode past the now empty British lines, his first impulse was to go straight to Keary, but there were other things that couldn't wait. Since he was going to ask Keary to marry him, he owed Deborah an explanation. After breaking the engagement he would tell Keary of his intention to join the American army. He had thought about this for a long time but hadn't really made up his mind until yesterday when he met General Greene's courier on the road.

He still couldn't believe it: With the British leaving Philadelphia and both armies on the move, General Greene had taken the time and effort to send a courier to free him. If men like this would be leading this new country, he was going to be part of it. And this meant more than lip service and waving banners. It meant fighting for the freedom of the country. He would probably lose Banetree anyway, but with a girl like Keary he could start over somewhere; without her, a king's palace was worthless.

Before leaving for the army though, he would sell all the slaves to plantations where he knew the owners personally and could be sure they would be well-treated. He would sell all families as an entity so they wouldn't be separated and would sell prime hands for a lower price, provided the new owners agreed to make homes for some of the aged.

He squared his shoulders and raised the knocker on Deborah's front door. Robinson showed first surprise then anger at Morgan's sudden appearance, but years of training surfaced and he quickly regained his composure. Leading Morgan into the parlor he bowed stiffly and said disdainfully, "Mr. Baines." Morgan knew his stock had dropped since the servants were always the first to know such things. He chuckled knowing Robinson would still be angry for the embarrassment Morgan had caused him by taking the costume that night. He could almost hear the tongue-lashing Deborah had given him and could picture the servant taking it, offering nothing but excuses interlaced with pathetic apologies.

"Oh, Morgan dear, how nice of you to call." Deborah acted as if he had not been gone more than an hour. "General, may I present Mr. Morgan Baines of Virginia? Mr. Baines, this is General Arnold, and of course you know Miss Shippen." Morgan laughed inwardly as he went through the formalities. There may have been a change of government in Philadelphia but the powers that be remained the same. Benedict Arnold was the hero of Saratoga and a household name throughout the country, but how he would fare against Deborah and her kind Morgan didn't know. Since a bad leg wound had made it difficult for Arnold to hold a field command he had been made military governor of Philadelphia and the belles who had "scarlet fever" only a week ago were now gathering around him. Thousands of dyed-in-the-wool Tories had left with the British but others who changed with the wind were devout patriots and in Arnold they had a governor whose favoritism was given more on the basis of wealth than devotion to the American cause.

Morgan felt relief when Deborah referred to him as an old friend and suspected she now had her cap set for General Arnold.

In this assumption he was right, for Deborah had indeed set her cap for the general. But her love—or what love she was capable of—was still reserved for Morgan despite the embarrassment he had caused her at the Meschianza. For a second she remembered that terrible night. First Captain Barnes, wearing her colors, was the only knight to be de-horsed and in the process practically ruined his expensive tin armor. Then at the last moment Major Andre had chosen Mercy Allen to be queen. Well, both Morgan and Keary would be green with envy when she married the national hero, Benedict Arnold.

"Mr. Baines, these letters came during your absence."

Robinson handed him a small packet. Etiquette prohibited him from reading the letters there but as his glance caught the handwriting of Captain Hardy, he excused himself as soon as possible.

In his haste to leave, Morgan didn't notice Deborah's eyes as she shot him a look that should have been in a scabbard. And of course he couldn't look a few weeks into the future and see her face when General Arnold announced his engagement to Peggy Shippen.

"Please excuse me, Deborah; I have urgent business and wanted to pick up my things before leaving." Deborah didn't protest beyond the required polite regrets at his early departure and Morgan was able to withdraw gracefully. He bounded up the stairs to his former room, where he had intended to pack and be on his way in the least amount of time possible. Once inside the room, however, he tore at Hardy's letter and soon his whoop of joy could be heard throughout the house.

Dear Morgan,
Mission successful as I sold the cargo in Brest for forty-six hundred pounds. Your half is desposited with Messrs. Brown and Hebert in Fredericksburg. Since I had no way to contact you I have taken the liberty of loading another cargo and will sail immediately under the same terms. With the French fleet active I anticipate our chances of success will be excellent.
Your most obedient servant,
John Hardy

Twenty-three hundred pounds would be enough to hold his creditors for at least another year, and from the date on the letter Captain Hardy was probably already on the high seas with another shipment. All at once his long-held dream of Keary going with him to Banetree began to seem possible. As he quickly stuffed his belongings into his bags he realized what a relief it would be to leave this house. Regardless of the fate of Banetree, he knew he could never have gone through with his marriage to Deborah.

"Molly, would you ask Jamie to come upstairs? I would like to talk to both of you." As Molly retreated down the stairs Keary poured a small glass of claret. She had done the best she could by both of them but still dreaded the meeting since it would mean good-bye. The two of them entered and sat uneasily on the edge of their chairs sensing an important announcement.

"First I want to say I could never have built this business without your help and could never leave without making provisions for you. But before I go into the other details, here is the deed to your house free and clear."

Molly gasped, "How did you know who owned it?"

"Mr. Willoughby handled it for me as he did some other things. In fact, I have sold everything and will be leaving for Virginia tomorrow. But before you panic I want you to know you have been well provided for." She rose and walking over to the table picked up a very legal-looking document. "This conveys all the shop equipment and stock to you. From this moment on you are the proud owners of the tinshop. I have negotiated a ten-year lease on the building at rent I feel you can afford and still make a good profit. You can continue business just as you have been doing and if you have any questions Mr. Willoughby will be glad to help you out. Does this arrangement seem satisfactory to you?"

"Oh yes." There were tears running down Molly's face, "But what are you going to do?"

"I'm going to Virginia and pay off as many of Morgan's debts as possible and see if I can't get his plantation on a paying basis."

"And suppose he doesn't want to marry you?"

"Then I shall have to change his mind. He wants to marry me whether he knows it or not." She took Molly by the hands and continued, "Now I'll have to say good-bye as my things are loaded in my new calash and I'll be leaving at first light. The new owner has already rented this flat and the tenant wants it immediately." After a long embrace Molly left blubbering while Jamie stammered, holding out his hand. Keary ignored his hand and threw her arms around his neck, hugging him tightly. He left hurriedly, unable to look back.

Keary was making one final trip through the flat to be sure she hadn't overlooked anything when she heard pounding on the door downstairs. She decided to ignore it, not wanting to be bothered with late callers whose emergency would probably be a leaking teakettle they wanted repaired. But the pounding became more determined and she sighed, realizing she wouldn't get any peace until she answered it.

As she reached the bottom of the stairs, her heart threatened to jump out of her chest at the sight of Morgan. Through the single pane of glass she could see him standing half slouched in that pose she loved so much with his insolent, yet charming grin. After fumbling clumsily with the lock, she finally managed to open the door and threw herself into his arms.

Jethro held the reins of the two horses, embarrassed at having to watch an embrace and passionate kiss that seemed to never end. He was finally given instructions where to take the horses and told to report to Mr. Stuart to begin his apprenticeship. He squeezed the five-pound coin, the most money he had ever had, and as he walked the horses toward the livery he wondered why Miss Keary never once took her eyes off Morgan all the time he was giving the instructions.

Morgan had planned his speech all during the long ride back from York, but it came out simply. "Will you marry me, Keary?"

"Oh yes, darling. Would tomorrow be too soon?"

"Tomorrow will be perfect since our honeymoon will not be that long."

"But I thought our honeymoon would be at Banetree and would last forever." They walked up the stairs as they talked, stopping every few steps for another passionate embrace.

"I can't stay at Banetree very long since I'll be joining the Continental army very soon. But we'll have a couple of weeks before I leave." He expected a protest but she sat on the couch pulling him down beside her and waiting patiently for him to continue. "I don't know if I can explain this very well but after seeing both sides close up, I believe independence is the best course for America. And if we are to enjoy the fruits of that independence, I feel an obligation to fight for it."

"I believe you explained it very well, my sweet, and while you're off fighting I'll take good care of Banetree and count the days 'til you return."

"That's the only bad part of it. Though there's no immediate danger, the debts are huge and the long-term financial outlook is none too good. Some people will say

I'm crazy to join the army at a time like this but I feel my duty to the new country should come before anything else."

"Don't worry, my love. I talked to Mr. Willoughby the other day and he told me something very interesting. It seems the courts favor the soldiers in this type of litigation and it will be almost impossible for your creditors to foreclose while you're in the army. So Banetree should be safe until after the war."

"Well, that's a relief. Now my only worries will be how I'm going to be able to stand the separation from you and how I'll raise more money once the war's over."

"Well, maybe I'll be able to visit you some during your stay in the army and as for the other worry, perhaps this will help." She handed him a draught for forty-five hundred pounds.

His eyes bulged in disbelief. "Where did you get this?"

"I sold everything I owned and only kept out enough for a new calash and *Diarmaid*."

"What the devil is a *Diarmaid*?"

"*Diarmaid* is a horse. He's one of those beautiful Narragansett pacers. Ever since I first saw him I knew one day I'd own him. The name is an old Gaelic one meaning a "freeman," which seemed appropriate for our new country. Some day I'll get a mare and start breeding them."

"That's fine but I still don't understand the money. Why did you sell everything not knowing—"

"But I did know. I knew you would come back and marry me and, after all, even an Irish wench should have a respectable dowry."

"You must have been reading my mind to be that sure of my intentions."

"Well, to tell the truth I wasn't that sure of you

intentions but I was positive of my own, and when I set my mind to something I get it one way or the other."

"I see." He gathered her in his arms and, brushing her lips with his, asked, "And when did you decide to be my wife?"

"The day you bought me."

His insolent grin faded into adoration. "Had I had an ounce of sense I would have marched you down to the preacher's that very day instead of letting Benjamin take you home."

"Well, that's nice to hear but it wouldn't have been necessary. Though I didn't know it at the time my prayers had been answered."

"Prayers?"

"Yes. I prayed you would buy me. So you see, Mr. Baines, you wouldn't have had to marry me; I would have gladly become your slave."

"And now I'm afraid I'm to become yours."

She rose, kissing his forehead in the process. "Wait here one minute." She was gone considerably more than a minute but when she reappeared he felt the agonizing separation was worth it. She wore the white silk dress she had saved from the Meschianza. "I've been saving this for a wedding dress but since we'll be getting married by the first preacher we meet on our way to Banetree tomorrow, perhaps we can have our wedding night a day early."

"Tomorrow? Do you think you can be packed in time?"

"I'm already packed."

"But you didn't even know I was coming. Keary, I can't figure you out."

"I know, darling, and I hope you never can. Love is so much more exciting that way."

Epilogue

It had been almost four years since Morgan, dressed in his new blue and buff regimentals and mounted on an Arabian stallion, rode away from Banetree. His travels took him back and forth across the Carolinas several times, as General Greene fought a brilliant campaign against Lord Cornwallis and other British generals in what proved to be the toughest campaign of the entire war. However, battles like Guilford Court House, Cowpens, Hobkirks Hill, and Eautaw Springs were already fading from the mind of this old soldier in tattered rags as he tried to urge the swayback old horse into a faster gait.

Morgan was a veteran of many long marches but in his eagerness to reach home before sundown, this one seemed the longest of all. As he passed the first notched tree and knew the old horse was too tired to move faster, Morgan dismounted and ran the rest of the way on foot.

Dusk was just settling over the long circular driveway when Keary spotted the lone woebegone figure stumbling up the drive.

"Morgan!" Her shriek could be heard the length and breadth of Banetree and far into Maryland. After a long embrace, several dozen "I love yous," and an exchange of longing tear-streaked grins, he picked her up in his arms and carried her past a gathering crowd of astonished servants to the second-floor bedroom.

The following morning as they rode around Banetree, Morgan was delightfully surprised to see everything so well organized and running smoothly.

"I wondered why your letters always sounded so cheerful and thought you were simply hiding the truth from me to help protect my morale. But from the looks of things there hasn't been too many problems to hide."

"Oh, there have been problems, love, but none too great for an Irish wench to handle."

"Well everything looks great; I just hope you haven't gone too far in debt."

"On the contrary. Banetree doesn't owe a penny and you, Squire Baines, have a surplus of over one hundred thousand dollars. And that's not counting all the wheat and corn I shipped to the army for promissory notes."

"Wheat and corn?"

"Yes. The army needed it and it turned out to be a blessing because I read that rotating crops is beneficial for the soil."

"Then where did all the money come from?"

"First I figured that Captain Hardy was taking too long on his voyages to Europe so we decided to take a cargo to the Sugar Islands instead. Though the tobacco didn't bring as high a price there as in Europe, it was easy to pick up a profitable return cargo and the shorter trips averaged more return overall. Next I lined up two more captains and started buying up all the tobacco I could from the other plantations."

"Wow! Tobacco must be selling at a very high price."

"No, actually it's a depressed market right now, but it

was good for a while. All in all we made a profit of almost forty thousand dollars on the tobacco."

"Then where did the rest come from?"

"Promise you won't get angry with me on your first day home?"

"I couldn't get angry with you if you had lost all my money, so I doubt I will for making me a rich man."

"Well, your cousin William stopped by and as soon as I saw how much he looks like you I got an idea. He's married now and has a small daughter. He wasn't doing too well financially, so I invited them to come for an extended visit. For six months I had him study everything to do with Banetree, pore over the books and family records until he felt more like you than himself. We even called him Morgan. When I was sure he could impersonate you, he left for England as Morgan Baines, a devout loyalist. By signing your name he was able to turn most of the family holdings in England into cash and return home."

"Well, I'm glad it turned out all right but I'm not sure I would have trusted William. As I remember he was always a bit of a rogue."

"That's one reason I had faith in him. It takes a bit of a rogue to pull off something like that."

"Yes, but the William I seem to remember might have kept right on going with the money."

"Not so long as I was holding his wife and child hostage. At any rate, I paid him fifteen percent of all the money he brought back, plus his expenses."

"Well now that we're rich landowners, I'd say it was time to start thinking of heirs."

"Methinks we got a pretty good start on that last night, love, but if you want to continue trying until we're absolutely sure, you'll get no objection from me."